SCARRED MEMORIES

The Possession Chronicles #4

By

Carrie Dalby

For Candice Marley Conner,

the first member of Team Henry,

and the band Europe,

thanks for the amazing music over the decades

Prologue

Frederick Davenport helped Mr. and Mrs. Easton clean their yard two days after the disastrous hurricane of September 27, 1906. The older couple needed his assistance as both their sons had families of their own to see to, and their vast yard was too much for them to handle alone. Frederick piled fallen branches in the middle of the driveway to burn while Lucy raked leaves into neat mounds. To him, she was as lovely in a work dress as she was clothed for a ball. Her blonde hair was pulled in a bun, though one strand fell over her ear in a delicate wave.

Over the past nineteen months, he'd grown closer than ever to Lucy as her social world shrank. Gossip kept Lucy's wounds fresh—often fueled by reports from Kate Stuart's *Snitch* magazine. Not even Grace Anne Marley would associate with Lucy when she returned from Europe and found her best friend with a ruined reputation. But the stories served to maintain Alexander Melling's notoriety among the men, as he was known to have "discovered the delights of the fair Miss E" before many had even taken notice of her.

Just as Lucy began to heal, Alexander approached her at the Halloween Flirts dance and set her reeling into misery once more. Then the holiday season was upon them, bringing back memories of the previous one when she was fool enough to open her heart to the scoundrel. January brought the news of Eliza Melling's death, followed by the carnival season Lucy chose to ignore. Her first book, *Azalea Blossom*, released that March. Though published under the pen name Olive Kent, Alexander knew the title as Lucy's. He had the nerve to send her two dozen red and white roses in congratulations, a nod to the day she met her publisher wearing a red rose from his bouquet.

Through the months, Frederick continued to come at least biweekly, often for tea on Saturdays. Occasionally, Lucy agreed to attend Trinity Church with him, which pleased her parents because she had only returned to the cathedral to attend Edmund's wedding service the previous May. On Frederick's lucky days, he was able to talk Lucy into accompanying him to a concert or performance. They'd sit near the back and left early to avoid the crowds and post-show chatter. Earlier that summer, Lucy began showing more affection with Frederick, kissing him before he left for home. He'd waited his lifetime for such signs from her, and it was a blow to him in August when the society column announcing Alexander's engagement to a New York socialite sent her back into the depths of despair. The cycle of pain continued with the Mellings intent on ripping Lucy's wounds anew every few months. But Frederick stayed by her side as her closest friend.

That post-storm afternoon, a well-meaning neighbor came by as Frederick and Lucy cleaned the yard. She noisily shared the latest gossip with Mrs. Easton on the front porch as though she did the family a favor by spreading the story of the demise of the one who'd wronged their Lucy.

"And the story is that Seacliff Cottage burned down with both the men inside it, though Mrs. Melling's companion and the driver escaped. The ship's captain stayed until the flames were gone, but there was no way to remove the bodies. The house is a total loss and the fiancée and Mrs. Melling are wrecks, as you can imagine."

Lucy dropped the rake and ran behind the house, but Frederick knew where to find her.

"I'm a fool, Freddy, an absolute ninny." The sobs took the use of her voice.

He sat beside her in the gazebo and put his arm around her, clinging to the fact that she'd called him by his nickname is such a pleading way. As the minutes ticked by, her tears began to slow and she shifted into him until he held her fully in an embrace. His gray work shirt was damp with a mixture of his sweat and her tears.

"You've been my constant, Freddy. Ever since I can remember, it's been you helping me after I hurt myself. Whether from a fall off a bicycle or losing my reputation, you've been here to comfort me. I know I've wounded and abused you in the past, and I'm sorry. Whatever reason you've stayed around, the Lord knows I've needed you."

"Lucy," he whispered as he wiped her wet face with his handkerchief. "I stay because I've been completely devoted to you since I was a boy."

"Don't say such things when you were married to—"

His finger went to her lips and he couldn't help but caress their rosy softness. He momentarily forgot to speak, gazing into her green eyes.

"You asked once why I never brought Harriet over while we were married. I should have explained it all to you and Eddie that Christmas. Maybe it would have saved you from much of your heartache—and if I'm to blame, please forgive me."

"No, never you." She took his hand.

"Harriet was the daughter of my father's best friend from his childhood in Pennsylvania. They were godparents for each other's children. Harriet's mother died when she was ten. At eighteen, she was in the beginning stages of consumption and her father's heart was failing. Her only living sibling was in the Klondike and her father knew he wouldn't outlive his daughter. With no relations to turn to, he wrote my father asking him to care for her. My father, as you know, wasn't in good health himself, but he accepted the charge. I sought to relieve the burden of her care by asking for her hand in marriage."

"You're too kind for your own good."

"I told Harriet my reasons for the marriage and she agreed to my terms."

"Whatever did you make her promise?"

"It was a marriage of convenience, to give comfort to our fathers during their final days. We got on fine, but there was no love between us. Harriet and I lived on separate floors within my home and I saw that she was well cared for with nurses throughout her last days. When she learned of my love for you, she understood I could never face you with a bride on my arm, even though our marriage was never consummated."

Fresh tears spilled from her red-rimmed eyes. "Freddy, you should have said something!"

"My pride is my sin. I didn't wish you to think less of me for marrying without love or think me silly to throw my life at the mercy of my father's covenants rather than following my heart." His hand went to her damp face and he lost himself in her tender gaze. "I waited years for your debutante season, but fate threw that twist at me months before my wait was over. Then two more years for marriage and mourning, but Alex beat me to you days before I could speak of my heart."

Lucy gripped his shirt. "You should have told me, Freddy! Propriety be damned, you should have spoken! You could have told me that Christmas or the night of the Dardenne masquerade when I spilled my heart to you."

"It's easier to say that now looking back like we are. But the way you stared into his eyes and smiled at him from across the room while you danced with me, and the way you ached for him even after his past was laid bare to you … I knew your whole being was consumed by Alexander. Much like the heroines in those novels you love, you craved the scorching fire of forbidden passion. But let's not berate ourselves with what might have been." He hugged her to him, kissing the top of her head. "Let's start today like we've been given a new chance. Now that you know the depths of my feelings, I'd like to ask your father for your hand in marriage, if you're willing to accept me after learning all that I've kept from you."

"I've cherished you always. You've seen me at my worst, and if you can still love me through those dark days, I know I'll be safe with you eternally." Her arms encircled his neck. "Kiss me, Freddy. We have much to make up for."

Frederick didn't hesitate to bring his lips to hers, and neither held anything back.

"You'll have me, then?" he whispered in her ear.

"With all my heart."

One

The mantel clock struck eleven. Lucy Davenport paced between the unlit hearth and the typewriter in the corner, her three-year-old daughter's legs spanning her round belly as she carried the girl. Lucy rubbed Phoebe's back as one little hand held tight to her mother's braid. A tabby cat jumped onto the sofa and watched the movement of Lucy's kimono as she crossed the room.

"The moonlight will keep away the shadows as much as your prayers protect your soul." Lucy kissed Phoebe's chubby cheek and lowered her to the hardwood floor, not trusting her coordination to climb the stairs carrying her daughter during the last months of pregnancy.

Phoebe gripped her mother's hand and they started up the straight staircase. In the light of the upstairs hallway, Frederick joined them. He scooped their daughter into his arms and kissed her unruly blonde hair.

"Another bad dream, Princess?" She nodded and snuggled against her father's paisley robe. "May Daddy tuck you into bed?"

"And Doff."

Lucy placed a hand on her husband's arm. "He followed her downstairs and is on the sofa. I need to turn off my desk lamp anyway."

She returned with the tabby and lowered the cat to the foot of Phoebe's pink canopy bed. After Frederick stepped away, Lucy bent over her daughter for one last kiss.

"The light is stronger than the shadows, but I'll leave your door open."

Frederick led Lucy into their bedroom, hugging her to him. "If these nightmares are any indication, she's as creative as you. I remember you waking up several times screaming while you were young when I stayed over with Eddie."

At the mention of her older brother, Lucy sighed. "Edmund teased me, but my mother was always patient. I hope I calm Phoebe as well as Mother did me."

Frederick lingered with a kiss on Lucy's mouth and untied the sash of her kimono. "You're marvelous, Goosy, but you need to think of caring for yourself and the newest one." He pulled back the red damask bedspread. "Hopefully you'll be able to write more during the day and not feel the need to stay up so late once we secure a mother's helper."

Lucy ruffled through Frederick's thick hair and settled her arms around his broad shoulders. She tilted her head up to gaze at the noble line of his straight nose, warm brown eyes, and the hint of a smile that always seemed to rest at the corner of his lips—soft and friendly.

"Are you trying to get me in bed, Mr. Davenport?"

"I'm trying to get you to sleep, Mrs. Davenport. There's a subtle difference."

She smiled, though it didn't reach her eyes. "I'll humor you this time."

Frederick placed their robes on the bench at the foot of the bed. Lucy made the conscious decision to lie on her side, facing away from her husband. After they'd eaten supper and finished with her favorite dessert, she'd settled Phoebe to sleep, sent Frederick to bed alone, and sat at her desk in the parlor because she knew she wouldn't sleep that haunted night.

September 28, 1910. Four years since fire had claimed the one she'd passionately loved. Four years in a world without Alexander Randolph Melling.

Her husband snuggled in behind her, a gentle hand reaching across her silk nightgown to rest on her belly. "At least try to relax, Lucy," Frederick whispered. "I know it's a difficult day for you."

Touched that he knew without her speaking of it, tears rolled down her face as she thought back on the date through their years of marriage: special outings and meals, each one carefully planned by Frederick. Of course he remembered the date. Frederick was with her when she'd heard the news the day after it happened. He had held her, as he often did, while she wept. Then he'd confessed his devotion to her and proposed.

She turned to her husband and held his hand. "I've lost count of the times I've cried over him, but it pleases me to know it's been your stalwart arms around me every time. I'm sorry if it pains you, Freddy. I still ache to think he might never have found deliverance from the demons that tormented him."

Frederick kissed the tears from her cheeks. "And what of his shadow that torments you? Do you think he'd be pleased that he's still causing you pain?"

"No, he wouldn't." Her lower lip trembled. "I know he didn't mean to do those hurtful things, that the words he spoke were in fear. But I also know I couldn't stay with him when he was drunk and being played by his father and friends. I don't regret leaving that day. Thank you for being there to see me home."

"I promised you that morning on the porch after the Dardenne masquerade I'd be there whenever you needed me. That's still true." He calmed her quaking lips with a kiss. "What can I do for you now?"

"Hold me through the night, Frederick. That's all I ask."

Two

Darla Beauchamp's knuckles were white on the railing of the ship. Though the island had disappeared on the gray horizon, she continued to stare south from the rear of the vessel. She'd left Dauphin Island dozens of times through the course of her eighteen years, but she'd only been in Mobile a handful of those instances. Now she had to call the city home though her heart overflowed with the sights and sounds of island life.

"Darla, you're welcome to sit with me." The captain's wife placed her hand on her arm. "Kade is at the helm with Douglas."

She turned to the woman, noting the way she kept an arm around her youngest though the girl was securely bound to her chest with swaddling fabric. Darla's own mother wasn't one to coddle, but an ache in her heart tugged at her throat.

Darla tucked a loose strand of her coffee brown hair behind her ear. "Thank you, Miss Maggie, but I'd like to stay here a bit longer."

"I know what it's like to leave home and sail to the unknown." Maggie squeezed her arm. "Don't underestimate your own bravery."

She took in the sight of Maggie Campbell. Even wearing a basic skirt and blouse with Tabitha strapped to her by means of tartan fabric, she carried herself with refinement. Darla knew the woman grew up in the country near the Alabama/Mississippi line, but had spent half a year in the household of a wealthy family in their home on the Eastern shore before she married. She was far from the typical islander, with her doting Scottish husband and an Italian priest for a pen pal.

"I'll be over in a few minutes, Miss Maggie." Darla turned back to the water, deep in thought of what awaited her at the home of her estranged relatives.

Darla's father, Reginald Beauchamp, was raised in an affluent household in Mobile. At seventeen, he'd eloped with his sixteen-year-old sweetheart, Virginia. They settled on Dauphin Island in 1890. Reggie, as he was known on the island, hired on with fisherman Emmett O'Farrell and saved until he had enough money to buy his own boat seven years later. A tropical storm three months back capsized the vessel, taking the lives of Darla's father and all three of her brothers. Darla was left to care for her grieving mother—the village midwife—but her mother's heart was too shattered to mend. Virginia Beauchamp passed away at the end of August. Since then, Darla had been at the mercy of her mother's friends—mainly Maggie, but also Claire Walker, who was now the island's prominent midwife.

On that day, September 30, 1910, after a month of being homeless, Darla was joining her Uncle Calvin, Aunt Ida, and their four children in Mobile. She allowed herself to daydream the past week about shopping trips and attending parties with her new family while Maggie helped her mend her clothes and make over a few donated dresses into pieces more fashionable for a young woman in the city.

As they steamed past Monroe Park on the south side of town, Darla straightened her black skirt and blouse before settling beside Maggie under the awning. Several other passengers traveling from the island to the city were on board, as well as a load of fresh seafood, but the captain's wife sat off to the side.

"I'll take Tabitha if you'd like, Miss Maggie." Darla smiled at the brunette just shy of a year old and held out her hands. Tabitha reached for her in return and Darla held the wrap as the girl was pulled free.

"Darla, you're a woman now, having dealt with grief over the summer and leaving home for the first time. Call me Maggie, like your mother did. There's a slim ten years between us. We're equals now."

She bounced the toddler on her lap and swallowed a lump that formed in her throat. "I don't see how I can ever measure up to you, but I'll try, Mi—Maggie."

Maggie put her arm around her. "I'll write you every week and expect a letter in return. I want to hear all about your adventures in the city, but remember what I cautioned you about. Feel free to ask and tell me anything. There isn't much that would shock me."

Darla blushed, recalling the warning she'd received about how "fast" some of the city men could be. "One was nearly my undoing" was how Maggie phrased it, followed by the news that another had tried to take from her that which she did not wish to give.

"I'll keep that in mind, thank you." Darla stood with Tabitha, allowing the girl to stretch her chubby legs by wobbling between the rows of benches while holding her finger.

When they'd made it to the end of the aisle and turned back, Captain Campbell approached his wife. He pulled Maggie into his arms and she stroked his trim, red beard as they kissed. Darla's blush returned as she thought back on the men she'd kissed in the past: two on dares, one passing first mate who'd caught her fancy, and another she'd had a crush on since they were in the one-room schoolhouse together. They'd gone courting a few times after she turned fifteen, but he'd joined the navy last winter and had no plans to return to the small island's lifestyle.

The captain motioned for Darla to come over. She picked Tabitha up, hoping to hide her warm cheeks behind the girl.

"Papa!" Tabitha leaned over Darla's arms, reaching for her father.

Captain Campbell took Tabitha, tossed her into the air, and held her to his chest. Darla hoped he would continue to show attention to his daughter as she grew because she knew all too well the loneliness of a father who gave all his energy to his sons. But with his kind blue eyes and the way he honored his wife, Tabitha would surely grow up knowing how much her father loved her.

"You feeling all right, Darla?" he asked.

"Yes, sir."

"Come on, Darla," Maggie chided. "No miss, sir, or ma'am for us. Equals, remember?"

"Captain, then?" she asked.

"If you must, but Douglas will do." He kissed his daughter's head as Tabitha snuggled into the curve of his neck.

"Or wharf rat if he has been naughty," Maggie added.

The captain raised an eyebrow at his wife, to which she responded by kissing him. Darla stepped away, resting her hand on the back of the bench in front of her. She'd stayed in the Campbell's home for several weeks, but still felt a flutter whenever they grew affectionate in her vicinity—which seemed to be every few minutes. From what she'd witnessed, her parents only kissed and touched when one of them came or left. Though startling for her to see at first, it did cheer her to know that passionate love was an option in marriage.

A deckhand brought three-year-old Kade to the Campbells. Dressed in a crisp sailor suit with a jaunty hat strapped to his head, the boy climbed on the bench next to where Darla stood and took a seat. He had his father's blue eyes and his mother's rich brown hair, both similar to Darla's own coloring, though the boy's face was oval like his parents' and hers was as round, and often as ruddy, as an apple. The captain kissed his wife and handed her Tabitha before returning to the wheelhouse in preparation for docking.

Gazing at the approaching city, Darla sighed and took her seat. Maggie seemed to know she wasn't in the mood for small talk and left her alone. But Kade buried his hand in her fist.

At her relatives' home, Darla would be the oldest. Calvin Beauchamp and his wife had four children, the oldest being seventeen and the youngest twelve. Three boys, but one fifteen-year-old girl who was twins with the middle son. Darla had always wanted a sister, and after the camaraderie with Maggie the past month, she anticipated time with another female even more. But she would miss the children and babies she was often surrounded with because of her mother's connections. Just last week, Darla assisted Claire Walker in delivering a baby boy in one of the homes on the island, and then stayed on with the mother the first three days as a helper so Claire could tend to her own family. With Darla's mother gone, Claire was the only one on the island to help with the new mothers, and she welcomed Darla's willing hands, even offering to hire Darla—something she considered in great length. But she'd chosen the Beauchamps over her surrogate family on Dauphin Island and prayed it was the right choice.

At the docks on Mobile River, Darla waited with Maggie and her children while the other passengers and cargo were unloaded. Douglas, in his fancy captain's jacket, escorted them off. He gave direction to a deckhand with a hand cart holding two trunks—everything Darla owned—to locate a hired cab.

"You'll be at the mercy of others in the city," Maggie told her as they walked to an automobile. "Island life is freedom to walk about at will, but in the city a young woman is chaperoned, or at least travels with a friend."

Darla and Maggie settled in the backseat of the hired car with the children while Douglas helped the driver secure the trunks on the back. Soon they motored north, turning west on State Street, a quaint, tree-lined road.

"It was Captain Walker who escorted me to the door when I became a lady's companion across the bay," Maggie reminisced. "A week after arriving, I met Douglas. Now he holds the title of captain and sees you to your new home. I hope you find someone as special as I did."

The automobile pulled to a stop under the shade of an oak tree in front of a red brick home with squared corners and scrolling wrought-iron trim across the front porch and second floor balcony. It looked to be two houses put together, complete with two sets of steps, one leading to the main door and the smaller set to a less opposing door and porch. The iron trim and green shutters gave it an air of refinement compared to the modest house beside it that sat narrow on the lot with functional square columns to support its porch ceiling.

Douglas stayed with the children while Maggie brought Darla up the front steps.

"You'll do well, Darla. Just remember who you are and understand differences aren't always a bad thing."

She nodded to her friend and turned to the door as it opened. A sour-faced maid answered. Having never conversed with a woman in uniform, Darla felt her tongue grow heavy and scuffed her shined boots on the wood floor.

Maggie stepped forward. "I'm Magdalene Campbell, here to see Miss Darla Beauchamp to her relations as was previously arranged."

Never had she heard the captain's wife refer to herself with her full Christian name, but if Darla had a fancier first name, she would have opted to use it at the door of a home like that. Trying to compose herself, Darla lifted her chin.

"This way, Ma'am, Miss." The maid curtsied to them and stepped to the side.

They were shown into a parlor ornamented with white dollies and silver—silver photograph frames, candlesticks, candy dishes, and figurines. The brightness of the pink walls and shiny objects nearly blinded Darla, so used to the dark plank walls of the homes on the island. But Maggie seemed just as comfortable there as she did in the home of their lowliest neighbor.

The lady of the house wore a fine blouse adorned with more lace than Darla had ever seen on a piece of clothing. Her skirt was a rich green, and her brown hair with the faintest touch of gray at her temples was swept into a lovely bun. She stood, looking at Maggie as though she saw an equal.

"Mrs. Campbell, I presume. I'm Ida Beauchamp. Thank you for seeing our niece here. I'm afraid my husband is still at work and the children at school, otherwise we would all greet you. Did you see her here alone?"

"My husband is in the hired car with our children." Maggie took the offered hand and immediately motioned to Darla. "It was our pleasure to see Darla here. We're fond of her and will dearly miss her company, but I'm sure she'll be a blessing to your household."

Aunt Ida looked Darla over, seeming to take in the faded-black mourning clothes and wind-blown hair. She took Maggie's arm and led her to the dainty settee topped with dollies on each of the three rises of the back. "Yes, but you must bring in your family for tea. Darla can fetch them."

"I'd be happy to help," Darla said.

Before she reached the front door she heard her aunt say, "She must take after her mother's family. She looks nothing like her father or his people."

"Virginia was a credit to the island. She trained under a midwife upon arriving and helped birth nearly every child born on Dauphin Island in the past two decades, including my own."

When Darla returned, her aunt appeared pale. Without so much as looking at her, Ida Beauchamp peered beyond Darla and settled on the handsome figure of Douglas in his captain's jacket with brass buttons, which little Tabitha played with as he held her with one arm.

"Mrs. Beauchamp, it's a pleasure to meet you." He offered his right hand and gave her his dashing smile.

"Captain Campbell, you and your family are welcome anytime." Color returned to her cheeks and she settled beside Maggie.

Douglas passed Tabitha to Maggie, pausing to lovingly touch his wife's shoulder—the most discreet display of affection Darla had ever seen between the two—and then stood beside the nearby chair, his hands behind his back.

"Darla," Maggie said as she motioned to an armchair.

She heated, remembering the manners lesson Maggie gave her—that a gentleman never sits until all the ladies in the room are settled. As soon as she lowered to the velvet armchair, Douglas took Kade on his knee.

The maid brought in tea and cookies. Darla sat as straight as possible, ankles crossed, hands demurely in her lap when she wasn't holding her cup. The next half hour was the most uncomfortable time she had ever experienced—even worse than listening to a laboring mother scream. Though her aunt practically ignored her, she was grateful for Maggie and her family being there to help smooth the transition.

After tea, Darla stood on the porch with Maggie and the children as Douglas oversaw her trunks being brought into the house.

Maggie took her hand. "I hope you settle in fine. Your aunt seems a bit uptight, but she might soften as time passes," she whispered.

Darla managed a smile. "Maybe if my manners were as fine as yours and the captain."

Maggie squeezed her hand as Douglas and the hired driver exited the house. "Relax and remember everything you've learned. If it doesn't work out, you know where you're welcome. You only need to send word and we'll be here for you."

Darla kissed Kade and Tabitha goodbye and received a hearty handshake from Douglas. "Joe or I will check in on you when we can," he promised.

Knowing two captains looked out for her best interest calmed Darla as she stepped back into the brick house.

Aunt Ida stood in the foyer, her arms crossed. "Now what am I to do with you?"

Three

Darla stared at her aunt, twisting her hands nervously.

"I had planned for you to share a room with Alice. We bought a second bed and she's been over the moon to play sisters, but that will never do."

She continued to stare at her aunt in disbelief.

"Mrs. Campbell informed me you've been training in midwifery and have helped deliver babies."

Darla smiled, proud of her skills. "I've been helping my mother since I was fourteen and then Miss Cl—Mrs. Walker since my mother took ill after the accident."

The woman huffed. "That might be well and good for an island girl, but things like that are not fit for a proper young lady to see before her own time comes. Why, the carnal knowledge alone of what you've been subjected to makes you unfit for the company of other young ladies, not to mention respectable gentlemen."

"There's no shame in bringing babies into the world, Aunt Ida. It's a sacred experience."

"Can you be trusted not to discuss anything of the sort with my Alice or any of our family or friends?"

Tending mothers and newborn babes—the one thing Darla did well—taken from her in the first hour of her new home. She brought a hand to her warm cheek and exhaled in an attempt to calm herself. "If that's your wish."

Aunt Ida sighed. "Until I can figure out what to do with you, go to Alice's room. Turn right at the top of the stairs. It's the second door down."

"Yes, ma'am."

For the first time in her life, Darla climbed a full set of stairs inside a house. She kept a hand on the oak banister and took in the details as she ascended. The cream color of the trim kept the house looking fresh but she wondered how it could be so clean with three boys running around. Her own brothers would have painted the house with dirt and grime by the end of the day.

Her cousin's room was something out of a catalog, all flowers and ruffles complete with a gilded dressing table covered with pretty things. While still youthful, the room had the air of someone on the verge of womanhood. The gorgeous dolls with China faces and shining curls were tucked away on a high shelf. A bottle of rose water sat on the vanity while the gold-trimmed brush, comb, and mirror set took center space.

Darla's weathered trunks sat atop the Oriental rug in the middle of the room, a ragged reminder of a different lifestyle compared to her relations. Not knowing which of the beds was hers, nor wanting to sit at her cousin's dressing table or tidy writing desk, she plopped herself atop one of the trunks and closed her eyes against the finery.

Not long after she settled, a rush of noise akin to a pack of wild dogs entered the house, which was soon quieted by a stern word from Aunt Ida. A steady tromp of feet marched up the stairs and turned the opposite way in the hall, heading away from the bedroom. Curious, she opened her eyes and was surprised to see a lanky boy with light-brown hair combed neatly to the side of his serious, long face. He wore gray trousers and an unblemished white shirt.

"Hello," Darla said. "Are you one of my cousins?"

"Yes." He motioned for her to come to the door. "Will you help me?"

"Of course." Darla smiled and went to the hall. "I'm Darla. What's your name?"

"I'm Felix." He offered her a set of handcuffs rather than his hand. "I'm supposed to wear these. Would you place them on me as tight as you can?"

The metal was cold and heavy in her hand. "Aren't these what police use?"

He nodded, a sheepish look in his dark eyes. "Sometimes I have to wear them when I've been bad at school. Will you help me, Cousin Darla?"

"Your mother has you do this?" she asked as she held open the hinge of the cuff and he set his wrist inside it.

He nodded but didn't look at her. Embarrassment? Would she be locked in a dungeon somewhere because Aunt Ida didn't think her fit to share a room with her daughter? As soon as both cuffs clicked into place, Felix ran down the hall and disappeared into another room. A second later, two bigger boys exited. The taller one with straight hair appeared to be younger. The more mature looking one with wavy hair stayed a step ahead.

"Who gave you the right to confine our brother?" he asked.

Darla took a step forward. "Felix asked for my help. You two must be Richard and Clarence," she said, using the names she remembered from the letter her aunt sent. "I'm Darla."

"We know who you are." The leader nodded to his brother behind him. "Clarence here lost the keys to those cuffs last week. Now what are we going to tell our mother?"

"Well … I … I don't know. I only did what he asked. He seemed certain he needed to wear them as punishment for his behavior at school."

"Do you find it normal to handcuff a boy for being spirited at school?" Richard pressed.

"I'm not acquainted with how things are done in the city, but we'd never do such a thing where I come from."

"Do you always go against your better judgment when you're told to do something?"

"No." Her voice was firm, almost raised. "I'm sorry, I meant to help."

Darla didn't notice the girl's arrival until she stepped onto the landing at the top of the stairs. Her brown hair parted in the center was pinned up in soft waves low on her head. Around the coiffure was a fashionable ribbon headband adorned with a loopy bow on the left side. Her white blouse was as fancy as her mother's and her waist the narrowest middle Darla had ever seen. Though her face was naturally long like her brothers, she had an air of refinement and beauty, and deep brown eyes that shone warmth while her brothers' held cold mischief.

Alice stopped beside her twin and poked older Richard in the back. "Please move so I can see our cousin."

He begrudgingly stepped to the side.

Alice rushed forward and threw her arms around Darla. "I've waited ever so long for a sister! I'm sorry for the loss of your family, but I'm glad you've come to stay with us." Alice steered Darla into their bedroom and shut the door on her brothers. "Now what has you looking so upset?"

Darla, still hot in the face from causing trouble, managed a smile for Alice. "It seems I've done something awful. Felix asked for help, so I did what he asked and locked the cuffs on him. Richard said Clarence lost the keys and now your mother will hate me."

"That's just like them. Never you mind any of it. It's all a game." She opened the door and told Clarence to fetch Felix. "Come see, Darla."

When Felix and Clarence returned, Richard smirked and disappeared into a far room.

"Come now, Felix," his sister said. "You know better than to let the other two talk you into tricking Darla. Show her what you can do."

He held out his still-cuffed arms and Alice made a show of tugging on them to prove they were locked. Before Darla could take two breaths, Felix was free.

Alice laughed. "We call him Houdini. Isn't it spectacular?"

"I've heard of Harry Houdini, but have never seen anything like it!"

"If I can talk Mother into letting me try the milk can escape, I'll be set for life." Felix gave Darla a broad smile.

Alice put her hands on her petite waist. "Now apologize for tricking your cousin. We want her to like us and be happy here."

Felix looked up the few inches that separated them in height. "I'm sorry Darla. It was only a joke."

"That's all right. I've had more than a few tricks played on me by my own brothers, but that was by far the best one."

"Glad to know you're a good sport." Clarence smoothed his hair even though it wasn't ruffled and grinned.

"You boys have had your fun, now it's my turn." Alice tugged Darla back into the room and closed the door. "Well, what do you think? Be honest now."

"The house is lovely and your mother seemed to like the Campbells—that's who I've been staying with this month—but I don't think she likes me."

"She's hard to impress but loves a good scandal, so long as it doesn't involve her family. I don't think she's gotten over what your father did. She almost didn't marry Father over it. They were engaged when your parents ran off together. Not a week goes by when she doesn't mention the ruination of the family's name by the likes of Reginald Beauchamp."

Darla groaned. "Then why did she invite me here?"

Alice danced about the trunks with an invisible partner. "Oh, she didn't. Father made her. He's been meaning to bring that branch back into the fold for years. Since you're the only one left, he had Mother send for you."

Confused at her gaiety, Darla frowned and crossed her arms as her cousin continued to waltz. Rich or poor, she'd seen enough on Dauphin Island to know if the lady of the house wasn't happy with something, nothing would go right.

"Don't worry. Mother isn't one to go against Father, though she'll do her best to undermine things. The blue bed is yours. It's nice how it matches your eyes. I didn't expect that. All the Beauchamps I know have brown. Do you favor your mother?"

It was a simple, honest question but tears stung her eyes. Afraid to speak, she nodded.

Alice gave her a quick hug, and then plopped onto the frilly pink bed against the opposite wall. "You might want to dress for supper soon. Mother likes us to be in the parlor when Father comes home at five-thirty."

"I don't have much to choose from."

"Is everything black?"

"Not at all. We aren't ones to go about in black on the island for months at a time, but it's one of my better outfits and I felt it appropriate."

A knock sounded on the door and before either could respond, it opened. Aunt Ida entered, her chin high, and glared at her niece standing beside her trunks. "Do not get too comfortable, Darla."

Alice sat up. "Why not?"

"It has come to my attention that your cousin is not a fit companion for you, dear. Have no fear, I shall find her a spot in another location."

"No!" Alice leapt at her mother, hugging her lace-covered arms. "You can't take her away before I get to know her!"

"I do not think you two have much in common and will be bored with each other, even if you find you can tolerate her."

"I can already see I'll love Darla. Have you ever seen such eyes on anyone else in our family? We need to shop for a pretty dress to match them. Can we go tomorrow morning? I'll use my own money to get her a ready-made dress if needed."

"There will be no need of that, Alice, though I do think a few new dresses will be in order for church and company. Reginald didn't abandon church when he ran off, did he? Were you raised with religion?"

"All of us children were baptized and received our first communion on the island."

"But I'm sure Mass at the cathedral will be a new experience for you, and one you will need to look your best for."

Darla motioned to her trunks. "If you'd like to check my clothes first—"

"That won't be necessary. I can only imagine the state of your clothing with the work you did." She shook her head. "But are both filled with your wardrobe?"

"No, ma'am, only one. The other holds what items of my family I wished to hang on to."

Aunt Ida nodded. "I will see that it is stashed away for you. The one with your clothes could fit in the bottom of Alice's closet, I think."

"There's room for both, Mother. Don't take her away from me. She just got here."

"Then see that she washes up, brush her clothes, and try to do something with that hair of hers."

Four

Lucy looked at the clock on the mantel. A quarter to five. *Who comes calling this time of day?* She rose from her desk, stepped over the blocks Phoebe had scattered on the rug, and went for the front door.

The cook—part-time housekeeper and full-time friend—came down the hall from the kitchen, wiping her hands on her apron.

"I've got it, Naomi, but thank you."

"As you please, Miss Lucy." She smiled and returned to supper preparations.

Before opening the door, Lucy smoothed her pale blue tea gown, adjusting the white sash that sat empire-style above the swell of her belly. She caught her breath at the sight of who stood on her porch.

"Good afternoon, Mrs. Beauchamp. Would you like to come in?"

"Yes, thank you, Mrs. Davenport."

Mrs. Beauchamp had not stepped foot into the Davenports' house since the week Lucy moved in, a polite call to welcome her to the neighborhood after she married Frederick. Lucy knew Mrs.

Beauchamp and the other women on the street weren't pleased to have a ruined woman as their neighbor, but while most of the others had become indifferent to her over the four years she'd resided there, Ida Beauchamp wasn't one to forget.

"Excuse the mess. Phoebe played in here most of the afternoon." She motioned to the girl lying on her stomach in front of the fireplace looking at an illustrated fairy tale book. "Phoebe, can you say hello to Mrs. Beauchamp from next door?"

Phoebe jumped to her stocky legs and curtsied, her loose blonde hair springing about her shoulders. "Ma'am."

Despite her usual frown, Mrs. Beauchamp smiled. "She's a darling creature."

"We love her more than anything." Lucy sat on the sofa with Mrs. Beauchamp. "Do you care for tea or coffee?"

"No thank you, I won't be here long." She folded her hands in her lap.

Lucy glanced at her desk, hoping her neighbor wouldn't focus on her typewriter or the stack of manuscript papers beside it. She clasped her own hands on her knees. "How can I help you, Mrs. Beauchamp?"

"I hope to be the one to help you. Calvin let me know your husband mentioned you are looking to secure a mother's helper of sorts. Not a full-time governess, but a young lady to help entertain Phoebe and whatnot."

"Yes, exactly right." Lucy winced as the baby inside her shoved a limb into her ribs. She rubbed the spot through her lacey gown and smiled. "This one is proving more active, tiring me more than Phoebe ever did."

"Must be a boy." Mrs. Beauchamp smiled. "Mr. Davenport will be pleased for his name to be carried on, I'm sure."

Not being one to get her hopes up either way, Lucy returned a polite smile. "We'll see when the time comes."

"Of course, Mrs. Davenport. The reason I'm here is about my niece. I am not sure if you heard, but Calvin lost his younger brother over the summer."

"Oh, I had no idea. I'm sorry for—"

"He'd been lost to the family for two decades already." Mrs. Beauchamp smoothed her skirt. "He was a black sheep, as is said. Quite a mark on the family name. He ran off at seventeen with his younger sweetheart. We never even knew if they married for sure, but thankfully they had."

Lucy felt her face heat, knowing her neighbor would be saying more biting remarks if she had not been in the presence of someone equally guilty of marring a family's name.

"At any rate, he settled on Dauphin Island and raised a family there as a fisherman. A storm took out his boat and all of his sons a few months back, leaving his wife and daughter to fend for themselves."

The cold way Ida tossed about a family catastrophe proved her heartless and Lucy did not waste much breath on her. "How incredibly unfortunate."

"His wife, the poor thing, seems to have died of a broken heart last month. Calvin took it upon himself to send for the girl as we are her closest relatives, though we had never laid eyes on her. The family was estranged, as you can imagine."

"Yes, Mrs. Beauchamp." Lucy knew all too well the sting of not being spoken to by relations—especially sisters-in-law.

"Well the girl—young woman actually, as she's eighteen— arrived this afternoon. I learned from her chaperone that her mother was the island midwife and she's been training with her for years. She has assisted in births and with the mothers before and after their day. I thought she might be perfect for what you're looking for."

"Thank you, Mrs. Beauchamp. I should like to meet … I don't think you've shared your niece's name."

"Darla Beauchamp, and I can bring her round tomorrow afternoon if that's agreeable."

"Yes, bring her for tea, thank you. Freddy will be here and he's a fine judge of character."

Mrs. Beauchamp sneered. "I'm sure he is."

Hiding the hurt, Lucy stood. "I'm sure you need to get back to your family, Mrs. Beauchamp. Thank you for stopping by. I'll expect you and Darla at three tomorrow."

After seeing her out, Lucy collapsed on the sofa and wiped her eyes. Doff jumped into her lap and meowed, begging to be stroked, to which Lucy obliged.

"Phoebe, it's time to pick up your toys. Daddy will be here soon."

Lucy's vision blurred as she watched her daughter drop blocks into the basket. The rumble of Doff's purring and her daughter's angelic features kept her from falling into complete hysterics. But Phoebe's fair features—pale skin, blonde hair, blue-green eyes—were a source of misery to her as well. If there were a bit of her father in her looks it would warm Lucy's heart to be reminded of her devoted husband. Instead, the pale glow Phoebe inherited from her mother was an open slate to memories of the one she lost her reputation with. When melancholy struck, Lucy often imagined Phoebe was Alexander's and wept anew for his baby she conceived while they were engaged, but lost three months after their separation—a secret she swore she'd bring to her grave, though the weight of it threatened to drown her in recent months.

"Friday evening isn't for tears. I'm yours the next two days." Frederick settled beside Lucy and wrapped an arm around her. He smelled fresh from the shower, as he always did after his hour at the gym.

Doff jumped off her lap and circled to Phoebe, batting a wayward block with a paw. Lucy shifted, leaning against her husband's strong chest. Frederick held her tight for a minute, and then tilted her chin up to look in her teary eyes.

"While both are from salt water, can you not accessorize with pearls instead of tears for supper? I could fetch the strand I gave you for your birthday."

She smiled and kissed him. "You always know what to do, what to say. I love you, Freddy."

"What's upset you?"

"The highly esteemed Ida Beauchamp saw fit to step inside our home this hour."

Frederick groaned. "Her husband is pleasant enough, but what did she put you through?"

Phoebe, having finished with her toys, climbed on the arm of the sofa beside her father and snuggled into an embrace.

"Besides her biting remarks about marred family names and character, she's offered her niece as a possible mother's helper for us."

"I doubt anyone in her family is capable of such work."

Lucy put her arms around both Frederick and Phoebe, hugging the two people still on the earth she loved most. "That's what I thought, but this niece is the daughter of Calvin's estranged brother. She was raised on Dauphin Island and her mother was a midwife. She's trained under her the past few years and is schooled in tending mothers and children."

Frederick kissed her forehead, and then Phoebe's. "Sounds promising."

"They're coming to tea tomorrow afternoon."

"Excellent." He set Phoebe on the ground. "Princess, will you help Miss Naomi set the table for supper?"

"Yes, Daddy!" She ran for the hall.

Frederick turned back to Lucy, a spark in his brown eyes. His hand caressed her abdomen in slow circles. Even through her dress, his gentle touch lightened her mood.

"What more can I do for you, Goosy?"

His fond words, including his nickname for her since childhood, chased away the remainder of her sadness. She arched back against his supporting arm, exposing her neck to him. "Kiss me, and then hold me again tonight."

"It would be my pleasure."

Five

With trepidation, Darla followed Alice to the parlor. Aunt Ida was on the settee with Felix, and Alice alighted on the opposite side of her mother.

"Come sit." Alice patted the adjacent chair.

Darla offered a smile to her extended family. Alice nattered on about something musical to her mother and Felix kept his head down. Maybe he thought Darla would tattle on him for his trick. Several minutes later, Richard and Clarence entered. They greeted their mother and situated themselves across from Darla. Then Calvin Beauchamp came into the doorway. His mustached, oval face and balding head were similar to Darla's father and she willed her eyes to stay dry.

"Where's my long-lost niece?"

Darla stood. "Hello, Uncle Calvin."

"Pretty as a picture, like your mother, but I'll not stand for you causing someone to skip town with you." He shook her hand warmly, and then kissed the back of it.

"Calvin, don't give her such ideas."

"Come now, what young woman doesn't fancy being swept away in a romantic plot?"

Alice smiled, a dreamy look in her eyes.

"Shall we pick a topic more suitable for the children?" Aunt Ida asked as her husband kissed her cheek.

"Of course, of course."

Darla managed well enough through the next half hour, answering questions about her deceased family members, especially her father and his work. Whenever something was asked that could lead Darla to speak of her mother and her profession, Aunt Ida changed the subject.

On the way into the dining room, Uncle Calvin took his wife's arm. "Take her shopping and buy her at least two Sunday and three receiving dresses, as well as a party gown. I'm sure she'll have no shortage of callers."

Aunt Ida stiffened. "I already planned to take her tomorrow morning."

The supper table was beyond anything Darla thought would be found in a castle. The silverware gleamed, the china sparkled. Three forks, two glasses, multiple plates. She didn't know where to begin or end, so she watched Alice beside her to see how she tackled each course of the meal. By the time she finished eating, her white linen napkin in her lap was marked with buttery finger prints and a few blotches of the red wine she was given with the meal—her first taste of the drink.

When they all retired to the parlor, she felt light-headed. Clarence set himself at the piano and Alice retrieved a fiddle from a black case in the corner. Alice tuned the strings and they each did a few scales.

"Clarence and I would like to perform a piece we've been practicing for Darla's homecoming. Mozart's Violin Sonata in F."

With a wild rush of fingers over the keyboard, Clarence began. Alice's bow was soon working the strings of her violin just as lively. Never having heard such music—for all she was acquainted with on the island besides church hymns were ragtime and down-home style tunes of the locals—Darla was captivated by the images the bright harmonies created in her mind, almost as though a new part of her brain opened like a rusty door. Though she was happy, tears came to her eyes.

So caught up with it, she sat dazed for several seconds before joining in the applause at the end. Alice curtsied and Clarence bowed. When her cousin sat beside her, Darla grabbed her hand.

"That was the most beautiful thing I've ever heard. How do you manage it?"

"Hours of practice. I've been playing since I was four, same with Clarence."

"I could listen all day." Darla sighed with longing.

"Good, because the boys are tired of listening to me. Fresh ears will be a blessing to have about the house."

Not long after, Uncle Calvin retreated to his den for a smoke and the children were released to ready for bed.

"Darla, stay after a moment," Aunt Ida said. "Alice, you may wait in the hall for her."

She stood before her aunt after the others left.

"I am sure you'll be pleased to hear I've set up an interview for you. The family next door is expecting their second child and is looking for a mother's helper for their daughter. I thought it would be just the thing to keep you occupied and help you earn a bit of your own way in the world, as that is what you're used to. You are expected at three tomorrow for tea. We shall be sure to choose a dress with that meeting in mind while shopping in the morning."

Thinking she expected a response but not knowing what to say, Darla kept it simple. "Yes, ma'am."

"Alice will show you how to use the taps in the bathroom. I want you showered and your hair washed so you'll be ready to be seen in town tomorrow."

"Yes, Aunt Ida. Good night."

By the time Darla was showered, her hair combed and braided, exhaustion settled into her bones. Alice chatted about different stores she hoped they would go to while she readied for bed.

"I'm sure mother will be on me about practicing tomorrow. That Mozart piece was the only time I touched the violin today. I usually practice two hours or more daily." She rotated her wrists and smiled. "It's a bit freeing to skip, though I do enjoy it. But I'm glad you're here now, Darla. We'll be the best of friends."

The luxurious bed was well beyond any comfort she had enjoyed, but Darla couldn't find rest in the lavishness. Thinking of her humble home and work-hardened parents left her feeling misplaced in the finery. *Father left a life like this behind him because he loved Mama so much.*

The last thing she remembered was hearing a faraway clock strike two, and then the sun was pouring through the open window.

"Rise and shine!" Alice called as she pulled a corset snug around her waist.

Darla looked upon her cousin's tiny middle as she tugged the cords ever tighter. "That looks painful. I've never had to wear one before."

"It's not so bad when you get used to it, though I wish Mother would allow me to save it for evening affairs. Ever since I came out she makes me wear one whenever I leave the house though they're terribly out of fashion in my set." She studied Darla, now in her underclothes by the closet. "If I had a womanly figure like yours, I'd not mind showing it off. You'll be positively striking in the right shapewear. Maybe even too alluring for Mother's standards." She giggled.

Darla looked down at her thick middle. It only looked small compared to her wider hips and full bosom. There was no doubt she was a solid woman, unlike the wisp-of-a-girl Alice. "I'm built like my mother, fit for labor and not refined past-times like fiddle playing."

Alice laughed. "The right clothing will lead to finding the right man. The right man will allow you as idle a life as you wish, Darla."

"But I like to work. I love to—" She stopped mid-sentence, remembering her promise not to discuss what she and her mother did.

"You love what?" Alice slipped her thin arms into the sleeves of a lace blouse.

Darla pulled on her best Sunday skirt. "I love to help people."

"There's plenty of charity work to remedy that."

After breakfast, Uncle Calvin drove his wife, daughter, and niece to the center of the shopping district with the instruction to telephone when they were ready to be picked up. Their first stop was the women's department of Gayfer's, where Darla was outfitted with the foundations of a good wardrobe—undergarments, shapewear, and hosiery. Aunt Ida fussed over concealing Darla's curves now that she had everything lifted into place. Tops with too many ruffles drew the eye even more, while plain necklines accentuated what was naturally there.

"This will be the death of me," Aunt Ida complained as they left the next store empty-handed.

"I wish I had your problem," Alice whispered to Darla.

It took until noon to find the minimum outfits Uncle Calvin insisted upon. Rather than joining the family at the dinner table, Aunt Ida went to bed with instructions for Darla to dress for her appointment after eating.

"I don't see why she has to rush you off to work," Alice said while Darla changed.

"I told you, I like helping people." Darla struggled to use the button hook to fasten her new boots. She'd only ever owned one pair at a time and now she owned three pairs of shoes.

"She could let you join a ladies aide society."

"If this works out, I'll just be next door for a few hours a day. You could use that time to practice when you aren't in school, and then we won't miss any fun together."

Alice sighed. "I suppose you're right. I need to start practice now, anyway. Come tell me how it is when you return. I've never set foot inside the Davenports' house."

"I think I've been in and out of every house on the island. Have you not lived here long?"

"Nearly my whole life, but Mother doesn't associate with Mrs. Davenport—some scandal from her past that she says I'm not old enough to hear about. You'll have to find out what it is and tell me."

Darla laughed. "I'll see what I can do."

"That is lovely on you." Alice tied the sash of the sky blue tea gown into a perky bow at Darla's back. "You're a flawless hourglass and I'm merely a willow branch."

"You're lovely, Alice. Perfect for fifteen, I'm sure of it."

"I'll be sixteen within the month. Mother allowed me come into society last New Year's so I'd be able to enjoy the festivities this holiday season. I was the youngest debutante this season, though they only allowed me to attend two Mardi Gras balls. I did get one dance with the gentleman I fancy, so it was worth the effort it took to talk my mother into allowing me out." She dropped her voice. "He turned nineteen this year."

Darla smiled to hold back what she wanted to say of herself at Alice's age—holding squirming newborns and cleaning up the afterbirth. As soon as she had Darla's hair firmly in a chignon, Alice went to the parlor to practice her violin. Alone for the first time all day, Darla perched on the end of her springy bed. Images of the sand and surf flitted behind her closed eyes while the sound of the gulls and waves filled her ears. Yearning to walk barefoot in the sand overpowered her. She had an hour before she was expected next door and nothing to do. Nothing. Never having been bored, she didn't know where to begin, especially with homesickness wafting over her like high tide. Knowing she couldn't leave the property, she opted to go into the backyard for fresh air, even if there wasn't a hint of salt in it.

She found her way to the backdoor off a downstairs hall near the kitchen and let herself out. Seeing the expanse of lush green made her regret buttoning on the new boots. The cool grass beneath her feet would be almost as nice as sand between her toes. Keeping to the brick path to avoid dirtying her footwear, she retreated into the shade of an oak. There she found a stone bench and listened to the sounds of the cardinals in the canopy while the music of Alice's violin flitted out the open window.

Not long after, the clang of the iron gate at the side of the house jarred her to alertness. Over the top of a hydrangea bush, she saw Richard and Clarence with someone dressed more respectfully in a suit and tie to her cousins' play clothes. They were huddled together, voices low—a scene she'd often witnessed with her own brothers when they were up to no good.

After a moment, Richard got under the parlor window and began howling.

"Richard!" Alice screamed.

The three scattered. Richard went back through the gate, Clarence to the backdoor, and the third boy came straight toward Darla, a hand on his derby to keep it on his head.

When he reached her bench, he stopped. "Hello there. You must be the cousin from the island." He tipped his hat and offered a creeping, closed-mouth smile. "Otis Youngblood, at your service."

"Thank you, Mr. Youngblood." Darla nodded and offered her hand. "Darla Beauchamp."

"Call me Otis, but don't let the company I keep fool you. Richard and Clarence are good boys, but I'm of age. I'm finishing off schooling and an apprenticeship in the records department in City Hall." He brushed back his dark hair before replacing his hat. "Mind if I smoke?"

Darla shook her head.

Otis bent his knee and rested the sole of a shoe on the trunk of the oak, leaning against it as he lit a cigarette. "From the way your cousins talk, I expected nothing but a country girl. How wrong they were." He winked.

Darla clasped her hands in her lap. "Aunt Ida insisted on making me presentable."

"I wouldn't give that old battle ax all the glory. You've got a lot going for you, Darla Beauchamp." He gave her an appreciative look. "Will you attend Mass with the family tomorrow?"

"Yes." She broke his mirthful gaze by looking at the bushes.

Otis bowed and then straightened. "Then I'll see you at the cathedral."

He strolled out the side gate, a trail of smoke following him like the exhale of a steamship's stack.

Six

At precisely three, the bell rang. Lucy hurried to the foyer, knowing Frederick would soon join her. Wearing her best smile, she opened the door expecting to meet Mrs. Beauchamp's smug face. What greeted her instead was a haunting reminder of her past.

Rich, dark hair.

Bright blue eyes.

Fine, lace dress.

Through the tears that stung Lucy's eyes, the girl looked like Eliza Melling—Alexander's younger sister who gushed over and supported their relationship from the beginning. The artist who drove Lucy's own brother to make foolish decisions because he lusted for her. Eliza the chaperone, who was in Seacliff Cottage when Lucy lost her innocence there. But Eliza died the winter before Alexander left the world.

The young woman wobbled slightly, as though she wasn't used to the heels on her dress boots. If it was Eliza, she would have carried herself elegantly. Not that spirits walked around ringing doorbells.

Lucy's hand on the knob trembled, as did her voice. "Are you Darla Beauchamp?"

"Yes."

Feeling faint, Lucy continued to grip the knob. "Is Mrs. Beauchamp not coming?"

"No, she's resting this afternoon, Mrs. Davenport. If you'd rather me come back when she can accompany me—"

"No, by all means, come in." She stepped to the side. "The sitting room is to the left. Make yourself comfortable."

Lucy hung at the back of the sofa, resting a hand on the curve of the upholstery. Darla took a seat in one of the armchairs and looked at her expectantly.

Frederick came down the hall. "Lucy, are you unwell?" He rushed to her side and placed an arm around her, his free hand feeling her forehead.

Darla immediately stood. Frederick's eyes went from the young woman and back to his wife several times.

Lucy leaned into him. "Let me wash my face and I'm sure I'll be fine."

"Excuse us a moment," he told Darla before walking Lucy to the half-bath. He ran water to dampen a cloth. "She reminds you of someone, doesn't she?" he asked as he moistened her forehead.

"It was like seeing a ghost standing there. She must think me eccentric."

Frederick went for the tears that spilled down her cheeks. "She'll think you the most amazing woman once she gets to know you, Goosy. And you, when you look at her again and get to know her, will find it's just a similarity in coloring that set you off, nothing beyond a vague outline from the past."

"The havoc Eliza caused—not that I didn't create enough with my choices."

"We've had a fresh start. Let the past stay behind, unless you want to think about last night." He kissed her neck and caressed the back of her cream-colored dress.

She held him tight. "You hold everything together when I begin to fall apart. You always have. Whatever did I do to deserve you, Freddy?"

"You put up with Eddie all those years."

"The best choice my brother ever made was having you as a friend." Lucy kissed him, rekindling the passion that stirred within her for the man she married. "I'm glad we have each other."

"You were worth the wait." He trailed a finger down her cheek. "Are you ready now?"

She nodded and took his arm, pilfering another kiss in the process. He escorted her to the sofa and shook hands with Darla.

"Frederick Davenport, Miss Beauchamp."

"Darla, if you please." Her smile appeared stiff, showcasing her nervousness.

When Frederick sat beside Lucy, she spoke. "I'm sorry for being odd at the door. When I saw you I was reminded of … an old friend who's no longer with us. It was a shock to me. I'm not usually weakened like that. I think it's the state of my body at present."

Darla smiled easier. "I've seen all sorts of changes in mothers as their time progresses. It's the most curious event in human life."

Focusing on the girl's broad face as opposed to her startling eyes helped Lucy transition her thinking away from the Melling in her memory—both Mellings, because she couldn't think of Eliza without reminiscing of Alexander. His cool complexion, the feel of his lean arms about her as he lifted her off her feet to carry her across the yard or to bed.

"Do you have much experience with mothers-to-be?" Frederick filled the quiet, covering for Lucy's wandering mind.

"Two babies last month, eight this year. I was only the assistant, but it's my fourth year helping. Often I stay to care for the mother or other children the first few days as the mother regains her strength."

"What is your favorite age in children?" Lucy asked.

"Between three and five, when they're curious about the world and want nothing more than to play and experiment with their limits."

Had her aunt informed her of their daughter's age? But the excitement in her eyes is too sincere.

Darla continued. "The Campbells, the family I've been staying with this past month, have a three-year-old boy named Kade I adore. The Walker's youngest, Abraham, is the same age. Those two boys together were a joy to observe."

Frederick put an arm around Lucy. "Our Phoebe turned three in August. She'll be in when the tea comes."

"Phoebe Camellia," Lucy whispered, blushing as she touched the ghost of a white camellia blossom upon her ear. She glanced at Frederick and saw the concern in his sympathetic eyes. Never had she explained her choice of a middle name for their daughter, but she was sure her husband discerned it connected to her first relationship. Frederick understood she held back a few sacred truths, but he never pressed for them though he read the pain in her eyes.

"It's a poetic name," Darla said.

"She's the finest girl around, but I expect no less with Lucy as mother." Frederick placed his hand on her knee. "Phoebe is capricious and a joy. She's happy to be read to or run about with imaginary dragons and won't shy away from a sword fight should she find two sticks. She takes her role as protector in Kingdom Davenport serious."

Darla laughed. "The best type of child."

"What we're looking for is someone to come a few hours, Monday through Friday, preferably in the morning, and keep Phoebe entertained while Lucy wr—"

"While I work on my projects." She motioned to her desk in the corner. Only her immediate family knew she was a novelist. Her books were well received nationally and locally, but she knew that wouldn't be the case for the latter if Mobilians knew who wrote the romances their young ladies and housewives treasured. "I have my station set up in here so I can keep an eye on Phoebe, but we do have a study I could relocate to, allowing Phoebe and her helper more places to play and explore. You'd be able to take dinner at home or here, and your time would be over by tea, unless something comes up. On days you're flexible, I might ask you to stay on if it's agreeable. Extra pay, of course."

"And the possibility of evening watches, for me to take my lovely wife to a show or other such amusements."

"That all sounds fine." Darla's words rushed together.

"Good to hear." Frederick stood as Naomi and Phoebe entered with trays.

Naomi carried the larger tray with teapot, milk bottle, cups, plates, and most of the food. Phoebe, in a blue, dropped-waist pleated dress and black Mary Janes, held a small tray with a few cookies and the bowl of sugar cubes. Frederick was all smiles as he praised his daughter for her job well done. He opened his arms to her and kissed her cheek before whispering in her ear.

Phoebe skipped over, held out her dress, and curtsied. "Pleased to meet you, Miss Darla."

The young woman's face lit with joy and she appeared to restrain herself from scooping the girl into her arms. "You must be Princess Phoebe, brave protector of Kingdom Davenport."

Phoebe leaned closer to Darla. "We have tea first, but I can train you after."

"I look forward to it." Darla offered a hand, palm up. Phoebe placed hers on it and Darla lowered her forehead to the back of the girl's hand. "I'm at your service."

Lucy grasped Frederick's hand and squeezed twice as her daughter's eyes widened in joy. Then she poured tea for the adults and a teacup of milk for Phoebe, who'd settled on the floor beside Darla after making her rounds with the cookie tray. Doff crawled out from his hiding spot and happily drank milk Phoebe poured into her saucer and placed on the floor beside her.

Frederick made conversation with Darla, but Lucy couldn't focus on the exchange. She stared into her teacup as her mind wandered to the proof of her next novel she finished reading the week before. It was the first full manuscript she'd composed since she'd experienced a love affair of her own. Her four published books were all stories she'd written before she was twenty. Though she improved upon the drafts when going through edits, they were completely imaginary and innocent. The new one, *Winter of My Heart*, had taken her over three years to write and another year to be brave enough to send to Mr. Noble, her publisher. While Mr. Noble proclaimed it her best work, Lucy worried over Frederick and her family reading it. All those who knew her would plainly see the ghost of Alexander upon the pages.

"Lucy," Frederick said as he touched her hand, "is it all right for Darla to take Phoebe into the backyard?"

Startled, she looked up. "Yes, of course. I'm sorry I drifted off for a moment." She smiled at Darla and opened her arms for a hug from her daughter. "Have fun and train her well, Phoebe."

"I think she's a perfect fit here," Frederick said after they left.

"Phoebe seems to like her already." Lucy added hot tea to her cup.

"And I think she's what you need as well. You're much too isolated. It will be good for you to have someone else about to converse with. You're often within that beautiful head of yours while the world passes you by." His hand rested on her cheek.

She leaned into his touch. "I'm not lonely. I have Naomi and you and Phoebe and all these stories in my head."

Frederick placed her cup on the table and brought them to their feet, hands on her shoulders. "When did you last leave the house?"

Lucy looked away from his intense gaze and sighed. "Supper with my parents Sunday."

"As much as I love being your husband and best friend, I know you need more in life." Frederick caressed her as he pressed against her curves for a kiss. "You need women to discuss motherhood with, fresh insight, and camaraderie. Someone to complain about your husband to, or whatever it is wives do when they gather."

She wrapped her arms around him, kissed him with a passionate flare, and snuggled into his embrace. "Freddy, I appreciate your concern, but I have nothing to complain about. I'm often emotionally exhausted. Between you and Phoebe and checking on my parents and writing, I don't think there's time or energy enough for me to cultivate friendships. Especially when most women still shun me for my choices before we were married."

"Goosy, you've hidden yourself away since your time with Alex." She winced. So often she heard the name in her own mind, it felt sharp to hear it from her husband's lips. "If people still think of you as that carefree spirit who almost married a Melling, it's because you've given them no chance to get to know you. Practically the only people who've seen you on my arm are the members at Trinity and your family. You need to be seen around town as you are now, an amazing mother and wife with a husband who's completely devoted to you."

"You've been more than patient with me and deserve for me to be known as your wife rather than ruled by the shadow of my past."

He hugged her to him. "You won't mind if I make a few plans for us?"

She breathed deeply as she grasped for an ounce of bravery. "I trust you won't overwhelm me."

"I know your wardrobe is limited right now. You might want to go shopping next week and pick out a few dresses."

"You know I never cared for shopping, but it's even worse in my current state."

"A state of amazement for the glorious creation we've made together." He gently pressed his palm against the swell of her body. "Would you want me to go with you?"

"Yes, please."

"Then I'll take half a day off next week and we can have Darla watch Phoebe while we shop and have dinner out." He kissed her. "You do want to offer her the job, don't you?"

Lucy nodded and clung to him.

"Then I'll plan for us, Lucy. You needn't fear."

Seven

The Davenports were much like the Campbells in their loving manners, though more subdued, so Darla felt at home after having tea. Though a delight, playing with Phoebe made her miss Kade—and in turn, his mother and sister. Darla completed a half hour of sword training and then Phoebe was ready to return to the house. They propped their sticks against the back stoop and tromped through the tidy kitchen, greeting the cook with salutes.

Darla followed Phoebe's lead and they walked in on Mr. and Mrs. Davenport embracing in the front room.

"Miss Darla, ready for battle!" Phoebe announced in her high-pitched voice.

The Davenports laughed and he bent to lift his daughter into his arms. "You're a great leader, Princess."

Darla smiled wistfully, wishing she'd heard encouraging words like that from her father. Mrs. Davenport took Phoebe to help her wash and Mr. Davenport motioned to a chair. Darla sat, making sure she kept her posture respectable. He settled across from her on the sofa.

"It's clear Phoebe is already fond of you, and we like you as well. Lucy and I offer you the position. You can talk it over with your aunt and uncle, but we'd like you to start Monday if that's good for you. Otherwise, whenever you can. We're happy to have you. You'll be paid each Friday afternoon, five dollars a week for your basic days. Special occasion rates will be decided before time. How does that sound?"

"More than generous. Thank you, Mr. Davenport. You have a lovely family."

He turned to look down the hall, then focused back on Darla. "Lucy's a private person and has been alone much of the time, with the exception of Naomi who's here most afternoons to cook supper and help with cleaning. She's known Naomi since they were both girls so she's like family. If Lucy seems distant, don't take it personally. It takes her a while to warm up to people, but she's as kind and vibrant as anything when you get to know her."

"I could already tell she has a true heart."

He smiled, making his pleasant features more pronounced. "She does, but she doubts herself often. I believe you'll be a great encouragement to her, Darla."

There was nothing but love for his wife in his gaze, but Darla had to look away. "I don't see how, but I'll do what I can for both your wife and daughter."

"All I ask is for you to be yourself." He stood. "I'm taking my family for a walk to Bienville Square. Would you accompany us or do you need to return?"

"I should ask Aunt Ida. Would it be all right to come back in a few minutes with my response?"

"Of course." Mr. Davenport saw her to the door. "We'll plan on leaving in quarter of an hour."

Darla went next door as quickly as her unfamiliar shoes would allow. Alice still practiced in the parlor. Aunt Ida was on the settee and motioned her in. Alice stopped playing mid-note.

"How did it go?" Aunt Ida asked.

"They offered me the position. I can start as soon as Monday if—"

"That's fine. Perfectly fine." Aunt Ida's thin lips managed a smile. "Work whenever you wish."

Hurt she wasn't allowed to discuss the particulars; Darla sucked in her breath and continued. "The family is preparing to go on a walk to the square and invited me to come along to give me more time with Phoebe before I start with her officially."

"Of course you can go."

"May I change to my old boots to—"

"Absolutely not. You may wear them around the house and yard, or even next door, but never about town." She looked her over. "You look decent, but borrow a hat from Alice for your walk."

Alice took her arm and they climbed the stairs together.

"How is it? Is the house creepy? Mrs. Davenport mean?"

"It's all nice. The house, though not as big as this one, is well-tended. Mrs. Davenport is elegant."

"I've only seen her across the yard or through a window." Alice pulled a stack of hat boxes off a shelf in her closet. "Mr. Davenport talks with my father when they happen to come or go at the same time. He's handsome enough. Richard says he goes to a gym several times a week. His arms and shoulders do look larger than most other men's, but fancy a married accountant bulking up. Makes me wonder what her quirks are."

"Her husband says she's very private."

Alice opened the top box and set it aside. "Must be because of that scandal. Any clue what it is?"

Darla laughed. "I've only been there an hour."

Alice plopped a white sunbonnet on Darla's head but immediately removed it. "Does he seem the type to lock his wife up? Is she there against her will? Maybe that's why he's so strong, to keep her imprisoned."

"Not at all. They appear to love each other very much."

"Any couple can put on an act when company's there. You'll have to watch for clues." Alice tried two more hats on her cousin before settling for a navy one with a wide brim.

"Phoebe brought me back inside after playing in the yard and they were in each other's arms most fetchingly."

"Did you see them kiss?" Alice nudged her toward the dressing table.

"Yes, before that as well." Darla studied her reflection in the mirror. "Thank you. That does look nice."

"I'm going to try to slip out front and get a look at them when you leave. Make introductions if you can."

"I'll do my best."

After stopping in the parlor for her aunt's approval, Darla returned to the Davenports' home and rang the bell.

"I'm able to come along, Mrs. Davenport."

"I'm glad of it, Darla. And please call me Lucy. We aren't as formal as others around here." She smiled and allowed her inside. "Freddy went up to get my shoes."

It was then Darla noticed the lady of the house was barefoot. She sighed in longing over being in control of her own self enough to choose freedom from footwear.

"Whenever you're here, feel free to go barefoot. I'm sure those frilly boots aren't what you wore around the island."

"Do I walk as terrible as that?"

"You're doing fine, Darla. And I'm sure no one will notice your feet with that lovely hat and your charming smile."

"Thank you, Mrs. D—Lucy."

"Goosy," Mr. Davenport called from the stairs, "do you want stockings as well?"

"No, it's too warm today." Lucy blushed, looking out the corner of her eye at Darla. "You won't tell anyone I'm venturing out stocking-less, will you?"

"No, but I wish that had been an option for me."

"Keep it in mind for next time. It will be weeks before autumn weather arrives. Summers in the city are awful, and what others don't know won't hurt them." A faraway look crossed her face, causing first a half-smile, then rolling sadness. "You just need to be discreet so no one learns your secret."

Mr. Davenport carried a doll carriage down the stairs. Phoebe trailed behind him with her mother's shoes. He set the buggy on the hardwood floor at the base of the stairs and grinned at Lucy. "She has to bring Pinky along for the adventure."

"And Doff," Phoebe said.

Lucy made her way to the stairs. "Doff will stay with Miss Naomi." She stopped to check the contents of the doll carriage and smiled at her daughter. "You did a fine job tucking in Pinky, and Daddy carried her down the stairs so gently it looks like she's sleeping."

She sat on the stairs and slipped on her shiny black shoes. As her husband helped her up, Darla noticed the strength beneath his suit jacket—broad shoulders and arms more fitting for a fisherman than a well-to-do businessman.

Darla lifted the carriage off the porch for Phoebe and saw Alice sitting on the side steps at her house. Her cousin approached like a proper lady, though Darla was certain she wanted to run.

"Phoebe, this is my cousin, Alice. We live next door. Alice, this is Phoebe, who I'll be helping with."

Her blonde head bobbed as she curtsied in her charming way.

"Isn't she the sweetest thing!" Alice gushed. The Davenports stopped behind Darla and Phoebe. Alice's brown eyes went wide with surprise as she looked them over.

"Mr. and Mrs. Davenport, my cousin, Alice," Darla said.

Alice wasted no time taking Mr. Davenport's offered hand. She smiled kindly at him and then threw all her attention onto his reclusive wife.

Lucy was prettier by daylight. Her porcelain skin and uncovered head shone in the dappled sun under the oak trees. "Pleased to meet you, Alice. Do you happen to be the violinist?"

"Yes, ma'am. My twin Clarence plays the piano."

"I love listening to you play. Whenever I catch a strand of it, I open all the windows on the west side of the house. It's much better than the gramophone."

"And if you're playing when I return from work, I've been known to waltz her around the front room before settling in for supper," Mr. Davenport said.

Alice clasped her hands over her heart. "That's the most romantic thing! I never dreamed my music was being enjoyed. My brothers try to quiet me, but I'll play all the bolder knowing I have an audience."

The Beauchamp's front door opened and Aunt Ida stepped onto the porch. She raised a hand in greeting, face unsmiling. "Alice, Clarence is ready for the duet!"

Alice took her leave and the group started down the sidewalk. Darla and Phoebe were in the lead, with instructions to take a right on Conception Street. Darla tried not to spy, but she noticed the way Lucy clung to her husband's arm as though frightened. There was a tremor in her limbs, but she kept her chin high and her green eyes were as bright as anything.

"Do you take lots of walks with your parents?" Darla asked Phoebe.

"Just Daddy. Momma works a lot."

Darla snuck another glance behind her. The Davenports had stopped. His hands cradled Lucy's face and he spoke softly before kissing her fully on the mouth. Darla turned away and waited with Phoebe at the next corner until they caught up. Mr. Davenport took the lead when their group crossed St. Francis Street, steering them to the only empty bench in Bienville Square.

Mournfully, Lucy stared up at a nearby building. Darla followed her gaze to the second floor window of a law office.

"Darla," Mr. Davenport said, "you may walk Phoebe around the square wherever she'd like to go. And here's two cents so you can each buy a bag of peanuts. She enjoys feeding the squirrels."

"Thank you, Mr. Davenport."

He cozied beside his wife on the bench, an arm around her shoulder and a smile on his face. Darla followed Phoebe, pushing her carriage. The girl was much remarked over with her fancy doll carriage and angelic features. If someone enquired of her parents, Phoebe would point to the bench. Often, the questioners' faces showed surprise, and half the time they ambled around the fountain to get a better look.

Whatever is Lucy Davenport's secret?

***

Darla returned in time to wash for supper. She'd enjoyed her own bottle of cola Mr. Davenport purchased for everyone and her stomach felt pleasantly satisfied as she joined her relatives in the dining room. Alice tried whispering questions during the meal, but a harsh look from her mother quieted all inquiries.

After the silent supper, the family gathered in the parlor. Clarence and Alice once again performed together, this time a piece by Chopin. Darla wondered if the Davenports were dancing in their house. Lucy had looked scared on their walk to the park, and then sad sitting on the bench. It wasn't until a couple stopped to speak with her and her husband that a true smile graced her pretty face. After the brief exchange, Mr. Davenport glowed with satisfaction. His love for his wife was evident in all he did, and it warmed Darla's heart. She knew Alice would pester her for information, but she didn't want to give away the Davenports' confidence.

Once they were bathed and in their beds for the night, Alice started in. "Mother fussed at me good for talking with the Davenports, even told me I'm never allowed to step foot into their house. But it was worth it to see them for myself. You're right. She's divine, even being in the family way. They're the most handsome couple I've seen around town and their daughter is precious."

"I think I'll be happy working for them. They're what my mother would have called 'good folks.' Do you know the name Easton?"

"There's an import company with that name. They bring specialty items over from Europe and Asia. My parents used them last Christmas. The owners attend the cathedral. Why?"

"Someone in the park referred to Mrs. Davenport as 'Miss Easton.' Her husband was quick to correct him and the man seemed embarrassed by the mistake."

"Maybe she's a relation." Alice shifted in her bed. "Mother only talked about Mrs. Davenport in hushed tones with her friends after she moved in."

"Will they be at Mass tomorrow?" Darla asked as she fingered the smooth sheet.

"Heavens no. They're Episcopalians."

"I've never met one before. We only have three churches on the island, so everyone is Catholic, Methodist, or Baptist." Darla yawned.

"That keeps things simple. Maybe you'll be able to meet the guy I fancy tomorrow. We often sit near him in church. Henry Adams." Alice sighed. "Isn't that the most wonderful name?"

"It's handsome and solid."

Alice giggled. "He's no Davenport with his muscles, but his shoulder was firm under my touch and his arm supported me without fatigue when we danced. He has the most gorgeous wavy hair and dark blue eyes that look brown from far away. And the cutest nose, but it's his lips are the best. Oh, I hope he's my first kiss!"

Darla smiled in the dark.

"Are you much experienced with kissing?" Alice whispered.

She laughed. "I may have kissed a few boys."

"A few! How many beaus have you had?"

"None. Well, maybe one would have counted. We went out several times at least. He's long gone now, joined the Navy."

"A sailor? How romantic."

"Practically all the men on the island are sailors in one way or another, Walt just made it official."

"Walt. There's a strong, handsome name."

"He's nothing to moon over now. He's been gone almost a year without so much as a letter. Not that I expected one, mind you."

"But you wouldn't have turned your nose up at it, would you?" Alice asked.

Darla smiled. "Probably not."

"**Goosy,**" **Frederick called** into the dark from the bottom of the staircase. "Are you down here?"

"Yes." She could barely make out the clock face across the room, the hands pointing to the one and three.

He came to her, trailing his touch from her shoulder until he reached her hand, which he brought to his lips. Lowering himself to the sofa, he took her into his arms.

"Can you not sleep?"

"A nightmare woke me." She leaned into his warmth.

"The old one?" he whispered as he stroked her braided hair.

"No, thankfully not." She shivered at the memory of the reoccurring dream she had often during their first year of marriage—Alexander screaming for help within a burning Seacliff Cottage. "But it wasn't much better."

Frederick rubbed her bare arms, dispelling her lingering chill. "Tell me."

"We were promenading through Bienville Square. You looked amazing in a crisp tuxedo, top hat, and tails while I wore an exquisite red gown that showed off a narrow waist."

"You're exquisite now." He kissed her temple and ran a hand over her motherly curves.

Lucy took a deep breath and tried not to think that his words and actions were something that Alexander might have said and done. Alexander Melling hadn't touched her in five years, but still she remembered. Whether it was a tender word from her husband, the smell of sandalwood, or the sight of a member of Mystics of Dardenne—like Sean Spunner who'd spoken to her in the square that afternoon—her first love was there to haunt her, reminding her of their recklessness and the pain she was left to carry alone.

But she was never alone.

Frederick was there through the whole affair, ready to rescue her.

She continued to describe the dream. "The square grew crowded and the people became hostile. I was yelled at and things thrown at me. They taunted you, saying you'd chosen an unworthy wife. After enduring the assault several minutes, you left my side. I was caught and branded with the letter A. It burned scarlet on my breast, where …"

"Where what, Lucy? You need to stop reading Hawthorne, but you know I'd never leave you."

She snuggled against Frederick, her face angled down so he wouldn't see the tears building. "They branded me where Alex often left passion marks."

"He would, wouldn't he?" Frederick guffawed. "I never thought of passion marks. Is that something you'd like me to do, Goosy?"

Lucy sat straight, caught somewhere between shock and frustration. "And here I am worried you'd be upset that I'm even thinking of those old events while you joke over it!"

"I'm not teasing. If you enjoy it, I'd be happy to indulge you in the pleasure." He smiled as he stroked her neck. "Being husband and wife is a form of lovers. Just as Alex didn't want me out-dancing him, I don't want to be second-best at loving you."

"You're not, Freddy. Not at all!" Lucy climbed into his lap and wrapped her arms around him. "You're my best friend, my protector, my husband. I'm eternally grateful to be known as Mrs. Frederick Lionel Davenport."

Then they kissed as they hadn't in weeks, long, deep, and playful.

"It appears our passion still burns hot, Mrs. Davenport."

"Always, Mr. Davenport." She kissed his hand and laid it at the neckline of her silk nightdress. "On our carriage rides home from events, Alex would tug down the hem enough to plant his kiss over my heart."

"Marking you as his." Frederick leaned his forehead against Lucy's, his breath warm and sweet on her face. "I'd never want to mar you, Goosy, but if you wish for a passion mark from me, I'd grant your desire."

Her heart flickered under his hand as her body pulsed with emotion. She tried to slow her mind to catch the right words to explain in the least hurtful way.

"I enjoyed the intimacy and attention, but I often felt it burning afterward as a reminder of my sinful actions. I'd see it in the mirror for days and be regretful, but I was so enraptured I craved more." Lucy ran her fingers through Frederick's thick hair. "But with you, Freddy, there's never regret with our actions. If I can help it, I'd rather not see something that will weigh my heart with memories of another, even if created by you."

Because I already have that constant reminder with Phoebe.

As though he heard the unspoken thought and wished to comfort her, he brought his lips to her neck and nuzzled against her ear.

"Tell me, Goosy. Tell me of the pain you've been holding all these years. I see it on your face and hear it in your voice. It grows heavier each day. You needn't carry the burden alone."

Lucy squirmed out of his arms and crossed the room to her desk. She ran her fingers over the keys of her Underwood typewriter and turned back to the sofa. Over five years ago, she'd sat in that room in the dark of the early morning hours, wrapped in a blanket provided by Frederick, and cried. She'd been bruised and scared after Alexander's roughness and the only person she wanted to see was Frederick. She depended on him to help her and he cared for her before seeing her to the cathedral. It wasn't the only time she'd found succor in his companionship. It was a pattern Alexander had recognized and envied—ultimate trust and love.

A cool breeze billowed the curtains, rustling the edge of a stack of papers under a decorative glass weight. Lucy's summer gown blew around her legs in the draft as she returned to her husband. Standing before him, she cradled her arms around her belly.

"I carried his child, Freddy. For three months, I bore hope he would find me enough inspiration to change his ways. At Edmund's wedding, I saw him in the back with Eliza and found the courage to pen a letter to let him know of my condition."

Frederick stood and took her into his arms.

"I finished the letter and meant to call a messenger the following day to deliver it. My parents had gone to see Opal, so I was alone. I imaged he'd read the letter in his office and rush across town to me. But that night, I started having pains. I should have called you, I know I should have, but I called a cab service and told the driver I needed discreet medical help. He seemed to understand and brought me to the other side of town, near where Naomi was raised."

He kissed her face and held her tighter. "You should have gone to the hospital, Goosy. You could have gotten an infection and died."

She shook her head, tears cascading over her cheeks. "After convincing myself Alex would come, I was too scared to lose my last hope. I didn't wish the hospital to contact my parents. Mother never knew what was going on. I'd told her I still had my monthlies so she wouldn't send me away. I didn't want to go away from you and wanted to be near in case Alex decided to come back for me."

She allowed Frederick to sit her on the sofa and tucked herself under his arm before continuing. "The lady at the clinic was kind and the bed was clean despite the humble conditions. By morning, I'd lost the baby—a tiny girl, no bigger than a hummingbird. I wrapped her in a swatch of fabric from my underclothes and named her Camellia Alexandra. She was buried in a nearby plot with other little angels who never had the chance to breathe."

"My God, Lucy. I always suspected something happened that spring. You wouldn't receive me when I came for weeks, but I thought you were depressed because of Eddie's wedding. I should have known, Lucy. I should have known!"

They cried together, clinging to one another and to hope.

"It was like God was telling me to let Alex go," she whispered. "When he came to me at the Halloween dance, it took all my control not to kiss his mournful lips. I couldn't go to him after hearing of his continued exploits, but I still hung onto my shattered dreams and worried over him, especially after Eliza died. And then he sent those roses when *Azalea Blossom* published, so I knew he still thought of me. It wasn't until his engagement was announced that I knew he'd never return. By then, I'd recognized how deep my feelings for you were, but I was still too muddled to do anything about it other than kiss you good night."

Frederick took her wet face into his hands. "I waited years to feel your lips on mine. It stung all the more when you pulled away after the news, but I've said it before and I'll say it again: you were worth the wait."

"And you aren't mad that I named Phoebe Camellia after—"

His kiss tasted of sweet understanding.

"Long ago, I accepted the fact that a portion of your heart was elsewhere, but I didn't know it was occupied by more than Alex. A mother's heart has room enough for all, Goosy. I won't deny your past or shun the memory of who it created."

"I'm sorry for keeping it from you. You had the right to know, and I should have known you'd understand."

He rubbed her chilled arms and then unbuttoned his sleep shirt, draping it over Lucy's nightgown like a cloak. "You've owned my heart since we were children. I've only wanted to love and care for you. Tell me Goosy, is this the last step on your road to healing?"

Lucy kissed his warm skin as she wrapped her arms around his bare torso. "Phoebe is so fair and looks nothing like you. Sometimes, I imagine she's Camellia Melling and wonder what my life would have been like had I carried her to term. But the daydream doesn't last long because I'm struck with sadness over the lack of you in the vision."

"Phoebe has plenty of my mannerisms, even if she's a miniature version of you. Hopefully she has the best of both of us, including your big heart and wild imagination. Now, may I take you to bed, my wife? Do you think you can sleep?"

"Anything is possible with you holding me."

Nine

After Sunday breakfast, Darla and Alice readied for church.

"As long as it's not raining," Alice informed her, "Father drives us ladies to Mass and the boys walk. I often walk home with them. There's usually a bit of mischief to be had along the way, especially if Otis is with us."

"I met him in the backyard yesterday before I went to tea."

"And you didn't tell me? Whatever did he say?"

"It was just after Richard howled at the window," Darla explained. "Richard and Clarence escaped to the front of the house and Otis ran for where I was sitting under the oak. He didn't say much. He seemed to know who I was and introduced himself, making a point to let me know he was older and more mature than your brothers."

Alice laughed. "He may be two years older than Richard, but his maturity is debatable. What else then?"

"He took a smoke and asked if I'd be at Mass today."

"He's a tease if there ever was one, but he must like you. He doesn't bother the girls he doesn't like."

"I found him odd."

"Oh, he's not so bad, just loves mischief, like Richard. I'm sure he'll have an appreciative eye for you today." Alice helped Darla sweep her hair into a low chignon and loaned her the same pretty hat she'd worn to the Davenports' yesterday afternoon.

Aunt Ida requested Darla wear the high-waisted navy skirt and the lace blouse she purchased the day before. The skirt hugged Darla's curves and made her feel sewn into the tapered thing. The refined lady in the mirror wasn't the same young woman who walked off Captain Campbell's ship two days ago.

The Cathedral of the Immaculate Conception entrance was barred by six massive columns at the top of the steps. Darla followed her uncle and aunt down the nave, nearly tripping over her feet as she gawked at the arched ceiling and ornate stained-glass windows.

Alice took her elbow and whispered, "On the right, in the black suit."

The young man looked up as they passed and neither girl looked away. He seemed to hold Darla's gaze, but she was certain Alice would have said the same thing about him looking at her. His wavy, dark blond hair was worn parted smartly on the side and he had a pleasant smile. Henry Adams nodded and turned his attention back to the hymnal in his hand.

Alice clung to Darla's arm. "Is he not fine?"

"Very fine," Darla admitted. "He's so handsome he's almost pretty. What does he do?"

"He's finishing college this semester in something mathematical. I heard he's looking for an internship."

They took their seats on a pew near the front, Alice's brothers joining them soon after. A lady in a large, black-veiled hat took the spot in front of Aunt Ida and turned.

"Mrs. Beauchamp." She spoke with a refined southern drawl. "I have something to discuss with you concerning your daughter. When would it be possible to speak with you at length?"

Aunt Ida's shoulders went back and her chest expanded like a proud bird as she fingered the brim of her hat. "I'd be delighted to receive you for tea this afternoon, Mrs. Melling, or whenever is convenient for you."

"I shall come at three. I will speak with you alone, and then with your talented daughter." She turned to the front without further comment.

Alice fidgeted throughout the service, but Darla, enraptured with the scope of the cathedral, could do nothing but stare. Afterward, Aunt Ida motioned for the family to stay seated until Mrs. Melling had retreated up the aisle. Then she had Alice by the arm.

"We must ride home at once. You need to eat, change, and reset your hair before she arrives."

"But I wanted to walk home with the others."

"Not today, Alice. There's no telling what this is about, but it's sure to be something wonderful for your future. Mrs. Melling is known to take on projects and if she has her gaze set on you, then you'll be impeccable before her eyes. Come along, Calvin. No time for small talk today."

Alice linked her arm through Darla's.

"No, let your brothers see Darla home. We must hurry." Aunt Ida quickened her pace and Darla was left standing in the nave with a smirking Richard.

"Don't worry, cousin. We'll make sure you get home," Felix said.

"Thanks." Her smile waned before it reached her lips.

In the shade of the portico, the Beauchamp brothers and Darla were met by Otis Youngblood.

"Do we have the pleasure of escorting your cousin home?" Otis asked Richard.

"If that's what you want to call it."

"Richie!"

All the heads in the group turned to the sweet voice. A young woman around Alice's age waved her mantilla at the oldest Beauchamp brother from across the way. Her strawberry-blonde hair curled around her heart-shaped face where it had come loose from her chignon. A light dusting of freckles sprinkled her otherwise creamy complexion and her lips were the type that looked like they were ready to grant a kiss at any given time.

Clarence nudged his older brother. "Your girlfriend's coming, *Richie.*"

Richard slapped his brother away and straightened his tie. "Good day, Sadie. May I help you?"

"I'm looking for Alice. I came across something that's just the sort of thing she'd be interest in."

Richard narrowed one eye. "Scandalous?"

Sadie shrugged and tried to look indifferent. "Possibly."

"Deals with anyone we know?" Clarence asked.

"Naturally, because we know everybody who's anybody in this town." She giggled.

Otis stepped toward her. "Is it anything that someone more mature could help you with?"

"Oh, I don't know." Her gaze passed over Felix and fell upon Darla. "I'd forgotten the cousin is here. Hello, island girl!"

"She's no girl," Otis said. "Darla Beauchamp is a young woman and her aunt aims to make a proper lady out of her, but not too proper, I hope."

"You rascal! Pay him no mind, Darla," she said. "I'm Sadie Marley, by the way. Alice and I are the best of friends, or we would be if she didn't spend so much time with that violin."

"Pleased to meet you." It was easy to smile at her, so amiable she acted.

Sadie turned back to Richard with a flourish. "Did Alice go home already?" When he nodded, she continued. "Tell her I'll be over after three with enough to keep us busy all evening."

"Sorry Sadie, but Alice and Mother have a guest coming at three. Mother won't stand for any distractions today."

She gave him a pert smile. "Who's coming that's more important than me?"

"Mrs. Melling."

Her bow of a mouth curved into an O. Darla half expected Richard to steal a kiss, but he merely bit his own lip and shoved his hands into his pocket. "Tomorrow, after school should be fine," he said.

"I won't be able to wait that long. Tell her to telephone me as soon as she can. If it's not too late, I'll come over."

"I'll tell her," Richard said. "May I walk you home?"

"No, I'm riding with Grace Anne and John today. They're hosting the family at their house for dinner. I should be home by three, and a telephone call from Alice better come through."

"I'll be sure of it, Sadie." Richard smiled and watched her descend the stairs.

Sadie crossed the road and joined a pretty woman with curly ash-blonde hair on the arm of a crisply-suited man.

"That's her oldest sister, Grace Anne," Otis said as he stood beside Darla, "and her husband, Dr. John Woodslow. Sadie is the next to youngest girl, and spoiled. I don't fancy the bloke that marries her, but Richard can't get her out of his mind."

"Shove off, Otis." Richard stomped down the stairs, his brothers trailing behind him.

Darla had no choice but to follow. She stayed a few steps behind her cousins as they headed north, and Otis matched her pace.

He looked at her with his closed-mouth smile. "We could slow a bit and I'd see you home. You could even make it proper by taking my arm."

"That's kind of you, but I'm happy to follow the boys."

"They don't make you nervous? I heard Felix pulled a trick on you your first day here."

Darla laughed. "So he did, but boys don't scare me. I had three brothers of my own, one older and two younger, so jokes and the like are nothing new."

"I suppose there isn't much that shocks you."

"Not really."

His eyes held more than enough mischief. "That's good to hear."

***

Darla spent the after dinner hours in Alice's bedroom, watching her nervously pace the plush carpeting. Aunt Ida had already seen to her daughter and Alice was given strict instructions not to sit until summoned. Her silk afternoon dress was white with embroidered Chinese florals across the bust—something Darla would have been scared to exhale in for fear of smudging it. To be sure the house was peaceful, Uncle Calvin took the boys on an automobile ride and they weren't expected back before supper.

When the doorbell rang, Alice held her breath.

"Don't worry," Darla said. "It won't be much longer now. Think about Sadie and what excitement she has in store for you."

"It does sound mysterious. How did you like her, Darla?"

"She's pleasant, but didn't stay long. She had to get to her sister's house."

"Grace Anne is elegant and caught the eye of a doctor, no less. I expect she's about the same age as Mrs. Davenport. These married women make me wonder which of my friends will be the fashion leaders in another decade. The affluent women set the pace for the rest of the town by hosting parties and running charity functions."

Darla's island community was all about skills, not fashion. The women with the best canning, quilting, and birthing knowledge were the most respected. They all did their part to look nice on the Sabbath, but clothing the rest of the week was about practicality. It wasn't a good idea to gut fish while wearing lace.

They waited a quarter of an hour before the maid knocked on the door.

"Miss Alice is requested in the parlor."

Darla took her hands. "Good luck."

Then it was Darla's turn to pace. The minutes ticked by until Alice rushed in. "She wants to meet you!"

"What?" She stared at her cousin.

"Mrs. Melling wants to meet you as you are to accompany me." Alice took her arm and hugged it.

"Accompany you where?"

"To my violin lessons with a virtuoso from Italy! He's to be the guest soloist at The Battle House Orchestra the rest of the year and is taking only three students while he's here. I'm to be one! Mrs. Melling is his sponsor and she's picking the students for him. The others are grown men already established in local orchestras and string quartets."

"How marvelous for you!"

When they reached the parlor door, both Mrs. Melling and Aunt Ida looked up.

"Mrs. Melling, this is Calvin's niece, Darla Beauchamp."

Darla crossed to the settee, smiled, and gingerly shook the lady's hand. "Please to meet you, ma'am."

Aunt Ida laughed nervously. "She was raised on Dauphin Island and just came to us Friday."

"And she already has a part-time job," Alice said, "but her hours shouldn't interfere with my lessons."

"You are allowing her to be employed?" Mrs. Melling turned on Aunt Ida. "How will that help her prospects with finding a husband?"

"She's used to working, and it's only a few hours a day helping with a neighbor's daughter. Nothing that would make her less desirable to a man of her station."

Darla, not used to listening to people discussing her without her input, crossed her arms and sat heavily on the loveseat beside her cousin. Alice patted her knee and smiled.

"But what work did she do on the island besides helping around the house? Surely there aren't many shops or schools to offer employment to young women."

"Alice," Aunt Ida said, "could you fetch a teacup for Darla?"

When Alice was gone, Aunt Ida leaned closer to her friend. "Her mother was the island midwife and she assisted. Darla continued to help with birthing as recently as last week. Naturally it's not something I want Alice privy to, so we do not discuss it in her presence."

"Dear Ida, women are doing much more these days than they are given credit for. Is that something you enjoyed, Darla?"

Despite knowing her aunt would object, Darla wouldn't lie. "Yes, very much. Both my mother and Mrs. Walker said I was a natural at it, with instinct to know what to do and a calming touch to soothe mother and child."

"Mrs. Walker? Any relation to Captain Joseph Walker?"

"Yes, Mrs. Melling, that's Claire's husband."

"Such a small world! Captain Walker made our weekly deliveries across the bay when I lived full-time in Seacliff Cottage. How is he? It's been four years since I have seen him. He was such a dear to me those months. He took tea with me practically every Friday."

"He and his family are very well." Darla smiled easily. "The Walkers have a fourth child now. Boys at the top and bottom with the two girls snug in the middle."

"How wonderful."

"Should I let them know you asked after them?" Darla asked.

"Of course, dear."

Alice returned with a cup and saucer and filled it for Darla.

"And the family she stayed with this last month is also connected to the Walkers," Aunt Ida said. "Perhaps you know the Campbells as well."

"The Campbells? Douglas and Magdalene Campbell?" Mrs. Melling's teacup rattled on its saucer and she turned pale under the brim of her black hat.

"Yes." Aunt Ida nervously fingered her skirt. "They took tea here on Friday with their children when they brought Darla."

"Of all the pain!" Mrs. Melling set her tea down with a clank upon the coffee table. "I must go. I shall meet the girls Thursday at four in the hotel lobby. Come ready with your best piece, Alice."

Aunt Ida hurried to follow Mrs. Melling to the door, apologizing for anything she'd said that upset her. By the time she returned to the parlor, she collapsed onto the settee, covering her eyes.

"I hope I haven't ruined your chances, Alice. That was the worst thing I could have said to Mrs. Melling."

"But why? What are people from the island to her?" Alice asked.

"Fetch me the brandy, dear. I need a bit to set me to rights."

Alice brought the decanter from a cabinet in the corner and her mother poured it directly into her teacup. "I don't know why I didn't connect the names before. She'll never forgive my cruelty."

"What is it, Mother?" Alice sat beside her mother and took her free hand.

After sipping the brandy, Aunt Ida sighed. "Magdalene was Mrs. Melling's companion when she lived across the bay. She was Magdalene Jones then, but Campbell was her chauffer. He came from Scotland that year, a relation to the carriage driver. The Campbells were at Seacliff Cottage when it burned. They were the last ones to see Mrs. Melling's husband and son alive."

Alice gasped.

Darla's mind raced. She knew Captain Campbell's uncle who passed away in February had been a coachman across the bay and that Magdalene had been a companion, but she hadn't placed them as working for the same family. Nor did she know why they left employment there. Could it have been because of the fire?

"I should have put it together. Magdalene isn't a common name." Aunt Ida drained the remainder of her drink. "Now your chance of working with Valentino De Fiore is in jeopardy."

It was Darla's turn to gasp. De Fiore was a name she saw often on Maggie's letters to her Italian priest—a friend she had met while working across the bay. Aunt Ida excused herself and went to lie down.

"How is it Mrs. Melling is arranging the students for the violinist?" Darla asked Alice.

"She's friends with his cousin, a—"

"Priest in Louisiana?"

"How did you know?"

"The priest is good friends with Maggie—Mrs. Campbell. They write each other weekly. They must have met when she worked for Mrs. Melling."

"And the plot thickens! Something scandalous must have happened there, I just know it. A society companion marrying the driver, friendship with a priest, and the men burned alive. Why couldn't the Campbells rescue the Mellings? Did they set the fire?"

"Alice! They're good people. I'm sure they had nothing to do with the fire."

"You'd swear your life on it?"

"Yes, I would." Darla stood.

"Even after seeing how upset Mrs. Melling got at the mention of them?"

"She was probably upset because it made her think of her husband and son, not because the Campbells are guilty of something."

Ten

Later that afternoon, the door opened and Darla
sat up from where she lounged on her bed. Alice led Sadie in the
room.

"I have to be home in time for supper, but I know you'll
want to go through these." Sadie plopped down in the middle of the
rug with a decorative hat box, her blue Sunday dress fanning out
around her. "Hello, Darla. Come join us."

Darla and Alice both sat near Sadie, creating a triangle of
intrigue around the mysterious floral-print box.

"I found this in the top of the wardrobe in Grace Anne's old
room yesterday. I knew it was a treasure, but I didn't know how
much until I asked her about it at dinner." She took the lid off and
tossed it across the room. "Ladies, here we have two years' worth of
Snitch magazines, edited by none other than Kate Stuart!"

"Kate Stuart?" Alice asked.

Sadie laughed. "Now better known as Mrs. Kate Lyons, wife
of the owner of Lyons, Melling, and Associates."

"I though the Mellings were all dead except Mrs. Melling,"
Alice said.

"But they are. Mrs. Melling sold Mr. Lyons the law practice on the condition he would keep 'Melling' in the title while she's alive."

Darla recalled yesterday afternoon in Bienville Square with the Davenports. The law office Lucy gazed at mournfully when they arrived was that exact building. *How did Lucy Davenport fit into the story?*

Sadie pulled out a few copies and passed them to the others. "It appears Mrs. Lyons was always a leader. She spent most of 1904 through 1906 compiling gossip on the single or newly married ladies in town. It came to an abrupt halt with the hurricane of September 1906."

"How was the island during the storm?" Alice asked Darla.

"It was awful, but we all banded together to help each other." She wanted to add that she'd helped with birthing a baby for the first time during it, but held her peace.

"Grace Anne told me there were a few tidbits about her in here, which I vaguely recall her being upset over at the time, but I don't remember the details. Not that she would have shared them with me. I was a mere child then. She assures me the stories in here are all about society ladies of her age group, complete with scandals and jokes. We're welcome to them, she says, but she won't tell us who's who. We have to discern that on our own."

"Thrilling!" Alice took her friend by the hand. "But first I have to tell you about my news. Mrs. Melling is sponsoring the guest soloist for The Battle House Orchestra, a young virtuoso from Italy named Valentino De Fiore. He arrives tomorrow and he's agreed to take on three pupils while he's here through the end of the year. She's chosen me as one of the prospective students! My first meeting is Thursday so he can plan for how to instruct me. If he accepts, I'll have lessons Monday and Thursday afternoons with Darla as chaperone."

"An Italian violinist named Valentino? How romantic!" Sadie squealed.

"Mrs. Melling said the posters would go up tomorrow and the article printed in the paper today, but I haven't had time to look for it since I found out."

"I could fetch the newspaper for you." Darla motioned to the magazines. "It's not like I would know any of these people."

Darla was glad her aunt wasn't in the parlor, but felt sorry for her if she was still nursing sadness over upsetting Mrs. Melling. Rather than being bored over gossip about strangers, Darla settled in an armchair with the newspaper and flipped through it. On the society page was a small article and advertisement about the coming of Valentino De Fiore. From the article she learned he was young for a soloist—twenty years of age—but had already performed all over Europe and the East Coast. The advertisement showed his handsomeness. If she were Alice, she wouldn't be able to think straight in the same room as him, let alone play music. She folded the newspaper carefully to mark the page and brought it upstairs.

"Darla, you were wrong about not knowing anyone in the magazines," Alice gushed as soon as she returned. "We started backward. Here, read this from the August 1906 issue!"

The talk of the month hails from the Eastern Shore. While the New York papers are linking our own A.R.M. to a NY socialite while they both summer in Newport, Mr. M's gracious mother is lounging in luxury near Montrose this season. Seen often at the Point Clear Hotel with a fresh face, M.J. of Seven Hills, and driven around Baldwin County by a handsome chauffeur, everyone is happy to see Mrs. M back in society after her heartbreak this past winter. May her lovely daughter continue to rest in peace.

Darla stared at the snippet twice as long as necessary.

"That's the Melling family, so that makes the chauffeur your captain and M.J. your friend, Maggie. Mother said her name was Jones back then, remember?"

"Yes. But what happened to Mrs. Melling's daughter?" Darla asked.

"She died that year in a horse riding accident." Sadie took the magazine back. "Grace Anne was upset for weeks over it, especially because the family didn't host a funeral in Mobile. She felt she had no closure because our parents wouldn't let her travel across the bay to see her buried in a common cemetery."

"Mrs. Melling lost all her family within a year?"

"Yes," Alice said, "same as you."

Darla shivered. "Now I feel sorry for the lady."

"I need to run, Alice. I'll be back in a few days to discuss your finds." Sadie hugged her friend and then Darla. "I'm happy you're here to keep her company. She spends too much time with her violin."

Darla smiled. "It was nice to meet you."

Alice saw her friend down, then pointed to the newspaper beside Darla when she returned. "Did you find the information?"

"Yes." Darla passed the paper to her cousin and watched her reaction as she looked over the article and photograph.

"I'm glad he isn't an old man, but I wonder how proficient he is in English." Alice looked to Darla. "It would be awful to spend half the lesson asking him to repeat himself if his accent is too thick."

Surprised she made no reference to his picture, Darla asked her opinion. "He looks intense with those deep-set eyes and long hair, doesn't he?"

Alice shrugged. "Looks like an old cabinet card photo. Those always have the subject dolled up. I bet he looks nothing like that now, even if he is only twenty. We need to make sure we bring the newspaper back when we go down for supper. Father might want it this evening since he was out all afternoon."

And with that, nothing else was said of Valentino De Fiore, though he was all Darla could think about that night.

***

After Monday morning breakfast, the Beauchamp children left for school and Uncle Calvin for work. Darla looked across the dining table at Aunt Ida, but she wouldn't meet her eyes.

"I'm heading over to the Davenports' now. I'll be home about the time the others return from school."

"No hurry, as long as you are home for supper, but we won't wait for you."

"I wouldn't expect you to."

"When you return, come through the side gate and use the back door so you don't disturb anyone."

"Yes, Aunt Ida. I hope you have a good morning."

On the front walk outside the Davenports' house, Darla paused. Was she considered the type of help that should use the back entrance? The front door opened and Mr. Davenport stepped out.

"Darla, I'm glad you're here." He leaned back inside. "Goosy, Darla is here! I'm sending her in."

Darla started for the steps. "Good morning, Mr. Davenport."

He smiled and shook her hand when they met on the porch. "Thank you for coming. I'll see you at dinner."

Phoebe joined them. "Need hug, Daddy."

He set down his briefcase and scooped her into his arms. "I hugged you three times already, Princess, but here's one more. You show Darla how we do things around here."

"Yes, Daddy." She squished his cheeks together and kissed him before he could set her down.

Mr. Davenport laughed. "I'll be back in a few hours, Phoebe."

With her fingers firmly held by Phoebe, Darla entered the house.

Lucy came in from the kitchen, an apron over her silk robe. "Sorry, but I haven't had time to dress yet. It will just take me a minute. Phoebe, why don't you show Darla your room. She didn't get to see it the other day."

Several minutes later, Lucy found them happily playing in the girl's room. Dressed in a loose-fitting blue silk dress, the lady of the house shone with happiness.

"She showed me how she makes her bed," Darla said with surprise.

"That's something my siblings all learned on our third birthdays. She's a big girl, and soon to be a big sister." Lucy's smile was radiant. "Freddy moved my things into the study yesterday, so I'll be in there. I'll leave the door open in case you have questions or need anything."

"Play outside?" Phoebe asked.

"Yes, Phoebe, as long as you stay with Darla." She pointed to her old boots. "I see you dressed for comfort today. That's great. I don't want you feeling stiff here."

The three separated in the downstairs hall, Lucy disappearing into the small study near the dining room. Darla spent the morning between Phoebe's room and the back yard. Every time they passed the study, she glanced in. Lucy would either be typing or pacing the floor in front of the opened window.

When Darla and Phoebe tromped in at eleven-thirty, Lucy was once again aproned and in the kitchen.

"We keep things simple at dinner, but you're welcome to stay for it. Freddy's coming home to eat. He does that more often than not." She stirred a pot of vegetable soup on the stovetop.

"Yes, thank you. I'd enjoy that. I don't fancy lunching alone with my aunt."

Lucy's laughter rang out like joyous bells. "I can understand. We usually start eating between twelve and a quarter after, so if you can see that you're both washed up by then, I'd appreciate it."

"Yes, Mrs—Lucy."

"And Phoebe likes to set the table. Thank you, Darla."

When Mr. Davenport returned, he greeted Darla and Phoebe before disappearing into the kitchen while Darla oversaw the girl setting the dining room table. Lucy's laughter in the kitchen caused Phoebe to giggle.

"Daddy teases Momma," she whispered.

Darla smiled at her. "They love each other very much."

"I love Doff!"

"Doff," Mr. Davenport said as he carried in a platter of delicatessen sliced ham and cheese. "Where's that cat hiding today?"

"On my bed!" Phoebe jumped up and down. "He played outside with us!"

"Then let that kitty sleep while we eat. Phoebe, would you get the fruit bowl from the kitchen counter?"

"Yes, Daddy!"

"Everything going well, Darla?" he asked as soon as his daughter was gone.

"It's been a pleasant morning. I've been curious though, what kind of name is Doff?"

"The fancy of my two girls." His brown eyes shone. "Phoebe was two when I brought him home. She petted him and declared him soft, but it sounded like doff. Lucy thought it the dearest thing ever and we've been calling him Doff ever since."

"That's sweet. May I help bring in anything?"

"No, I just need to fetch the soup and my wife. We'll be here in a jiffy."

Darla couldn't help but smile. The Davenports were infectious with their love. No hint of sadness crossed Lucy's face as she'd seen several times on Saturday. Darla took her meal alongside Phoebe so she could help the girl with anything she had trouble with. She sat in a specialty chair made to match the other dining chairs, but the seat bottom was half a foot taller so she was at the correct height for her size.

Mr. Davenport wiped his mouth and looked across the table at his wife. "The new intern started today. I thought we could host him for supper one day this week, but dinner might be better—less formal so as not to overwhelm the young man."

"That would be fine."

"We can ask Naomi to fix something hot so we don't put you out. Were you able to work much this morning?"

"Yes." She held up three fingers. "It was a good morning."

"Excellent! You pick the day to host, and then I'll plan our shopping day from there." He turned to Darla. "One day this week, I'd like to take Lucy out for shopping and a meal if you could stay longer that day."

"Any day but Thursday is fine. I'm sorry for any inconvenience, but starting next week, I'll not be able to stay late on Mondays or Thursdays. Alice was offered the chance to study violin under a visiting soloist. I'm to be her escort when she goes to meet him this Thursday, and should all go well, accompany her to her lessons twice a week after school."

"What an honor for her," Lucy remarked. "And it's no trouble."

"Is it the young Italian at The Battle House?" Mr. Davenport asked. "I read about him in the paper."

"Yes, the very one." Darla wiped a smear of butter off Phoebe's cheek. "Mrs. Melling stopped by after Mass yesterday to extend the invitation to Alice."

Lucy stood so fast Darla didn't understand how she stayed upright.

"Excuse me." Lucy disappeared up the stairs.

"I'm sorry, was it something—"

Mr. Davenport shook his head. "No worries, Darla."

"Mrs. Melling is Valentino De Fiore's sponsor," she explained. "Is Lucy familiar with her?"

His smile was bitter. "More than she'd like to be, though it's been years since she's spoken to her. I read she was sponsoring the man but never thought it would come up in conversation."

"I'm truly sorry to upset her."

"She'll be fine shortly, but I'll see to her."

Darla was left in the dining room with Phoebe, fully understanding how awful Aunt Ida felt yesterday when her words chased Mrs. Melling from the house.

Eleven

"Goosy," Frederick said as he let himself in the bedroom. "Are you all right?"

He sat on the bed and wrapped her in his arms.

Lucy accepted his offered handkerchief and dabbed her eyes. "It was a shock to hear the name so casually."

"Mrs. Melling is the violinist's sponsor, that's why she met with Alice. She's setting up students for him."

"Ida Beauchamp and Ruth Melling must be friends. They're so similar with their cutting remarks and looking down their noses at me. I was never good enough in Mrs. Melling's eyes and I'm forever stained in Mrs. Beauchamp's opinion."

Frederick's hand trailed from her jaw down to her neck. He nestled against the hollow of her throat, kissing her with his warm lips. "But you're golden in my eyes, Lucy. Always and forever."

She positioned herself to be kissed more, lying back on the bed. His brown eyes brightened as her mood lifted.

"You glow more each day with beauty and love."

She caught his hand and brought it to her lips. After kissing his palm, she placed it on her belly, allowing him to feel the movement. "It's been a while since we ended up on the bed midday. You've awoken my passion as well as the baby."

He laughed and kissed her ear. "Tonight, Goosy. As for that acrobat within you, I hope the babe is gentle on your ribs." Frederick's hand lingered as he smiled. "Thank you for mothering our children."

"Freddy, you're the key that unlocks my happiness." Lucy caught him by the collar and pulled him closer. "Now please go back to work so you can return all the sooner."

They kissed several times, and then he led her down the stairs on his arm.

After hugging their daughter goodbye and assuring Lucy he'd call with the day for the dinner so she could ask Naomi to help plan for it, Lucy, Phoebe, and Darla were left in the dining room.

"I'm sorry if I said something—"

"No worries, Darla." Lucy gathered Frederick's dishes. "You know how pregnant women can be with moods. All is well, and I'm glad to hear about your cousin. It's a splendid opportunity. If you could help me bring the dishes to the kitchen, I'd appreciate it."

The telephone rang the next hour, and Lucy stopped typing midsentence and picked it up from the box mounted on the wall between the kitchen and dining room.

"Davenports' residence."

"Are you ready for me to have wires run to the study so you can get one of those desktop models?"

She laughed. "Now that I'm working in the study, I'll think about it. It is a bit difficult to pull myself up some days and it will only get worse."

"Dinner with the intern Thursday. That should give Naomi plenty of time to plan and prepare. Now, would you rather go clothes shopping tomorrow or Wednesday?"

"Let's get it out of the way and go tomorrow."

"I'm going to make a reservation for the Trellis Room. If Darla can stay all day, that's good. Otherwise, ask her not to come until two and we can leave for shopping then. Tell her an extra dollar, all right?"

Once Darla was secured for the next day, Lucy returned to work on her newest project, a mystery involving a young mother and an eccentric neighbor. She was vaguely aware of the comings and goings of Darla and Phoebe until she heard Naomi come in at three.

"Afternoon, Miss Lucy," she said from the doorway. "How's the new girl working out?"

"Phoebe adores her." Lucy stood and stretched. "It's about time for me to take over. Freddy's invited an intern from his office over for dinner Thursday. Would you be able to help prepare something? I can give you money and the shopping list so you could bring things when you come Wednesday afternoon or Thursday morning."

"That'd be fine. I'll start thinking about it while I prep supper."

"And Freddy and I are going out tomorrow afternoon. Shopping and supper, so it will just be Phoebe and Darla tomorrow evening."

"First a walk to Bienville, now a full outing. What's gotten in to you this week?" Naomi winked her blind eye.

Lucy hugged her old confidante. "You know my past. I've allowed it to creep up on me, shadowing my present. For now and the future, I'm trying to break free from it."

"For all your heartache, you've had more love in your life than most, Miss Lucy. I've seen you with your husband, and before that with your old fiancé. I know it didn't turn out well, but you had some good moments with him. Focus on those." She patted Lucy's back. "Remember how excited he was to learn you slept with his handkerchief under your pillow?"

She laughed through a sob. "The love in his eyes was my undoing. They were steely blue when upset, but bright as a spring sky when all was well. I feel unfaithful to Freddy when I think of Alex, but it's difficult not to, especially during certain times of the year."

"Mr. Frederick's a fine man. He loves you more than you know."

"I've been consumed by Alex so long I'm afraid I don't know how to let go." Lucy stepped back, distancing herself from her friend. Her gaze fell on Phoebe and Darla coming out of the living room. She didn't realize they were inside. Heat from embarrassment over what they might have overheard colored her cheeks.

"Any request for supper tomorrow, girls?" Naomi asked.

"Shrimp and grits!" Phoebe pulled Naomi's skirt. "Shrimp and grits!"

"Is that all right with you, Darla?"

"Anything is. I'm easy to please."

"Shrimp and grits it is." Naomi tickled Phoebe and the girl ran off laughing. "I'll stop at the market on my way over tomorrow for the shrimp."

"Thank you, Naomi." Lucy turned to Darla. "And whenever you can make it over tomorrow is fine. No rush. I'm not sure how much wr—work I'd get done before we leave. It's been so long since I went out on the town I hardly know how to dress."

"I'm sure you'll be lovely," Darla said.

"Thank you. I feel weighted down much of the time."

***

"Writing six pages yesterday was wonderful, Goosy." Frederick brushed through her hair as she sat at the dressing table. "And you feeling free enough to come to bed with me at a decent hour was even better. I hope your days continue to go well with Darla here."

"What should I wear?"

Frederick leaned down and kissed her neck. "Whatever you wish."

"I fear what I'm seen in today will set the tone for the future of Mrs. Davenport. How do you wish your wife to be known? Light and frilly? Dark and mysterious?"

"You're already considered mysterious, Goosy. You hardly leave the house." He set her brush on the table and pulled her into his strong arms. She relaxed into her safe spot as she clung to him in return. "But you'll be gorgeous no matter what. Everyone will be looking, so wear something you'll be comfortable in despite the stares."

"Then nothing red to match my blush." *And because it was Alex's favorite color.*

He kissed her forehead. "Greens, blues, and pinks have always been my favorite, though I love you no matter what you wear."

"I know you do, Freddy. I just want to be sure I'm presentable on your handsome arm." She straightened his blue tie and smoothed his navy jacket. "You're wearing your best day suit and I need to be equally matched."

Frederick touched her skin above the low neckline of her nightgown. "Our hearts are matched in every way possible."

They kissed and held each other until they heard Phoebe in the hallway. Frederick saw to her while Lucy fixed breakfast in the kitchen.

Lucy tidied the small table in the kitchen when Darla knocked on the door.

"I fear you'll find me incredibly lazy still wearing my robe two mornings in a row."

"It's nothing to worry about," Darla said as she entered. "I'm sure you didn't want to spoil your going out clothes when you cooked breakfast."

Lucy laughed. "Nor do I have the energy to change multiple times this morning when I'll be trying on clothes all afternoon. Freddy took a sack lunch today. I'll need to leave before one-thirty to meet him at the office. I want to let him show me around the business before we leave. I usually only go in at Christmas to help distribute gifts to the staff. It's time I get out more, especially since I might miss the Christmas visit with the baby due near then."

Darla followed her into the kitchen. "Why haven't you gone out much?"

"I've never been one for big events, but before I was married, I made several mistakes that became widely known. Most ladies, like your aunt, look down on me, so I've kept to myself."

"All this time?"

Lucy nodded and turned to wash her hands at the sink. "And poor Freddy. He's so patient and never complains, but I know it has to hurt him not to have me beside him at the typical festivities for those of his station. He turns down invitations on my account, and I don't want him to feel like he needs to do that anymore."

Darla's blue eyes seemed to brighten with the information. "What's changed your mind? Oh, I'm sorry, I don't mean to pry. Forget I asked."

"Time has been the main thing, but also one of my projects and this pregnancy. I want to give Freddy back all the support he's shown me."

"Let me know if you need anything. I'd be happy to help if I can."

Lucy spent a few hours writing, then took lunch with Phoebe and Darla while still wearing her kimono. At one o'clock, she descended the stairs wearing a navy Every Size Maternity Skirt she'd mail ordered the previous month and a mint green blouse with lace detailing at the neck and cuffs. Her hair was swept into chignon and topped with a navy ribbon.

Darla lay on the rug in the living room reading a book aloud to Phoebe.

"Do you think I'll be okay in this? There's so little I have that fits me right now."

"Momma!" Phoebe ran to her and threw her arms around her legs. "I go shopping too?"

"Today I need you to help Miss Darla." Lucy kissed Phoebe and took her hand before looking to Darla. "Naomi will be here about three. She has a key and lets herself in the back. If you need us before five, call the office and one of the workers can find us, otherwise telephone The Battle House."

"We'll be fine." Darla smiled. "You look lovely. Try to enjoy yourself."

***

When Lucy walked into Davenport Allied Accountants, the secretary gasped.

"Mrs. Davenport, it's good to see you. You're looking well."

"Thank you, Ms. Neves." Lucy smiled at all the workers and tried not to twist the strap of the leather purse in her hand. "Is Frederick in a meeting or with a client?"

"Not last I checked," one of the clerks said. "I'd be happy to get him for you."

"I'd rather surprise him myself, thank you."

She made her way through the maze of desks and file cabinets and past several men hunched over counting machines. They glanced up when she crossed before their tables and stared open-mouthed as she continued to the back office. The oak door with FREDERICK L. DAVENPORT, OWNER lettered on the frosted glass inset was a few inches open. Lucy peeked in to be sure he was alone and then closed the door behind her.

Frederick looked up from the papers on his desk and a slow smile spread across his face, causing the dimple on his right cheek to show. He crossed the room and wrapped her in an embrace. "You look fabulous. How was the walk over? Not too tiring, I hope. I wished you would have allowed me to pick you up."

Lucy kissed him and rested her head on the shoulder of his white shirt. "It's not too hot today and no one tried to make small talk with me. I think I startled the workers, though."

His laughter rumbled through her chest as they continued to hug. "I don't think you've been in since last December. Would you like to go around and meet the new hires and say hello to the old faces?"

"Only if it's you showing me around."

"You won't be able to rid yourself of me all afternoon, Goosy." He placed his hand on her hips. "Is this the skirt you ordered? It looks nice with the blouse."

"Yes, but I'm afraid I won't be able to use the shirt much longer. It's cut loose, but I'm almost to the seams. If I wasn't wearing the maternity corset, I might not have been able to button it."

"We'll find you plenty of functional clothes to fit you the next two months that will allow you to be natural and comfortable. Nothing but pretty things to wear on outings and at home. Now let's say hello to everyone and then we're hitting the shops, starting with Mademoiselle Bisset."

"Bisset! She won't have anything for someone in my condition."

"Oh, but she does." He quickly kissed her lips and pulled on his suit jacket. "I've already spoken to her and she looks forward to dressing you once again."

Twelve

Darla was pleased to see Lucy's smiling face when the Davenports breezed into the house at a quarter to eight. Mr. Davenport's arms were full of boxes, which he carried immediately upstairs. Lucy went straight for Phoebe, cozied in the corner of the sofa with Doff.

"Ready for bed, little one?"

"Momma!" Phoebe stood on the sofa and reached her arms as far around her mother as she could. She kissed the swell of her mother's shirt. "And baby!"

"Slip your shoes on, Princess," Mr. Davenport said when he returned. "You can help with the rest of the pretty things for Momma. There may be a surprise for you also."

Once they were outside, Lucy turned to Darla. "Was everything fine?"

"Phoebe was a little sad come suppertime, but we made a game of it. Naomi pretended to be a waitress at a restaurant and Phoebe was visiting royalty. How was your time out?"

"Overall, it was wonderful. Freddy was elated to show me around the office and help choose clothes for me. He's so sweet and charming that those shop girls fawned over him as much as me. And

Mademoiselle Bisset was the worst." She laughed. "I think he lined up dresses with her beforehand. I used to shop there when … before we were married. My father and now my brothers have helped her secure orders from France over the years and she was always fond of me and my mother stopping in."

Darla's pulse quickened. "Securing orders?"

"My family owns an import company, Easton and Sons. Father is retired, but my brothers run things now." Lucy sighed. "I don't see them much. Their wives hate me."

So she was Miss Easton!

Frederick and Phoebe came through the door with the last of the parcels.

"It does seem like you had a successful afternoon," Darla said.

"Freddy bought more than necessary."

"No, Goosy. It will all be worn by you and enjoyed by everyone in your vicinity." Phoebe followed him up the stairs with a small box of her own.

"How was supper out?"

Lucy frowned. "That was the worst of the day, though the discomfort wasn't constant. Lots of stares and whispers, but a few people actually stopped to talk and seemed genuinely interested in us as opposed to just seeking gossip."

Darla felt her cheeks warm. "How do you feel now?"

"Amazing." Lucy's smile was brilliant. "Freddy and I needed the time out together, thank you. We discussed on the way home that we should try to get out once a week, not for anything as long as today, but at least for a walk or see a show or take a meal out. And I'm going to go out more with him and Phoebe. Real family outings like we did on Saturday afternoon."

"That will be great for all of you. Let me know when you need me, besides Monday and Thursday afternoons."

"We will, Darla. And thank you."

Mr. Davenport and Phoebe returned, the little girl carrying a black and white stuffed rabbit.

"See what Daddy got me?" She ran to Darla to share her newest treasure.

She pretended to scratch it behind its ears. "That's a handsome rabbit, Phoebe. I look forward to seeing you play with it tomorrow. Make sure you and the bunny sleep tonight so you're rested in the morning."

"I will, Miss Darla!"

Mr. Davenport had an arm around Lucy but his other hand pulled a dollar bill from his pocket. "Here's for your extra time today, in case you should need it before Friday."

"I can wait, but thank you."

"No," Lucy said, "take it. You'll be going to the hotel Thursday with Alice and you might see something that strikes your fancy along the way."

"All right, but any other time you can wait for Friday."

They said their goodnights and Mr. Davenport stood on the front porch to see that she got to the side gate without issue.

The Beauchamp family was all in the parlor. Clarence pounded out a lively tune on the piano and Alice studied a score on her music stand, moving fingers along the violin strings but not using her bow. Richard and Felix were playing Parcheesi in the far corner while Uncle Calvin read the newspaper and Aunt Ida worked a piece of lace with a crochet hook.

"Darla's home!" Alice put down her violin and met her in the doorway. "Did you get terribly bored being alone with the little girl? I wanted to come over after supper, but Mother wouldn't let me."

"Don't sound so dramatic, Alice." Aunt Ida set her crocheting on her lap. "I'm sure Darla is tired and would like to get ready for bed. Why don't you go up before the rest of the children so there isn't a rush for the bathroom?"

Uncle Calvin looked over his paper. "If she wants to sit with the family, there's no need to rush her off to bed. She's a grown woman, Ida."

"It's no trouble. I'll have tomorrow evening with you all. I think I would like to settle in for the night, thank you."

Alice tried to follow.

"You need thirty more minutes of practice," her mother told her.

Darla took her time in the bath. Then she rested on her bed with the box of *Snitch* magazines, waiting for her cousin to come. The top magazine was folded open like Alice had it marked to be shown. She picked up the January 1905 edition and scanned the page, her gaze settling on familiar initials.

Previously shy Miss E. seems to have had a bumper Holiday season. Before the clock struck twelve on New Year's Eve, she'd collected not one but TWO handkerchiefs from some of our city's most handsome men:

A.R.M. and F.L.D.

Both of whom she was seen dancing zealously with at the Order of Mayhem's ball. Well played, Miss E!

Miss E was likely to be Miss Easton, especially since F.L.D. could be Frederick Davenport. The A.R.M. looked familiar. She hunted through the other editions Alice had remarked upon the last two days and found the answer in the article about Maggie and Douglas. A.R.M. was Mrs. Melling's dead son!

***

After a night of fielding questions from Alice, Darla looked forward to work Wednesday. She'd given her cousin only scant amounts of information about the Davenports and refused to commit to the opinion that Miss E was Lucy, though she believed it to be true. Alice had linked Alexander Melling's initials herself and felt the F.L.D. was Mr. Davenport.

At the Davenports', Darla spent the morning outside with Phoebe, chasing butterflies and pushing her doll carriage with Pinky, her china faced doll, and the new rabbit, Rummy, up and down the street. When she passed by the entry hall table on their way in for dinner, she spied the newly delivered mail, the top envelope addressed to *Frederick L. Davenport.* Both men in the article were accounted for.

While they ate, rain began but conversation was pleasant.

"I ran into Maxwell," Mr. Davenport said to Lucy. "He was on his way to a lunch counter and told me he's taking dinner at your parents' house Friday and for you to expect an invitation. He said to tell you he missed your wit at the monthly family dinner last week."

Lucy set down her sandwich and glared at her husband. "Lottie and Mary Margaret were awful in August. I couldn't go through with it again."

"I know, and we all agree on that and don't blame you. Everyone was hot and irritable that day, but Maxwell spoke to Lottie and she's promised to hold her tongue from now on. Eddie was supposed to speak with Mary Margaret, but we all know how Eddie says one thing and does another. We're not sure what the outcome will be with those two."

"If I do get invited Friday, they'll expect Phoebe. Then what do I do with Darla?"

"She would be welcome too. I spoke to your mother yesterday morning and told her we'd hired a helper and how much work you're getting done."

"Would you want to go across town with me when I visit my parents?" she asked Darla. "I go at least once a week, sometimes on the weekend with Freddy, but often during the week as well."

"I'll go anywhere and do anything to help out. I'm here to ease your burdens, Lucy, however that falls." She handed Phoebe another piece of the apple she'd sliced for her.

"See," Mr. Davenport said, "all will be well. And when it comes to your sisters-in-law, remember that compared to the charm you Eastons were born with, those who married into the family are sour."

"Not you, Freddy, just the women."

"Your older sisters did marry amiable men."

"But I got the most handsome and pleasant of them all." Lucy's smile broke through the previous sadness.

"Is your family large?" Darla asked Lucy.

"Yes, a big Catholic family. My mother birthed ten of us, though only seven are still alive."

"Catholic? Alice told me you were Episcopalian."

Frederick laughed. "I've been so since birth, but Lucy was baptized before we were married. She grew up in the cathedral where your family goes. Her parents and brothers and their families still attend."

"And what of your sisters? Are there many Miss Eastons?"

"None that live in the city. The only one unmarried is the youngest but she's only sixteen. My three older sisters were all married before I came out in society."

Pending any news from Alice or Sadie about other affluent families in Mobile with a name beginning with an E, if the articles in *Snitch* dealt with an Easton sister, it would have been Lucy.

"Is your younger sister away at finishing school?" Darla asked before taking a bite.

Lucy dabbed her mouth with a napkin. "No, she's in an asylum."

A piece of apple lodged in Darla's throat and she started coughing.

Frederick stood to help, but she waved him away as she drank iced tea to wash it down.

"I'm not going to lie about it," Lucy said when the room quieted. "Most people already know. Please excuse me." She exited the dining room and shut the door to the study. A moment later, the sound of typing filtered through the wall.

"She probably got an idea she needed to record," Mr. Davenport offered. "At least she finished her sandwich first."

Darla twisted the napkin in her lap. "I'm forever saying the wrong things."

"No, Darla. Lucy has hidden away from so many things that it startles her to confront the truth, but it's the only way to help her heal. You're good for her."

"Is her sister really in an asylum?"

"She's been locked up for over five years. Opal is her name, should you ever hear someone mention Opal Easton. The sister and two brothers between Lucy and Opal passed away in ninety-seven and Lucy always blamed her for their deaths, though it was yellow fever that took them. Lucy was sick too and I've always thought she felt guilty for surviving when the others didn't."

"I know that feeling," Darla whispered.

Phoebe finished eating and drinking her milk and reached for Darla to pull her chair out. "All done, Miss Darla!"

Mr. Davenport nodded, and Darla set the girl free. "Princess, can you play in the front room a few minutes?"

"Yes, Daddy!"

He turned back to Darla, a faraway look in his eyes. "Opal was always a bit odd. She couldn't attend school from the age of eight because of her outbursts."

"How terrible."

They both listened to the typing for several seconds.

"She was jealous of Lucy. Her outbursts continued to increase and the day before Lucy's wedding, she started throwing things and screaming. Lucy was in a weakened state and Opal managed to knock her down. She struck her head on a table edge when she fell. I had to pull Opal off Lucy and confine her until help arrived. Lucy was unconscious for a full day, and in the hospital for several more. Opal had to be medicated and committed at only ten years of age." Mr. Davenport stood. "I'll help you get the dishes to the kitchen, and then I'll need to be on my way."

They worked silently, then he disappeared into the study and Darla went on to the living room. When Mr. Davenport came down the hall, he left the study room open.

"All is well," he whispered to Darla. Then louder, "Be brave, Princess. I'll be home for supper."

The only way Darla could focus on Phoebe was to read. The two spent the next hour reading Grimm's Fairy Tales on the sofa until Phoebe wanted to look for a gingerbread house in the yard. Since the rain temporarily stopped, Darla spent the next half hour trying to wrap her head around being attacked by a sibling, all the while following Phoebe through the mud around the hydrangea and azalea bushes. Her brothers could be cruel in their jokes, but physical violence against her never was an issue.

When Naomi arrived at two-thirty, they helped her carry groceries into the kitchen as the next round of showers arrived. They washed up for a snack and settled at the tiny kitchen table. While they were eating cookies and milk, Lucy came in. Her face was hard, green eyes distant. She smoothed a hand over Phoebe's blonde hair and set about fixing a cup of tea.

"You look like you could use a nap, Miss Lucy."

"I'm fine, Naomi, but thank you."

"No need for lies with me. Something is weighing on you. You go lay down and I'll bring your tea to your room when it's ready."

"Do I look that poorly?"

Rather than being rude, Naomi gave direction. "Miss Darla, please escort Miss Lucy upstairs."

Lucy's laugh was hollow, but she didn't protest Darla's hand on her elbow.

"Sleep good, Momma."

"Thank you, Phoebe."

They were both silent until they reached the second floor landing. Lucy's voice was a hoarse whisper. "Sometimes I feel like I'm going crazy, that Freddy will have to lock me up one day."

"I'm sure that's not the case." Darla walked her to the large bed and tried not to stare at the intimate details in the grand room—the silk nightgown laying over the dressing table chair and Mr. Davenport's robe on the bench at the foot of the bed.

"Maybe that's why he's been so patient with me and allows me to hide from society. Why he hasn't pushed me to attend social functions. What if Freddy thinks me unfit to mother his children because of my insane sister?" Lucy collapsed onto the bed face first.

Darla immediately reached out to help her roll over. "You're in no danger, but you must treat your body carefully. Here, curl on your side. Let me tuck a pillow between your knees, it will lessen any back discomfort."

"Freddy hired you to watch me because he doesn't trust me with myself anymore, doesn't trust me with Phoebe, especially since I told him about what I imagine sometimes."

She'd seen pregnant women in hysterics before, but never so despondent and with logical reason for the melancholy. Darla tucked Lucy's loose hair behind her ear and took her hand. "Mr. Davenport has no worry over your sanity other than you not thinking well enough of yourself. He loves and trusts you. I'm here to entertain Phoebe so you can work on your projects."

Her laugh was bitter. "He'll not think the same way of my projects when he lays eyes on the next one. No one will."

Sobs wracked her body such that Darla feared convulsions would set in. The pillow under Lucy's head became saturated by tears and still she didn't slow. But Darla's confidence in her ability to help Lucy overpowered any doubt or fear.

Darla ran to the top of the stairs. "Naomi! I need lavender or cinnamon, quickly!"

Naomi came to the hall and looked up. "Is she unwell?"

Darla gripped the railing. "Sobbing uncontrollably. I need lavender or cinnamon to hold under her nose."

"She keeps lavender sachets in the linen closet, the door next to the bathroom."

Darla found a small bag of dried petals and crushed it in her hand to release more aroma as she rushed back to the bedroom. She tucked it near Lucy's damp chin and encouraged her to breathe while she flipped the red blanket from the other side of the bed around her quivering form.

"Come on, Mrs. Davenport, breathe in, breathe out. Slower now." Darla rubbed her back over her blue tea gown in circular motions. "It's nothing to hurt you, just an attack of emotions all women in your condition are subject to. Nothing more, nothing unreasonable."

Lucy's chest heaved in rapid succession as she fought to slow the tears.

Darla continued to soothe her with the massage. "You've had a full week, with much to reflect on in the meantime. Your body is telling you it's had enough and needs to relax. Can you smell the lavender yet? Breathe deeper, Lucy."

Naomi came in with a steaming cup. Darla motioned with one hand to the nightstand and the cook placed the cup and saucer there.

Lucy wiped at her face as she took more calming breaths and seemed to see Naomi through her tears. "Please don't tell Freddy. He worries too much about me as it is."

Naomi put her hands on her hips and narrowed her blind eye. "That man loves you and deserves to know if you've had a rough afternoon."

"But he might think—"

The cook's finger pointed right at Lucy. "He'll think you're growing a baby in that little body of yours and need more rest."

"But Opal—"

"Is that what this is about? Miss Opal is completely different than you. You needn't fear in that regard."

"But my nightmares, the feelings of doom that wash over me at times, my sin—"

"It's that wild imagination and tender heart of yours, Miss Lucy. Sit up when you can and Miss Darla will help you with your tea. Then you need to rest." Naomi shook her head. "For all your softness, you're the most stubborn lady I know."

In between rain storms, Darla walked the sidewalk with Phoebe and her doll carriage. They were out when Alice returned from school.

"I thought you weren't working late today." Her cousin fell into step beside them.

"I wasn't going to, but Mrs. Davenport isn't feeling good this afternoon so I'm waiting until her husband comes home."

"Guess I'll practice straight away then. Sadie might come next hour."

"I'll be over as soon as I can."

When the rain chased them back inside, Darla read aloud to Phoebe in the living room. They were on the sofa when Mr. Davenport came home.

"Hello, Princess." He lifted Phoebe into his arms and hugged her. "And hello, Darla."

"Did Naomi call you?" she asked.

"No, why?"

Darla's voice was quiet. "Lucy had a rough afternoon."

Mr. Davenport lowered Phoebe to the floor. "Could you set a tea party in your room? I'm sure Pinky and Rummy would enjoy it. I'll be up to join you soon."

"I save you the biggest piece of cake, Daddy!" She gathered her doll and bunny off the sofa and scampered up the stairs.

His eyes settled on Darla. "I had the feeling I should come home early and skipped the gym to get here. What happened?"

She told him of Lucy's mood when she emerged from the study, her remarks about Opal, the hysterical crying, and her fears over her own issues.

His face paled. "I've never compared her to Opal. Her conscience is what weighs her down, not madness. Opal had no concern over her actions or being spiteful to others. Lucy is sensitive and protective of those she loves. She holds in her hurt to spare others until it erupts like this. I must go to her."

He mounted the stairs two at a time.

Thirteen

Lucy could smell his comforting presence when the door opened—adding machine ink and cooling aftershave. Wanting to know what he'd say and do, she feigned sleep while he crossed the room.

"I pray you'll find the peace you need because my love will never be enough to heal you."

She didn't mean to hurt Frederick, but Lucy knew in that moment exactly how he felt because she had been at that end of a relationship. When Alexander had doubted himself, when he resisted the urge to change his life for the better, she was left with the painful repercussions and feeling helpless. Alexander had even told her on their last day together that if her love wasn't strong enough to cure him, nothing was. *Why have I carried the pain and twisted it to do the same to another?*

Lucy raised a hand, hoping he would take it. "I'm sorry, Freddy."

"You spend too much time in the depths of despair." He kissed her hand and sat on the edge of the bed, holding her watery gaze with his earnest one.

"I'm ready to move on. I've been trying, really I have, and then Opal's shadow appeared, casting all my problems in a sinister light." *Just as Alex's father and his past did to him.*

Frederick fingered her hair back from her face and smiled in the sweet way that made Lucy's heart soar every time. "You have nothing to fear in that regard, Goosy. You worrying about it shows how truly sane you are because you care—the very thing Opal never did."

"I hope you're right," she whispered.

"You needn't carry more pain around." He gently ran a hand over her rounded belly. "Our baby, the love people have for you, and a testimony of God are the only things you need."

Lucy kissed him with depth of feeling as she caressed from his face down to his shoulders. When her hands went under his suit jacket, he pulled her up as he stood. Wrapping his arms around her, they clung together in a moment of urgency.

"I love you," she breathed the words against his chest.

"And you hold my heart." After resting his head against hers a minute, he straightened. "I have a tea party to get to in the next room. Would you care to accompany me?"

"No, Phoebe needs her time with you. I'll go down and see about helping with dinner."

"Don't push yourself. Why don't you relax with a book in the living room. Darla might still be down there."

Frederick removed his jacket and tie, then went on to Phoebe's room. After stopping at the dressing table to brush through her tousled hair, Lucy left it loose and descended the stairs.

Darla sprang from a chair in the living room when she saw her. "Are you feeling better?"

"Yes, thank you for helping. Freddy will pay you extra for your time."

"That's not necessary. It was just another hour and I didn't stay for the money." She stepped closer. "Is there anything more I can do?"

Lucy shook her head, her veil of hair flowing behind her with the movement. "You were a huge help to me, Darla. I'll see you in the morning."

Quarter of an hour later, Frederick found Lucy in the study standing before the built-in bookcase. He fingered the hair that fell about her waist before slipping an arm around her. His touch and nearness aroused her tender emotions.

"Can I help you find what you're looking for?" His hand shifted to her hip as she turned to him.

"You could if what I'm looking for was tangible."

"That coquettish smile tells me what you seek." Whether his kneading grasp at her hips was what he preferred or something he'd seen her enjoy under Alex's hands she didn't know, but she loved it. Again, their kisses turned urgent. Lucy's hands went for his buttons as a clatter of dishes sounded from the next room.

Frederick pulled away enough to raise her chin with his finger. "Amid all your other emotions this week, it's nice to see your passion for me heighten. But unless you want me to ask Naomi to keep an eye on Phoebe and keep dinner warm, we need to slow down."

For a moment, she rested her forehead on his shoulder, fingering the row of buttons on his white shirt. Not liking even Naomi to be privy to their intimacy, she clasped her hands behind her back and took a step away.

"There's something else we could do for the moment."

A hand reached out and caressed her jaw. "Anything, Goosy."

She pointed to the shelf with copies of her books on it. "Author copies for the new book will arrive in the next few weeks.

We need to make room for them, and I want you to read it as soon as it's here."

"No making me wait until publication day and waking me up at midnight to start it?" Frederick's eyes shone with merriment as he pulled her back into his arms and kissed her firmly on the mouth.

"I want to give you ample time to read it before you hear people discussing it."

"As long as the character causing the winter in the heroine's heart doesn't resemble me, I'm sure I'll be fine."

Lucy laughed and hugged him. "Your love is spring sunshine and blossoms, Freddy."

"And spring comes after winter." His finger traced her eyebrow, then trailed down the side of her face. "I believe I understand your concern, but you should know by now that my love for you doesn't waiver."

Just as their kissing rose to the next level, there was a tug at Lucy's dress.

"Momma feel better?" Phoebe asked.

Her smile broke the intimate kiss with Frederick but his taste lingered on. "Yes, Phoebe. I'm much better now. Is supper ready?"

"Miss Naomi says ten minutes." She reached for her mother to pick her up.

"Here," Frederick said as he lifted her, "why don't my girls go cuddle on the sofa and I'll check on Naomi."

He carried Phoebe in one arm, and the other hand rested on Lucy's shoulder. After seeing them settled amid the cushions on the sofa, he retreated to the kitchen. Lucy held Phoebe and whispered more of *The Continuous Story of Princess Phoebe* that she'd been narrating to her since the day she was born until they were called to supper.

***

Thursday morning, Lucy changed from her nightgown into one of her new dresses while Frederick shaved in their adjoining bathroom.

"I want to grow a mustache or beard, what do you think?"

"A mustache and goatee would be handsome on you. Start it on a Saturday, though." Lucy straightened the blue and gold band at the empire waist of her cream-colored dress. It was an art nouveau detail on the Roman-inspired ensemble and it allowed her belly to be draped within the pleats.

"So it looks like I had a rough weekend when I go to the office Monday?"

"Exactly." She laughed as she sat at the dressing table to fix her hair. She twisted it into a high, soft bun, knowing it would slowly work its way into a low chignon by noon.

Leaving her shoes off, she stood in the bathroom doorway and waited for Frederick to finish drying his face from the hot rinse after shaving. His skin was pink and smooth around his grin, his brown eyes full of love.

"That looks even better on you today than it did when you tried it on at the store." His hands went about her. "Ah, no corset this time. It's meant for the natural shape of a woman. You fill it out perfectly."

She melted under the touch of his fingertips and even more when his lips found her collarbone.

"You keep this up and you'll be late for work," she whispered as she played her fingers down his bare chest.

"We're as close as ever, Goosy. Let's enjoy it." His hands cupped her curves as he backed her toward their bed.

"Momma! Daddy!" Phoebe knocked on the bedroom door.

"Just wait until there are two." Frederick gave her a final, nuzzling kiss. "We'll have to be creative and quick when the mood strikes."

Laughing, Lucy opened the door. "Good morning, Phoebe."

"Ooh, Momma's a princess!"

From behind, Frederick wrapped his arms about Lucy's chest and looked over her shoulder at Phoebe. "You're the princess. Momma is a queen."

A shiver coursed through Lucy's body, both from the familiar words and position. Feeling her tremble, Frederick turned her around. He stared into her eyes several seconds before a frown set in.

"I'm sorry, Goosy. I'd forgotten how he called you that."

And often held me from behind, resting his chin on my shoulder. She forced a smile. "Normally I wouldn't ... but it's been a long week with the anniversary and everything else going on."

"Shall you be empress? Duchess? President?" He kissed her after each offered title.

Her smile was genuine. "I'll be queen of Kingdom Davenport as long as you're my king."

Phoebe hugged both their legs. "Doff hungry. I hungry!"

"Just something simple, Lucy. We'll have a big dinner."

When Frederick left for work, Lucy followed him to the front door for another embrace.

"We'll be here about twelve. Be sure you rest a bit this morning."

Darla came up the front walk, so Frederick held the door open for her before leaving.

"You're radiant, Lucy. A perfect hostess." Darla looked down at her own everyday dress. "Should I change?"

"You're fine for now." Lucy went in the living room and curled on her side in the corner of the sofa. Darla settled in the chair across from her. "Why don't you try to get Phoebe to play outside this morning? Then you could change into what you'll need to wear to the hotel this afternoon before dinner. You can have Phoebe stay inside after we eat to keep your clothes fresh."

"I don't want to run out on you during my work hours to change."

"I think it might be in your best interest. The intern coming for dinner is quite handsome." Lucy laughed softly at the blush on Darla's cheeks. "There's no harm in looking your best, even if you don't plan on catching a man's eye."

"Easy for you to say. I'm sure you had no shortage of callers and admirers in your courting years."

"I can assure you that my social calendar and parlor were both empty until I was twenty. Not a bite or a nibble before then." Seeing the shock on Darla's face, she continued. "I found out that winter my lack of beaus was because of my brother, Edmund. In an attempt to protect my virtue, he threatened all his friends and any other man he saw looking at me. He was a notable boxer in school so they all kept away. Only one was brave enough to risk his safety for the thrill of meeting with me that year."

"Mr. Davenport?"

Lucy shook her head. "No, but he returned to us that Christmas as well. He was absent from our lives two years, but he was always welcome. From when I came into society until that winter, Frederick was married and then in mourning for his first wife."

"He was married?" Darla covered her mouth, seemingly embarrassed from her outburst. "I'm sorry. I just can't picture him with anyone but you."

"Neither could he," she murmured. Then Lucy's smile returned tenfold. "That's another story, one for Freddy to share if he wishes."

"I don't mean to be nosy."

"It's nothing to worry about. I assume everyone in town knows all my secrets, or at least some version of them. I'd rather you ask questions of me than your aunt or someone else. I'm sure their understanding of things is quite exaggerated."

Embarrassed by her prodding, Darla stood. "I should see to Phoebe now."

"She's playing in her room. Freddy wants me to rest and I find it difficult to sit around. It's nice to talk. I never thanked you for your help yesterday. You're skilled and comforting. If possible, I'd like you to be there with me when my time comes."

"I'd be honored to, but if I'm needed to be with Phoebe, I'd be happy to do that as well."

Lucy nodded. "You'll be close by in any case."

"Yesterday, after you left the dinner table, Mr. Davenport told me a little about your sister, how she attacked you the day before your wedding. That must have been awful for you both. Especially with him not knowing if his bride was well as you lay unconscious in the hospital."

"I wasn't to be married to Freddy then."

"He said your wedding day and I assumed—"

"He was with me when Opal attacked, but I was engaged to another. Freddy was my dearest friend and he'd seen me home from Mass that morning, after …" She ran her hand over the swell of her body and smiled faintly. "Frederick knew everything. Some people feel sorry for him for ending up with me, as though I lied or tricked him into it, but he knew the truth as it happened. He was there to see it all unfold. I can't blame others for doubting my intentions for him because I didn't realize the depths of his love for me until over a year later."

Darla's face held an expression of confusion.

"I'm saying just enough for you to breed more questions, aren't I?"

She smiled. "Afraid so."

Lucy laughed. "Then let me tell you the basic facts. I was engaged to Alexander Melling, a dashing young lawyer and the son of Mrs. Melling, who you met Sunday. We started seeing each other over Christmas six years ago and were engaged a month later. The passion we shared was overpowering to my naïve self. Though twenty, I had never courted nor even danced with more than a handful of men at social functions. I allowed him to sweep me away and we became physically involved just weeks before our wedding. My guilt, coupled with his unsavory past and family influences, were our undoing. Our relationship ended explosively not once, but twice, and with witnesses on the way down. I was often mentioned in gossip circles, both vocally and in print. I spent a year and a half trying to shut out the world. Freddy was my only constant. He was there through it all and patiently waited for me to heal. I'm afraid he still is."

"I only knew my aunt forbade Alice from associating with you because of a scandal."

"Ida Beauchamp and the like still see me as a ruined woman. Even last weekend in the park, someone referred to me as Miss Easton because he didn't associate me with Freddy. To him I was still Alex's girl. I'm trying to remedy that. I'm happily Mrs. Davenport now. It's time the city knows it."

Fourteen

While Darla watched Phoebe swing on the little platform seat hung from one of the oak tree branches in the Davenports' yard, she mulled over everything she'd learned. Without a doubt, Lucy was the Miss E listed in *Snitch* so often. Gathering handkerchiefs, stealing away with Mr. Davenport during a Mardi Gras ball while engaged to Mr. Melling, and shamelessly being seen coming out of her fiancé's home in the middle of the night—it was all there.

Still, she wondered how Maggie Campbell fit into the story with the fire at Seacliff Cottage that ended the lives of both Mr. Mellings. Lucy had been talkative without slipping into one of her moods, but Darla didn't want to press too hard, especially with a dinner guest coming. Deciding to approach the subject in her next letter to Maggie, Darla tried to enjoy the remainder of the morning.

At eleven, she brought Phoebe inside. The girl was dirty from playing in the damp earth, but the sound of the typewriter clanged through the closed door to the study. Darla returned to the kitchen to seek advice from the cook.

"It sounds like Lucy's working. Should I wash Phoebe and help her dress for dinner?"

"That would be good." Naomi stirred the contents of a pot on the six-burner stove. "If Miss Lucy comes out, I'll let her know."

"Doesn't she look lovely today?"

Naomi smiled. "She always does, but that dress is something else. Mr. Frederick sure spoiled her this week."

Darla ran a shallow bath for Phoebe and helped the girl wipe the grime away.

Wrapped in a towel, Phoebe ran down the hall. "Can't catch me!"

"Phoebe Camellia!" Lucy's stern voice rang out from the stairs. "No running in the house, young lady."

Phoebe looked back at Darla, giggled, and dove into her bedroom. Darla waited in the hallway for Lucy. She seemed slightly breathless when she reached the second floor.

"We had more fun than expected outside, so I gave her a quick bath."

"Thank you, Darla. I'll get her dressed so you can get yourself ready." Lucy smoothed over the waistband of her dress. "I'm thinking about changing myself."

"But you look wonderful!"

Lucy shrugged. "I thought so this morning, but now I'm thinking it might be too ostentatious for a luncheon."

"Keep it on. You look amazing. If you want to keep it casual, stay barefoot."

Her laughter twinkled. "All right then. Freddy will be pleased. He let me know this morning how much he liked it."

Lucy blushed, but before Darla could reach the stairs, Lucy stopped her. "One more thing. My mother called while you were outside. We're going to my parents' home for dinner tomorrow. Maxwell, my oldest brother, will pick us up around eleven-thirty and we should be back before two, so it won't be any extra time for you."

"I look forward to meeting your family."

Darla let herself in the back door at the Beauchamps'. She washed her hands and face in the upstairs bathroom and hurried to the bedroom to change into the sky blue tea gown she'd worn for her job interview last Saturday. After buttoning on her new boots, she brushed through her hair and swept it into a chignon.

When she reached the bottom of the stairs, Aunt Ida stood with her arms crossed.

"And what do you think you're doing by going to work in one of your new outfits?"

"I'm sorry, Aunt Ida. I thought I mentioned it to you in the parlor last night. The Davenports have company for dinner today, a worker from the office. Lu—Mrs. Davenport asked me to dress for the occasion."

"So Mr. Davenport and another gentleman from the office will be there?"

"Yes."

"All right, but only for special things like that. I don't want you wearing out your new threads by playing with the child in your pretty clothes."

"Yes, Aunt Ida. And tomorrow we're going to the Eastons for dinner. A brother named Maxwell is to drive us."

"Maxwell Easton, now he's a credit to his parents! He and his lovely family are fine members of the cathedral. The suffering Lucille put her poor mother through is unthinkable. And her father! Why, he even had to retire not long after word got out about her running wild with—oh, never mind. I hate for you to be associated with her, but despite her bad choices, she is from a fine family and married a respectable gentleman."

Mr. Davenport's automobile was parked when Darla returned. Not wanting to cause a scene by entering the front door, she rounded the back.

"Get on with you!" Naomi fussed at her. "They're all in the living room."

Darla tried not to totter in the heeled boots as she walked the hallway. Lucy's laughter rang out, followed by Mr. Davenport's smooth voice.

"Our Phoebe is ready to be a big sister. She's caring for her doll as well as anything. And here's Darla. She started helping with Phoebe this week, a great asset to our household."

All eyes turned to Darla in the doorway but she kept hers down. Phoebe rushed over and hugged her legs, almost toppling her. Darla recovered by placing a hand out for balance.

"Easy, Phoebe," Lucy coaxed. "Bring Darla in to take a seat."

As Phoebe led Darla around the sofa, she got her first look at their dinner guest. Dark blue eyes stared at her and a smile of recognition brightened his charming face as he stood. It was none other than Alice's Henry Adams.

"Miss Beauchamp, isn't it? I saw you arrive at Mass Sunday with your relatives. I'm Henry. Henry Adams. It's a pleasure to meet you."

She accepted his hand with what she hoped wasn't a blush on her face. He was even better looking up close, and she anticipated Alice squealing in excitement when she told her later. "Thank you, but call me Darla, please. It's nice to meet someone else in town."

Phoebe settled between her parents on the sofa, and Darla and Henry in matching arm chairs across the coffee table from them.

"I've only been in Mobile two years myself. I moved from Chatom for schooling and don't aim to go back." He grinned sheepishly. "Sometimes my country still shows."

Darla laughed. "I grew up on Dauphin Island, but I'm still too new to say where I'd want to settle. As of right now, I miss the island terribly, even though there are lovely people like the Davenports here."

When Naomi came to tell them dinner was ready, Phoebe dashed for the dining room and Frederick took Lucy's hand.

Henry stood before Darla and offered his arm. "May I escort you to the table?" He leaned closer and dropped his voice. "I think that's what I'm supposed to say."

She tried not to laugh because she didn't want to be seen as a giggling girl, though he did bring her joy. "I'm not sure myself, but it sounds refined and I happily accept. What does your family do in Chatom?"

"My grandfather's a judge in Monroeville, but my father decided to breed horses. I did a lot of farm chores growing up. I don't miss the sights and smells of mucking the stables, but I do miss the riding."

"I've never been around horses. We only went where we could walk or sail."

In the dining room, Henry pulled out her chair and Darla sat beside Phoebe. Once Henry settled across from her, Mr. Davenport offered a prayer and they began passing around the platters of roast, vegetables, and rolls.

Henry was unpretentious and Darla was completely at ease with him as she was with the Davenports. She wondered—beyond his looks—what Alice saw in him because she seemed set on high society and he was anything but. The group spoke of farms, fishing, business, and food. By the time dinner was over, Darla's face was sore from smiling.

"This has been great fun," Lucy remarked over a slice of pecan pie. "We should do it weekly."

Darla looked across the table at Henry. His eyes darted to Mr. Davenport, a modest smile on his face.

"Maybe Wednesdays, to give us something to look forward to in the middle of the week," Mr. Davenport said as he pushed back from the table. "You all take your time, but excuse me. I need to check something from this morning's paper."

"I done too!" Phoebe raised her hands. Darla wiped her face and then the girl ran for the stairs.

"Would you like to come back, Henry?" Lucy asked.

"Yes, very much. I admire Mr. Davenport and now that I've seen his family, I have something more to aim for in my life." He looked at Darla briefly. "It's a blessing to be among friendly, welcoming people. A huge improvement to my rented room."

Lucy's radiant smile made Darla feel dark and plain. "I'll set it up with Freddy. I'm sure we'll all look forward to it."

From down the hall, Mr. Davenport called out, "Lucy, could you come here a moment?"

As Lucy excused herself, Henry stood. Rather than returning to his seat, he made his way around the oval table to Darla.

"If you're finished, I'd be happy to bring you to the living room."

She looked down at her last bite of pecan pie. "I'm not one to waste good food." She held her position until she finished chewing.

"I'd have enjoyed the meal with the Davenports, but you made it delightful." Once she stood and her hand was on his forearm, he rested his other hand atop hers a moment. "You're the nicest young woman I've met in the city."

Darla laughed. "But I'm not even from the city."

"Precisely."

They made it as far as the living room when Phoebe cried out for help from upstairs. Darla dashed to her aid and a minute later carried down the doll carriage with Rummy and Pinky tucked inside.

"Off on an adventure then?" Henry smiled.

"Always," Darla replied. "This girl loves to explore."

"Mr. Henry come, too!" Phoebe bounced, her beribboned hair springing about her shoulders.

"I think he'll be going back to work with your daddy soon, Phoebe."

"I go see!" She skipped toward the study.

Henry crossed into the hallway, stopping a few feet away from Darla. "I hope we meet again soon."

She clasped her hands before her and tried not to smile. "There's always next Wednesday."

"And Sundays. Do you ever go to morning Mass during the week?"

"It wasn't something we had the time for on the island."

"Keep it in mind. It's a nice way to start the day."

Mr. Davenport returned carrying Phoebe on his shoulders. The twelve-foot high ceiling gave ample room for the fun. "Afraid your stroll with the girls will have to wait until next time, Henry."

"It was a pleasure to meet you officially." Henry offered his hand and Darla readily accepted. Then, turning to Lucy, who'd paused by her husband, he took hers. "And thank you for hosting me, Mrs. Davenport. I look forward to spending more time with your family and friends."

After the men left, Lucy smiled at Darla. "Was I not right about Henry's handsomeness?"

"Very correct in that regard. I'm going to take Phoebe for a walk with her dolls. We'll keep to the sidewalks and stay clean."

"I'll work for a while then. Knock on my door before three if I'm still in there so you can be on your way." Lucy fingered her lips and sighed with contentment. "The afternoon can't pass soon enough."

Fifteen

When Darla and Phoebe returned from their walk, they settled in the living room. The music of the typewriter keys clinked while Darla read Phoebe a story about a girl no bigger than a thumb. By the fifth page, Phoebe slept soundly against the armrest of the sofa. Darla slipped off Phoebe's shoes and covered her with a crocheted lap blanket. Going toward the kitchen, Darla paused outside the study long enough to listen to the typing. It stopped after a smooth run. The sounds of paper being pulled from the machine and then crumpled were followed by an exasperated grumble.

Darla knocked on the door. "Are you okay, Lucy?"

"Yes, come in."

Lucy paced the floor, tossing a wad of paper between her hands like a baseball.

"Sorry if I disturbed you. Phoebe fell asleep on the sofa and I wanted to check on you before I leave."

"No worries, Darla. It's nothing serious, just the hazards of my profession." She paused mid-step, her pale green eyes staring.

"I always thought a woman's hobby was only that—projects. Are things that different in town?"

Lucy shook her head, causing her low knot of hair to loosen further. As though annoyed, she ripped at the hairpins and pulled her hair loose. "I'm a writer," she whispered.

"Do you write a newsletter for a ladies group or poetry?"

Lucy's laugh rang out. "I don't belong to any ladies groups but I have been known to pen poems. People always knew I wrote, but only my immediate family knows what I've written. I'm a novelist. My first book was published the year after everything happened with Alexander, so I published under a pseudonym to safeguard myself against the gossips."

"You have an artist's soul, flowing and deep."

"And you have a healer's soul, compassionate and perceptive." Lucy took her hands. "I feel I can trust you, Darla. You've done so much for us since you've come and deserve to know the truth. Do you read much?"

"Not as much as I'd like. We only had the Bible, a reference on herbs, and a birthing book at my house. But my mother's friend, Claire Walker, has a little collection at her house she let me borrow from. Her best friend lives in California and sends her new books several times a year."

"How fortunate for her, and you." Lucy led her to the bookcase recessed into the wall. "Can you guess which ones are mine?"

Darla perused the titles and fell upon the shelf with the pastel covers, with three copies of each of the four books. "You're Olive Kent? *Azalea Blossom* is one of Claire's favorite books! She and her friend Loretta reread it every March and discuss it in their letters!"

"Claire is a close friend?"

"She was more so to my mother, but she's who I worked with this past month. My mother trained her in midwifery. Before marrying, she volunteered as a nurse during the Spanish-American War and also taught at the Creole School on Mon Louis Island. She's very smart."

Lucy laughed. "I'm sure she is to captivate a young woman like you. How would you like to send her an autographed copy?"

"Oh, could I? She'd love that!"

"Next time we go shopping I'll buy one at the bookstore. It's quite fun to have the clerks talk about my books without knowing I wrote them. I get the most candid critiques that way. Freddy thinks it's shameless because the books are so well received locally and I never hear anything negative beyond certain parts being too slow to a reader's liking."

Darla laughed. "Oh, I'd eat it up if I were you. I've read *Azalea Blossom* and *Forever in Love*, but not the others. Those two were charming, though."

Lucy fingered the spines on her collection. "These copies are all spoken for. One of each for Freddy, Phoebe, and for the new arrival. Freddy's and Phoebe's are inscribed but I'm waiting until after the baby is born to address those. When the children are old enough, the books will go into their own rooms."

"That's a lovely notion. I have my mother's books and a few other items from the house, but nothing personalized. No notes."

Lucy put a hand on her shoulder. "Come now. It's not a time for sadness. You had a lovely dinner with a handsome fellow who couldn't keep his eyes off you. In an hour, you're heading to one of the finest hotels in the state to meet a famous violinist—who is also quite handsome. Freddy showed me the article about him in the newspaper. And tomorrow you get to take dinner with the Eastons."

Darla smiled. "And Olive Kent."

"Not a word to your family, please."

"Of course not, Lucy. I'll be on my way. Phoebe is tucked on the sofa."

When Darla came in the backdoor, the maid informed her Aunt Ida was out visiting friends. Darla decided to wait in the parlor for Alice. Not worried about being watched, she took her time and looked around the cluttered room. Besides the silver frames and figurines along the tabletops and mantel, there was a bookshelf tucked in the corner behind a flowery armchair. Chuckling to herself, Darla touched each of Lucy's books and settled in the armchair with the copy of *Magnolia Wind* and read until her cousin came home.

Alice changed from her school clothes into an ankle-length black skirt and fine white blouse. A hired car was ready at a quarter to four to drive them so they would arrive at the hotel fresh, though they had to walk home afterward. Alice sat erect, like a crystal candlestick that would shatter if handled wrong, so Darla kept quiet. She stayed a half step behind her cousin when they entered the hotel, awed by its grandeur.

Mrs. Melling sat in the lobby in a fancy hat and gray silk dress that shimmered under the light. She waved them over. "Turn around, girls."

They each turned before her as she looked them over. "That's a much better look for you, Darla. That skirt your aunt had you in Sunday was almost obscene. It's clear you have the body of a woman, but one doesn't need to showcase how womanly you are on the Lord's Day. Alice, you look fine. The bow is a nice touch. Come, I will take you to his room."

The elevator operator saw them to the fifth floor and Mrs. Melling led the cousins to the far hallway. "They're keeping the rooms next to and across from his empty as much as possible, though I doubt guests would complain about the music," she whispered to them before knocking on the door.

Alice stood in front of Darla with Mrs. Melling, so she didn't see her cousin's expression when the door opened. But Darla's eyes went large, trying to soak up every detail of the exotic man before them. His chin-length black hair was nearly the same style as the photograph from the newspaper, but at present was tousled with an air of sensual recklessness that fell about the open collar of his shirt. He smiled at Mrs. Melling before stepping forward to a make kissing motions quickly on each cheek without contact.

"Valentino, here is Alice Beauchamp. Alice, the magnificent Valentino De Fiore."

He looked over Alice, who clutched her case to her chest and touched a hand to her shoulder as he greeted her in the same manner.

"Come for her at five, *Signora* Melling." His accent was lovely and his English understandable. "Come in, *signorina*. Set your things at my music stand."

Mrs. Melling headed back down the hall and Darla stepped in after Alice.

"And who are you?" His dark eyes bored into Darla's soul with burning heat.

His nearness caused her heart to pound as she looked up at him from her two-inch deficit in her heeled boots. "Darla, Alice's cousin and chaperone. In our country we don't send young ladies into a hotel alone."

He threw back his head and laughed.

"How fortunate Alice is to have such a dear cousin. You are most welcome, Darla." With the lightest touch—one she wouldn't have imagined a man capable of—he took her elbow as he leaned in. Rather than the motion of kisses he'd given Mrs. Melling and Alice, Valentino's lips touched each of her cheeks with a lingering quality. Then he whispered in her ear, "*Hai dei bellissimi occhi*. You have beautiful eyes, *signorina*. I could make wonderful music for eyes like yours."

Hand still on her arm, Valentino escorted her into the room. He pulled a chair out from the desk, facing it toward her cousin. Alice was in the far corner near the window. Cleared of furniture, the space housed only a music stand for sheet music and a floor stand supporting Valentino's violin and bow. Darla felt the heat on her cheeks and jumpiness in her knees as she tried not to follow every move he made.

He motioned to the bag Darla held. "Her music?"

Darla nodded and passed it to him. He opened it and dumped the booklets and sheets onto his large bed.

Rifling through them, he shook his head at Alice. "Mozart, Vivaldi! Have you no imagination or zest to go beyond the ordinary?"

"There is one I work on when my family isn't around, something that drives my mother crazy. I've not perfected it, but—"

"What is it?" His stare was electric.

"Paganini's Moto Perpetuo in C."

He laughed again, throwing his head back. All he did was bold and impassioned. It made Darla yearn for his touch all the more. Never had she been so affected by a man, but she'd yet to meet one that dripped with as much carnal appeal as Valentino.

"That is one of my signature pieces, did you not know? I would love to teach it to you properly. Play it!"

"But Mrs. Melling said I should come with my best piece. Paganini is just a game that I'm not good enough for yet." Alice was close to tears.

Valentino strode to her in two purposeful steps. "Even if you do not play it well, it shows you have conviction. I do not need to hear your brilliance in your performance pieces. *Signora* Melling already knows of their worth and this meeting is because she deems you worthy. Show me what you hope to master and I will guide you from there."

"Yes, Mr. De Fiore." She lowered her head.

"Call me Valentino. And play, now!" He raised his hands as though conducting an orchestra and flourished them at her.

Waiting while she tuned the strings, he leaned against the desk beside Darla and crossed his arms. Alice fumbled with the bow and dropped it. Valentino huffed and raised his voice. "Why are you nervous, *signorina*? You have secured me as teacher but I must not be expected to witness this display every time."

"Your teaching her is certain?" Darla looked up at him. "She was under the impression that this was an audition."

He glanced at Alice, still struggling to tune her violin, then returned his gaze to Darla. "Will you chaperone her every time?"

"That's the arrangement with my aunt."

His smile was roguish as he lifted his head toward Alice. "*Signorina* Beauchamp, you need not fear. I will take you on. You may relax because however you do with Paganini today, you will master it by the end of the year. Here, we will step out so you may prepare in peace. If you need the music for it, check my case on the side table."

He pulled Darla to her feet and led her into the deserted hallway, leaving the door open a crack.

"Now it is time for my studies. I have waited my whole life to see eyes like yours. They remind me of the Mediterranean Sea, where I sailed from when I left Italy." He nudged her against the wall, their bodies mere inches apart. "Tell me, Darla, do you close your eyes when kissed?"

Her heartbeat pounded in her ear as she smelled Valentino's cologne. She wanted to reach out and touch his beautiful hair. "Only if so moved by the one I'm kissing."

"You are the most fascinating creature I have laid my eyes on since I arrived in Mobile. I am certain you will close your eyes in rapture when our lips meet." His hand alighted on her hip. "But now I must go listen to your little cousin."

Emptiness filled each cavity in her soul when she lost his touch. Instinct told her he was a romancer, that he wanted to play her like his violin as he probably did with many women around the world, but part of her craved his touch once more. Darla followed him back into the room and sighed as she reseated herself.

"You are tuned, Alice. Please begin." Valentino stood between the cousins, a smug look on his face.

Alice played the strangest thing Darla had ever heard. Her bow moved like a saw and her fingers raced up and down the strings. Her body tremored to keep the pace and her hair ribbon jiggled like it was caught in a whirlwind.

After no more than fifteen seconds, Valentino interrupted. "Stop! You must take off that hideous thing on your head. It twitches like my grandmother who is prone to fits in her old age. Do not wear any ornamentation from now on. Be like your cousin and keep things simple. Pretty ladies do not need to draw attention away from their faces."

Alice removed the band and ribbon with one hand. Taking pity on her, Darla took the accessories. "Keep your chin up," she whispered. "He's monstrous."

Valentino winked at Darla on her way back to the chair. She placed the ribbons on the desk and ignored Valentino's pressing gaze. She no long wanted a kiss and didn't look forward to sitting through an hour of him barking orders at Alice twice a week.

"Start again."

Alice made it almost a minute before he stopped her. "Enough, enough! It is better than I expected, but you watch me."

In a moment, his instrument was under his chin, bow at the ready. While Alice's body had seemed to fight the music, Valentino's rapid movements flowed with the sound as though he became one with the score. His eyes appeared closed as his hair danced to the rhythm of the song. Once again, Darla was captivated by him—this time through the passion that resonated through his violin.

When he finished, his eyes resumed their focus around the room, falling first upon Darla's enraptured gaze. He licked his lips and raised his eyebrows in complete confidence that he'd master the tune as well as her yearnings. Trying to regain her indifference, she shrugged and looked at the flowered wallpaper.

"Well, Alice?"

She slowly raised her head. "I'll never be as good as you."

"True." He brandished his bow and brought it against her backside for a light spanking before setting his things back on the holder. "But you will be better than you were yesterday."

Alice tried to hold back tears but one slipped out.

"No tears, lovely Alice! You are good, very good for your age. With me you will find greatness."

More tears fell.

"No ribbons and no tears. In here you are a woman, not a girl." He gripped Alice's chin like he was testing the ripeness of fruit, and a moment later his mouth was on hers. "See? I do not kiss girls, only women. Dry your tears and play one of the things you had prepared for me so you may tell *Signora* Melling how well you performed without lying."

Alice calmed her breathing and wiped her eyes with a handkerchief from her pocket. "Yes, Valentino. I just need a moment to clear my head."

"Take a turn in the hall. That always works for me."

She nodded and placed her things on the bed on her way out. Darla rose to go with her but Valentino barred her way with his arm. "Musicians need solitude before a performance."

"You seem the type to grab whatever thing catches your eye at any given time."

He took Darla's hand and pulled her two steps forward so she wasn't in line with the open door. "Jealous, are you? I had to kiss her to save her from sadness and prove she is mature enough to handle this."

"And what if she isn't? She's not yet sixteen and you appear to be a taxing instructor."

"She is a tender young thing, but I will do what is needed to draw the music from her." Valentino fingered the lace at Darla's collar. "But with you, the longer you hold on to anticipation, the better it will be. Trust me."

"And what of your anticipation? I'm sure it will feel as good for you as anything does for me. Maybe even better." She bit her lip, tossing his game back at him.

He grabbed her waist with quick but gentle hands. "I can already tell we'll make beautiful music together. Where can I find you?"

She stepped back to her spot by the desk. "Here, on Monday and Thursday afternoons."

Alice rushed into the room. Without a word, she scooped her things off the bed and settled herself in the corner, though she didn't need the music stand. "Vivaldi, a movement from 'Winter,'" she said confidently.

This one was as soft as the Paganini was fast. Darla recognized it as one Alice had practiced much that week and she always enjoyed hearing it. Valentino stood with his arms crossed, scrutinizing Alice's stance. Her eyes were closed so she didn't suffer from his harsh stare. He let her play the complete movement and then smiled.

"See, it is as I said. Precise and lovely, though your posture could use some help to allow more passion to flow through your body. The score is melodic enough that non-musicians would not notice the lack of heart you feel, but to a trained ear you have much to learn to reach the top." He stood before her. "May I position you?"

She blushed slightly but nodded. His hand went to her shoulders first. Then he had her raise the instrument and bow as he adjusted her elbows and wrists.

"Play a few notes."

She did.

As his hands slid down Alice's sides to her tiny waist and then to her non-existent hips, Darla nearly erupted.

"Your chaperone knows this is purely for teaching, so it is not improper, is it, Alice?"

She shook her head and glanced at Darla, who rolled her eyes.

Valentino's hand was then on Alice's middle. "Now, tighten your muscles here, like a singer would, but keep the slight angle with your hips. Then your knees—"

"That's quite enough, Valentino." Darla's voice was sharp. "You may tell her what to do with her knees."

"*Sì*, Chaperone." He laughed and winked at Alice as though it was their private game. "Step your feet apart and allow your knees to bend so you may dip and sway with the music. Now play those same notes again and feel the difference."

Darla was sure he was full of himself and only looking for an excuse to make her jealous, but she had to admit the notes sounded fuller.

"*Buona!* It will take time before it becomes natural for you to stand that way. Practice before you begin playing. Now move around and see if you can return to the stance."

Valentino stepped back to allow her space to maneuver. He bent over the desk on the pretense of checking a piece of stationary on the shelf. He trailed a callused finger over Darla's hand. "For you I have other positions in mind," his lyrical voice whispered. Then louder, "Take the position, Alice!"

He went to Alice and repositioned her to meet his requirements. Three more attempts, each time fewer adjustments needed.

"Now walk the hall for a minute and return to the position."

As soon as she was outside, Valentino was beside Darla touching her dark hair. "It is soft and luxurious. Does it cover you fully when it is down?"

She slapped his hand away. "Do you really think you'll ever find out?"

He leaned against her side, bending to her ear. "I am a virtuoso and always learn everything about the curiosities I find in my travels. I will discover all your secrets, *amore mio*."

Darla hated herself for the thrill that ran the length of her body. He was a collector of women without a sincere bone in his body that didn't relate to music.

Alice breezed into the room as Valentino straightened. He followed her to the corner and watched her settle into the pose.

"No, no! Your hips and waist are still wrong. Come"—He motioned to Darla—"let me show her with you."

She stared at him.

"Come on, Darla." Alice's eagerness couldn't be ignored. "It will help me understand what he's doing to see it done to someone else."

Darla forced her feet to carry her across the room. Valentino immediately placed his violin and bow in her hands.

"Careful to not touch the horsehair. Oils from skin are very bad for it. See how Alice holds the bow lightly between her fingers? There is an art and balance to holding it. Very good."

His hands were on her shoulders, adjusting them to the proper angles and tucking the violin under her chin with a lingering caress on her cheek. "I do not wish to frighten you, but that beautiful instrument you are holding is worth enough to buy several automobiles. Please do not drop it."

Drop it? She wanted to smash it over his head when he trailed his hands from under her arms to her waist, then on to her hips, forever smiling at her as he lowered to his knees. "You see, Alice?" he said over his shoulder as he maneuvered her body. "A slight angle, but loose so when your knees are bent, your whole body can flow while remaining strong."

"Yes, I think so."

Valentino still knelt before Darla. She cleared her throat and glared down at him. He stood, keeping his hands about her. "You are a natural with positioning, Chaperone. I would love to dance with you sometime."

"Valentino, I think I got it!"

He turned to Alice, poking at elbows and middle to test strength. "*Sì*, Alice. Well done. You may pack now."

"And what about me?" Darla still stood posed with his priceless violin.

He waited until Alice bent over her music scores to sort the mess he'd made of her papers before making his move. His hand traveled the length of her arm supporting the violin. "Do you like the feel of it in your hand?"

"Not especially, though it's pretty to look at."

He laughed, deep and joyful. "You are the most fun of all, Chaperone." He replaced his violin then took the bow as a knock sounded.

"This lady will be the death of my passion," he muttered as he went to the door.

"How did it go? Is Alice not everything I said she is?"

"*Sì, sì, Signora* Melling. She is fine. We are to work on Paganini together. Alice, the first three lines for Monday. And *Signora*, there is no need for you to meet us here each time. I will see you at the shows."

"Are you sure it is safe?"

"They are good girls and she is chaperone." He pointed to Darla with indifference. "Besides, there are always workers about the halls delivering things to the rooms."

"Very well, Valentino. I will see the girls out this time."

"Alice," he said, "I should very much like to see how families in Mobile live. A supper invitation to your home one evening after lessons would be agreeable."

"Of course, Valentino. I'll ask my mother straight away and send word."

“I look forward to the invitation.” He came to them all for kisses to say goodbye as he had greeted each of them. Only Darla's cheek facing away from Mrs. Melling received a real one.

Sixteen

"You look lovely today, Darla. How was the meeting yesterday?" Lucy asked as soon as the young woman was in the door Friday morning.

"Awful." Darla removed her hat and hung it on the coat tree in the front hall. "The lessons are in his hotel room and he's an absolute flirt, yet he barks orders at Alice and thinks he owns the world because of his brilliance. He could see my appreciation for his looks the moment I walked in and pounced. When he played, I nearly melted into his arms and he knew it. But after seeing his behavior, I want nothing to do with him. Yet I'm bound to go to him twice a week with Alice."

Lucy's arm went around the shoulders of Darla's white blouse as she led her to the sofa. "You must remain strong. Do you believe you or Alice are in danger?"

"No, and I think I can deal with his advances. He managed to send Alice or us into the hall a few times and used the privacy to speak flattering words and give little caresses, but he never sought privacy with Alice, though he used the excuse to position her properly to have his hands all over her."

"A cad to be sure!" Doff jumped onto the arm of the sofa and purred to be petted, to which Lucy obliged.

"But it worked. It really did improve her sound so I can't call him out on it. And then he positioned me with her watching to help her understand how she needed to hold herself." Darla covered her face with her hands. "And so help me—his touch is as amazing as his playing!"

Phoebe dashed into the room. "Miss Darla sad? We go to Nana and Papa's house today!"

Darla uncovered her face and smiled. "I am happy about that, Phoebe. I want you to show me all the wonderful things there."

Lucy stood and reached a hand for Darla. "Let me fix some tea. We can sit in the kitchen and chat a little longer. Phoebe, will you build a block castle here for Darla? I think she'll want to play in a few minutes. Doff can help you."

"Yes, Momma." Phoebe pulled her basket to the center of the room and set to work, the cat circling her efforts.

In the kitchen, Lucy propped the swinging door open and set the kettle to boil.

Darla paced the room. "I've never met a man so bold before, and I hardly knew what to do. When I teased him back, he seemed to enjoy it. If I ignored him, he changed his tactics. I thought I'd gotten over the infatuation after witnessing his haughty attitude, but then he played and my resolve washed away. He knew exactly what he was doing. It appears he's a virtuoso of the violin *and* a master seducer."

Lucy sighed and hugged herself. "Alex was like that. All romance and flowing words that rivaled the great poets. He knew what to say, how to keep me at bay until I craved his touch so much I welcomed everything."

"I don't want that to happen to me." Darla reddened. "I don't mean anything against you, Lucy."

"I know you don't."

"You were engaged to be married and in love. Though I admit to Valentino's attractiveness, I don't see a future with him nor wish one. He's working me on purely carnal desires and it frightens me that I can be swayed in such a way. I thought myself too practical for that."

Lucy smiled. "Maybe setting your sights on another man would help keep you grounded around Valentino. Someone like Henry."

"Alice has had a crush on him since last year! She came out into society at fifteen just so she could dance with him once this season. He's practically all she talks about when in bed at night. I told her he took dinner with us when we walked home from the hotel. She was excited and asked all about him because she's hardly spoken to him. But then she turned jealous when I told her it was going to be a weekly occurrence. I can't in good conscience allow myself to open to Henry because it would destroy my friendship with my cousin."

"But you like him?" Lucy set two teacups on the counter.

"It would be very easy to imagine spending my future with someone like Henry."

"There's nothing as attractive as a numbers man." Lucy giggled. "This writer married a sensible accountant."

"But he doesn't appear to be dull."

Lightness filled her chest. "He isn't dull. I said sensible, and that he is, but he's also romantic, supportive, my best friend, a fabulous kisser, and an amazing dancer."

Darla laughed. "You glow when you talk about him and he glows when he talks about you. And when you're together, it's truly breathtaking. That's what I want for my life—mutual love and respect. A relationship like Frederick and Lucy Davenport. And a precious child like Phoebe wouldn't hurt either."

Lucy's laughter turned to tears. "Then don't do what I did. Don't hide from who your heart calls you to because someone else pulls stronger. Don't get swept away with physical feelings when your heart tries to show you where your peace lies. I lost nearly two years I could have had with Freddy because I was dazzled by Alex. I'm only fortunate because Freddy was patient enough to wait for me. Not many men would do that."

The front door opened. Darla went for the hall, which Lucy appreciated because she was still crying.

"Daddy!" Phoebe squealed.

Lucy washed her face at the sink. A moment later, Frederick came in.

"I left a file I brought home last night and had to come back for it."

Lucy turned off the water but stayed facing the sink. "You could have sent a clerk or the intern for it."

"I know." Frederick's hands went around her new pink dress, another draped column–style, and he snuggled against her back. "But I'm selfish and wanted to steal another kiss."

"You can't steal what's given freely."

"You steal my breath every morning I wake up beside you. I gave you my heart years ago and have lived each day for you since then."

She turned and wrapped her arms around his neck.

He fingered her cheek. "Why are your eyes red? Are you being sentimental today?"

"Thinking back on our journey. Darla said we both glow when we speak about each other and that we're 'breathtaking' together. How's that for a compliment?"

"I'd say that sounds like my beautiful wife." His kiss was tender but she demanded more.

Phoebe scampered in while Frederick kissed her neck.

"Sorry, Mr. Davenport and Lucy," Darla said. "I tried to catch her."

"Did we look as breathtaking as that felt?" Lucy teased Darla.

"Very much so. Come on, Phoebe. Let's give your parents some privacy." Darla pushed back through the swinging door.

Frederick tugged Lucy closer.

"Are you sure you don't want to join us for dinner at my parents?"

"I was thinking about it, but with this trip to get the file, I'll need to be in the office so I don't have to stay late and cut into my gym time. I'll have someone bring me a sandwich from a deli or something. You have fun and tell everyone hello for me."

"I'm sorry you had to spend your time running back here." Lucy pursed her lips, which Frederick kissed.

"I'm not. These moments with you are worth eating a cold lunch alone in my office."

***

Maxwell Easton came to the door at eleven-twenty. Lucy welcomed him with a hug. "You look dapper with your mustache waxed."

"And you look like you swallowed a bowling ball."

Lucy scoffed. "I'm not as bad as that. And besides, I feel terrific, not heavy at all."

"Give it another month."

Phoebe threw her arms around his legs. "Uncle Max! Uncle Max!"

He scooped her up and tickled under her arms. "Little Phoebe, you get taller every time I see you. You ready to be a big sister?"

"Yes, Uncle Max. Doff is big brother!"

"A cat for a brother? I'm sure your mother would think that's the best type of brother to have."

"I might have wished to trade Edmund for a cat at a few points in my life." Lucy smiled. "Since you're early, could you stop by the bookstore so I can dash in with Darla to buy something? Darla, this is my oldest brother, Maxwell Easton. Maxwell, meet Darla, our new hire as a mother's helper. She's kin to the Beauchamps next door."

Maxwell laughed. "And Ida Beauchamp lets you near Lucy?"

Lucy playfully backhanded his arm. "Her father was Reginald Beauchamp."

"Was?"

"He passed away this summer," Darla said. "And my aunt isn't fond of me."

"I'm sorry to hear that. Reginald was friends with one of my friend's older brothers growing up. I often admired his daring when the older boys were about. But yes, Lucy, load up and we'll be on our way."

Lucy breezed through the door of the bookshop, Darla at her heels.

"How can I help you?" Mr. Lloyd asked.

"We're looking for a copy of … what's it called?" she turned to Darla.

Darla blushed, but played along. "Azalea … Azaleas in Bloom?"

The shop keeper smiled. "*Azalea Blossom?*"

"That's it!" Lucy clapped her hands. "My friend said I simply had to read it."

"It's been one of our best sellers for years," Mr. Lloyd said. "I'll show you to Miss Kent's books. She has four out, in case another catches your fancy. And if you enjoy them, a new one releases at the end of the month. She's a favorite for most of the ladies in town. I've ordered four cases of the first run and I think we'll sell out within the week. The ladies enjoy reading about familiar locations and I don't think they mind the romance, either." He winked as he handed her the pink hardcover with an azalea blossom embossed on the cover.

They completed the purchase and were both laughing by the time they reached the sidewalk. Lucy climbed in the front with Maxwell and he looked into the bag.

"You didn't!"

"I couldn't help myself. The man said Olive Kent was a local favorite and he's already ordered four cases of her new book."

Maxwell nodded over his shoulder. "Is she part of the inner circle?"

Lucy laughed. "Yes, sworn to secrecy by blood pact."

Darla leaned forward. "I forgot to tell you, my aunt has all your books. I started reading *Magnolia Wind* yesterday. It's lovely."

"Don't fluff her head any more than the bookseller did." Maxwell pulled into traffic.

When they neared the Mellings' old law office, Lucy clutched her hands in her lap and stared at the sight of a woman in purple stepping out the front door. Her large hat shaded her face, but the sun glinted off the gold watch around her neck. Maxwell rolled to a stop because a wagon three vehicles up paused to unload a box into a store front.

Looking up, the woman met eyes with Lucy and smiled like a predator that'd caught its prey. She crossed to the edge of the sidewalk and waved like royalty.

"Lucille Davenport, it's been so long since I've seen you I wondered if you were unwell. But it looks like you are expecting a new addition soon." Her gaze traveled to Maxwell. "Hello, Mr. Easton. It's good to see you being brotherly to Lucille since her other brother wants nothing to do with her from what I hear."

"You should know by now, Mrs. Lyons," Lucy said, "that what you hear isn't always true. You might want to think before passing on information."

The woman leaned in the open window. "Made a stop at the bookseller? It is a shame you never published, Lucille. I was looking forward to reading between the lines of your novels."

"A true disappointment." Lucy knew her smile didn't match her words, but she couldn't hide the giddiness from knowing that her books were safe from Kate's talons.

"The traffic is moving. Watch your toes, Mrs. Lyons." Maxwell's voice was curt.

When they were a block away, Maxwell patted Lucy's knee. "You held your own well."

She clenched her fists. "That Kate! I want to rip her eyes out whenever I see her. Oh, but her and Rupert deserve each other! They're both vile creatures and have to be the coldest couple in town. Do they take turns domina—"

Maxwell laughed. "Don't forget the little ears in the backseat, Lucy."

She huffed and remained silent the rest of the drive.

After they parked in the Eastons' driveway, Phoebe ran up the front steps while Darla stood by the automobile staring at the house.

"Are you okay?" Lucy asked.

"I've never seen anything like it. It's beautiful, like a castle."

"It's a Queen Anne style, so it's royal in that regard. Can you believe it was built from a kit? A house from a catalog, like for a doll. Funny, isn't it?" She took the young woman's arm and followed Maxwell into the house.

After introductions were made and they settled in the parlor for a few minutes, the sound of a car pulling in came through the open windows. Lucy's heart leapt at the thought of Frederick surprising her. She sat forward and watched the doorway. When her clean-shaven brother walked in, she sat back with a sigh.

"Eddie, dear!" Their mother reached around her granddaughter to take her son's hand. "I'm glad you could take your lunch hour with us."

Edmund greeted his father next, and then turned to Lucy on the settee.

"Be nice, children," Maxwell teased.

"Lucy." Edmund leaned over and kissed her cheek. "You look well."

"Thank you. That's a handsome suit you're wearing." She motioned to Darla, who'd just come in behind him. "And this is Darla Beauchamp, my mother's helper for Phoebe."

When she saw him blanch, Lucy took heart knowing he had the same reaction she did when seeing Darla for the first time. As unkind as the thought was, she hoped he felt uncomfortable with the reminder from his past.

Seventeen

Darla found Maxwell charming but Edmund— Eddie as his parents and brother called him—gave her a creepy feeling. He kept staring at her across the dinner table, his hazel eyes like a cat eyeing a dead mouse. But Mr. and Mrs. Easton were wonderful. The men tended to speak of their business affairs, but Mrs. Easton doted on Lucy and Phoebe, and often asked after Darla's own comfort.

When dinner was finished, Edmund stood. "Excuse me. I need to get back to the office." He rounded the large table to his mother's side to kiss her goodbye, and then patted Phoebe's blonde head. "Stay sweet, little Phoebe. And Lucy, I hope to see you at the family supper this month. I missed you last time."

"I plan on it, Edmund."

After Edmund's exit, they settled in the parlor. Phoebe was given leave to show Darla the house, so she tromped up the stairs and peeked in every bedroom and bath at the girl's insistence before going into the lovely yard.

"This was Momma's fairy castle and now it's mine!" she said of the gazebo surrounded by giant azalea bushes.

"It's very pretty, Princess Phoebe. I'd love to play here sometime, but I think Uncle Maxwell needs to get back to work." Darla took her hand and led her to the kitchen door.

"I'll let Freddy know," Lucy said to her parents when Darla and Phoebe entered the parlor. Maxwell helped her stand and she turned to them. "You girls ready?"

"Stay with Nana and Papa!" Phoebe threw herself into her grandmother's arms.

Lucy looked at her mother and then her father, both wearing smiles and nodding their consent. "Let me call Daddy and arrange for him to get you after work."

Phoebe clutched her grandmother. "I stay until tomorrow."

"Oh, Lucy, let her. She can sleep in your old bed, no trouble. Just have Freddy drop by some clothes and whatever else she needs."

"Rummy and Pinky!"

"Very well, but you be good for Nana and Papa." She kissed her daughter.

"That will give you time to discuss things with Freddy," her mother whispered.

They said their farewells and then Maxwell drove Darla and Lucy back across town.

"What do you think of the offer?" Lucy asked her brother when he pulled to a stop before her house.

Darla slipped out the back to give them privacy, but still heard the discussion as the automobile windows were open.

"It would only be feasible for it to go to you, me, or Eddie, but I think you're the logical one. You lived there the longest and help them the most."

"You don't think Edmund will cause trouble?"

"Do you think Mary Margaret would want that house? She's tied to her parents' circle and they like being downtown close to all the social events. Don't worry about it. If Freddy agrees, I'll back you two up. Now enjoy your free time." He winked.

Lucy backhanded his arm and laughed.

Once she stepped out, Maxwell leaned over the seat and waved. "Nice to meet you, Darla."

"The same to you, Mr. Easton."

Lucy sighed. "I need to call Freddy and pack a bag for Phoebe. I think I'll walk it to his office to save him the trouble of coming here to pick it up."

"I could go with you. I have nothing to do until Alice comes home and don't like the idea of you walking that far alone."

"But you could read, unless of course you'd rather have the chance to see Henry. I wouldn't blame you." Lucy's laughter filled the hall as she stepped into the front door and set the book bag on the entryway table. "I'll make the calls first if you want to collect Phoebe's doll and bunny for a start."

Darla wasn't trying to listen, but she heard Lucy phone Naomi and cancel her for supper. Then the secretary at the office put her through to her husband and her voice dropped to a whisper.

When they were upstairs, Lucy pointed out which of Phoebe's clothing and supplies to pack. Her toothbrush and hair brush, with the toys on top of the neat pile all fit snuggly in a small suitcase. Darla carried it downstairs as Lucy answered the ringing doorbell.

"Pardon me for bothering you, Mrs. Davenport, but I was told next door that Darla Beauchamp would be here."

"Captain Walker!"

Lucy stepped to the side as Darla took his free hand and smiled at the jovial man.

"Lucy, this is Captain Walker, Claire's husband."

"Do come in, Captain Walker. Any friend of Darla's is welcome here."

They settled in the living room and he passed a brown sack to Darla. "Here's a taste of home from the ladies. Some cookies from Claire and bread from Maggie. I think there's a couple letters in there, too."

"It means the world to me, thank you! I picked up something for Claire today. What great timing." She looked to Lucy.

"I'll get it for you." Lucy took the book from the entry hall and brought it to the study to sign.

"You'll never guess who I met last weekend," Darla said to the captain. "Someone who told me to pass on that she asked about you and wished you and your family well."

Captain Walker's crooked smile looked amused. "Who might that be?"

"Mrs. Melling. She said you looked after her during the months she spent at her Eastern Shore cottage. I didn't realize how you met the Campbells and that their time across the bay ended with a fire."

His smile disappeared. "It's not something they like to discuss. Maggie went through some rough times there, but it's good of you to pass on the information."

"I figured as much. Mrs. Melling was quite upset at the mention of Douglas and Maggie."

"It's not for me to say more, but you may send my regards in return the next time you see Mrs. Melling." He stood and straightened his jacket. "It looks like you ladies have a busy day ahead. I won't keep you. I promised Claire and Maggie I'd look in on you on your first week away. I'll report that you're well and dressing like a real city lady."

Darla's hand went to her hip in the slim-cut skirt as she stood and looked down at her shiny boots. "I'd much rather be barefoot in a calico walking the beach."

"All the same, you look right nice."

Lucy joined them in the foyer and passed the bookstore bag to Darla.

"Here, Captain. Tell Claire I managed to secure a rare signed copy. And thank her and Maggie for the food."

"I will." He turned to Lucy in the door. "Based on the reception I received next door, I must thank you for looking out for Darla's best interests. She's blessed to have this refuge against the coldness of her aunt."

"I'm sorry. Was she rude to you?" Darla asked.

"Not to me, but there was indifference in all things pertaining to you. Stay well, Darla. I'm sure you'll see me or Douglas before too long."

"I look forward to it."

"Come by anytime," Lucy added. Once the door shut, she said to Darla, "The captain was very agreeable, as Jane Austen would say."

"The captains are the finest men on the island."

"Let's rest a moment." Lucy steered her toward the sofa. "I could put my feet up before we leave and you could read your letters."

"You wouldn't mind?"

"Not if you share a cookie."

Darla retrieved the letters and two oatmeal cookies from the bag. Lucy sat with her legs stretched across the sofa and Darla took the closest armchair. She opened Claire's letter first.

Dear Darla,

I hope this package finds you well. Maggie and I wanted to send you a taste of home to mark your first week away from the island. It's been quiet since you left; the opposite of your life at present, I'm sure. I hope to encourage Maggie to train with me while you're away. Mrs. Collier will be the next one to birth, as you know, and I think she'd be fine with Maggie in attendance. I hope all is well with you.

Sincerely,

Claire Walker

Darla sighed and nibbled the cookie. Lucy seemed to be daydreaming, maybe thinking up something for her next book. After another bite, she slid open the second letter.

Dearest Darla,

Forgive the shortness of this letter. I wanted to get it out with the care package this morning, so expect a longer note by mail. Yesterday I received my weekly letter from Claudio. He informed me that one of his cousins, Valentino De Fiore, is to be in Mobile for the remainder of the year. A friend of Claudio's is sponsoring Valentino's stay with a local orchestra and has arranged a few violin students for him to earn some extra money while he's in town. Claudio was concerned to learn that his cousin is to have a young female student as he is known to lead the hearts of many ladies astray. (And if he looks anything like his cousin, it is to be believed!) The name of one of his pupil is Alice Beauchamp, which I think is your cousin. If that's so, please watch out for her. I'd hate for anything to happen that might compromise her innocence.

On a happier note, Claudio will be coming to Mobile in November to see his cousin perform, and Douglas and I will at last be able to visit him after these four long years. We will, of course, expect to see you as well when we come to town.

Much love, and stay alert!

Maggie

"It's as I feared."

Lucy looked over. "What's that?"

"Maggie's note. She's friends with Valentino's cousin—a priest in Louisiana. When he heard Valentino had taken a female student he voiced his concern to her. She recognized the name as my cousin's and wants me to watch out for her because, let me read her exact words … 'he is known to lead the hearts of many ladies astray. (And if he looks anything like his cousin, it is to be believed!)'"

Lucy's confusion showed on her furrowed brow as she chewed the last of her cookie. "How strange you know someone who is connected to Alice's teacher."

Darla swallowed hard and took a deep breath. "It's odd, but there's a reasonable explanation."

As though sensing the importance of what she was about to say, Lucy swung her legs down and turned to Darla.

"Please don't get up, Lucy. I wouldn't want you to risk a fall if what I say upsets you."

"What is it?"

"It's been a puzzle to me this week, but things are slipping into place, unveiling the past as it relates to Alexander Melling."

"Alex?" Lucy paled.

"It all started on Sunday, or maybe Saturday when I came here the first time. Alice was desperate to discover what scandal you have in your past that would make her mother ban the family from mingling with you. She wanted me to spy and figure out what happened. Alice had ridiculous ideas, like your husband was holding you here against your will in some sinister plot because he's too muscular for an accountant."

Lucy tried to laugh, but it didn't sound true. "He doesn't go as often as he used to, but when we married, I insisted he still go to the gym three times a week. That was his coping strategy when … never mind. Did you discover all the secrets here?"

Darla shook her head at the pointed question. "Most I learned next door. When Mrs. Melling came after church she asked about what jobs I did before coming here that made my aunt allow me to work. I found it odd Aunt Ida didn't mention you by name, but rather referred to you as a neighbor. I'm not allowed to speak of birthing babies around my cousins, but when Alice was sent out of the room, I mentioned Claire—calling her Mrs. Walker. Mrs. Melling asked if she was a relation of Captain Joseph Walker and I told her she was his wife."

Every time she said "Mrs. Melling" Lucy winced, but Darla couldn't tell the information without mentioning the woman.

"Captain Walker delivered weekly goods to Mrs. Melling when she lived in Seacliff Cottage. That was her vacation home across the bay."

A haunted look shadowed Lucy's eyes. "I was acquainted with the house."

"Apparently it was where her daughter died, and she lived there half a year while in mourning."

Lucy nodded. "Eliza had a horse riding accident in January '06. Mrs. Melling stayed on until Alex was engaged to Beatrice Kirkpatrick. I'm sure Mrs. Melling never found fault in *her*."

Darla shivered from the coldness in Lucy's voice. "Well, Aunt Ida was eager to impress Mrs. Melling, and after she asked about the Walkers, she let her know I had connections with the Campbells, too. When Mrs. Melling heard the name she grew angry and left quite suddenly. It was only then that Aunt Ida put the names together. Maggie, known as Magdalene Jones to society, was Mrs. Melling's companion before marrying. She married the chauffeur, Douglas Campbell. They were at the property when it burned, the last ones to see Alexander and Mr. Melling alive."

Lucy sprung from the sofa, eyes huge and hands trembling. "I must get Phoebe's things to Freddy."

"You don't look well."

"I'm fine. You may talk while we walk or you can go home for the day, your choice."

"I'm coming with you."

"Why, because you haven't gathered all the secrets you need yet?" Lucy's usually soft eyes were like an oak with the brilliance of a setting sun behind the leaves. "What more do you need to answer all of Alice's questions? That I'm familiar with Seacliff Cottage because that's where Alex bedded me the first time might fulfill her curiosity. Or the fact that I'm Olive Kent. That's enough to ruin me for life, so tread carefully with that one before sharing it."

"Lucy, I don't tell what I learn here. You've become a dear friend to me. I'd never betray your trust."

"I've been betrayed too many times in my life, both by family and friends. It was silly of me to trust someone I'd just met. Please go."

"But Lucy, I only told you about Alice because I'm sharing everything with you. I haven't told her any—"

"Go!"

Darla ran next door and immediately went for the telephone in the kitchen, ignoring the glare from the cook. She asked the operator for the accounting office and tapped her fingers on the phone box while she waited.

"I need to speak with Mr. Davenport immediately. It's about his wife." She kept watch out the window for Lucy.

After a minute, Mr. Davenport's voice came through the line. "Lucy?"

"No, it's Darla. Lucy was going to bring Phoebe's suitcase to you, but we started talking and now she's terribly upset and it's my fault. She made me leave and I fear she'll try to walk to your office alone. I'm watching your house from my aunt's, and if she leaves I'll follow."

"I'll be right there!"

Darla went out the backdoor and paced the length of the smaller porch on the side of the house, praying Mr. Davenport would make it home before Lucy ventured out.

Eighteen

Lucy's tears fell, not from anger at Darla, but from hatred at herself for snapping at the young woman. In her heart, she understood Darla wasn't one to betray, but the fact that her cousin wanted information, her aunt knew things about the Mellings that she never knew, that Darla herself was friends with people that knew Alexander … she couldn't tolerate hearing more until she absorbed what she'd just learned.

The front door burst open.

"Lucy!" Frederick was at her side on the sofa before she could respond. "Whatever is the matter?"

"Freddy, I made a muddle of things with Darla. She was being honest with me and I yelled at her to leave."

He put an arm around her. "I'm sure she'll get over it."

"No, I was too cruel."

He took her face in his hands and kissed her forehead. "How do you think I came to be here at two-thirty in the afternoon? She ran next door and called me, frantic over having upset you and concerned for your safety."

Lucy buried her head on his chest and curled against him. "You did the right thing hiring her, Freddy. She has the key to understanding everything."

"What's there to understand?"

"Why Alex had to die." He stiffened and Lucy imagined he forced his arms to stay around her when he really wanted to push her away. "I always thought he died because the Lord knew it was the only way I'd let him go, but what if there was another reason? Darla knows the people who last saw him. Her friends were at Seacliff Cottage when it burned." She paused and still he didn't say anything. "You're mad, aren't you?"

His arms tightened around her and he kissed her head. "I'd just hoped we were past this, at least until December."

"But don't you see? This could be it! If I can speak with who was there, find out if he'd reconciled things in his life, know that he was right with the Lord, I—"

"But what if he was just as messed up as he ever was? What if he died miserable? What if he started the fire? What would it do to you to know—rather than imagine—he died bitter, angry, and sinful?"

Silent tears rolled from her eyes. "But then I'd know and wouldn't have to project any more fanciful stories. I could pray for him one last time and be done—"

Frederick's fists clenched. "Do you really believe that?"

"I like to hope it," she whispered. "I'm sorry, Freddy. Every time I think I'm better, something of him comes back to me and it's fresh again."

"You've allowed yourself to suffer too long. It's been almost five years, Lucy. Five years!" Frederick released her and stood. He ripped his suit jacket off and threw it at the armchair, towering over her as he loosened his tie. "In two months' time, I'll see the sadness in your eyes when you see the first sprig of mistletoe hanging somewhere. I'll see the wistfulness on your face when you hear the cathedral bells calling people to midnight Mass. I'll see the damn longing in your eyes when the clock strikes midnight New Year's Eve. And God help us all when the Mystics of Dardenne masquerade comes around, followed by Valentine's Day!"

Frederick was her unconditional love, forever patient and caring. What type of woman was she to turn him against her? She had finally crossed the line and it cost her the one she never wanted to give up. The memories of Alexander's assault, Opal's attack, being chased through the duplex by a manic Alexander intent on having his way with her before she left him—none of it was more fearful than seeing the anger on Frederick's face.

With quivering lips and a racing heart, she held his gaze for what she believed was the last time. "Are you going to strike me?" Her voice cracked as his countenance fell.

He sank to his knees before her. "God no, Lucy. Never." Encircling her in his arms, he kissed her neck. "You know me better than that. I'm sorry I yelled. Can you forgive my harsh words?"

"Yes, Freddy." The words escaped her in relief and his strong embrace helped her trembling ease. "You haven't gone to the gym since Monday, have you?"

"Not with our shopping and supper out. The week got away from me." Frederick leaned back, gazing at her face.

"You need that, you know." She trailed a finger down from the bridge of his straight nose. "Be sure you go after you get Phoebe's bag to her."

He smiled. "Don't try to change the subject, Goosy."

Frederick wouldn't play like that if he was angry. His dimples only winked during genuine smiles. And he wouldn't have softly admonished her if he planned to hurt or leave her. She should have realized all that before, but the fervor on his countenance in the moment of his anger was out of her experience with him. Her arms went around his neck and she kissed her husband to let him know she was his no matter what haunted her.

Frederick laughed. "Now you're really trying to change the subject."

She tugged off his tie and unbuttoned his collar. "Can you blame me?"

"Oh, Lucy." He trailed the sweep of her rounded neckline with a loving touch. "Darla's wearing a hole in her aunt's porch waiting to hear where she stands with you. Whatever happened, whatever was said, there needs to be reconciliation so she doesn't worry until she comes back Monday morning. Call her over and I'll start some tea."

Frederick pulled her up, then hugged her a moment before going to the kitchen. Lucy stopped to remove her shoes before stepping onto the porch. Darla looked at her expectantly from next door. Lucy motioned her over and tried not to feel the pang of guilt Darla's smile evoked. She ran to her, a daring feat in her slim skirt and new boots. Before she could speak, Lucy gave her instructions.

"Frederick is making tea. Go into the kitchen and tell him everything you told me so he's caught up with the news before you continue."

Darla took two steps and paused as though she wanted to say something.

"And Darla, I'm sorry for the things I said. I do want to know what you've discovered. I think it will help me."

"I'm sorry I upset you."

Lucy paced the living room until Frederick and Darla came in with the tea. Then she pretended to be placid while Darla spoke about Sadie Marley bringing a box of Grace Anne's old *Snitch* magazines and Alice going through them with the express purpose of finding information about Lucy. The discovery of the notice about Mrs. Melling's companion and driver from the summer of 1906 had her heart racing.

"Alice thought you might be the Miss E written about, but I knew for sure when you told me some people still think of you as Miss Easton. But I never told Alice when I learned the truth, though she knows A.R.M. is Alexander and suspects F.L.D. is Mr. Davenport." Darla looked at her. "That woman who spoke to you today from the sidewalk, that was the Kate who wrote *Snitch*, wasn't it?"

Lucy nodded and took a sip of her tea.

Frederick laid a hand on her knee. "You spoke to Kate?"

"Cruel fate stopped Maxwell's automobile in front of Lyons, Melling, and Associates on our way to my parents' for dinner." Lucy set her cup on the table and paced, not caring if her agitation was known. "And then Edmund joined us for the meal, though fortunately he didn't stay after eating. But I bet he wish he never came."

"Why's that, Goosy?"

She pointed to Darla. "Because I could tell he thought the same thing I did when he looked at her, but his memory of Eliza Melling is more cumbersome than mine."

Darla's mouth opened in shock and Lucy returned to pacing.

Frederick looked to Darla and offered a smile. "It's your dark hair and blue eyes, nothing more."

She nodded and drank more of her tea before continuing. "Maggie is still friends with the priest, Claudio De Fiore, that she met while working for the Mellings. She and her husband will be coming to town next month to see a performance while Father De Fiore is here visiting his cousin. I might be able to arrange for you to meet them so you may ask the questions you seek about Alexander. But I'll warn you, even Captain Walker says Maggie doesn't talk about the fire. She doesn't talk about the Mellings at all. I never knew who she worked for before coming to the island."

"I beg you to plead with her to speak with me!"

Frederick stepped between her and Darla, taking Lucy by the shoulders. "Don't get your hopes up, Goosy."

She leaned around him. "Invite them to dinner or supper or tea. Please let them know how much this means to me! I have no closure."

"You had closure the day I saved you from his hellish duplex." Frederick's voice held a hint of pain.

Darla stood and stepped to the side. "I'll see what I can do about a meeting, but I need to go now. Thank you for tea."

Lucy held her position until the front door shut. Then she collapsed against Frederick.

"Let me get you into bed." He looked at the clock. "Why isn't Naomi here yet?"

"I telephoned her and told her to take the afternoon off because with Phoebe gone, I figured I could cook for you and me easily enough."

"I'd rather not leave you alone. Would you want to ride with me to deliver the bag?"

She shook her head. "No, I'll rest. You see to Phoebe and stop at the gym. I've heard your strength has become legendary. You don't want to disappoint your adoring public by skipping too many workouts."

"Don't do this to yourself."

"Do what?" she asked bitterly as he led her up the stairs.

"Fall into self-pity and push me out."

"Just let me rest. I'm sure I'll be back to rights soon."

Without speaking, he helped her out of the high-waist dress and hung it on the closet door. His eyes wandered from her bare feet up her silk chemise, lingering at her chest before meeting her gaze.

"You've always brushed my feelings aside, Lucille." Her eyebrows rose at the use of her proper name, and his lips curved into a sad smile as though happy she'd registered the slight. "I'm asking you to remember that though I've been devoted to you most of my life, there's a limit to the pain I'm willing to endure. Both the pain you inflict on yourself and your family with your brooding obsessions. I'm the one you promised to love and cherish before God, not Alex. He ran from you more than once to spare you pain, now you need to run from his memory to get away from the pain you keep causing yourself."

His lips on hers felt like Alexander's had before he walked out once he saw to her immediate needs after his violent hour—full of regret and waning devotion.

"Freddy—"

He pressed a finger to her lips. "Rest. I'll be home by five-thirty."

Lucy didn't think she'd sleep, but the next thing she knew, the sunlight filtering through the drapes was softer. The timepiece read five o'clock. She washed her face and decided to dress in one of her new gowns. Its base was turquoise with panels and trim of fine gold lace, the largest draping her bulging torso. She twisted her hair into a romantic chignon and descended the stairs as Frederick came in the front door.

"Welcome home."

Guilt over hurting him so much stung her heart as he smiled at her with complete adoration. "You're radiant, Goosy."

He met her at the foot of the stairs and wrapped her in his arms. He smelled fresh from the shower, his hair damp.

"How was Phoebe and your time at the gym?"

"Good on both accounts. The princess is being spoiled, as I'm sure you guessed. I took thirty minutes on the rowing machine, ten minutes with a punching bag, and five sparring rounds in the ring with Chuck and Thomas." He kissed her cheek. "And did you rest or spend all your time dressing up?"

"I woke at five. What you see before you is a washed face, a new dress, and a refreshed hairstyle, nothing more."

"Nothing more than my ravishing wife. Do you want to go out for supper again?"

"I just want to be pretty for you."

"You are, every day." His kissing was more subdued than their other encounters that week, but it held more passion than his parting one. "Shall I call the Trellis Room to see if they have an opening this evening?"

"On a Friday night, it's doubtful." She let her arms trail off his shoulders when he went for the telephone.

"Seven-thirty, a secluded table for two." He took her hand when he returned. "What shall we do until then?"

Lucy turned to him and fingered his open collar. "Get you out of this and into a tuxedo for one thing. Tonight you need to dress to match me."

Frederick took her hand and started up the stairs. A depth of heartache etched into his brown eyes when they reached their bedroom. He unbuttoned his shirt, then stood with arms out.

"What would you have me wear?"

His attitude was defeat. Resignation. As it was Lucy who brought him to that point, she wanted to lift him back to his pedestal she loved to admire him on rather than see him on his knees like he awaited a beheading.

"I never meant to hurt you." She undid his cufflinks and set them on his dresser. "I'm sorry for being an emotional wreck these past weeks." *Years.*

Frederick stayed silent as she pulled off his outer shirt. She tossed it onto the bench and her hands went to his belt. The memory of her hands on Alexander's waistband as they stood before each other in his bedroom at Seacliff Cottage played through her head like a moving picture show, but she held her gaze and concentrated on her husband. Her real husband, not the one she imagined marrying.

"I know what it feels like to be on that end and it's unforgivable," she whispered.

He shook his head, a pensive smile soft on his lips. "Forgiveness is possible. I've been forgiving your moods and misplaced longings through four years of marriage. It's when the same infraction happens for the hundredth time that makes it more difficult to forget the dozens of other instances."

"Sometimes things look worse before they improve. I feel a change inside me." Her arms encircled his neck. "Have we not enjoyed some amazing moments lately? Last Friday night, for one."

"That was great." His hands went to her hips, but his smile was short-lived.

"Freddy, pardon my imperfections. I want us to be strong together. For your sake, and Phoebe's, and the new one."

He shifted a hand to her belly. "And what of your sake, Goosy?"

"I'm used to being broken."

"That's exactly what I've been trying to get you to understand! There's no reason for you to wallow through life broken." His hands cradled her face and his lips brushed hers. "You don't need to play martyr. You have a family who loves you and wants to enjoy, love, and spend time with you. Do you think harboring the heartache and pain makes you a better person?"

She smiled. "Maybe a better writer."

"As much as I love your glorious imagination and skill with words, I'd rather have a healthy, happy wife and mother to my children than share a bed with a successful writer who moons over the monster that abused her. Am I to be a Friday night lover while you think of Alex the rest of your life?"

Lucy jerked out of his arms, eyes wide and mouth open in speechless horror.

"And don't think this is sudden on my part. I'm growing weary of being victim to your pain. Every year, I hope it will be the last one you sink into depression over his anniversaries but there's no improvement. And this year it's worse than ever." He tucked her into the curve of his broad chest. "I knew he would be in your heart, but his portion is nudging me out. Can you deny it?"

"No, but I'm fighting for your space, Freddy. I'm trying, really I am." His soft undershirt was soon spotted by her tears.

"I'm telling you my feelings in hopes that it will strengthen your resolve to hold to what we have." His tender touch traveled her back, traced the curve of motherhood, and came to rest with one hand on her hip while the other caressed her jawline. "Cleave to me, Lucy. Our future can be bright together and you don't have to hurt."

Their kiss started gentle, but Lucy unbridled her passion. Torn between the living and the dead—though both were alive in her heart—she didn't differentiate between the man in her mind and the one she touched. She gave her all to the moment, eyes shut in reverence for the internal images though the sensations of her body bringing abundant pleasures as well.

Afterward, Frederick held her in his arms, his breath warm on her shoulder as they lay in bed. Lucy rested her hands atop his on her torso, both their hands rising from the movement within.

"Frederick," she started, her voice low. "My parents want to give us their house."

"Why? Where are they going?"

"It's getting too much for them, even with the extra rooms closed off. Rather than hire on another worker, they want something smaller after the holidays. They told me today after Edmund left. Maxwell agrees with us having it and is willing to settle any issues that might arise from Edmund, even though he doesn't think he and Mary Margaret would want it."

"I wouldn't feel right about taking it, but we could buy it from them if that's what you want."

"It would be further from work, church, and everything for you."

"But Phoebe loves it there. And we both know it's a magical place to spend one's childhood." Frederick switched to lying in front of her. "The forts, battles, and races. And you were always my fair maiden to rescue."

"Phoebe's a warrior. She'd be the one rescuing others and protecting her little brother or sister."

"Just one sibling?" He kissed her. "We could fill the house like your parents did."

Lucy's heart raced to see the spark back in his eyes. "Let me get through this birthing before agreeing to anything more. I haven't done well this time."

A fingertip trailed her curves. "You haven't had swelling issues or bad sickness."

"I fear I'm not well in my head, in my heart."

Frederick kissed her forehead. "We're working on that, but it's probably the combined stress of the new book and the pregnancy. Let's get ready for supper."

Nineteen

Just as the Beauchamps finished supper, the doorbell rang. The maid was gone for the day so Uncle Calvin answered it.

"Frederick, good to see you. And Mrs. Davenport, you look prettier than ever."

Aunt Ida sucked in her breath with a hiss. "Children, go to your rooms this instant."

They did, but they all went slowly, peeking into the front hall as the Davenports were led to the parlor. Lucy wore a turquoise gown with a delicate gold shawl around her shoulders, looking like a gilded ornament on Mr. Davenport's arm. When the cousins were halfway up the stairs, Uncle Calvin called for Darla.

"Darla, with all the commotion this afternoon, I neglected to give you your wages." Mr. Davenport handed her an envelope.

"It could have waited, but thank you."

"It's no trouble. We're on our way out, as you can see. Have a good weekend."

"Thank you, Mr. Davenport. And I hope you enjoy yourself, Mrs. Davenport."

Lucy smiled meekly and seemed to tighten her hold on her husband's arm.

"We'll let your family get back to your activities." Mr. Davenport nodded to Uncle Calvin. "Please apologize to your wife for the interruption."

As though they had crowded on the upper landing, all the cousins rushed down the stairs as soon as the front door clicked shut.

Alice sighed. "Isn't she the loveliest? And Mr. Davenport looked dashing in that tuxedo!"

Aunt Ida stormed into the room. "I thought I made it clear you are not to speak to or about them, Alice."

Uncle Calvin scoffed. "Frederick Davenport has been a good neighbor for as long as we've both been here and nothing has changed since he married Lucille. They're quiet and there are less comings and goings than there was with his first wife with all those nurses at odd hours."

"I'd forgotten he was married before," Alice remarked. "He must like to keep his wives inside. She never went out either."

Aunt Ida practically snorted her distaste. "It's none of your business what he does with his wives, but that first one was a Yankee with consumption. He was saddled with her when he was but twenty, the poor man."

"You won't see me settling down at twenty." Richard crossed his arms. "I aim to make a name for myself and take my time finding the right woman."

Alice turned up her nose at him. "Good luck finding one who would have you."

"I bet he'd ask for Sadie Marley's hand tomorrow if she wanted him to." Clarence laughed, but when Richard lunged at him, he ran out of the parlor.

"Clarence, come back!" his mother called. "You have to practice the duet with Alice. You need to be perfect when Valentino De Fiore comes for supper on Monday."

Clarence returned as Alice tuned her violin, but Richard stayed out of sight and Felix soon slipped away. Darla settled back in the armchair and closed her eyes, allowing the Chopin piece to drift through her soul.

***

On Sunday, the Beauchamp family arrived to Mass fifteen minutes early. The boys stayed in the square, cutting up with friends, but Alice took Darla by the arm and brought her to the portico hoping to find Henry. After only a minute of standing between the columns, he found them.

"Miss Beauchamp and Miss Beauchamp." He tipped his gray hat. "I hope you're both well this morning."

"Yes, Mr. Adams." Alice inclined her head and stared at him longer than he kept eye contact.

He turned fully to Darla. "I wanted to inquire after the Davenports. I saw Mr. Davenport rush out Friday afternoon and heard there was some trouble with his wife."

"Oh, she's fine now. They both are." She smiled at him. "It's just how things are with women in her condition."

"Yes," Alice elbowed her way closer. "They stopped in Friday night on their way out. I've never seen her look finer. They're a handsome couple."

"So they are." Henry refocused on Darla. "I'm glad all is well. Hope to see you Wednesday. Good day, young Miss Beauchamp."

Alice watched him enter the cathedral, mouth open. Then she stomped her foot. "Of all the insufferable things to say, he called me 'young!'"

Darla stifled a laugh. "You are younger than me. He was probably differentiating so you'd know he was addressing you."

"But 'young?'" Alice smoothed her red skirt and lifted her chin. "If a man like Valentino De Fiore calls me a woman, I must surely be one."

An enclosed black automobile pulled directly before the gate and a uniformed chauffer stepped out. He opened the rear door for Mrs. Melling, who wore a crisp black dress. Valentino then exited, straightening his suit and smiling for the world to see.

On the portico, Mrs. Melling settled her eyes on Alice. She whispered to Valentino and then he set upon the cousins like a bee to flowers.

"Good morning, my beautiful ladies." He greeted them with kisses for each cheek and a wink for Darla. "You must sit with us, Alice. I want to keep you close, and you must allow me to accept your mother's supper offer in person. I will arrange for an automobile to drive us to your house after your lesson tomorrow. It will be a wonderful way to end what will be a glorious afternoon."

Valentino was introduced to Uncle Calvin and Aunt Ida, then Alice was whisked away with him to Mrs. Melling's regular pew. During Mass, Darla caught Henry looking her way and smiled.

On the way out of the cathedral, Alice made a show of prancing past Henry on Valentino's arm but he hardly seemed to notice the violinists. Instead, he held the door for Darla to exit.

"I'll see you Wednesday," she said on her way out.

On the sidewalk, Mrs. Melling and Valentino were readying to leave. Darla joined Alice to keep her from being left alone. Alice waved good-bye, then scanned the crowd.

"Do you think Henry noticed me with Valentino? Maybe seeing me with an older man will help him understand I'm not a child."

"I can't say one way or the other," Darla replied.

Sadie went by with her family. "I'll be over this afternoon!" she called.

Sadie came at two o'clock, more eager to hear about Valentino than what all they found in the magazines. To afford them more privacy against her spying brothers, Alice locked the bedroom door and she and Sadie sat with their backs to her bed, whispering. Darla read from her aunt's copy of *Magnolia Wind* on her own bed, but when Alice started speaking of the way Valentino taught her, Darla set aside the book.

"He took my chin"—Her voice rose with excitement—"and then he kissed me! Right there in the middle of the session. He declared me a woman."

Sadie squeezed her hands and sighed. "He must be the most romantic man in the city."

Darla went to her drawer and pulled out the note she'd received from Maggie in her package Friday. She sat across from the others and handed it to them. They held it between them and read.

Alice threw it at Darla when finished. "You're just jealous that he kissed me and not you."

"Why would I be jealous over a cad like him? You see it right there—even his cousin knows him to be a scoundrel. I'm only letting you know so you can stop yourself from falling for him. And that goes for both of you."

"I wouldn't mind being played by him." Sadie giggled. "His fingers are so long and—"

"They felt good on me." Alice's eyes sparkled and Darla could see the romantic notions Sadie fed her would lead to trouble. "He touched me practically all over as he positioned me properly. I think I'll accidentally forget everything I learned so he'll have to do it again."

"Alice, he's not the type to take seriously," Darla said. "You'll only end up hurt, either when he leaves or before."

"You just want him for yourself! I saw the way you looked at him when he played."

"Anyone would look at him with longing when he plays—he's a master at his craft and music is passion. But I'm not interested."

"Keep telling yourself that," Alice said, "but your eyes betray the truth."

***

At three o'clock Monday afternoon, Darla knocked on the study door, thinking it odd she hadn't heard the typewriter all afternoon. Lucy had stayed in the study except when she joined them for the noon meal, but she wasn't talkative. Mr. Davenport didn't come home to eat and when Darla questioned her, Lucy only replied that he had to make up his time for what he missed Friday afternoon.

Lucy opened the door, red-eyed and weary looking.

"I need to leave now," Darla said, "but if there's something I could quickly do to help, I'd be happy to."

"No, there's nothing you can do."

Phoebe followed Darla to the door. "I come, too!"

"No, you need to be Momma's helper this afternoon." Darla paused long enough to hug her. "I'll see you in the morning, though."

She left the Davenports to wait for Alice to return from school, changing from her old island dress to the slim-fitting skirt and blouse, vowing to go clothes shopping without her aunt on a coming Saturday. She'd be able to afford at least two new outfits in another week or more, but she continued to make-do with what her uncle had bought.

On the way to the hotel, Alice kept her violin case in the hand between them as though a barrier. As they drew closer, a coy smile played across her face and her steps became bolder. Darla followed her into the elevator and down the deserted hall. They both paused outside the closed door and listened to the sweet melody coming from within.

Alice sighed. "Dvořák's 'Song to the Moon,' the most romantic song ever written."

It was pure sensuality to Darla's ear and she rested against the wallpaper to hear more. When the notes trailed into nothing, she kept her head to the wall, eyes closed while her mind held to the visions of a heartbreaking moonlit night on the beach, full of yearnings and broken promises. The next thing she knew, the door opened.

Valentino stood in front of them grinning. "It sounds better without a wall between us. Come, I will play again for my ladies."

Alice giggled and followed without question, but Darla took her time. Once they were all inside, Valentino looked them over and shook his head.

"No, it is not good. Your parents pay me to teach, not entertain. You must come to one of my concerts this weekend. But if you do well, I will play for you after the lesson, Alice. If you are not so good, I will only play for Darla and you will learn to improve your practice. Come, show me how you position yourself."

Alice removed the violin and bow from her case and stood defiantly bad. Valentino, still holding his own instrument, brandished his bow at her with a scowl.

"I have no time for infants, Alice. You displease me."

She straightened herself into the proper stance, but Valentino had already turned his back and thrust his violin at Darla. "Come, you are wearing the perfect outfit for this."

He pulled Darla out of the chair with one arm. Wanting to keep him from touching her as much as possible, she took the position as best as she could remember.

"See, Alice? Darla remembers better than you. Shall I stop teaching you and take on a new student to teach scales to?"

"No, Valentino. I'm sorry! I remember now. Forgive me."

He looked back at her pleading eyes and smirked. "There is no time for games, Alice. You are to be a woman here, *sì?*"

"Yes!"

"Then see how your cousin positions her glorious hips and her shoulders are back while remaining fluid." Valentino circled Darla and pointed to the locations before handing her his bow. "Show her how a woman holds it."

Valentino's dark eyes were sultry, matching the innuendos of his words. She raised the bow to the proper angle as Alice scowled.

"*Brava*, Darla. You win a song for sure."

The hour passed with Valentino's cutting remarks, him poking Alice with the tip of his bow when her posture changed, and Alice's angered glances at Darla in between the same agonizing opening notes to Paganini. To tune it out, Darla thought back on the lunch with Henry last week, how he played at being a gentleman to her while she knew he was well-versed, even if not comfortable with it, to help her feel at ease. A smile must have found its way to her face, for when the sounds of the lesson quieted, Darla found Valentino smirking at her.

"You find your cousin's problems amusing, no?"

"Not at all. I was thinking of something else. Please forgive me."

His smile showed that he did, just as Alice's glare told Darla she did not.

"See if you can get through the first page Thursday, Alice. And if you value your lesson, you will stand appropriately the first time." Valentino waved her out as she packed her case. "Go in the hall to wait for us. I must give your chaperone her song. Darla, sit on my bed so Alice can take the desk chair into the hall."

Darla sat as close to the edge as possible, trying not to think she was sitting where he slept, especially when the stirring notes of the song began. Valentino stood a few feet in front of her, stealing glances her way when he didn't have his eyes closed. The score was gorgeous, as was the way he swayed to the music.

As soon as it was over, she looked away and tried to regain her composure. Valentino handed her his violin and retrieved his case, laying it on the bed beside her.

"I am packing my things, Alice," he called out the open door. "You shall see me play after dinner because I will perform for your family."

"That's kind of you," she called.

He looked at Darla, leaning close to take the violin from her. "And for you, I will grant an audience whenever you wish it."

"Thank you, but that's not necessary."

"But I must have a private performance with you before I leave. I count on you."

"I'm afraid you're going to have to find that audience elsewhere."

Valentino snapped the closures on his case shut and looked to the hallway. "Finding the replacement is not difficult."

Darla stood, infuriated. "She's not but a girl and you know it."

He smiled and placed a finger on her nose. "My touch can make any girl into a woman."

Darla's face went hot. "Mrs. Melling wouldn't stand for it, not to mention her parents!"

"I'm sure my cousin let my sponsor know how I am. He is a priest and will try to protect all from the influence of sin, but he does not understand that to love is a gift from God." Valentino ran a finger over her cheek. "Mrs. Melling set my students, my lessons. Tell me, Chaperone, why would she secure me a pretty girl and her cousin and have me teach her in my chamber while my other two students are taught on the main floor?"

Twenty

Lucy was glad when Friday afternoon came. She'd written over twenty pages but felt Darla always watching, listening for changes in her routines, checking her demeanor for oddities, so she could report to Frederick when he got home. Having walked a tightrope of emotions for five days, Lucy was ready to fall exhausted into a cocoon of quiet for the weekend. No company, no shopping, no trips, no church. She wanted to curl under her blanket and hibernate, especially as it was October twelfth.

The doorbell rang as she came out of the study just before three in the afternoon. Darla started down the stairs from Phoebe's room, but Lucy waved her away.

"Delivery from New York, Mrs. Davenport. Just a small one, but I could bring it in for you." The man lifted his cap and motioned to her stomach.

"Yes, thank you."

He hurried to his wagon parked at the curb and carried the wooden crate inside.

"On the sofa is fine. It will make it easier to unpack." She retrieved a quarter from the entry hall table drawer where Frederick kept loose change for the purpose of tipping deliveries or to give

Phoebe a little spending money on their way to the park. "Thank you very much."

After he was gone, she settled next to the crate and saw it was from Noble Publishing House rather than anything she'd mail ordered. Lucy could give Freddy his copy of *Winter of My Heart* as an early anniversary present that evening as they were celebrating four years on Monday. Maybe he would stay home all weekend with her, reading.

"Naomi?" she called out. Lucy hadn't heard her arrive, but she called out once more just in case.

Darla and Phoebe came down the stairs. "We haven't seen Miss Naomi yet," Darla said as they joined her in the living room. "May I help with anything?"

"I need to get this open." She pointed to the crate. "And to the study. Not necessarily in that order, just both things."

Darla easily picked it up. "Any straight metal tool would do to leverage the top loose."

"Freddy keeps things like that in the shed out back." Lucy patted the edge of the desk for the crate to be placed. "Should be easy to find."

With her arms free, Darla turned to Lucy. "Will you come with me? It's nice out today, and a little fresh air might bring some color to your cheeks."

Lucy froze, remembering a winter evening nearly six years past when her mother sent her out for fresh air because she looked pale. Like then, she was pale over her anxiety about Alexander. Back then, it was worry over his transgressions. Now it was over how she'd portrayed their relationship in the novel. What would Frederick think—as well as her parents and siblings?

"Momma see our fairy house," Phoebe sang. "Come see our fairy house!"

Lucy ran a hand over her daughter's pale hair and looked into her green-blue eyes. "Yes, Phoebe Camellia, I'll come see your fairy house."

The three went out the kitchen door and across the yard. While Darla entered the shed, Phoebe took her mother by the hand and led her under the oak tree beyond the stone bench. Lucy knelt in the grass beside Phoebe and stared more at her daughter than the acorn furniture and leaf blankets that she pointed out.

"It's all lovely, my Camellia." She pulled her onto her lap and kissed her cheek.

"I love you, Momma."

"I love you too."

A few minutes later, Lucy stood, taking Phoebe by the hand.

"Will you play with me?"

Lucy looked down at her daughter. "I'm tired, Phoebe."

"You nap with me next time, Momma, and then you can play."

"I'll nap tomorrow."

Back inside, Darla was quick with prying the top of the crate open. As she was about to lift the lid, Lucy cried out.

"Stop! I can get it from there, thank you." Ushering Phoebe and Darla from the room, she pulled the study door shut behind them.

In the hallway she said, "You received your pay when Freddy was home for dinner, didn't you?"

"Yes," Darla replied.

"Then feel free to leave. We'll see you next week. Thank you." She knew she sounded cold, but at that moment she couldn't carry on a pleasant conversation to save her life.

"All right, Lucy. Goodbye, Phoebe." She bent to hug the girl. "Take good care of the castle and I'll see you Monday morning."

A moment after Darla went out the front, Naomi was heard in the kitchen.

"Let's go see what Miss Naomi has for supper," Lucy said cheerfully.

While Phoebe helped Naomi put groceries away, Lucy locked herself in the study. Upon removing the crate's top, she caught her breath. The book was exactly the same color as Alexander's eyes—ice blue. While her other books had simple embossed flowers, birds, or a heart, this one held a cloaked lady in profile. She ran her fingers over the image and remembered the red cloak she'd left at her parents' house because it brought back too many memories of her winter with Alexander.

"Happy Birthday, Alex," she whispered as she fingered the image. "We never got to share either of our birthdays together, but I've thought of you on each of your milestones."

Spying an envelope atop the stack, she clutched the book to her chest and read the letter.

Mrs. Davenport,

You'll see the printers and binders took more care with this one. This is your best work and your sales to date prove you're worth the extra effort for a detailed cover. Be ready for more exposure with this, my dear. I might have to insist on bringing you to New York for interviews after New Year's, as I know travel for you before then will be impractical and against medical advice. You will hear from me after the release.

Sincerely,

Wilson Noble

She brought the letter and the first book to the desk. Sitting in the chair, she removed her favorite pen from the drawer and opened the book. Lucy gently flipped through the pages, gazing at the layout and the lovely details, like the camellia blossom surrounding the first letter of each chapter. Then she turned to the cover page and simply inscribed:

Frederick,

Your love warms my heart.

Love,

Your Goosy

Phoebe ran through the hall, the patter of her buckled shoes distinct in the otherwise calm house. With a rush of anxiety, Lucy left the study and called out to Phoebe.

"Get ready to leave, Phoebe." Lucy went in the kitchen. "Naomi, I'm going to walk Phoebe to the office. We'll ride home with Freddy."

"Y'all be careful out there."

Lucy wore her navy adjustable skirt and a new, short-sleeved lace blouse. Wanting to protect herself from any elements and staring people, she pulled a gray caplet from the downstairs closet and pinned on a sunhat. Once Phoebe placed on her own hat, Lucy adjusted the white collar on her bishop-style dress and, with Rummy and Pinky in the carriage, they went down the sidewalk.

The first few blocks were quiet, but then the stares and whispers began. In her mind, Lucy heard them.

"That's the Easton woman. She's the one Alexander Melling ran out on."

"I heard she cheated on Alex with her current husband."

"I knew she was sinful."

"She looks as crazy as her sister with those green eyes."

The messages scrambled inside her head as she fought to keep her chin high. When they reached Bienville Square, she took her favorite bench and waved the peanut man over so Phoebe could feed the squirrels. The girl parked her doll buggy and sat on the edge of the bench, swinging her short legs as she tossed the nuts to the furry crowd.

"Lucille Easton Davenport." The slimy voice crept up her spine as the man stopped in front of her. "Kate told me she saw you with your brother last week, but it's been months since I've laid eyes on your glowing form. If I had confirmation Kate would look as succulent as you, I'd have her in the family way in an instant."

She stared at his crooked nose and thought of Alexander's final declaration of his unworthiness that involved Rupert and a young woman named Twila. "Mr. Lyons, you have both a lady and a young girl in your presence. I'd appreciate you reining your speech to reflect such company."

"You claim the status of a lady now? Does marriage to a gentleman allow you to take such liberties after the wild days in your youth that had you disrobed—"

"Please shut up."

Rupert laughed. "Alex always had the best taste and an eye for fresh talent, but why did Frederick settle for someone else's cast offs, even if they look as good as you? He always seemed the saintly one."

There was truth behind his words and it stung. Lucy stood and looked at her daughter. "It's time to go, Phoebe. Just dump the rest of the bag, the squirrels will be happy to receive them."

"Don't rush off on my account, Mrs. Davenport."

Rupert's thin-lipped smile further soured her stomach, but Lucy ignored him.

"Is that man a friend, Momma?" Phoebe asked as she pushed the doll carriage.

"That man is no one's friend."

The internal disparaging remarks were louder as they walked the last few blocks to Davenport Allied Accountants. The anxiety that pushed Lucy out her front door had turned to anger when Rupert approached. Then it melted into despair. She cursed herself for leaving the safety of home and wanted nothing more than to hide within her husband's arms.

It was after four o'clock when Lucy held the office door open for Phoebe. Her daughter pushed the doll carriage into the building like she was royalty arriving at court for inspection.

"Why bless my stars, it's Phoebe Davenport," Ms. Neves said as she rushed to greet her.

Several clerks near the front—including Henry Adams—came forward to welcome the boss's family. Lucy didn't mind it when people made more over Phoebe than her. She took pride in having a sparkling daughter and would stay on the sidelines if given the choice. Phoebe was soon introducing Pinky and Rummy to the group. Only Henry lifted his head to smile at Lucy as she slipped past them to get to Frederick's office. His door was closed and the murmur of voices could be heard. She sat on the spindled bench in the hallway. Every few minutes she gazed to the front to check that Phoebe was behaving herself, but the girl could do no wrong with that crowd.

At four-thirty, Henry approached her. "He's with a new client, but should be done soon. May I get you some coffee?"

"No, thank you, Henry. I'm fine." She said no more, and he excused himself.

A minute later, the voices within Frederick's office rose as they approached the door. One was decidedly feminine and his laughter was plainly heard.

"—gather the rest of the paperwork from the list I gave you, Mrs. Smith, and that will be everything we need. I look forward to seeing you next week." Frederick's hand was on her elbow to escort her out and it sent a pang of resentment through Lucy's unraveled mind. He smiled as he said his farewell—and he looked handsomer than ever with his week's growth of a mustache and goatee. Then the grin faltered as he looked into the hall. "Lucy, what a surprise!"

His smile was back and brighter than before, but the change stabbed her. He helped Lucy stand and then brought her before the woman in black. "Lucy, do you remember Judith McGowan Smith? Mrs. Smith, my wife, Lucy."

"Yes, Lucille, the infamous Miss E." Judith smiled like a cat—plenty of mischief behind the politeness. "Mr. Smith suffered heart failure over the summer. I'm afraid I've been making a muddle of the finances since then. Your husband's such a dear to help me straighten things out. He's going to help me curb my impulsive appetites." Judith patted Frederick's muscular arm and practically winked at him while nausea swelled within Lucy.

"I'll see you next Wednesday, Mrs. Smith. Be sure to bring the papers."

Frederick walked her to the front of the office, where he introduced Phoebe. Judith—seeing his adoration for his daughter— had to gush over his child.

Lucy cried in Frederick's chair when he returned.

He shut the door. "Goosy, whatever is the matter?"

With his words, her pain turned to daggers. "Just exactly what are the *appetites* Judith needs help with? And how often does she touch you if she has no shame in doing so before me?"

"Lucy, it's not like that." He pulled her into his arms.

"How long has she been coming to you?"

"This was her first appointment, a consultation. Nothing more."

Lucy pulled away and crossed her arms over her chest. "I insist you assign her to someone else."

"My father always started the new clients, got a feel for what was needed for the job and then assigned them to one of the accountants as he saw fit, keeping only the most important clients for himself. That's what I do as well—you know it."

"Well I didn't know you had widows with hungry appetites and wandering hands knocking on your door."

"Goosy, I'd never—"

"After that display you must think me daft to turn away from the day unchanged in some way. And she didn't just fawn over you. She's dragging Phoebe into her plans."

"You're searching for plot lines in real life." Frederick's fists clenched.

Lucy stepped away. "That's where the best material comes from."

Frederick caught her arm and turned her to him, brown eyes searching for the source of her anger. "Have I ever given you reason not to trust me?"

"No, but I've never seen someone flirt with you like that either."

"You don't get out much."

Lucy couldn't have hurt worse if he'd punched her. As though seeing the distress on her face, he kissed her forehead.

"I didn't mean it like that, Goosy." He hugged her to him but she stood like a pillar. "I've been true to you forever. There's nothing anyone could offer that would pull me away from you, from our family."

She looked up at him. "Then you'll assign Judith to one of the others?"

"As soon as I can, but in the meantime I'll bring someone with me to our meetings if that would make you feel better. Henry might be good. I'll tell them both it's for training purposes so neither is uncomfortable."

Lucy's green eyes narrowed. "After that shameless display, Judith deserves to be uncomfortable."

"Jealousy and venom aren't your style, Goosy." He kissed her quickly on the lips, then again, slower. And a third time with the motion to open her mouth.

The sensation was like kissing a new man as his facial hair changed everything. It was beyond the prickly phase and she began to enjoy it more, though she could no longer fantasize it was Alexander she kissed because he always kept his face smooth.

Lucy tried to communicate to Frederick how much she needed him, feeling down his arms as the kissing continued.

"I have every reason to be suspicious of the attention other women give you. I admit I've been neglectful and I'm trying to repair that. You're handsome, strong, and successful. You're romantic and an amazing father, too. My new mission in life is to accompany you as often as possible so all the women in Mobile with ulterior motives will know that you're by no means available."

"Goosy, you're fire and ice, but you know I love you."

He took her hand into his and they gathered Phoebe and hhe. Once they were in Frederick's automobile and on the way home, Lucy looked to the setting sun and tried to get the image of Judith Smith touching her husband out of her head.

Twenty-One

Wednesday was a bright spot for Darla. She had survived two more lessons with Valentino after his bold declaration of longing for a "private audience," as well as one of his performances with The Battle House Orchestra—which she attended with the Beauchamp family. Alice remarked on the way Darla had swooned at his solos and practically threw herself at Valentino Monday afternoon as payback. He'd played right along with her in what Darla could only assume was an attempt at making her envious. But the only thing Darla cared about was the smile Henry gave her after Mass. Though Lucy had been cold to her lately, Darla hoped lunch with Henry and Mr. Davenport would be pleasant. At a quarter to twelve, Darla helped Phoebe set the table. The study had been quiet most of the morning but Lucy currently paced the hall. Seeing her clutching her stomach, Darla went to the doorway.

"Lucy," she said, "are you experiencing any discomfort?"

"Yes, in here." Her fist went to her heart.

"Would it help you to talk about it?"

"What if I'm too late to save my marriage?" She kept walking toward the living room, so Darla followed. "I've caused this myself, hiding away in the house while Freddy is out in the world surrounded by appreciative eyes."

"You're getting out more, and your husband adores you." Darla stopped beside her in the front room. "Did you not have a fine time during your anniversary dinner at the new restaurant?"

"Yes, but it might be too little too late. Everyone sees me as inferior to Freddy, like he just needs one more excuse to leave me. Even the men in town think me unworthy of him." She took Darla by the shoulders. "I always thought it was worth the trouble and pain, but it's all catching up to me now."

"What's that, Lucy?"

"My love affair." Her look of panic turned to sorrow as she released Darla. "I never thought Alex ruined me, but I guess he finally has and—more importantly—my relationship with Frederick. I've been neglectful of him all these years because of the memory of Alex. Whether by my own thoughts or the gossip of others, I've failed the one who's been with me the longest."

Darla placed an arm around Lucy and led her toward the sofa. "Mr. Davenport looks at you the same way Maggie's Douglas looks at her and they're the most in-love couple I ever did see. He's completely devoted to her, as I suspect your husband is to you and you to him."

Lucy shook her head and dropped to the sofa. "I still love him, Darla. I lay sleepless at night after all these years for want of him. My body aches for Alex while I cling to Freddy. I'm scared I only married him because Alex died. I love Freddy dearly, but I'm even more frightened some woman is going to swoop between us and I'll be left with two holes in my heart."

It was as though Lucy had tossed an anchor to Darla. Her confession cried for help while Darla was dragged down by it. She would pen yet another letter to Maggie that afternoon in hopes she would agree to speak with Lucy about Alexander Melling. Her last reply was that she would "think about it," but Darla feared her new friend wouldn't survive childbirth with the weight of her emotions threatening her happiness.

Before she could respond, Lucy was back to pacing and Phoebe called for help in the dining room. When the table was complete, Darla brought Phoebe into the living room and they sat on the floor while the girl built a castle out of blocks. Lucy never slowed. She walked the hall until twenty minutes after the hour when the men arrived.

"Sorry we're late," Mr. Davenport said as he removed his jacket. "One of our appointments was more involved than expected."

Lucy flung herself into his arms before he could hang his suit jacket. They exchanged murmured words and several kisses, and then Lucy took his brown jacket and Mr. Davenport went to wash. She then hung Henry's coat and led him into the living room.

"Was it the meeting with Mrs. Smith that kept you longer?"

Henry paused to greet Darla and Phoebe before returning his attentions to Lucy. "Yes, she loves to shop and had receipts and charge account statements from more stores than I've ever been into. Not to mention a full house staff. I don't think anyone ever explained the simple fact that you can't spend more than you have, especially now that she's living on a fixed income of savings and interests on fluctuating stocks."

Lucy shook her head. "Women like her play dumb to get extra attention and favors. She knows exactly what she's doing."

Henry shrugged. "I don't know, but I feel sorry for the one that will be assigned her when we're done setting up her files."

Darla smiled. "Better be careful what you say, it might be you."

"Mr. Davenport assured me he gives the younger clients to older, established accountants so they can impart fatherly wisdom and hopefully be better received. And he also said he was grateful you weren't like that with money. He proudly stated you're a sensible shopper and not the least bit frivolous—a true treasure to a husband."

Lucy laughed. "It's good to know I'm appreciated for something, even if it's as unromantic as finances."

"Ah, but to an accountant there is nothing more attractive." Mr. Davenport came up behind his wife and leaned over the back of the sofa to kiss her cheek. "Though your beauty and wit is a close second."

Lucy glowed with his sweet words and attention.

"Still," Henry remarked, "Mrs. Smith is going to need to remarry soon if she wants to keep the lifestyle she's used to."

And with that, the light went out of Lucy's eyes. Henry excused himself to wash his hands, and they all gathered around the table a minute later.

Once they were into the meal, Henry spoke.

"I didn't have time to mention it, but there was a card for me when I arrived at the office this morning." All eyes looked to him, Darla's most expectantly. "It's an invitation to a dance hosted by a society called 'Halloween Flirts.' Is that a real thing?"

Lucy smiled. "I can't believe they're still doing it. It's an old tradition. Come Halloween, one or more of the young women's social groups band together and rename themselves that to host a party on Halloween night."

"Did you ever go?" Darla asked.

"Once, in '05."

"And you, Mr. Davenport?" Henry looked to him.

"I escorted Lucy that year. I also claimed a few dances with her at Mardi Gras balls when she was twenty." He winked at Lucy.

"We should go to one next season. Enjoy it fully together for the first time." Lucy's voice was quiet, determined.

Frederick tilted his head to the side and smiled. "That would be nice, Goosy. We'll see how things settle down after the baby is born. Well, Henry, do you plan on going?"

"I've no idea who invited me or if I'd even know any of the attendees."

"I'll be there," Darla said. "My cousins Richard and Alice are bringing me."

"Well then, I'll be sure to go. I'd like an excuse to see more of you."

***

"No, no, no, Alice!" Valentino brandished his bow. "You are too slow on the uptake."

"I'm sorry, Valentino."

"I work with you nearly three weeks and you are still on the first page. Am I not a fit teacher, *signorina*?"

"I'm treated like a child all day at school and then I come here and you expect a competent woman. It's too much to change in an instant." Alice flashed her sad brown eyes.

"You are a woman always." He embraced her and fully kissed each cheek. "When you finish school, you must concentrate on music and love making. The two go together beautifully."

"That is not appropriate advice, Mr. De Fiore." As his flirtations increased, Darla insisted on calling him by that rather than his overly familiar Christian name.

"It is getting more difficult to control myself. Alice is blossoming before my eyes each day." He took Darla by the arm. "Come, chaperone, you must walk the hall with me while she tries once more without me looking or else I do not know what I shall do. You, Alice, play! You have three attempts—I will be listening."

As soon as they were in the hall, Valentino stood before Darla, one hand holding hers. "You wound me, Darla. What have I done to cause such coldness?"

She raised her eyebrows. "Let me start with you trying to seduce my young cousin."

"She is sixteen next week and plays like a woman." He pointed to the air. "Listen."

Darla rolled her eyes. "If you cared for me, you would not try anything with Alice. If something happens to her I'll be blamed. I'd lose my spot in their household, which would cause me to lose my job and become homeless. Is that what you want, to tarnish a young woman and ruin my life all at once?"

"I only make things good. I promise, *amore mio.*"

He kissed Darla quickly on the lips and stepped into the room. As though she was on the deck of a ship in a storm, everything wavered in chaos around her. All she could focus on was the tingling sensation of his touch.

By the end of the hour, he declared Alice master of the opening of the score. He played the second page for her and assigned the first two lines to be completed by Monday. A hotel employee approached Valentino's room as they left.

"Mr. De Fiore, a letter for you."

Alice slowed her steps and Darla matched her stride.

"Wait, *signorina,* tell me of this," he called to them.

Alice was at his side in an instant and glanced at the card he handed her. "It's a party for Halloween. Dress in a costume and come dance with lovely ladies, like me."

"It is tradition? Lots of fun?"

"*Sì,* much fun." Alice giggled.

"I shall come. No lesson that day. Instead save a dance for me. You as well, chaperone."

Twenty-Two

Thursday, October 27, the afternoon before the release day of *Winter of My Heart*, Lucy dressed herself and Phoebe for supper at her parents' house. Maxwell, Edmund, and their wives were invited to come for after supper drinks, but Lucy didn't know if they accepted. To be safe, she prepared three copies of her book—signed as "Olive Kent" in case anyone at their homes ever picked one up and looked inside.

Lucy wore the turquoise and gold gown once again as she wanted to save her new pink one for the orchestra the following weekend. She dressed Phoebe in a rosy lace dress and they spent the next hour on the sofa reading aloud from a Hans Christian Anderson collection.

When he came home, Frederick kissed them each on the head on his way to change into a fresh suit. Returning to the front room, he took the time to pull Lucy into a full hug then scooped Phoebe into his arms and carried her to the automobile.

The three rode snug in the front seat. In the middle, Lucy clutched the parcel of books for her family. "I'm scared, Freddy."

He patted her knee as they motored down Dauphin Street. "It's a beautiful story, Goosy."

"You really think so?" The book was a fantasied version of her relationship with Alexander—complete with a happy ending after several missteps, though none were as horrific as what she actually encountered.

"Yes." He lifted her hand to his lips. "You're brilliant and your heart shines through with clarity."

Lucy wondered if her heart was laid too bare in the book. They hadn't been intimate with each other since she gave Frederick his copy two weeks ago. When he released her hand to turn onto Catherine Street, she placed it lightly on his knee. Once parked, Phoebe crossed the yard in a flash. Lucy slid the books onto the seat and turned to her husband.

"You know I love you, Freddy." She brought her arms around his neck. "I can share everything with you, but sometimes I think it hinders us. That all my bad outweigh any good you might receive."

"No, Goosy." He rested his hands on her shoulders and leaned his forehead against hers. "You're a complex, amazing woman. I wouldn't trade life with you for anything."

Their kissing grew intense and her hands roamed under his suit jacket. "I want you, Freddy."

Frederick laughed. "Not in front of your parents' house."

"It'll be mine in a few months." She linked their fingers together and kissed him. "I'm going to buy it, Freddy. I'll buy it with my royalty money you've had me save these past years. You've bought everything since we've been married, but now I want to buy something for us, for our children."

"You don't have to, but I'll not stop you if that's what you desire." He helped her out of the automobile.

"It is." Lucy hugged him when she stood. "It will be our fairy kingdom, from the turret bedroom to the gazebo."

Frederick put his arm about her as they walked to the porch. "We've had some magical moments in the gazebo."

Lucy smiled and leaned her head against his shoulder. She'd been proposed to within those metal walls twice, first by Alexander, and then by Frederick. She tried to focus on her time with her husband, memories of when he carried the train of her Christmas dress to keep it out of the puddles and when they read together during spring evenings. But the memories of sneaking out in the night to meet Alexander were more passionate, his gift of the fingerless gloves more evocative than Frederick's steady attentions. Even Frederick's proposal was over-shadowed by the news of Alexander's death—or perhaps only made possible because of it.

Despite her brooding, they had a pleasant supper and then everyone settled in the parlor with drinks for the adults.

"I'm going to buy the house from you," Lucy told her father over his glass of brandy.

"No, Lucy, it's yours without money. I'd like it to stay in the family and you've done your share of helping around here through the years."

"If she buys it, it would help things look fair to the other siblings." Frederick took a drink. "The girls are all too far away with their husbands' jobs, but you never know if feelings would be hurt. Maxwell is all about Lucy getting it, but there's no telling what Eddie will say."

"You think it best?" Mr. Easton asked his son-in-law.

"I do, and Lucy has the money at her disposal. We can have the property assessed and offer a fair price after the first of the year. The paper trail and money exchanged should settle any grudges that might arise."

"All right then, Freddy." Mr. Easton shook hands over the agreement and then hugged his daughter. "You're really doing what you love, aren't you?"

"Yes, Father." She settled back on the settee with her family.

"Lucy, it seems every friend I talk to mentions seeing you about town lately, either walking, shopping, or dining out." Her mother smiled at her. "It's great to hear everyone gushing over how you glow, especially when you're on Freddy's arm."

Lucy snuggled against Frederick's side, much like she often did with Alexander during their engagement. "He takes great care of me and I love to spend time with him. It just took me a while to brave the cruel world."

"If Maxwell or Edmund aren't expected, I should get my girls home," Frederick said as Phoebe yawned.

"Their wives both said it would be too difficult to find someone to watch the children on a school night, but they'll all be here Sunday."

"I'll leave their books, if that's okay."

"Of course, Lucy." Her mother picked up her copy and ran a finger over the image on the bottom right of the cover. "It almost looks like you wrapped in that cloak you loved to wear that winter you and Al—" Mrs. Easton put her wine to her lips and looked away.

"It's all right, Mother. It doesn't hurt me to talk about him." *It hurts not to.*

"Remember we're leaving for Susan's Monday morning, if you want to bring her copy on Sunday and save yourself the postage."

"That will be good. What day do you return?" Lucy asked her mother.

"Thursday, and then we'll not leave until your new one arrives. I'll be at your disposal, though I know you have a great helper now with Darla."

Frederick slipped out from beside Lucy so he could pick up his sleeping girl.

"I'll sit in the back and hold her," Lucy whispered to him as her father went ahead to open the front door.

Mrs. Easton took her daughter's arm and walked her to the porch. "Lucy, dear, I know I told you once that you and Alex would make the best-looking grandchildren, but you and Freddy … well, Phoebe's just precious."

Lucy smiled and looked at her mother. "But she looks nothing like Freddy. She could be Alex's if it weren't for the fact that there's two and a half years between the events."

"Lucille Amelia, what a thing to say!"

"It's true. She's my constant reminder of him."

***

Monday morning, Lucy stood watch over Frederick as he shaved around his goatee. "What made you decide to try the new style?"

Frederick pulled the straight blade through the remainder of the shaving cream. "Just a whim."

"It makes you look harsh when you're not smiling. I bet it scares your opponents when you're boxing at the gym." He laughed and then rinsed his face. Lucy was ready with a fresh towel and a kiss. "It gives you an edge. An erogenous, commanding air and I love it."

"Good because I'm all for you, Goosy."

She played her fingers down his chest and pressed her silk dressing gown against him. Their kissing culminated with him carrying her to their bed, a sad smile on her lips because she didn't think Alexander would have been able to lift her when she was close to her last month of pregnancy. Frederick laid her down softly and sat beside her, trailing a hand over her body with gentle caresses.

"You're stunning, Lucy. I thank God for you every day, doubly so on the days you run hot."

Lucy laughed and pulled him to her. "But for now we must wait."

She referred to the doctor's advice from the house visit Saturday—that she was to abstain from sexual intimacy until after the baby was born, to protect her body and the baby from shock or stress, as well as to keep the risk of infection down.

Frederick's smile completed her as he trailed a finger down her cheek to lift her chin. "You're always worth the wait."

The kiss was fathomless, their touches enflamed. They continued on in each other's arms until Phoebe knocked on their door. Frederick pulled Lucy up and she went to the door while he finished dressing for work.

Phoebe held Doff out to her mother. "It's Halloween! Doff is wizard. He needs hat!"

Lucy took the cat. "We could make him a paper one, but I don't think he'd keep it on. Pinky might be more suited for a costume than Doff."

"And one for Rummy, too!"

"Sounds like my princess will have a busy day with all those costumes to make." Frederick buttoned on his shirt. "Will the costumes be ready for inspection when I return from work?"

"Yes, Daddy!" She ran out of the room, Doff following her.

Frederick turned to Lucy. "Remember I have a luncheon appointment today and won't be home at noon."

"You aren't taking meals with young widows, are you?"

"You needn't be jealous about Mr. Van Antwerp, Goosy. He was my father's favorite client."

"Allow me to cook a breakfast worthy of the important business man I'm married to."

Lucy was still in her robe when Darla arrived nearly half an hour later than normal.

"Sorry, Lucy. Alice ran me ragged with last minute costume preparations. You know, I can't be sure, but I think she had something to do with Henry and Valentino receiving invitations. Do you think my cousin is the type to be in a society that hosts these dances?"

Lucy adjusted the sash above her belly. "I'd be surprised if she wasn't."

Darla frowned. "Can I talk to you about something?"

Enveloped with sadness because Darla's unspoken language proved that she'd been a poor friend to the girl the past weeks, she silently promised to offer cheer that day. "Of course, would you like some tea?"

"No thank you." They settled on the sofa in the living room while Phoebe continued her costuming in her room. "It's about Valentino. You remember how Maggie told me of his cousin's warning?"

"Yes."

"I showed Alice the letter, but she started flirting with Valentino because she's jealous of my time with Henry. He's a complete cad and gives her the attentions back! The other day he was so bold as to tell me that his cousin had to have made Mrs. Melling known of his affinity for women." Darla blushed. "And Lucy, he said Alice is the only student he teaches in his chamber. The others he teaches on the main floor. He said it was all Mrs. Melling's doing and made it sound like we were an offering to him from his sponsor. When I wrote Maggie to ask after Mrs. Melling's character, she assured me, though a well-respected lady, she'd personally been on the receiving end of the lady's schemes, one of which ended with her virtue nearly stolen from her."

Lucy took Darla's trembling hand in an attempt to mask her own feelings. *Please don't let it have been Alex!* "Yes, Mrs. Melling can be cruel, but I don't wish to think so ill of her that she would sacrifice a young lady's purity."

"Maggie has no cause to lie, and it helps explain why she doesn't talk about her time with the Mellings."

"And even more reason why I must speak with her. Has she given you an answer about that?"

Darla nodded. "They'll take tea here Friday afternoon."

"Thank you, Darla!" Lucy threw her arms around her. "I might be able to put an end to all this and enjoy the concert."

"I bought a new dress for it the other day. I went shopping by myself and used my own money. It felt glorious."

Lucy laughed. "Having your own income is freeing. Next we need the right to vote, especially since I'll be a property owner soon."

Darla looked at her as though eager to know more, but not wanting to be impertinent.

"My parents' house, sometime after the holidays when things settle down with the baby. But don't fret, there's time to figure it all out, and though it wouldn't be as simple as walking next door, we'd want to keep you on as long as possible. That is, if you aren't ready to settle with a family of your own by then."

Laughing, Darla took her hand. "There's no need to worry about that, Lucy. And there's plenty of time to discuss the details later."

Twenty-Three

Darla's talk with Lucy was interrupted when Phoebe needed help with costumes for her favorite toys. Lucy went on to her study, but when Phoebe was sent to bed for quiet time after lunch, they communed again in the living room.

"What are your costumes?" Lucy asked.

"Alice is a gypsy fortune teller in purple and silk with lots of gold jewelry and a headscarf, and I'm to be a witch. Richard is going as a devil. Clarence is in no hurry to grow up, so he doesn't attend parties like this yet, though he and Alice are sixteen now."

"And what are your clothes like?"

"A solid, shapeless black dress with a black cape. I think Alice is trying to hide me from Henry tonight, or at least make me as unappealing as possible."

"How are the sleeves?"

Darla sighed in frustration. "Big and droopy. They cover my hands they're so long."

"And the fabric? Is it someone's real dress?"

"Not at all, just a cheap piece from the store fashioned into a pull over sack dress."

"Come with me."

They went up to her bedroom and Lucy disappeared into the closet. She returned with a slim, rectangular box. "When you get home, cut the sleeves of your dress into cap length. With the billowy fullness, they should easily become fluttery, just the thing for a Halloween Flirts dance. And then you wear these."

Lucy lifted the lid and removed a pair of black lace fingerless gloves.

"Oh, I couldn't Lucy. Those are gorgeous!"

"You can and you must." She placed the gloves in her hand and retreated to the closet. She returned a moment later with a gauzy, forest green scarf. "And you cinch this around your waist like a belt. It will give shape to the dress. There's no reason for you to attend your first city party looking frumpy."

"Thank you!" Darla hugged Lucy. "Now I actually look forward to going."

The doorbell rang while they were still upstairs.

"Let me get it." Darla rushed downstairs and set her borrowed accessories on the table in the foyer before opening the door.

A man from the local florist held a large vase of red and white roses. "Delivery for Lucy Davenport."

"Oh, how lovely. She'll be down in a minute."

"No need to see her, just sign on my clipboard, Miss. Line seven." He passed her the form.

"Thank you," Darla said as she received the vase. She turned around smiling. Lucy gripped the banister at the bottom of the stairs, all color draining from her face. "They're for you. Do you think Mr. Daven—"

"He'd never send roses like that. Never." Lucy began to tremble. "Is there a card?"

Darla set the vase on the coffee table and took Lucy's arm. "I'll look after you're safely seated."

Lucy sat ridged in one of the armchairs, hands tremoring. Darla took the little envelope from her.

"Open it and pass it to me. I don't think I could manage unsealing it right now."

Darla didn't want to be nosy, but it was easy to read the typed inscription at a glance before she handed it to Lucy.

Lucy,

All my love, always.

"Who could be so cruel?" She threw the card and sobbed.

Not sure what to do, Darla grabbed a small towel from the downstairs washroom and brought it to Lucy to dry her tears. They increased as the minutes passed. Fortunately, Naomi came not long after.

"Can you help me get her to bed?" Darla asked.

"Yes, but what's the fuss about?"

Darla pointed at the roses and Naomi shook her head. With one on each side of her, they walked her upstairs.

"Now Miss Lucy, don't give it too much credit. Someone played a cruel trick instead of a treat today. I'll get rid of them and—"

Lucy sprung off the bed. "What if they're from Alex?"

"And however would that happen?" Naomi pulled the loose navy house dress off Lucy and handed her a clean handkerchief from the dresser.

"I don't know, but who else would know how he signed his notes?"

Naomi grunted. "Was it in his hand, then?"

"Typed by the florist." Lucy blew her nose and fell back on the bed.

Darla pulled the blanket over her still-quaking form. "If you turn on your side, I'll bring a pillow for your knees."

Lucy grabbed her hand. "Thank you Darla. And don't let my sorrow ruin your day." Her green eyes, though red-rimmed and swollen, were intense. "You go to that party and dance with Valentino if you must, but be sure Henry gets more time with you."

"I will, Lucy. Thank you."

"Naomi will listen out for me and Phoebe. You can bring my things back tomorrow."

Darla squeezed her hand in return. "If you're sure."

Lucy nodded. "Shut the door on your way out, both of you."

As soon as Naomi pulled the door behind them, Lucy's sobs began anew.

"What do you think the roses are about?" Darla whispered.

"There's no telling. Her old fiancé sent her a bouquet like that the day she met her publisher, to wish her well. Though it was a year since they'd parted ways, he sent her another delivery the day her first book released. Tore her up something fierce, and it should have been a happy day. I thought Mr. Davenport would swim across the bay and punch the man for the heartache it caused her."

"Was that when Alexander Melling was living at Seacliff Cottage?"

Naomi narrowed her good eye at Darla. "You know the stories?"

"Lucy's told me some, but not everything."

"It was before he went east. The only people who know about the roses would be Lucy, Mr. Davenport, her parents, and Mr.

Melling himself. Unless of course her siblings heard tell, but they wouldn't have had reason to be privy to the notes. Mr. Maxwell would never do something like that and it'd be a rough thing for Mr. Edmund to do. He was a joker, but not one to inflict that much of a wound."

Darla descended the stairs with Naomi. "What are you going to do with them?"

"Leave them for Mr. Davenport to see." She paused in the living room to pick the card off the floor and set it on the table by the vase. "God bless her, she loved him so much. It was difficult to watch her pain all those months. Years, really. Mr. Davenport's the only man I know who would have stayed by her side all this time when it's clear she still pines for her first love."

Phoebe ran down the stairs with her doll, rabbit, and a basket of paper costume pieces. "Miss Darla, help! Pinky and Rummy losing capes and hats!"

"Miss Darla is about to leave, Sugar."

Darla rested a hand on Phoebe's shoulder. "I'll go get my sewing kit and be back in a minute."

Phoebe wandered down the hall and peeked in the empty study. "Where's Momma?"

"She's in bed, not feeling good," Naomi answered.

Darla picked up the gloves and scarf. "I'll be back soon, don't you worry."

She slipped in the back door of the Beauchamps' house and tucked the borrowed items under her pillow. Then she spread the witch's dress on her bed and cleanly trimmed the sleeves before laying the cape over it. With her scissors repacked in her sewing basket, she returned to the Davenports.

Phoebe sat at the top of the front porch steps, basket in her lap, while Naomi stood inside the open door to keep an eye on her.

"I've got Phoebe," Darla told the cook. "You listen out for Lucy."

Naomi nodded and pushed the door closed. Darla set to work sewing the decorated newspaper capes around the toys with blue yarn, and then made chinstraps for the pointy hats while Phoebe watched in rapt attention.

"Now Doff," the girl proclaimed as she pulled the last, slightly larger hat from the basket. "I catch him, you tie."

Darla followed her to the door. "Your mother might be sleeping, so we have to be quiet."

Phoebe put a finger to her lips before entering. She easily caught her cat on the sofa and Darla settled beside them.

"Don't take this personal, Doff," she said to the cat as she tied a ribbon under its chin to secure the wizard hat.

Phoebe giggled and, clutching the tabby to her chest, ran for the kitchen to show Naomi.

Darla waited on the sofa, unsure if she should see to Lucy once more before leaving. Whenever she tended Lucy, she felt her mother beside her, guiding her in what to do, what questions to ask. It was almost a compulsion to draw closer to her mother as it was a fondness for helping Lucy—and it made her feel guilty. Before she could decide, Mr. Davenport came in the front door.

"Seems to be a big project on the porch."

"Phoebe and I just finished with the costumes. I'll clean it up before I leave."

"No trouble, Darla." Mr. Davenport's smile immediately dropped when his gaze fell upon the coffee table. "What are those doing here?"

Darla lifted the card off the table. "It caused such turmoil last hour when they came. It upset Lucy to see them, and when she read the note—"

Mr. Davenport snatched it out of her hand and crinkled it in his fist upon reading it. "What sort of game is someone playing with her? Where is she?"

"She was sobbing, but Naomi and I got her into bed to rest."

He started for the stairs.

"Please, Mr. Davenport, I don't wish to alarm you, but at this stage of her pregnancy, high levels of stress can cause complications. She's so emotional and I worry about her."

He rubbed a hand over his whiskered chin. "So do I Darla, every day. Come with me, please."

Outside the door, he motioned Darla to wait. Lucy was curled on her side. Her body appeared to be trembling.

"Lucy, I'm here."

"Hold me, Freddy. Let me feel your arms about me."

"Darla's here too. I want her to ask you some questions about how you and the baby are feeling." He removed his shoes and placed his suit jacket on the bench.

"Come to me, Frederick, please." The wild desperation in her voice prickled Darla's neck.

He waved Darla in as he climbed onto the bed on the far side of Lucy. Darla's cheeks heated at being in the same room as the couple while they were in bed. He kissed Lucy's cheek before lying behind her on top of the blanket, following the curve of her body with his own. Then he pulled down the blanket and traced her belly through her underclothes.

"I'm here, Goosy. I'll always be here for you."

Darla tentatively crossed the room, trying not to fantasize about being so close with a man that his mere presence would help her feel better.

"Lucy, have you felt the baby move since you've been in here?"

"Yes." She lowered her husband's hand to her middle. "Daddy's home."

His eyes closed and a smile found its way to his worried face. "Strong as ever," he whispered.

"Have you experienced any pains in your back, abdomen, or groin?"

"No, but sometimes I get aches in my back, mostly lower."

"Changing your position often will help." Darla looked to Mr. Davenport. "You can use the heel of your hand and apply as much pressure as she's comfortable with to relieve the ache. And remember the pillow between her knees when she lies on her side."

"Thank you, Darla." Mr. Davenport trailed his hand across Lucy's belly.

"Yes, thank you." Lucy exhaled, as though trying to still her quaking voice. "But now you need to go prepare for your party. Don't worry about me. I expect you to tell me all about it in the morning."

Twenty-Four

Having set her hair into twin braids before supper, Darla only needed to dress after the evening meal, taken an hour early to allow the three attending the party ample time to prepare their costumes. Darla waited until Alice added her accessories before slipping on the altered sack dress.

"Don't tell me one of the boys snuck in here and cut your sleeves!" Alice rushed across the room and fingered the new length.

"It was my doing." Darla pulled on one of the lace gloves. "Lucy loaned them to me. Aren't they wonderful?"

Alice's initial scowl turned to a smile at the mention of their neighbor. "I bet her clothes are lovely. She looked gorgeous when they stopped by. I can't wait to see them at the concert Friday night. I intend to study her every move."

Darla said a silent prayer for Lucy's well-being as she tied on the scarf, adjusting the width and position of it before the dressing mirror to best accentuate her curves.

"Look at us. I'm still a willow branch though a year older." Alice sighed. "You look terrific, but keep the cape pulled around you when we leave so Mother doesn't see the adjustments."

Darla held her tongue about mentioning Aunt Ida's sharp angles that matched her personality. "Had we the opportunity to stand our mothers side-by-side, they would look much the same as us. Some things don't change with age."

Alice adjusted the purple scarf about her head. "Well at least we don't look like our fathers."

"Uncle Calvin looks a lot like my father did, minus the sunburnt skin." Darla slipped a quarter into each of her pointy black shoes so she would have money if needed but wouldn't need to carry a purse. "I wish I could have seen them together—seen all our families together. It's sad we missed having cousins when growing up. I bet you would love the island. Think of what it would have been like as girls to sleep out on the beach on a summer night, our brothers running wild or night fishing while we whispered stories back and forth or you playing the violin by moonlight."

"No use crying over what might have been when we have a party to get to." Alice twirled, her silks billowing out most becomingly. "If I keep moving maybe Henry won't notice how straight they hang off me. Do me a favor and don't stand too close. It's simply not a fair choice looking the way you do. We should keep Sadie between us when we aren't all dancing."

A knock at the door saved Darla from responding to Alice's ridiculous ideas. She pulled her cape closed while Alice answered.

"You girls ready?" Richard's voice was muffled through his red devil's mask.

"Just about," Alice said as she paused to apply lip color.

Richard clapped his red leather gloves together. "Come on, you both look fine."

Alice shoved a little brush into her wrist bag and skipped for the door.

After the short drive, Richard dropped them in front of The Battle House Hotel and went to park.

Darla looked to Alice. "Shall we wait for him?"

She laughed. "I make a point never to enter a party with my brother."

They presented their invitations at the door and gained entrance to the grand ballroom, transformed into a haunted forest complete with looming tree trunks and spider webs. Alice ran to a group of friends, leaving Darla standing to the side. Since her cousin wasn't nearby, she flipped her cape behind her, exposing her gloved arms and accentuated hips.

"Good evening, Darla."

She turned to her name. "Henry, I'm glad you're here." She took in the sight of his Union officer costume and laughed.

A smile grew upon his pleasant face. "I figured the sight of this would be as scary as anything else."

"Just be careful you don't get lynched on your way home."

"I've got a regular jacket at the coat check. You look great, by the way." He touched a lace hand, causing a rush of warmth to spread from Darla's hand to her face. "Those are real nice."

"Thank you. Lucy loaned them to me, and the scarf." She touched the trailing ends of it. "The costume was drab before those changes."

"I don't see how anything on you could be drab." He held her gaze a moment, a bold grin on his face. "Would you care to dance?"

"Gladly." She accepted his offered arm and was grateful he chose a spot on the far side of the dance floor so they wouldn't be near the arriving guests.

The string quartet played a traditional waltz. Gratitude over the make-shift lessons Alice had given her the past few weeks filled Darla with relief. Felix was the unfortunate one caught by his sister to stand in for a partner with Darla, but the awkwardness of dancing with a twelve-year-old cousin was worth it to be able to stand comfortably before Henry. He placed a hand at her waist and took her gloved hand in his.

Darla looked him in the eyes. "I'll warn you, I'm not much practiced in fine dancing."

"That's all right. I'm here to spend time with you, dancing or not."

She adjusted her hand on his shoulder and smiled.

"Is that agreeable to you, Darla?"

"There's no one else I'd rather spend my time with."

Henry's hand at her waist tugged her slightly closer and his features relaxed as though secure in their mutual feelings. They waltzed around the floor, only gazing at each other. When the song ended, the music leader announced the next dance was ladies choice and double rush.

"What's 'double rush?'" she asked.

"It means ladies can cut in." Henry smiled. "Well, are you going to ask me to dance?"

Darla laughed. "Would you care for another dance, Henry?"

"I'd be honored." He bowed to her.

"Good, just don't expect me to lead."

They both laughed until Darla was startled by a tap on her shoulder.

"Excuse me, Darla." Alice moved to nudge between them, but Darla stepped back, not wanting to make a scene over Henry.

She quickly left the dance floor and found a spot near the refreshment tables. A dozen young ladies flocked to the entrance, including Sadie Marley. The grouping of witches and fairies converged on a single form before they moved as a herd into the ballroom. Valentino De Fiore, with nothing more than a white hotel sheet tied about him like a toga and a circlet of laurel leaves upon his head, stood amidst the young ladies. Darla laughed, for there was nothing more fitting than Valentino to be draped in bed clothes in the middle of a Halloween Flirts party. According to Valentino, the hotel's orchestra was enjoying a bumper season and the tickets for the coming weekend's performances were sold out. He approached Darla with his brazen air, the ladies falling instep behind him as the song ended.

"Darla, *amore mio*, you are perfection for Halloween." One of his hands went to her waist, the other to her chin as he kissed each cheek. "And what of me? It is clever, no?"

"Yes, Mr. De Fiore, very clever." She stepped out of his reach.

"See how close they are? Valentino greets her with kisses every time she comes or goes," Alice told Henry as they approached.

Valentino looked to the sound of Alice's voice. "Ah, my little flower, do not tell stories to make a man jealous. I greet you the same." His hands went to her shoulders as his lips pressed against her cheeks. Then he turned to his harem. "Ladies, my prized student, Alice Beauchamp, a woman of the violin and scholar of love."

Not wanting to watch the shameless display, Darla side-stepped the group and went for the punch table.

"Miss Beauchamp, how good of you to come with your cousins." Otis Youngblood, dressed as Count Dracula took her arm. "May I offer you a glass of punch?"

"Yes, I was just going to get one, thank you." She reached for the cup.

Henry rushed over. "Don't take it from him, Darla."

Otis smirked. "What do you know, country boy? You don't even know what side we were on in the war."

Darla looked to him. "It's okay, Henry."

He leaned closer and whispered. "He has a flask with him and most likely spiked it."

"Oh …" She turned to Otis. "Did you add a dash of something?"

"Just a little, to help you enjoy the night." His tight-lipped smile was as creepy as ever with his powdered face.

"Then I respectfully decline. I'm more than capable of enjoying myself without the aid of alcohol." She stepped away from Otis and took Henry's arm. "Thank you."

"May I get a drink for you?" Henry asked her.

"Yes, please."

With drinks secured, they found their way across the room to a dim corner with empty chairs. Once they were settled, Henry studied her face.

"I never cared for your cousins or their friends. Alice is nice enough, but those brothers of hers are trouble. I pity the guys she'll date, though I do hope she isn't fool enough to go for one of Richard's friends, like Youngblood. Are you acquainted with him?"

"Just a few times. He never sat right with me, though tampering with my drink was beyond my suspicion."

"In the country, we'd just offer it open and the girl would probably accept. Would you?"

"Not at a party like this, but at a barn dance or something, yes." Darla smiled at him before drinking her punch.

"What is the story with you and Valentino De Fiore? Alice tried to talk you and him up big, so I knew it must be false, especially after you stepped away from his touch when all the other young ladies were pressing in for that honor."

"The only good thing about him is his playing. I'm Alice's chaperone for her lessons Monday and Thursday afternoons. He's nothing but a Romeo and he knows I despise his flirting, but he keeps on. I'm a captive audience for him two hours a week and he fancies to make me his Alabama lover because the stories are he leaves a woman heartbroken in every place he stops. My only fear is that he'll use Alice when he admits to himself I'm not going along with his seduction. But the music he makes is magnificent and he knows it." Darla sighed. "Some songs make me feel like floating away in ecstasy."

Henry's stare was intense, the blue of his eyes almost black in the shadowed room. "You have a soft spot for music?"

"It appears I do, though I didn't know until I came here."

"If I were to secure tickets to an orchestra's performance, would you like to attend with me?"

"I'd go anywhere with you, Henry." The words came out softer than she wanted. She was sure she sounded too lovesick and it would scare him away.

"I wouldn't want to take you there and have you moon over the soloist the whole time."

"If you were holding my hand, I'd only have eyes for you, no matter who was playing."

They finished their punch in silence and returned to the dance floor just as a ragtime band took the stage.

"Do you cakewalk?" Henry asked.

"I'm not half bad, according to island standards."

"Having grown up around horses, I've been known to choose my moves directly out of the corral. That's your warning."

"Warning notated." She grinned at him as he took her hand in his.

When the Joplin tune started, they were ready. Henry was quick and light on his feet as he pranced. After a few seconds, Darla recognized his style and speed, matching it. Soon they dropped hands but kept beside each other, Darla lifting the edge of her skirt with one hand, the other delicately gloved one waving to the side in time to the jaunty music. By the time the song ended, most of the participants on the floor were watching rather than dancing and even the band clapped for them.

Henry was quick to take her hand back. Without a word, he led her off the floor and served punch for them once more. He took a sip as he brought them toward the corner.

"It's spiked now," he warned.

Darla laughed as she sat. "I don't care. It's been too long since I danced liked that, thank you, Henry. You're splendid."

"If you're only half up to island standards, those islanders must be the best strutters in the state."

Alice, practically dragging Valentino on her arm, came over. "You were holding out on me, Darla. There I was making sure you learned to waltz when you should have been teaching me! I'll not soon forgive you."

"*Sí*, my pet, you were glorious." Valentino bowed to her. "The most fascinating of American dancing I have ever seen."

"There's not much to it," Henry said. "Would you care to take the next dance with me, Alice?"

"Oh, I'd love to!"

Henry drank the rest of his punch and offered his arm to Alice, who cut her eyes at her cousin as they passed. Darla took another drink and looked to Valentino.

"Are you going to ask me to dance?"

He slipped into the seat next to her and placed his arm around her shoulders. "I prefer slower dances that allow me to cling to my partner. We will have to wait until the quartet returns, unless you want to go to my room and I can give you that private performance."

She shrugged his arm off. "That's not going to happen, but I'll be pleased to see the concert Friday night."

"My eyes will only be for you. Every note I play will be my soul speaking to yours." He stood. "I will come for my dance soon, Darla. You will not be disappointed by my moves tonight or my playing Friday."

By the time Valentino took half a dozen steps, he had no less than four adoring fans following him. When the song ended, Henry saw Alice off the floor and she took hold of Valentino when he walked by.

Henry returned with a smile. "I'm glad you weren't swept away by Romeo."

"There's no temptation for that to ever happen, though he did threaten to dance with me when the quartet returns."

"Should I see you home before then?" he teased.

"I'm not leaving Alice here now that she's drinking the punch."

"Well then, shall we get some refreshments and settle in for a long night?" A smile curved at the corner of his mouth and the urge to kiss him flooded Darla's thoughts.

"That sounds fine."

A Lady's Choice with a Double Rush was called by the band leader as they carried plates to an empty table. Sadie hurried to Henry.

"Would you dance with me, Mr. Adams?" she asked.

He lifted his plate of sandwiches and cakes.

"Just set them down and I'll hold a spot for you," Darla said.

"All right, then." He placed them on the table, then pulled a chair out for Darla. He leaned over her once she was seated, a hand on her shoulder. "I'll be back soon."

His kind touch sent a thrill through her as powerful as Valentino's music. A minute into the song, Richard stopped at the table. Arms crossed, he plopped into a chair opposite Darla.

She swallowed her cake and looked at her cousin's masked face. "Have you asked her to dance yet?"

He pushed the devil's face on top of his head. "I can't strut like that."

"You're welcome to eat with me and Henry when he gets back."

"You think he'll want to come back after dancing with Sadie?" Richard smirked. "Thank you for the offer but dining with the country boy is not on my list of fun for tonight, though I suppose he's what you're used to. Maybe even a step up since he's from the mainland."

"He's well above any of the city boys I've met, that's for sure."

"Cousin, you are peculiar." Richard stood and slid his mask back into place before walking away.

While others danced, Darla's gaze flitted between Alice promenading around the room on Valentino's arm and Henry's prancing steps with Sadie. It could have been her imagination, but it looked like he held back a bit. She fancied that it was his way of saving his best moves for when he danced with her.

"Did you enjoy it?" she asked when he returned.

"Not half as much as I enjoy dancing with you."

"The proper city girls don't know how to cut loose, do they?"

He laughed. "It's more than that, Darla. But Miss Marley is a bit free tonight. I think she's had the punch. She said Alice made her dance with me as a way to poke back at you and she promised she'd get Valentino to dance with her tonight as payment. How do you like that?"

"They're all welcome to their schemes so long as I'm on the sidelines rather than dancing with partners pushed upon me by others. Do you like finding out you're being used?"

"I'd rather know than not."

She narrowed her eyes. "And the fact that a girl wishes to make you notice her by hanging on the likes of Valentino all night doesn't affect you?"

"The only girl I'm worried about is you." He placed a hand on her knee under the table.

She felt her cheeks warm. "That's good to know."

Henry removed his hand and they fell into their regular pattern of mealtime conversation, though they had to lean in to be heard over the music. In close proximity, his eyes were as blue as his Union jacket.

After eating, they got in a few more dances. Once again, the crowd made room for them as they shimmied and stepped to the beat. Then the ragtime band left the stage for the return of the string quartet. Without asking, Henry and Darla stepped together, transitioning from the parallel cakewalk back to the more intimate holding of the partner with the waltz.

"I've enjoyed myself immensely," he told her.

"You're a wonderful dance partner and spending time with you is always a delight."

During the second tune, Valentino approached.

"I'll give him the rest of this dance, but then will you cut in or whisk me away if needed?" Darla asked.

Henry smiled. "I'm at your service."

"*Signorina*, I have come at last." Valentino stepped between Henry and Darla from the side. "You have cast a spell on me with your dancing tonight. I must have a turn with you."

Henry moved to the sidelines while Valentino took Darla into his arms.

"You seem to have been doing fine without me." She stared at his brown eyes rather than his thin toga.

"Ah, but it takes many to fill the void you leave in my heart. Alice is not second choice unless there are a dozen along with her. They love me, why do you not love me?"

"I think you're more concerned about my lack of affections for you than you are about your true feelings for me. I'm not a conquest or game, Valentino. I prize sincerity, not flirtation."

"And this man you've been dancing with, he gives you that?"

"He does. We've become friends this month and enjoy similar things. He's sweet without having the false notes of someone looking for a quick romance to fling away when bored."

"I would cherish your memory. The touch of your lips would burn forever in my mind." He pressed against her in a most intimate way. "And the feel of our bodies together would be—"

Darla jumped back, and her left hand slid off his shoulder, but he didn't release the one he held. "This dance is officially over."

In an attempt to try covering being spurned, he immediately took her arm and escorted her to the side. He kissed her hand when they stopped and whispered, "Then Alice it shall be, and maybe her little blonde friend too."

Twenty-Five

Thursday afternoon, Alice practically floated to the hotel for lessons. From what Darla had witnessed and Alice herself had gushed about, Valentino verbally smothered his student with adoration from the moment he'd been turned down by his first choice at the Halloween party three days ago. He spent the remainder of the dance with Alice in his arms. A few well-placed kisses found her face and his hands often caressed her flowing clothes.

Alice had practiced the same pages of her violin music intently the past two evenings, much to the distraction of her family. Wednesday she didn't even ask after Henry. It was good in a way because Darla didn't have to tell her Henry had come over after eating to ask Aunt Ida for permission to bring Darla to a Saturday matinee at Lyric Theatre. Alice would find out soon enough, but Darla would rather have her cousin mad at her over the increased attentions of Henry than have her pining after Valentino.

When they reached the hotel room, they both paused to listen to the music from within.

"Saint-Saëns, 'The Swan.'" Alice sighed. "He plays it wonderfully."

Alice waited until the music stopped, but instead of silence it was followed by boisterous conversation in Italian. A cloud of anger moved across her face and she knocked forcibly.

When a handsome priest with dark hair and eyes opened the door, Alice gasped while Darla sprung for him. "Father De Fiore!"

His smile was broad, the light within him so bright Valentino appeared dull beside him. "You must be Darla, dear friend to Magdalene." He embraced her and kissed her cheeks. "And your cousin, Alice. You must both call me Claudio, as we are among family."

"I didn't know you were coming today," Darla said. "I expected to meet you tomorrow after Maggie and Douglas arrive."

"No, we—I came on the train today as a surprise. But as soon as the hotel staff saw me, they telephoned *Signora* Melling. She is sending her driver to get me for supper as Valentino has practice with the orchestra tonight."

Darla leaned to the priest's ear. "Could you ask her to have Alice's lessons moved to the main floor?"

Claudio frowned and placed a hand on her upper arm. "Is there mischief?"

She nodded. "I fear for my cousin's heart."

"I will see what can be done." He squeezed her arm before stepping back.

Valentino had a finger under Alice's chin and whispered something that made her giggle.

"Valentino," Claudio said as he went to them, and then he spoke rapidly in Italian.

Seeming to understand that her teacher was being scolded, Alice retreated to the corner. Her face turned the color of an azalea blossom as she readied her violin and set her music on the stand.

The two cousins went back and forth several times, Valentino sounding more irritable with each exchange. When he turned to Alice, he snapped. "Begin, and do not make a mockery of this song."

Ten seconds in, she fumbled over the notes.

"No, no! You are not fit to play!" Valentino's hand cut through the air as he made slashing motions toward her.

"*Calmati!*" Claudio jumped in front of him.

Alice looked up, brown eyes soft. "I'm fine with his attentions, Father De Fiore."

"I told you to call me Claudio." He laughed. "But I see how he is with you. If that is what you are used to, fine. But it shall be known that your relationship is for music only, not love."

"Music is love." Valentino danced to Alice and trailed a finger across her cheek. "I teach her to make beautiful music and she loves me in return."

Claudio berated his younger cousin in Italian. As though to save Valentino from the scolding, Alice started the song again. The men quieted and watched in awe as she played with precise quickness and passion. As she neared the end of her practiced section, Valentino shouldered his violin and took over seamlessly where she left off.

His face was full of concentration. While he knew each note, the speed took effort. As soon as he was done, Valentino stepped to Alice and kissed her on the lips.

"*Brava, Alice, Brava!*"

Alice smiled. "The glory is to my teacher, who ignites the passion within me."

Darla rolled her eyes and Claudio crossed his arms.

"If he were my teacher, I could not do what you just did," Claudio said. "You must learn to take credit for your own talent and dedication. A teacher can only do so much. The rest is up to you."

There was a knock at the door, and being closest, Darla answered it.

"The automobile is here for Father De Fiore," a bellhop said.

Claudio's shoulders sagged beneath his black coat. "I hate to leave after meeting you both, but I must. Will I see you tomorrow at the concert?"

"Yes," Darla said, "we're coming with Alice's parents."

"Good! I shall see you then, as well as the Campbells. It shall be a good day." He kissed Darla's cheeks in farewell and turned to Alice. "You are wonderfully talented, Alice. Do not let feelings get in the way of your learning."

Darla walked with Claudio to the door. "I will speak with *Signora* Melling, and will talk to Valentino about his behavior." He stepped into the hall and pointed next door. "I am staying there all weekend. I will keep an eye on him and try to talk sense into his head, but he is most stubborn and loves to be adored. It is a curse, to be sure."

"Thank you, Claudio."

Behind them, the music began again.

"I am surprised my cousin did not take a liking to you rather than Alice."

Darla's cheeks warmed. "He did, but after a month of me turning down his advances he gave up."

"You remind me of someone I once knew, but her personality was much different."

"Eliza Melling?"

Claudio's smile was bittersweet. "*Sí*, but how did you know?"

"I've been told that before, by the lady I work for."

"And who is that?"

The door opened across the hall by an unshaven man in a gray suit.

Darla's eyes switched back to Claudio from her brief glance. "Lucy Davenport, a neighbor of my aunt and uncle."

The door across the hall slammed shut.

Claudio cleared his throat and ran a finger around his stiff collar. "I wonder why Magdalene never mentioned that to me."

"Do you know the Davenports?"

"I know of them."

"They'll be at the concert tomorrow night as well. I can make introductions if you'd like."

"*Sí*, that would be most interesting."

***

Lucy spent most of Friday morning pacing the house. At eleven, Darla sent her to bed to rest. While Darla played with Phoebe in the backyard, she kept an ear and eye out for Lucy but she was still in bed when Darla checked on her at noon.

"Naomi's making sandwiches. Would you like one?" Darla asked.

"I don't know." Lucy grabbed her hand. "What if Maggie doesn't like me and refuses to tell me anything?"

"Then you'll be no worse off than you are right now. But really, she's kind. I'm sure she'll see your need and be able to tell you enough to satisfy your curiosity."

"What if Freddy doesn't get here in time? He said he wants to be here when I receive any news. What if he gets stuck at work and we have tea but never talk?"

"Now I know why he calls you Goosy. You're being a Silly Goose if I ever heard one." Darla pulled her up. "On with you, let's eat a little something to keep your energy up. A cup of coffee might help, too. I doubt you slept much last night."

She gave a shallow laugh. "I didn't, which means Freddy didn't either. I'm most selfish, but if I can't sleep, he can't sleep. He knows I'm not resting whether I'm beside him in bed or down at my typewriter and he does all he can to help me. God knows I don't deserve him."

"Don't say such things. You two are perfect for each other."

Lucy slipped her feet into her house shoes at the foot of the bed and smoothed her skirt. "That's what I thought about me and Alex, but no one says that about Freddy. Maxwell even said Alex and I were a good match. He respects Freddy and knows his impeccable character, but he's never said we're good for each other. I often feel like I'm a chain around my husband's neck, slowly tightening."

She went pale. Darla took her arm and sat her back on the edge of the bed, feeling her pulse in her wrist.

"You mustn't think that way, Lucy. You're making yourself ill with fretting."

Her lower lips trembled. "But he's slipping away from me, I can feel it."

"It's you who's slipping away. You're falling into melancholy. Your husband loves you."

"But he doesn't like me anymore." She shook her head. "I've hurt him too much. I always have. I flaunted myself before him when I was with Alex but still ran to him when I was in pain. I expected complete support and love while I only offered him the satisfaction of helping me."

Darla's stomach began to twist, but she forced herself to place a hand on Lucy's shoulder. "It can't be that bad, Lucy."

"But it is." Her shoulders heaved under the emerging sobs. "Half the time I'm with him, I close my eyes and pretend he's Alex."

Repulsed by the confession, Darla left her to cry and hurried to the kitchen.

"Naomi, she's falling apart. Could you make some coffee?"

Naomi twisted the tea towel in her hands. "Friends of yours or not, I think today will be the final straw for that girl. She ain't up to this stress in her condition."

"Mr. Davenport tried to talk her out of it, but she's convinced it will bring her closure. I've let Maggie know how delicate Lucy is, and I'm sure she'll tell any news with the lightest of hands." Darla looked to Phoebe sitting at the corner table, munching a cheese sandwich. "Everything okay, little one?"

"Yes, Miss Darla. How much longer until Papa comes?" Phoebe asked about her grandfather coming to get her for an overnight stay.

"Less than an hour. After you eat, we'll make sure your bag is ready. Come up when you've cleaned your plate."

Darla returned to Lucy. She was still on the bed, weeping. Darla wet a washcloth in the bathroom.

"Let's start cleaning those tears. You don't want to be red and puffy when Mr. Davenport and the Campbells arrive."

Lucy took the cloth and wiped at her face without purpose. "It's no use. Let me get in the shower. I wanted to change anyway."

To quiet her anxiety, Darla made the bed while Lucy showered, then she helped Phoebe check her bag and made sure her bedroom was tidy.

"Why don't you bring Doff down to the sofa? I'll be there in a few minutes," she told the girl.

"Momma sick again?"

"No, but she's not feeling strong today."

"I strong!" Phoebe held up her arms to showcase her muscles. "Strong like Daddy!"

Darla laughed. "Your daddy is raising you to be a strong girl, and that's a true blessing."

Phoebe gathered Doff into her arms and carried him downstairs. Lucy came out of the bathroom wrapped in a robe, her blonde hair falling around her narrow shoulders. She looked utterly lost and young, but with the worry of an old soul etched onto her pretty face. Her left hand cradled her rounded abdomen but the look on her face wasn't motherly.

"Are you having pains?" Darla asked.

"What?" Lucy looked down and patted her belly. "No pains there. Freddy makes strong babies."

Darla frowned. "That's your baby too, and you're the one doing all the work right now with growing and protecting the babe."

"Freddy still protects us, and this one is going to be completely Davenport and no Easton. I can feel it."

While Lucy dressed, Darla waited at the top of the stairs, listening out for both Phoebe and her mother. The front door opened and Mr. Davenport came in.

"Daddy!" Phoebe ran to him.

He lifted her to his chest with one arm. "I had to come home early and see my princess before you go on your adventure to Nana and Papa's house."

She kissed his cheek with a loud *smooch*. "I love you, Daddy."

"I love you more, Princess." He set her down and removed his navy suit jacket.

Lucy emerged from the bedroom, dressed in the Greek-inspired column dress with a fringed, blue shawl. Darla offered an arm and walked down the stairs with her. Mr. Davenport followed their progress, a slight smile gracing his serious face. He met them at the bottom of the stairs and took his wife into his arms.

"How are you feeling, Goosy?" He kissed her cheek as though testing for a response, and then went for her lips after she smiled.

"Darla insisted I lay down for an hour so I feel decent."

He tucked her under his chin. "Good to hear."

"Your coffee and sandwich should be ready, Lucy," Darla said. "I'm sure there is plenty for you, Mr. Davenport."

"Thank you, Darla." He turned toward the kitchen and walked with his arm around Lucy, looking like the perfect couple—if one didn't know what went on inside Lucy's head.

"Now Phoebe," Darla said, "let's get your bag."

"And Pinky and Rummy."

"Do you want to bring your carriage, too?"

They were back in the living room with bag, buggy, bunny, and doll when the doorbell rang.

"Papa!" Phoebe attached herself to her grandfather's legs and Darla had to pull her away to allow Mr. Easton entrance.

With a good-natured laugh, he stepped inside. "Thank you, Darla. And I'm excited to see you too, Phoebe. Nana has some cookies baking this afternoon. Did you eat your dinner?"

"Yes, Papa. It's all gone in here." She lifted her dress and patted her tummy.

"We're still working on modesty issues, I'm afraid," Mr. Davenport said as he joined the others trying to hide their smiles. "Thank you for offering Phoebe a mini-adventure."

"No problem, Freddy. You know Evelyn loves to dote on your girl. And speaking of which, where's my girl?"

"Finishing up a light dinner in the kitchen. Naomi is there, too." Mr. Easton went for the back of the house with his granddaughter and Mr. Davenport looked to Darla. "How was she today? And you know I don't mean Phoebe."

Darla nodded. "She paced all morning until I made her lay down. Then she had a crying spell when I got her up to eat. She took a shower to relax and clean the tears."

"I can't thank you enough for your help." He retrieved her weekly pay from his billfold. "You can go freshen up or whatever it is you ladies do these days. If you want to return a little early so you're here when the Campbells arrive, that's fine."

"Thank you, Mr. Davenport. I do hope the afternoon goes well."

"You and me both."

Twenty-Six

Lucy emerged from the kitchen on her father's arm, the memory of Opal saying she was their father's favorite loud in her mind.

He kissed her cheek. "You and Freddy have fun tonight, Lucy. And there's no rush to get Phoebe in the morning. Telephone when you're up and we'll decide then."

"Thank you." She hugged him and bent to Phoebe.

"I've got her." Frederick lifted Phoebe and held her while Lucy kissed and hugged their daughter.

"You be sweet for Nana and Papa. I love you, Phoebe Camellia."

Phoebe took her grandfather's hand at the door and Frederick followed behind with her suitcase and doll carriage. When he returned to the house empty-handed, he led Lucy to the corner of the sofa and sat at the opposite end. He pulled her legs into his lap and removed her gold slippers so he could massage her bare feet.

She leaned the side of her head against the back of the sofa and smiled at her husband. "You always know what to do for me. I wish I were half as considerate of your needs as you are of mine."

His brown eyes turned to her. "All I require is your love and devotion, Goosy."

"I do love you."

He nodded and turned his attention back to her feet. "But you don't seem like you're with me half the time. Even when we're lying together it feels like your mind and heart are elsewhere."

"My stories occupy many of my thoughts."

Frederick frowned. "I'm sure *Winter of My Heart* occupies much space in your life."

In an attempt to change the direction of the conversation, Lucy squeezed his arm. "Mr. Noble called this morning and said the literary circles in New York have chattered about it all week. They're clamoring for Olive Kent to make an appearance."

"And is he willing to wait until January to try talking you into anything?"

"He knows I'll not consider any travel plans until after the baby is born. Do you think I should go?"

"You've worked hard to meet your goals and deserve to relish in them however you see fit. Just remember, the first time you make an appearance in New York, the truth will eventually filter to Mobile and everyone will know who you are."

Lucy nodded. "That's what gives me the most pause. I like our quiet life together, Freddy. It's safe and secure. Every day you make me pleased to be your wife."

"Have you really been happy with me?" Frederick worked his hands up to her calves.

She took a deep breath. "It pains me you have to ask. You're nothing but goodness and love for me, Phoebe, and the new one. I'm happy with you, with our family."

"But part of you still yearns for more." He trailed his fingertips down from her knees to her feet, and then stopped.

"Not more. Just—"

"Someone else," he finished for her. Frederick lowered her feet to the ground and stepped away. "Shall I change suits for the tea?"

She stood and straightened his red tie before wrapping her arms around him. "You're perfect. You can slip the jacket back on before they come, if you want." She gazed up at his dignified face and felt the curve of a smile breaking through her sadness.

A hand skimmed around her middle to the small of her back and his other cradled her cheek. "You're still my fair maiden, Lucy."

The kiss started soft, but as Lucy's hands roamed over her husband's shirt, it deepened. In turn, he caressed her curves as they made their way back to the sofa.

"You're my knight, my protector." She gasped between kisses as Frederick hovered over her. When his kisses moved to her neck, she arched back in hopes of his attention being directed down. He didn't disappoint. His warm lips moved to her collar bone. "You make everything right in my world, Freddy."

"Lucy," he whispered, "if we could be like this always. Connected, passionate, nothing between us but love, we'd have it all."

He gently lowered himself until he was barely resting on top of her and received a kick from the baby.

Lucy giggled. "That space is already taken."

Frederick sat up and pulled her into his lap, pressing a hand against the swell of her middle. "This one's livelier than Phoebe was. What have we gotten ourselves into?"

"What do you expect from a byproduct of our activity?"

His laugh was loud, bringing her to the realization she hadn't heard it lately. His seriousness was because of her moods. She silently vowed to share more love and laughter with him.

"Never give up on me, Frederick."

"I haven't given up, though it's been a trying year."

Darla's knock came on the front door a few minutes later. Lucy was still in her husband's arms, but he hollered for Darla to come in.

"Sorry, maybe I came a little too early." After looking at Lucy, Darla smiled. "But you look much improved."

"Freddy's arms are my balm." She kissed his cheek, then patted her hair. "Though I should probably tighten this up a bit."

Frederick fingered a loose tendril. "It gives you that artistic, free-flowing style that's perfect for a writer."

"But they don't know I'm a writer. You didn't tell Maggie, did you, Darla?"

"I've told no one."

"There goes that excuse." She went to the mirror over the fireplace and undid her chignon as she finger-combed her hair.

"Would you like me to get your brush?" he asked.

"If you wouldn't mind."

Frederick took the stairs two at a time and raced back. As he brushed through Lucy's hair, he spoke to Darla over his shoulder.

"Are the Campbells the type to want a formal tea?"

"Freddy, you know I couldn't serve a formal tea to save my life," Lucy interjected.

"What I mean is, should I wear my jacket or would the captain be pleased or shocked to remove his as well?"

"Oh, he'd be happy to unwind while he's here. They're very personable and unpretentious. They were married a few weeks before you and their son is less than two months older than Phoebe. I think you'll find you have much in common, besides the link to the Mellings."

Lucy twisted the length of her hair, then wrapped and tucked it into a loose bun, picking her hairpins off the mantel to shove them in at intervals to hold the style together. "I hope so. If she refuses—"

"They're coming and agreed to talk." Frederick turned her to him and kissed her on the mouth. Then leaning his head against hers, he hugged her to him. "It will all work out for the best. And you look gorgeous."

"And you need to smile so you don't look too serious."

He laughed. "I will. But I'm going to shave it into a moustache soon."

"It will give you an even greater air of respectability, don't you think, Darla?"

"From what I've seen, mustaches are definitely a businessman's look in the city."

Frederick looked over Lucy's shoulder into the mirror, rubbing his goatee. "Maybe I'll do it for tonight."

"After tea you could go to the barber and have a proper shave," Lucy said.

"I think I will."

The doorbell rang and Lucy gasped.

"Get the door, please, Darla. And be sure to hang their jackets and anything else." Frederick took Lucy's elbow and laid her silk shawl around her that had fallen off during their intimate time together. "Don't worry, Goosy."

The sound of excitement in Darla's voice helped encourage Lucy to be brave, but she still clung to her husband's arm when the Campbells came into the living room. Douglas was incredibly handsome with a ginger beard and weathered features—a true captain if she ever saw one—while Maggie was a classic brunette beauty, simply dressed for the city in a dark skirt and cream blouse. She came directly for Lucy, arms open.

"Lucy, I heard of you several times at Seacliff Cottage and was curious who the woman was that captivated Alex and sent Mrs. Melling to hysterics whenever mentioned. You're even more beautiful than I imagined."

Lucy hugged her in return, an incredulous air swirling inside. "They spoke of me a year after the fact?"

"To Mrs. Melling you were 'that blonde' or 'that writer,' to Mr. Melling—depending on his mood—you were an asset or a mistake, and to Alex you were his one great love. Some of his final words were about you." Lucy caught her breath, and Maggie rushed on. "But I'm getting ahead of myself, forgive me."

Formal introductions were given and Frederick stayed by Lucy, taking one side of the sofa with her in the middle and Maggie on the other side. Darla was in a chair next to Maggie, and Douglas sat across the coffee table in an armchair.

"Should I help Naomi?" Darla asked Lucy.

"No, you're a guest today."

Darla clasped her hands in her lap and looked between the women. "I met Father De Fiore yesterday."

Maggie's smile was luminous. "How's Claudio? I look forward to seeing him."

"He's most kind. He's going to try to help solve the situation of Valentino's outrageous flirting with my cousin."

"And is he still striking to look at?"

"He shines with the light of God and makes his cousin look boyish." Darla blushed.

Douglas groaned. "Don't get Maggie started on Claudio. It will be bad enough to take dinner with him tonight. The jokes between them—they're incorrigible."

Maggie laughed. "We grew close in our months together. But you get to enjoy the fun, Darla. We stopped next door first and your aunt gave you permission to take supper with us at the hotel before the concert, but would prefer for you to sit with the family for the performance.”

“Oh, thank you! But I was curious, how did the Mellings befriend an Italian priest?” Darla looked to Lucy and she smiled, knowing Darla helped turn the conversation to what mattered most.

“He met Alex on the ferry a Friday afternoon at the end of February ’05, as he reported for training with Father Angelo,” Maggie said. “Alex was on his way to Seacliff Cottage for the weekend to ride Janus and get away from his heartache in the city.”

Frederick took his wife’s hand.

“According to Claudio, Alex attached himself to him. He was a deacon at the time, not yet a priest, but Alex shared his troubles, all of which I don’t know other than his heartache over a broken engagement and his poor behavior.”

“That’s an understatement,” Frederick muttered.

Douglas smirked. “I can imagine.”

“Freddy, don’t,” Lucy whispered.

“What?” Frederick’s voice rose. “Can we not all admit that Alexander Melling did insufferable things? Or had he changed?”

Douglas motioned to Maggie. “Most of it is her affair to share, but I will say his final twenty-four hours showed growth and change I never expected, though I only knew him through stories until a few days prior.”

All eyes fell to Maggie and she took Lucy’s hand. “I’ll tell you about my time with him in Seacliff Cottage, but you’ll have to help tell the story because Alex linked it back to you.”

“Me?” Lucy felt the color drain from her face.

Maggie nodded. “Do you wish to speak privately?”

“Freddy knows everything. Darla’s heard plenty as well. And your husband has a kind face. I don’t see him judging me.”

"Then there's no need for embarrassment for any of us." Maggie squeezed her hand. "Well, for starters, Mr. Melling hired me to be a companion to his wife so he and Alex could return to their typical work pattern after Eliza passed away. I think it was the first night there, Alex told me I was a peace offering to him from his father."

"He hadn't reconciled with him in the year since?" Lucy asked.

"Apparently not. I hardly saw them speak to each other that weekend. At first I thought Alex was upset over Eliza's death, but the more I learned the more I understood it to be over you and whatever part his father played in the broken engagement. Alex told me I reminded him of you and I was there to help him heal."

Lucy clutched Frederick's hand. "He was still upset over me? I know I should be saddened, but it makes me feel better to know he was suffering along with me."

"He deserved to suffer," Frederick muttered.

"He went through much but there were more layers to him than I understood from that weekend." Maggie touched a garden book that was displayed on the coffee table. "Several times, I saw him with a book when he was alone. It was pink and looked terribly out of place in those dark rooms. I didn't remember the title until I saw it later at Claire Walker's house, *Azalea Blossom* by Olive Kent."

Lucy covered her face with her hands and began to rock back and forth. Frederick's arms went about her and she leaned into his chest.

"Tell them, Freddy. We can trust them."

"Olive Kent is Lucy's pen name. It's a well-guarded secret among her close relatives, Darla, and now you."

"So that's how Darla got the autographed book for Claire!" Maggie laughed. "Oh, she was pleased to get it. She even gave me her old copy."

Freddy hugged Lucy tighter. "Lucy picked the name after the broken engagement because of the gossip surrounding her. She didn't want her book to be ill-received locally because of what happened in her personal life. But Alex knew the book's title. They were engaged when she submitted the manuscript to Mr. Noble. It doesn't appear he told anyone else, but the day it was released he had roses sent to her—the same type he had delivered to her for good luck the day she met the publisher."

"And someone sent her the same thing on Monday," Darla added. "Even used his signature line. Her newest book just came out last Friday."

"I'm under orders from Claire to purchase a copy for her while in the city." Maggie looked to her husband and back at Lucy. "But that's odd about the flowers. We get a bottle of Scotch sent to us from Louisiana every year for our anniversary. Claudio doesn't claim doing it and it's never signed."

Naomi arrived with the tea, setting it on the coffee table. Frederick introduced her to the Campbells.

"Do you need help or anything else, Miss Lucy?" she asked after presenting the food tray.

"No, thank you Naomi." She looked to the others. "I'm not one to fuss over formalities, but I usually pour the tea."

"I'd be happy to do it," Maggie offered. "It's no trouble."

"Thank you."

Maggie saw to everyone's tea. Her hands, well-manicured despite being slightly work-hardened, moved elegantly. Lucy never thought of proper ladies in the country, but Maggie opened her eyes to new possibilities—both in life and fiction.

When Douglas came to get his tea from Maggie, Darla switched to his seat. The captain winked at her before taking her old spot by his wife. His hand immediately went to Maggie's knee with a caressing touch and she leaned to him for a kiss, almost like a reflex. Lucy snuggled against Frederick and watched the way the Campbells constantly shared attention back and forth through touches and knowing glances. It brought a tear to Lucy's eye because that was how she and Alexander used to be.

"Darla told us you have a three-year-old son," Frederick said to Douglas. "Our Phoebe turned three at the end of August."

"Aye, Kade turned three in June. We also have a daughter, Tabitha. She just turned one last month. Do you have your hopes on a boy or girl this time around?"

"No preference, but I love my girls." Frederick kissed Lucy's cheek.

After eating, Maggie continued the tale. "That weekend was completely otherworldly. I might as well say it. We learned the next week that the house was infested by demonic activity."

"What?" Frederick stiffened beside Lucy.

"Claudio helped bring it to light. It took the assistance of a priest and constant blessings and exorcisms to clear the space. We battled it all summer, as Douglas witnessed when he came, but that first weekend with Alex I completely lost my senses."

"How do you mean?" Darla asked.

"The demons played upon our emotions, stirred our lusts. Alex and I went back and forth playing at seduction, but only one of us was affected at a time—*oppressed* Claudio called it. I was swayed until Alex became conqueror and then I fought for freedom."

Lucy's teacup began rattling on her saucer as she remembered the words of Consuela all those years ago—*Alexander the Great, my conqueror.* Frederick placed her cup on the table and pulled her closer, stroking her arm.

"Did he—did you—" Lucy couldn't get the words out.

Maggie's smile was tainted with memories. "We never went all the way. The times we came close were when he was the oppressed one, but there were plenty of moments I wanted to ride that passion to the summit. He was sensual and amazing. He spoke all the right words, but then the demon took over and he turned despicable."

"I know exactly what you mean." Lucy leaned her head against Frederick's shoulder as she gazed at the other woman. "He was generous, loving, and full of tender passion until the demons of his past took hold of him. Then he turned into his father, all dominance, pride, and selfish needs."

Maggie squeezed her hand. "Mrs. Melling saw the attention Alex gave me and arranged for him to go east with their cousins for the summer. Then Mr. Melling and his wife had a falling out because Claudio and I were cleansing the house. Mr. Melling refused to come on the weekends. We thought we were free of the demons when he stopped coming, but we were wrong."

"But how did they come to be there?" Frederick asked. "It's difficult to comprehend."

Maggie laughed. "Think how I felt as a Methodist seeking blessings and exorcism from a Catholic, but I couldn't deny what I experienced and witnessed." She turned serious. "Demons are invited in when sin is committed. We all thought it was through Mr. Melling because he was having an affair with the maid. It wasn't until Alex returned in September that we learned the root of the original sin."

"Forgive me, Maggie!" Lucy clutched her hand. "I had no idea!"

Maggie smiled. "I don't blame you."

"I was so in love with him, I thought I knew what I was doing. We were engaged and had a horrific time at his stupid masquerade the night before." Tears fell as Lucy rushed through the words. "I thought going to Seacliff Cottage would give us the privacy to talk and make amends. Eliza traveled with us so we wouldn't be seen crossing the bay alone. We did talk and smooth things over, and then we were in his room before a fire with a picnic and half undressed. It all made sense to me then. I felt I needed to show him how committed I was, despite learning the depths of his sinful past. He recited my poetry and carried me to his bed. I wanted him, wanted him to have all of me, but as soon as it was over, I was ill with guilt. I thought the pain was only between me and Alex, but I've seen how it's affected me and Freddy, and now you and those within

Seacliff Cottage. How much evil have I allowed into the world by my choices?"

"Goosy." Frederick pulled her to his chest. "The burden is not yours alone. And you've been re-baptized since then. You must let it go."

"But I can't!" Her body shook with sobs. "I crave and love him even today. He's in my blood, in my head, and heart. Everywhere I look, I think of Alex. I worry for his soul, his salvation."

They let her cry a moment while Frederick murmured in her ear and caressed her.

Maggie knelt before her. "Lucy, dear, can you hear me?"

She nodded, her cheek rubbing across the wetness on Frederick's shirt.

"He found peace." Maggie gripped her hand. "Those days were a complete mess, but Alex confessed, forsook his sins, and gave himself to the Lord during the hurricane. The day before he died, we reconciled. He even came to decent terms with Douglas and they hated each other—that's how clear his conscious became. Hurricane or not, we had peace for that last bit, until Mr. Melling came and polluted the house. Alex became oppressed for a bit, but he fought for me—for us—again."

"He usually took blows rather than gave them." Lucy wiped her eyes with her husband's handkerchief. "Rupert is the only one I ever saw him strike."

"Rupert Lyons?" It was Maggie's turn to look peaked. Douglas took her hand.

"Yes." Frederick said. "It happened at Alex's masquerade Lucy mentioned. He was in with the rowdiest group, along with Rupert, Lucy's brother, and a bunch of others. Lucy was never one to flaunt herself, but that night she covered her hair, painted her lips, and wore an amazing gown that showcased her lovely form. The drunken members didn't recognize her. While Alex saw Eliza out of the party, Rupert came to Lucy. She didn't know who it was because of his costume, but he grabbed at her and said vile things. When Alex heard of it and figured out who it was he broke Rupert's nose."

Maggie gave a half-laugh. "I always thought his nose looked crooked. That's who accosted me, practically with Mrs. Melling's blessing. She sent me out with him unchaperoned, though Douglas and I were engaged. He tried to rape me in Eliza's sepulcher."

Douglas rubbed Maggie's arm as though she had chill bumps under her sleeves. "I got there just in time to stop him from the unthinkable."

"Oh, Maggie." Darla bit her lip to keep it from trembling.

Maggie turned to her young friend. "Now you know why I never spoke of the Mellings. So many horrific things happened at Seacliff Cottage, but at least the best thing in my life did as well. I met Douglas there and that one good outweighs all the bad."

Twenty-Seven

Darla sipped her cooling tea, trying to understand everything she'd heard. Lucy still cried, though silently. Mr. Davenport kept his strong arms about her, exchanging knowing looks with Douglas because both their wives seemed to have a soft spot for Alexander Melling.

"I'm glad he found peace." Lucy sniffed. "But what were his final words you mentioned?"

Maggie looked to Douglas and briefly rested her head against her husband's shoulder. "It's a bit horrific what happened in the end. It might shock you."

"I need to know!"

"Goosy, if you stop now you'll still have the peace of knowing his conscience was clear at the end." Mr. Davenport kissed her cheek. "You don't need to know the details."

"But I do! If I leave my imagination to fill in the rest, I'll be as bad off as before."

"He loved you to the end, Lucy. What he did, he did for all of us—me, Eliza, and you."

"Eliza?"

"It was believed that Eliza died from a horse accident but we learned the truth that summer," Maggie said. "I found burrs sewn into her saddle pad. They were placed there by the maid—the one Mr. Melling was having an affair with. When Douglas's uncle confronted Mr. Melling with the evidence, he was yelled at for not destroying the tack like he was told. Mr. Melling knew about the supposed accident, yet he hid the truth. Alex learned of it when he came home in September and was livid."

"I always knew the man was despicable"—Mr. Davenport's voice practically shook with anger—"but that's against all decency."

"Alex knew how vile his father was and tried to keep me away from him. He only wanted to be with me, but his father sought to undermine our relationship and what changes Alex made."

Maggie nodded. "Claudio, after learning about it, found Mr. Melling making advances toward me and almost killed him. But months later, it was Alex who finally did."

Lucy paled. Darla crossed to her side and motioned for Maggie and Mr. Davenport to clear the sofa. Maggie moved beside her husband and Mr. Davenport slid out from beside Lucy. Darla rolled Lucy onto her side and tucked a little pillow between her knees.

"Come on, Lucy." She stroked her hair and gripped her hand with her other. "Take a deep breath in. Try to relax."

She continued to talk Lucy through breathing while she crushed Darla's hand in her anguish. Mr. Davenport paced the room, alternating between looking at Lucy with concern and clenching his fists.

"I'm okay now," Lucy whispered to Darla. "Let Maggie continue."

"Your body's had enough stress. I'll not let you put yourself and the baby at risk to hear what became of a man long gone from you." Mr. Davenport dropped to his knees before her. "I'm here with you now, Lucy. Isn't that enough?"

Lucy shook her head, tears rolling off her cheeks as she curled further into herself. "I'm sorry, Freddy, but I have to know. Will you hold me while I listen?"

Darla, Maggie, and Douglas stared at the couple. Lucy's expectant face was desperate and it was clear she was half a second from shattering.

"Come on, Goosy." He stood and scooped her into his arms. Then he sat on the sofa holding her.

Lucy reached up and touched his cheek. "I've never deserved you."

"Don't talk like that." He nestled her to his chest and whispered something that made her smile through her tears, but also caused fresh ones to fall.

"Freddy …" Lucy met his lips.

A minute later he looked at his guests apologetically. "Please excuse us."

"I assume it's like watching me and Maggie." Douglas laughed and took his wife's hand.

"Almost." Darla retreated to the other armchair with a half-smile.

"Just you wait," Maggie said. "You'll find someone whose arms you never want to leave."

Darla felt the heat rise to her cheeks and hoped Lucy wouldn't say anything about Henry, but the hostess turned to Maggie.

"Would you finish the tale? Don't bother stopping, just get it all out no matter what happens. I'll be listening."

Maggie looked to Mr. Davenport and he nodded. "Very well, but remember we've never told anyone except Claudio. During the hurricane, we were all trapped in the main house: Alex, Douglas, Uncle Simon, Claudio, and the former maid, Lydia. She'd come by with her newborn daughter in hopes of getting financial support from Mr. Melling. As the storm raged, you can imagine what happened within the walls. Alex trying to seduce me, Douglas angry or oppressed himself, me fighting my own desires, and Claudio too. Claudio forgave Lydia for her hand in Eliza's death but Alex wouldn't. He saw her as an extension of his father's sins."

Maggie paused to gather her thoughts. "The baby, Georgiana, was ill and we lost her that night. Then Lydia ran off. We had a horrendous time but survived. By the time the weather cleared, Alex helped Claudio cleanse the house and offered to dig a grave for his half-sister while Douglas drove Claudio back to Daphne."

Douglas rubbed her shoulders and whispered in her ear.

Maggie sighed. "It was when Douglas was gone and Alex was digging the grave that Mr. Melling arrived. Uncle Simon was in the carriage house and I'd run back to Seacliff Cottage to retrieve our coats. He found me there and had me cornered, but Alex rushed in and attacked."

Lucy's hand went to her mouth to cover a cry.

"It was no match. Mr. Melling threw him against the doorframe and knocked him out. He was dragging me upstairs when Alex woke. I saw his countenance descend into darkness, but he talked his father into handing me over to him so he could finally have his way with me."

Maggie wiped a tear from her alabaster cheek. "I had Alex push the wardrobe in front of the door so his father couldn't get in, but when Douglas came back he couldn't get to me either. He fought Mr. Melling in the hall while I sought to help Alex out of his oppression. When both our struggles ended, Mr. Melling was beaten near death and Alex was furious with himself for once again falling victim to his demons."

Lucy cried and her husband rocked her in his arms.

"When we were getting ready to leave, I was in the hall with Mr. Melling, thinking he was unconscious, but he rose and came at me. Douglas pulled me away but Alex went for his father. His vengeance surged and he lifted Mr. Melling over his head so his jacket caught the flame of the gas chandelier." Maggie's voice quivered and Douglas stroked her arms. "Alex told his father that it was punishment because he wouldn't leave me alone, allowed Eliza to die without justice, and ruined his prospects with you, Lucy. He couldn't let him live after all he'd done and would continue to do. Alex caught his own shirt on fire and dropped it on his father, commanding us to run. He was still standing beside Mr. Melling when Douglas carried me down the back stairs. He died to save us, to give justice to his sister, and to make amends over your broken engagement."

"But he was to be married!" Lucy cried out.

"He still loved you, Lucy. He told me he'd rather die than live a lie. He couldn't go through with the wedding but he knew he couldn't break it either. Death was the only way out for him, too."

Lucy buried her face on her husband's shoulder and Douglas offered Maggie a handkerchief. After several minutes of the sentimental scene, Darla spoke up.

"I know it was difficult, for everyone, but I think it will help in the long run. Would anyone like more tea or coffee?"

Several minutes later, Darla returned with fresh supplies. Lucy was still in Mr. Davenport's arms, but Maggie pulled her chair close enough to the table to see to pouring for everyone.

Seeing the cinnamon stick and grater, Douglas raised an eyebrow at Darla. "Good memory you've got," he said, his Scottish accent thicker than normal.

"People's oddities are often memorable," Darla said.

He laughed. "So I'm odd, am I?"

Maggie smiled. "The strangest, most wonderful man I know."

Lucy calmed enough to sit beside her husband and drink a cup. Mr. Davenport declined, and kept an arm around her. The talk slowed and then turned to the concert.

"I look forward to the performance," Maggie said. "And more so of seeing Claudio. I'll ask him in person about that Scotch that comes yearly. I don't think he'd lie to my face about it."

"Yet you think a priest would lie in a letter?" Darla asked pointedly. "He seemed forthright when I met him."

"Oh, he is, I just don't understand the present. It's something …" Maggie pressed her lips together a moment. "It's something more suited to Alexander than Claudio."

"And my roses." Lucy and Maggie's eyes met.

Frederick rubbed Lucy's arm. "More likely someone with mischief on their mind is looking to stir things with those Alex was closest to."

"I was in his presence for the total of a week," Maggie said. "I hardly consider myself in close confidence of him."

"But what you experienced together," Douglas said, "is what makes the bindings strong."

"Our shared sin and torment?" Maggie gave a hollow laugh. "I put up with more from Mrs. Melling."

"Do you think it could be her sending things?" Darla asked.

"No," Maggie and Lucy said at the same time.

The men laughed.

Not long after the coffee was drunk, Darla went next door to change into her new dress so she could go to the hotel with Maggie and Douglas. Alice came in from school while she pulled the plum gown over her cream camisole, which showed between the deep V-cut of the dress.

"It's even prettier on you than I imagined. You were smart to pick one without a train, and the velvet trim will take you through the holidays well," Alice said as she fingered the sash and overlays. "But why are you dressing so early?"

"I'm going to the hotel with the Campbells. Aunt Ida gave me permission to take supper with them, but I'll meet you all at the concert."

"Valentino says priority seats are reserved for us. I wonder if he got them for his cousin's friends as well."

"Possibly. Would you tie the bow for me? You're the best at bows."

"It's too bad Valentino thinks them juvenile." Alice sighed. "And how are the Davenports today?"

Darla thought back on the flood of Lucy's tears. "They're getting on well with the Campbells, which I'm glad of. It feels like bridging my old life with the new."

Alice turned Darla sideways so she could see the profile of the bow in the dressing mirror. "And do they know they are both connected to the Mellings?"

Darla hesitated. "Yes. Thank you, it's lovely. What should I do with my hair?"

Alice dug through her ribbon drawer and came out with a cream-colored velvet band. She brushed through her cousin's hair and worked it into a bun with loose ends that created a soft fullness in the back. Then she pinned the ribbon like a headband, securing it under the knot of hair.

"Thank you, Alice."

Alice kissed her cheeks, an annoying habit she started that week to show her dedication to Valentino, no doubt. "I'll see you in a few hours."

***

Supper in The Trellis Room with the Campbells and Claudio went by too quickly. Darla's face was sore from laughing, though she didn't understand half of their humor because Maggie and Claudio had more private jokes than seemed possible.

The priest led the way with Darla on his arm to the grand ballroom, which was set for the performance. When they passed the sign in the lobby, it was surrounded by several young ladies cooing over the photograph of Valentino under the headline of "This weekend only: Tchaikovsky's Violin concerto in D Major, Opus 35 with Orchestra. Shows Friday and Saturday evenings, and matinee Sunday featuring visiting soloist and world-wide sensation, Valentino De Fiore!"

"I do not know what to do with him," Claudio said. "He is too full of pride, and for good reason. The women love him—well all but you."

Darla laughed. "I love the music, not the man."

"Your mother must have taught you well."

"She was a fine woman," Maggie said from behind them.

"With excellent taste in friends," Darla added.

While they waited to enter the room, Darla heard her name spoken by a voice she didn't expect to hear that night. She turned, dropping her hand from Claudio's arm.

"Henry, how good to see you!"

He wore a basic tuxedo, much like Douglas's. "I don't mean to interrupt, I just wanted to let you know curiosity over what moves you got the best of me and I was able to purchase a ticket."

"That's wonderful! We can talk about the performance tomorrow." She took his hand and squeezed it before letting go. Then she turned to Maggie. "I'd like you to meet one of my closest friends from the island, Maggie and her husband, Captain Douglas Campbell. And their good friend, and Valentino's cousin, Father Claudio De Fiore. All of you, this is Henry Adams. He's interning with Mr. Davenport."

"I'm glad to meet you," Maggie said, offering her hand.

Douglas shook his hand and placed his other on Henry's shoulder. "I'm a tad like a crazy uncle to Darla, so I best not hear of anything troublesome happening."

Maggie lightly punched her husband in the stomach, causing everyone to laugh.

"Do not mind them," Claudio said. "Everyone knows it is the priest you need to stay on the good side of."

"I'm pleased to meet so many people with Darla's best interest at heart, but I don't wish to intrude. I only wanted to let Darla know I was here." He turned to her. "I look forward to seeing you tomorrow."

"Thanks for stopping. I'm glad you got to meet my friends and they you."

As soon as he walked away, Maggie poked Darla in the side. "He's very handsome and polite. Why didn't you tell me about him?"

"I told you in my letters that an intern was taking weekly luncheons at the Davenports."

Maggie's hands went to her hips on her lacy blue gown. "That's not what I mean."

"And now I know why she doesn't have eyes for my cousin." Claudio laughed. "Darla's heart is elsewhere."

"The three of you are worse than my brothers would be." Darla's cheeks flushed.

"You just let me know if he doesn't treat you well," Douglas said with a smile. "I can arrange for a one way trip across the bay."

Twenty-Eight

Lucy felt as though she floated through the hotel lobby on Frederick's arm. Alex loved her to the end and Frederick loved her still. Her heart was lighter than it had been for months and her silk gown like air against her skin. The pink train skimmed the floor behind her and the Renaissance-style chiffon sleeves draped her limbs with a poetic beauty.

"Freddy, isn't that Henry over there?" Lucy nodded toward the intern standing beside one of the potted trees.

"So it is. Would you mind if we stopped to say hello?"

"Not at all."

"Henry, it's good to see you out this evening." Frederick shook his hand.

He looked the couple over and smiled. "Thank you, Mr. Davenport. You look as lovely as ever, Mrs. Davenport."

Frederick moved his arm around Lucy and she leaned into him. "Have you seen anyone else we know?"

"Mrs. Smith is here, and another client whose name I can't remember. The bald man who loves to buy automobiles. And Darla. She's here with friends from the island and a priest."

Lucy's reaction to the first name set her stomach souring, but the information on the Campbells gave her hope. "Where are they? I'd like to meet Father De Fiore and see the others again. Darla looks as pretty as ever today."

"Up near the entrance." Henry shoved his hands into his pockets. "And yes, Darla looks beautiful."

"Thank you, Henry." Frederick clapped him on the back.

Half a dozen steps later, Frederick was accosted by Judith Smith. She wore a tight black gown with a low neckline, which she angled at him in the best possible way.

"Mr. Davenport, my financial savior!" Her talons went around Frederick's free arm then trailed down to his hand. "And Lucille. It's amazing how girlish you manage to look even in your present state."

"Good evening, Mrs. Smith." Frederick awkwardly shook her hand with his that she'd captured and slid it free, setting it on top Lucy's on his other arm.

"I didn't know it was possible, but you look even more handsome with your new style, Mr. Davenport." Judith studied his mustache and smiled beguilingly. "And so you don't worry over my funds, I'm here as a guest of the Lyons. Kate thought it was monstrous that you don't allow me to spend more than a few dollars a month on entertainment and took pity on me."

"I advise you, Mrs. Smith. That's not the same as denying. The choice is yours."

"So you won't deny me anything, Mr. Davenport?" Her fingers brushed over his shoulders before they lowered.

"Oh, you can be sure he'll deny anything that isn't righteous." Lucy's tone could have created icicles in July.

Judith faltered before finding her footing and striking back. "I wouldn't say that, Lucille. He did marry you after all." And then she was gone.

Frederick moved his arm to support Lucy around her back. He kissed her ear and held her close. "Ignore her."

"Can you see now what I tried to warn you about weeks ago?" Lucy clung to him, not caring who saw the display.

"Yes, Goosy, you were right. And next week her file gets passed to Mr. Peabody for managing all future concerns."

Lucy laughed over his choice—the first accountant hired by his father when the office opened more than two decades ago. "That will serve her right, though I pity Mr. Peabody."

It was easy to spot Douglas's red beard across the room. Frederick led them through the crowd toward the Campbells. Maggie was striking in blue and it made the captain's eyes brighter than ever. Douglas saw them approaching and smiled in greeting. Then Darla and the priest turned.

Father De Fiore took both Lucy's hands in his and kissed her cheeks. "I would know you anywhere, Lucy. You are even prettier than those sketches Eliza drew all those years ago. I sense your kind soul, and coupled with your beauty, I better understand Alexander's obsession with you."

"Father De Fi—"

"Claudio. I am Claudio to all those who knew me before the priesthood, and all those who are connected to those dearest of friends." He turned to Maggie and smiled. "Magdalene, is she not the perfect image of all that would do well for Alex? The greatest of matches."

Lucy startled at the Biblical name—so much more fitting for the woman than the nickname—and knew she would never think of Magdalene as Maggie again.

Douglas cleared his throat. "Claudio, this is Lucy's husband, Frederick Davenport." He motioned to him, for which Lucy was forever grateful because she couldn't find her voice.

Claudio laughed and bypassed the offered hand for a hug. "I mean no disrespect. It is only that I have heard of Lucy for years and she is ingrained with Alex in my head."

"Years?" Magdalene questioned.

Claudio turned to her as an usher arrived.

"Family and friends of Mr. De Fiore, please come this way."

"We'll see you later," Douglas said to the Davenports.

Lucy watched Claudio take Magdalene's arm and strained to hear his words. "Do not hate me, *posseduta*, but do you not remember when I said the bonds formed within Seacliff Cottage shall be stronger than the forces that tried to tear us down?"

"Yes," she said as they stepped away.

"I trust you not to be angry with me, but I think you will understand when …" his voice trailed out of range and anxiety loomed over Lucy.

"Shall we find our seats as well?" Frederick asked her.

Lucy nodded and held fast to his strong arm as he offered their tickets at the door. The Campbells, Beauchamps, and Claudio were front row center, but Frederick led Lucy to the third row on the side aisle seats. The orchestra warmed up, a sound Lucy always found invigorating and comforting at the same time. She watched Claudio and Magdalene whispering as the room filled. At one point, Magdalene stood and seemed to search the crowd, then she was back to the priest's side and turned anxiously to her husband—her expression fearful. The lights dimmed and Douglas took her hand, forcing her to sit.

Frederick set the program in his lap and looked to his wife. He fingered the beading that marked the neckline and crossed between her breasts, accentuating her further developing bosom.

"You look extraordinary tonight, my fair maiden," he whispered as he linked their hands together. "I'm glad we came."

"I love you, Freddy."

She kissed his cheek, thinking of what he'd whispered to her when she'd asked him to hold her while they heard the final part of Alex's story: *You brought me through childhood with wonder and magic. You gave me your first dance and your smile every time we were together. You allowed me someone to fantasize of throughout my boarding school and college years. You gave me the dream come true of marrying my first love. You gifted me my beautiful daughter. You give me a reason to come home from work every day. I love you.*

Lucy settled her head on Frederick's shoulder as the conductor came out. Applause for the conductor of The Battle House Orchestra was nothing compared to the onslaught of whistles, claps, and shouts when Valentino De Fiore took the stage.

As soon as the Tchaikovsky movement began, Lucy melted into a dreamland of romance and emotions. She kept her eyes closed until the solos. For those, she sat as captivated as the others in the audience while Valentino allowed the music to flow from every muscle of his body. He removed his tuxedo jacket after the first movement and a stage hand rushed to take it from him. Lucy began to understand the strength Darla possessed to withstand advances from such a charismatic individual. When he was between parts, he seemed to stare down at the front row where Darla and her cousin sat.

During the solo in the third movement, a young lady a few rows back fainted and had to be carried out. Afterward, Valentino and the orchestra received standing ovations. Several young women rushed to the stage and tossed roses at him. He posed and bowed for five minutes before leaving the stage. Then he returned to do it all again.

After the concert, Frederick stood in the aisle, watching for a break in the crowd. An usher approached them.

"Excuse me," the man said to Lucy. "Someone in the back wanted to know if it was possible for you to autograph this."

He handed her a copy of *Winter of My Heart* and she paled.

"I'm sorry, I think you must have her confused—" Frederick began.

A shadow fell over Lucy and she turned. Rupert, Kate, and Judith stood behind her, watching the exchange.

"No," the usher said, "the guest told me she would refuse, but to insist upon it."

Frederick's voice turned hard. "I'll not have you pester my wife. There is obviously a mistake."

Judith laughed. "Really, who would think Lucille had the talent of Olive Kent?"

Frederick glared at her, and while it warmed Lucy to see his irritation over the woman, she prayed he'd hold his tongue.

"No," Kate's cool voice said behind her, "it makes perfect sense now that I think of it. The book is a pathetic love cry for Alexander Melling, though the hero's family owns a respected architectural firm rather than a law office."

"Alex, an architect?" Rupert scoffed.

"His name was Samuel in the story, and Sam to those he was close to."

The usher scuffed his feet. "I'm sorry to cause a problem, I'll just—" He reached for the book but Lucy snatched it to her chest.

From her silk purse, she pulled a pen. Opening the book, she found it odd the binding felt loose though only a week old. Lucy boldly scribed *Olive Kent* in fluid cursive. She snapped the book shut and handed it to the usher.

"You may tell your benefactor that this has been my most costly autograph."

She reached a hand to Frederick, who helped her up. She embraced him with passion and, after kissing, she leaned to his ear. "I guess there's no point in me not going to New York now."

Lucy turned to the group behind her and managed a smirk. "I'm sure your cleverness in figuring out who I am will be the talk of the town, Kate. Enjoy your measly time in the spotlight. I've been enjoying my success for years."

With a huff, Kate grabbed Rupert's arm and they stalked out of the room, Judith following close behind.

Lucy's knees went weak and she sunk to the chair, grabbing Frederick's hand. "Where did the usher go? See if you can find out who he gave the book to."

Frederick hastened up the aisle in pursuit but returned minutes later with no information.

Twenty-Nine

After the concert, an usher escorted Darla, Claudio, the Campbells, and the Beauchamp family into a cozy reception room.

Aunt Ida came to speak with Claudio while her husband poured her a glass of champagne. "Father De Fiore, I expected Mrs. Melling here tonight. Is she unwell?"

"All is good for her." Claudio stepped closer. "She knew who my guests were and decided to wait until tomorrow's performance to attend this week's show."

Aunt Ida glanced toward the Campbells and gave a forced smile. "They are a lovely couple, but I understand they bring old memories to the surface."

"*Sí*, both good and bad, but it is wonderful for me to see them again." He looked over the Beauchamp children around the room. "I was in attendance at Alice's last instruction. She plays wonderfully."

"Thank you, we are proud of all she has accomplished."

Uncle Calvin arrived with drinks and passed glasses to his wife and Claudio.

"And your niece Darla is a gracious young woman. I am sure she is a credit to your family and is blessed you have taken her in."

Not wanting to overhear what her aunt might say to that, Darla crossed the room and joined Alice on a red settee.

Alice took her cousin's hands. "What shall I say to him when he comes in?"

"Tell him what an amazing job he did."

"He had to have seen the tears in my eyes."

"Don't worry about modesty in that regard. You can't over compliment Valentino."

Alice laughed. "I think you're right."

As soon as the discussion between Darla's aunt and Claudio broke up, Maggie pulled the priest into the far corner. They appeared in rapt conversation, as they were before the concert began. At that time, Maggie looked ready to dash across the concert hall, but now she looked defeated, worried.

"Excuse me, Alice, but I'll be back." Darla made her way to Maggie and Claudio.

When she passed the door, Valentino waltzed in and took Darla into his arms, spinning her around. "I was glorious, no?"

"Yes, Valentino. You were wonderful and I studied your every move. Now put me down, please."

He kissed her cheeks and leaned to her ear. "I only have eyes for you this night. Your dress is perfection." He set her down but kept his hands on her waist a moment longer, caressing her velvet sash.

Claudio rushed over and Valentino stepped away with a shrug. Alice was quick to fill the void and grew misty-eyed while explaining how the different movements aroused a myriad of emotions within her while her family gathered around.

Darla continued to Maggie and Douglas in the corner.

Maggie clutched her hands. "We have to find Lucy."

Douglas hugged his wife and Darla stood beside them uneasily while the Beauchamp family gave their regards to Valentino.

"Come along, Darla," Aunt Ida called to her a few minutes later.

Douglas crossed to Aunt Ida and Uncle Calvin. "Would it be all right if Darla stays with us a bit longer? I know Maggie would appreciate more time with her. We'll hire a cab and ride along to bring her home so she's never unchaperoned."

"Certainly, Captain Campbell." Uncle Calvin shook his hand. "It was a pleasure to meet you and your wife. I hope the remainder of your stay in Mobile is enjoyable. It was a splendid show. Splendid."

After they shuffled out, Valentino brought Darla a glass of champagne. He placed it in her hand without asking if she wanted it and took her elbow, steering her toward a settee for two.

"And now we are together without your dear little cousin."

"I thought you'd given up on me, that you were all about Alice now."

"Never, *amore mio*." Valentino lifted the hand from her lap and kissed the back of it. "My cousin reminded me that Alice is much too young so my passion for you is rekindled."

Darla rolled her eyes and pulled her hand free.

Claudio came to them. "I have to step out a moment Valentino, but I trust you will behave yourself. If not, Douglas will beat you in such a way you will not be able to play in tomorrow's concert."

Douglas raised an eyebrow and snarled like a mad dog.

Valentino shifted an inch away from Darla and grimaced. "I will behave."

After Claudio left, Douglas stood beside Valentino, causing him to leave to refill his champagne.

"Thank you," Darla whispered.

Douglas winked at her. "I have half a mind to go find that Henry of yours."

Valentino returned to his seat and placed his hand on her knee. Darla immediately brushed it off and was about to reply to Douglas that she wished he would find Henry when the door opened. Claudio entered, followed by a man in a gray suit and hat, clutching a copy of *Winter of My Heart* in his gloved hands. Darla recognized him as the man who'd opened the door across the hall from Valentino's room when Claudio left Thursday afternoon. In that brief second the day before she registered no details about him, but with him standing a few feet away, she saw the icy blue eyes under the shadow of his hat. They matched the blue of Lucy's book and Darla gasped.

Maggie bravely stood before the man for several seconds, he with a slight smile, she with a frown. Removing his hat, she exposed his dark blond hair and touched his unshaven cheek with her other hand.

Throwing her arms about his neck, Maggie clutched his hat behind him. "Thank God! And thank you for saving me that day. Though now that I know you're alive, I want to kill you for putting me through that!"

Alexander Melling's arm went around her and he kissed the top of her head. "It was the only way, Magdalene. I had to protect you, find justice for Eliza, and mend my broken relationship with Lucy. I needed to burn the path of my sins so I could start fresh without the shadow of my Melling name."

Maggie took a step away. "You smell the same, feel the same. But still, in all these years you couldn't—" She slapped his hat back on his head. "The anniversary bottle of Scotch!"

Alexander laughed. "And do you still only have a taste for—"

She punched him in the stomach and it was Douglas's turn to laugh. "It's clear to see Alex still gets you riled up."

Claudio smiled. "It has been difficult to keep the truth from you these years, but I made a promise and had to keep it."

Maggie stepped to the priest and punched him as well, though not nearly as hard.

Valentino laughed and raised his glass. "I like this woman. She does what I only dream of doing to Father De Fiore."

"That's because she's Methodist." Alexander's words caused the friends to laugh.

Douglas approached Alexander. "I for one am glad you disappeared, though you still visit Maggie in her dreams from time to time."

"Do I now?" His impish smile was charming and Darla saw a glimpse of the young man Lucy must have fallen for.

Douglas shook his head and chuckled. "Still the same Alex."

He turned serious. "I'm the one who was with you the final day at Seacliff. I haven't gone back to my old ways, but there's one thing that still haunts me. I hoped she'd be here because they played Tchaikovsky and Claudio confirmed my thoughts after speaking to Darla yesterday. It took all my restraint to keep from running to her when I saw her tonight."

"No!" All eyes turned to Darla as she stood. "It would break her! Maggie gave her a sense of peace this afternoon by telling her you were right with the Lord before you died. If you go to her now, she'll shatter. The stress on the baby, the—"

Alexander came to Darla. "You have no idea of the depth of my feelings for her."

"But I know the depth of her feelings for you! If you love her, if you respect Mr. Davenport, you'll stay away."

"I can't. I love her too much. And after reading the new book, I know she still loves me." He pulled the novel to his chest. "I sent roses to prepare her for my coming."

"It sent her into hysterics! Between the pregnancy, her obsession with you, and the book's release, she's been on the verge of a nervous breakdown. The stress could harm her, harm the baby. It isn't right for you to come to her now."

"I can no longer stay my love."

Darla stepped closer. "Mr. Davenport loves her. He's been caring for her all these years and been her constant. You need to leave her alone."

"You don't understand." Alexander laid his gloved hand on her shoulder.

She knocked it aside. "I understand plenty and know more than you think I do. If you go to her there will be no question what will happen. She loves you. She aches for you daily. She has a daughter she fantasizes is yours. If you go to her, she'll leave with you, *if* she lives through the emotional stress. Do you really want to be responsible for another murder?"

"Another—I must see her!" Alexander rushed out the door.

Darla lunged for the priest. "Claudio, stop him! He'll ruin their marriage completely! His memory has brought enough havoc on it already."

Thirty

While Frederick made tea, Lucy sat in the dark living room waiting for him to join her. Through the open window, a breeze fluttered the sheers, and a shadow from one of the ferns hanging on the front porch swung back and forth. Footsteps raced up the stairs, then hesitated. Curious, Lucy stood. Her bare feet crept toward the front door. A quiet knock, one she wouldn't have been able to hear unless nearby, tapped on the other side of the entrance.

Expecting it to be Darla, she turned on the foyer light and unlocked the door. Doff dashed out from behind her as soon as the entry was open.

The man on the porch removed his hat and held it next to a copy of *Winter of My Heart* in his gloved hand. "I understand my request for an autograph caused some trouble. I wanted to apologize for that, and for what I did to you five and a half years ago. Can you ever forgive me, my queen?"

Tentatively, she raised a hand to his face. He stepped onto the threshold and sighed as she fingered the burn marks under his shadow of a beard.

Her fingertips brushed his lips and she stared into his eyes as her knees weakened. "My angel, am I dreaming?"

Alexander entered the rest of the way, an invisible cloud of sandalwood surrounding him. He set his book and hat on the credenza and took her gently by the hand. "I'm truly here. I've thought of you always, but after reading this book I had to come. Your words recaptured my heart and soul as your poems did when we were so happy together. I love you more than ever."

His eyes shone clear and blue, a testament to his devotion as Lucy's heart raced with the reality of him before her. "And I'm not dreaming?"

Alexander's smile broke all doubt. "I'm with you again, my queen."

Lucy did what she always dreamt—she wrapped her arms about his neck and gave herself to him. His gloved hands roamed the back of her silk gown, slow and sinuous. He didn't take advantage of her opening mouth for several seconds, as though he wanted to reacquaint himself with her one step at a time. He tasted of mint and humility, which made Lucy crave more. Reflexively, her hand moved to the buttons of his gray jacket and his mouth traveled to her throat.

Behind Lucy, the tea tray clattered to the floor.

Alexander raised his head, his look of yearning fading to remorse. "I'm sorry, Freddy, but I couldn't stay away any longer."

"She's never fully been mine, but I didn't expect to lose her to a man that was supposedly dead." Frederick's voice thundered through the house as he approached. "Did you send the Campbells to trick me into false security with the tale of your death?"

Lucy clung to Alexander's arm, not wanting to lose him despite her husband's anger.

"They thought I died in the fire, but I escaped through the front door after Douglas carried Magdalene out the back. Only Claudio knew. He helped tend my burns and brought me to Louisiana with him so I could start a new life. But I couldn't run from my past. Lucy stayed in my heart all these years." He hugged her to his chest. "I've read all her books, but after *Winter of My Heart*, I had to come. You can't blame me for loving her."

Frederick's biceps strained against his white dress shirt as he yanked Alexander from his wife. "And you can't blame me for ending your life for good this time!"

"Freddy, no!"

Frederick gripped Alexander's neck. "Get away, Lucy!"

Alexander turned purple within the deadly grasp but Lucy couldn't over-power Frederick's athletic build. Tears ran down her face as she pounded on his arm. "If you hurt him, you're hurting me!"

"And how much have you hurt me, Lucy? How much damage have you caused my heart by your actions and misplaced affections? I can no longer attempt to protect you from yourself when you plainly have no care for how you treat me or our family. I'm willing for you to finally taste the pain you've given me all these years!"

The front door swung open, Douglas in the lead position. Quickly assessing the situation, he slammed into Frederick's side, causing him to release Alexander, who collapsed to the floor gasping for breath. Lucy dropped to her knees beside him.

Douglas had Frederick by the wrists, trying to calm him. "I know what it's like to see one's wife in Alexander's arms. Allow the veil of red to pass so you can focus on what's important."

"This is all my fault," Claudio said. "Allow me to make amends. I did not foresee Alexander rushing to your home."

Fredrick pushed out of Douglas's grip and charged for Claudio. "You're aiding in this adultery, priest! You've harbored him all these years and then you set him upon the city he forsook. Why don't you bring him to his mother and let her control him? Maybe her dislike for Lucy will be able to keep him away from *my wife!*"

Frederick's punch landed in Claudio's face and he stumbled back.

"Mr. Davenport!" Darla cried. "Think of Phoebe! Don't do something that would put you away from your daughter."

Lucy turned to Frederick as he staggered toward the living room.

"Don't you dare touch me after what you were doing with that monster!" Frederick pulled off his bowtie and threw it on the floor.

"He's changed, Freddy." Lucy advanced but Frederick retreated. "You've known I've loved him all this time and then I learned he was right with God and it gave me peace. Now he's here to give us another chance."

"A man right with God doesn't come to take another man's wife!"

Lucy stood against his accusations with her head high. "He didn't take me. I willingly placed my arms around him and initiated the kiss. I'd do it again if given the chance. You heard the names Opal called me that day and now you know them to be true. But it's not any worse than me fantasizing about Alex through four years of marriage. My sin might have been invisible to everyone else, but the Lord knows I've been with Alex in my heart and head at least half the times our bodies have been together."

Frederick's brown eyes held enough anguish to sink a ship. Regret tried to surface within Lucy's heart, but she knew her words were true and couldn't take them back. She wouldn't take them back. They were out there for everyone to hear and judge her by.

"I do love you Freddy, but I've always loved Alex more."

He pushed her to the side and struck his fist through the thick plaster wall beside her old typing desk. Alexander, back on his feet with Magdalene's arm linked through his and Claudio on the other side, was the next target. Frederick charged at him, but stopped a few feet away, clenched fists trembling for want of striking as blood seeped from his knuckles.

"I should have kicked you out of the hospital that day you came back for her! I should have told her brothers you'd had your way with her so they would have disposed of you then and there. But no, I was too worried about protecting Lucy's feelings! I wanted what would make her happy, and I knew how much she loved you. I knew her heart would break whether with or without you that day and allowed her the decision to accept you back. You don't deserve her and she's pathetic if she allows you back after what you did. But I'm the foolish one! I'm the one who stayed beside a woman who never fully loved me. Even Eliza warned me that year. She said I'd never have Lucy's passion because it belonged to you. I'm the ignorant fool who tried to create a family with her though she's set on tearing it apart!"

"Freddy, please," Lucy's voice cracked. She stepped toward him, a hand reaching out. "I've needed you these years. I'll need you still."

"I'm done trying to heal your pain. You can suffer like the wretch you've become for all I care, but you'll not receive an ounce of my sympathy. For all your self-righteous anger toward Mrs. Smith, you're no better than her in your actions. No, you're much worse!" Frederick ran up the stairs, slamming the bedroom door behind him.

Lucy's knees went weak but Darla caught her. With Douglas's help, they laid her on the sofa. Though awake, Lucy stayed in a half-stupor of shock and pain, aware of her surroundings but unable to communicate. She stared straight ahead at the coffee table while listening to the buzz around her.

"Maggie, can you prepare a chamomile tea?" Darla said as she placed one of the pillows between Lucy's knees. "Douglas, there's a sachet of lavender in the closet at the top left of the stairs. It's nestled in with the towels, please fetch it quickly. And Claudio, pray!"

"And what can I do?"

Just love me, Alex!

"Go back to the hotel," Darla said with a venomous tone.

"I'm not leaving unless I'm carried out feet first or Lucy's with me."

"That's not going to happen, Mr. Melling." Darla sounded old, bitter. "Mr. Davenport won't let her leave as long as she's carrying his child. He loves his children too much to turn either over to you."

"I didn't come to steal his family from him. I came to apologize to Lucy and see if she still felt for me as I feel for her. And she does."

"A mother is the heart of a family. You're tearing the Davenports apart by claiming Lucy."

"I'm not claiming," Alexander whispered. "I leave it all up to her."

"And a fine mess of it you've made." Darla knelt and touched Lucy's forehead and cheeks with her warm hands. "Are you cold, Lucy?"

"I feel nothing." Her words tumbled out like spilled marbles.

Douglas came back with the lavender. Darla tucked it under Lucy's nose and took her hands. "Can you squeeze my hands?"

Lucy had to focus to comply with the command.

"Good," Darla replied. "Can you do it tighter?"

Lucy's efforts took almost a minute before Darla had her stop. Then Darla slightly pressed on the swell of Lucy's belly in different locations through the evening gown.

"What are you doing to her?" Alexander came closer, but still out of Lucy's line of sight. "You'll hurt her."

"I'm a midwife and am checking for the response of the baby, so back off."

"How old are you?" Alexander's voice sounded concerned.

He loves and cares about me! He always has.

"Eighteen, but I've been training four years. Now shut it so I can listen."

"You remind me of my sister, though her passion wasn't helping young mothers."

"I'm sick of being compared to Eliza Melling. Now hush!" Darla took Lucy's pulse before settling back. "I think you're okay,

Lucy. Just a bit of shock. Lay there until your tea is ready. Do you need anything?"

"Alexander," she breathed.

Darla scoffed. "That's the last person you need."

"I've always needed Alex."

Darla looked sideways and shrugged. "It's your life, though I feel for Mr. Davenport and Phoebe." She went for a chair across the room.

"We need a few minutes of privacy."

Darla huffed. "Do you trust him, Captain?"

"Aye, come on. You too, Claudio. You can pray in the kitchen."

When they were gone, Alexander sat on the floor in front of Lucy. "I'm glad you're okay."

"Did you come for me like they say?"

"Only if you'll have me, my queen." He stroked her cheek and smiled.

"Why are you wearing gloves when you always despised them? I want to feel your skin on mine."

"I'm not the same man I was when you knew me. I've been through hell and back and have the scars to prove it."

With deliberate motion, she raised a hand to his stubbly cheek. She smiled, remembering the time she'd gone to their duplex when he didn't show up for Mass and found him in the middle of shaving.

"I can see the discoloration under your growth, but you're as handsome as ever to me, Alex."

"The hair never grows longer than this. I find it easier to leave it than shave daily and expose the damaged skin. But my face is the least of my disfigurements."

"The fire?"

"And the demons. Did Magdalene tell you about those? What I tried to do to her?"

"Some, but probably not all."

"She tried to spare your feelings, I'm sure. Magdalene's naïve, artistic ways reminded me of you and the demons capitalized on it. They wanted another virgin taken within the walls. What you and I shared was beautiful, but wrong." Alexander leaned forward and kissed her lightly on the lips. "It would have been even more special had I waited for you until our wedding night, but patience was never my strong suit. Can you forgive me?"

"Yes, Alex. Show me your wounds."

He pushed the coffee table out of the way and took off his jacket. "I'll not ask you if you want me until you see them all."

Underneath the gloves, his hands were mottled red and brown with his natural skin color, puckered with scarring from burns. He undid his cufflinks and rolled his sleeves. The discoloration reached his elbows.

"Bite marks from my father. That's what I had to endure to see him to the end."

"I always knew you were brave." She kissed the back of each hand.

"You and Magdalene always thought better of me than I did. Now from my time with Magdalene." He turned sideways when he slipped his shirt off so Lucy received the full effect of the unveiling at once. "That's where I tried to claw the demon from me rather than hurt her."

"Alex …" Lucy sat upright and trailed her fingers over the pinkish scars on his chest where he used to be smooth and perfect. "Freddy might say it's the skin you deserve but I think it's beautiful. It's symbolic of what you survived and now you're stronger than ever. Just as our love will be."

He stood and gently pulled her to her feet so he could fully hug her to him. Her fingers skimmed across his unmarred back and over his shoulders while he felt the silkiness of her pink gown around her hips and back, carefully avoiding the space supporting Frederick's baby. To compensate for the swell of her body, he shifted her slightly sideways.

Lucy kissed him and leaned to his ear. "Mark me. Mark me as yours." She tugged the beaded neckline aside, exposing the top of her left breast.

His eyes sparkled like the bay on a sunny day as the tears swelled. "My queen, I've missed you."

She clung to him as his lips found the tender spot and left a passion mark for the first time in over half a decade. But to Lucy it was like he never left. Alexander briefly nestled into her chest, and then raised his head to look into her eyes.

"You don't have to be afraid to touch me, my angel." She moved his hand to her belly. "My first and last shall be with you."

"Your first?"

She laid her cheek against the scars on his chest. "I wrote you a letter after seeing you at Edmund's wedding. I was going to send it while my parents were out of town so you would come to me, but the night before I was to send it I started having pains. I went to a clinic and they did what they could, but it was too late. Camellia Alexandra passed away before she had a chance at life."

Tears dampened both their faces. "I should have been there with you, Lucy. I was a fool for too long. I might have deserved punishment, but you didn't need to suffer like that."

Banishing the thought of their last day together and his hideous revelation about Twila, her hands circled around his back.

"I don't think there was anything anyone could have done for me then. I didn't even let Freddy near me for weeks. He didn't know about the pregnancy until last month. The secret grew too much to carry alone and I finally shared my grief. Alex, I've been suffocating.

I've been half empty, broken without you in my life. I need you to breathe, to feel alive."

Magdalene returned with Lucy's cup of tea. "Alex, her husband is upstairs!"

"I had to show her my scars before seeing if she'd accept me."

They relaxed their embrace and Magdalene eyed his hands and arms. "How did you get to Claudio when you were so injured?"

"My legs are fine. I walked through the woods all afternoon and came to him in the evening." He helped Lucy sit, then picked up his shirt.

She handed Lucy the cup. "That's much like what my father endured, though his burns encompassed his whole upper body. But your scratches look better than they did that year. May I touch them?"

"My body belongs to Lucy. Ask her."

Lucy gazed hopefully at Alexander before turning to Magdalene. "They were for your sake."

Magdalene traced the raised lines on his chest when Claudio joined them.

"I think Alexander will give Valentino a challenge at being the most desirable man in Mobile."

"That's not funny. If you hadn't already taken a few punches tonight, you'd be in trouble."

"Mighty Magdalene gives a mean strike," Claudio said as he fingered around his blackening eye, "but Frederick has you beat."

Darla and Douglas stopped to clean broken remnants of the tea tray.

"Let me finish cleaning so you can talk to Mr. Davenport," Darla told him. You're the only one who can come close to understanding."

He straightened. "I hardly know the man. What can I possibly say?"

"He's much like you. Honorable, good, patient—though he's been tested to the brink." Darla put her hand on the captain's arm. "Think of what might help you if you were in his position and guide him that way."

He nodded and went for the stairs.

"I appreciate what you're all trying to do, but if you need to leave—"

"No, Lucy." Magdalene sat beside her. "We'll not leave you with Alex and Frederick. It wouldn't be safe. We'll stay until a temporary solution is found, at the very least."

"But your aunt and uncle, Darla, they'll worry."

Darla didn't contradict Lucy's words as she continued to wipe the floor.

"We don't want to get you in trouble or not be allowed to have you out with us anymore." Magdalene looked to her friend.

"How can I possibly sleep?"

"You have to try," she said. "You don't want to have puffy eyes for your date with Henry, do you?"

"No, but may I stop over tomorrow and see if there is anything I can do?"

"Of course," Lucy said. "Thank you for all your help."

"And come for me if you experience any pains or—"

"We will, Darla."

When Claudio walked Darla next door, Alexander buttoned his shirt but left his sleeves rolled up and his gloves off. They all collectively held their breaths when footsteps came down the stairs.

Thirty-One

Frederick, stone faced, sat in the chair across from Lucy. His bandaged knuckles rested benign on his lap. "What is it you want from me?"

"A divorce." She hadn't thought farther than holding Alexander, but in the moment she knew what needed to be done. After saying the words, her path unfolded within her mind. "I can go live—"

"You're staying under this roof until my child is born. Phoebe was born here and the new one will be as well. You may have the guest room for yourself. I'll move your things tonight. That will help Phoebe transition to us being separated." He pointed to Alexander standing behind the sofa. "And that monster is to keep away from what is most precious. Lucy is under doctor's orders to abstain from sexual intimacies the duration of her pregnancy and I'll not have you defile her while my child rests within."

A tear slipped down her face. "Freddy, you're being too harsh! I would nev—"

"I have no trust for what either of you are capable of doing, nor what vile diseases he might have from his times in whorehouses. I'm making myself clear in front of these witnesses." He stared down Douglas, Magdalene, and Claudio in turn. "If Alex attempts to join himself with Lucy before the baby is born, I'll not be held accountable for the fury it unleashes in me."

"Frederick," Alexander said, "I give you my word that I won't go that route. I would never go against the doctor's orders for anything that could harm her."

He scoffed. "Then it's Lucy I should be worried about disobeying the doctor. She never did follow the guidelines given to her after Opal's attack."

"You're being too cruel." Lucy choked on a sob.

"I'm being realistic. It's not my fault you've lived in half a fantasy these years. I'm done protecting you. I'll do all I can to protect my children, but you're on your own."

Alexander's hand went to Lucy's shoulder. "She has me."

"I'll still buy my parents' house after the baby is born and move into it after the first of the year. I'm sure they'd have me sooner if you want to be rid of me."

"You're staying with me. If something were to happen, this house is closer to the hospital. The doctor is used to making house calls here and Darla's next door. You have to stay. There's no other option. Do you understand?"

Lucy nodded.

"And if you think I'll allow you custody of my children, you're sorely mistaken." Frederick stood. "I'll move your maternity clothes and toiletries to the other room so you can get some rest."

"Please, Frederick, allow Douglas and I to help," Magdalene said as she stood. "Claudio can chaperone down here."

The three climbed the stairs and Alexander took a seat beside Lucy. "I must tell you something in regards to what Freddy brought up. If you change your mind, I'll not blame you."

"Alex, you can tell me anything, just let me love you." She kissed him and took his hands into hers, not shying away from the texture of the scarring.

"When Claudio and I left Daphne after the fire, we stopped in Mobile. My face and arms were bandaged and needing care several times a day. I sent Claudio on errands and waited at the train station. He visited my mother and while there, I had him take a check from my banking papers and my stash of money from my room, as well as my sketches of you that Eliza did and your poems, which I kept in that poetry book you left behind when you moved out of the duplex."

"Do you still have it? Would it be terrible of me to ask for it back?"

"I'll bring it to you when I return." He kissed her cheek. "I predated a check for Claudio and had him go to the bank to cash it, saying it was a present to celebrate him receiving the priesthood, and he wasn't sure if it was in good form to cash it or not since I had passed. The bank, knowing my family and seeing a priest before them, cashed the five hundred dollars. That and the money he secured from my room was enough for me to live on until I could get myself settled in Louisiana." Alexander squeezed Lucy's hand. "But I didn't want Claudio to feel obligated to come help me morning and night with my bandages. I sent him to find Consuela."

"Alex …" Tears fell down her face while Claudio watched in silence.

"My intensions were good that time. I'll admit that after you left me, I visited the district to try to find solace, but gave up when it made me miss you more and compounded my guilt. After the fire, I was reborn. I wanted to help someone else out of hell, so I offered Consuela to come with me. I paid for her travel and a second room in Monroe. In return, she tended my wounds for her boarding. I planned to ask her to marry me once I recovered and had a job, figuring it would be comforting to have someone who knew me by my side. Two weeks later, I knocked on her door to see if she wanted to go for an afternoon walk and she had a paying man with her."

"How awful, and after what you did for her."

"It helped me understand why I couldn't change just because you loved me. I changed after your time in the hospital because it scared me into wanting to, but as soon as my old temptations were there the night Eddie kidnapped me, I grabbed for the familiar comforts of alcohol. It wasn't until I saw how vile my father truly was that I was able to put preventing myself from becoming like him to the forefront of my life choices. Lucy," he whispered as he played his hands over hers, "since the fire I've not had any alcohol nor have I been with anyone. I've been inspected by doctors and screened for diseases and I'm miraculously spared from the ailments men like myself often find themselves struck with. I'm not perfect, but these four years I've been as saintly as possible, all in preparation of hoping to one day be worthy of you."

Lucy covered his face with kisses and wrapped her arms around his neck. "Thank you for telling me. Has she come to bother you since then?"

"She did at first, trying to get money, but she stopped after a while. You needn't worry about her coming around anymore. She died last year from complications with syphilis. Now you know why Freddy was so adamant about me keeping away from you until after the baby is born. I don't expect him to listen to my tale or understand that I know I'm not infected because my lifestyle was unsavory."

"I understand, but what have you been doing for work?"

"I used the name Alex M. Randolph and took the Louisiana State Bar in the first quarter of 1907. I passed and got in with a small firm. I take the undesirable cases, the ones that are easily settled out of court and the clients who can't afford to pay well. Most of the time, I'm more legal consultant than lawyer, but it suits me. I've made a humble living, enough to rent a small apartment, purchase new releases from Olive Kent, and take the train to track down my first and last love affair."

He kissed her on the cheek and held her closer. "But I'm sure my mother would be mortified by my cheap suits and Eliza is probably rolling over in her grave at some of my color choices. I proved to myself I didn't need the Melling name or the cushion of money to have a decent life. Decent, but not satisfying. Satisfaction only comes when I'm with you."

They melted together in a wash of salty kisses.

After a minute, Claudio cleared his throat. "I must ask you both to stop. It is getting to be too much to tempt fate. While she is yet married, you need to restrain yourselves. We do not want a repeat of Seacliff Cottage."

Alexander placed his arm around Lucy's shoulders and she curled against his side. "Let me ask you as a friend, Claudio. Do you not see how well we fit together? How perfect she is for me?"

"*Sí*, and it is wonderful to see you joyous. But as a priest, it shouts against all reason. I want to cringe at seeing you touch another man's wife and pity the Father on the other side of the confessional when you attend."

Alexander's laughter vibrated Lucy's soul with a lust for life she hadn't felt in years.

Magdalene returned. "I'm going to help you ready for bed, Lucy. Frederick wants someone with you in case you weaken."

Alexander helped her stand and they kissed. "We'll figure the rest out tomorrow, my queen."

When Lucy turned toward the hall, Frederick stood in the doorway. She wanted to hug him, to tell him how sorry she was, but she knew it was too soon. Instead, she allowed Magdalene to escort her upstairs.

Once she was washed and ready for bed, Lucy laid in the double bed, feeling the great empty space around her in the unfamiliar room. Since marriage, she'd never slept without Frederick and the reality of being alone in a new room set her heart racing. She cracked the window, then lay back and strained to hear any conversations or fights that might be happening downstairs.

Nothing.

Quiet for five, ten minutes, more.

Then Frederick stepped into the doorway, backlit by the hall light. Lucy clutched the blankets to her chest.

"They're returning tomorrow afternoon. That will give us time to collect Phoebe and let your parents know what's happening without rushing in the morning. Sleep as long as you can."

She rolled to her side. "Thank you."

"Let me get you an extra pillow."

He brought the pillow from her side of the bed and tucked it to support her knees and back.

"I said some harsh things tonight, but please know that I don't want you to suffer. I don't hate you. I hate what your relationship with Alex did to you—to us."

"I'm sorry you're pained, Freddy. I'll always love you."

***

Lucy's sleep wasn't as troubled as she expected, but she woke disoriented several times when she needed to use the bathroom. At eight, she dressed in a red tea gown she retrieved from the closet in the master bedroom. It's wasn't one of her maternity pieces, but the waist hit above her belly and the loose fabric tented her abdomen without being tight. She wanted to wear Alexander's favorite color and it was the only thing that fit. After the baby was born and she was ready to shop, she'd buy several red dresses because her closet was mostly pastels. Frederick was subtle but Alexander made her bold.

She walked the length of the downstairs on her way to the kitchen. A tightening in her chest stopped her short when she entered the room. She expected to see Frederick drinking coffee and reading the paper or doing his Saturday morning pancake baking though Phoebe wasn't home.

There was no one.

Overwhelmed with numbing fear, she sat at the little table and stared out the back window.

Half an hour later, the sound of someone coming in the front registered in her foggy brain. Then Frederick pushed through the kitchen door holding a paper bag.

"Goosy, are you all right? You look pale."

Lucy stared at him. His hair was damp and his tweed sport-coat was unbuttoned. "I thought you left me."

"I told you last night I don't wish you to suffer." He put the bag on the table and laid a hand on her belly, his handsome face tight. "I'll see things through with you, as much for my love for you as for our children. I didn't sleep much and got up at five-thirty. I went to the gym for a couple hours, then stopped at the bakery to bring us breakfast. I heard you up several times in the night and figured you'd sleep long after I returned. I'll leave a note next time."

She brought his hand to her lips and kissed it. "You're kinder than I deserve."

Frederick brewed coffee and brought plates to the table. "I'll do my best to be polite, but there are some things I won't stand for, especially in my house."

"You've always been kind to me and I wish to repay that. If we could be friends that would be wonderful."

"And once again, you ask too much of me."

"I'm sorry, but in my mind you're this giant of compassion and service, heroic in your ability to help and heal. I forget that you have feelings and needs because you've been so selfless in seeing to mine."

"I don't want Phoebe caught in the middle, nor do I want her to witness you being intimate with Alex before everything is finalized. I told him before he left and I'll tell you now, you may be friends when Phoebe is around, but nothing more until you move out."

"You'll allow Alex to visit me?"

Frederick brought their coffee to the table. "As long as there's another adult here, but he stays on the first floor."

"You're being much fairer than I expected. After all you said last night, I feared living under lock and key, though I had trouble envisioning you as a tyrant."

"I spoke out of anger and pain, but you needn't expect that as the norm." He placed a pastry on each of their plates and stared at her with disdain. "I hope you know what you're doing. Just as you said yesterday, your sin with Alex before marriage affected more than just the two of you. Your choice to end our marriage affects more than just us. The ripples could be felt for generations, in all our families."

"I know, but I have to try, Freddy. I've been dreaming of life with Alex for six years. I'd be more lost to you now if I stayed with you after holding him again. I need to be true to my heart."

Frederick offered no conversation while they ate. Afterward, he called the Eastons and let them know they wanted to get Phoebe before noon. He stopped by the study and looked in at Lucy hunched over her journal. "We need to leave at a quarter to eleven. We're taking a luncheon with your parents before coming back."

"What time—"

"The others won't be here until two o'clock." He nodded to the candlestick-style telephone on the desk. "I'm glad it worked out well for you."

"It's a great convenience to have it within reach while I'm working." She rushed to him and threw her arms around him before he could block her. "I'm sure I'll appreciate all that you do even more these final weeks. I do love you."

"I love you too, but it's clear who was on your mind when you dressed today. He's a fool if he doesn't realize what he has in you."

A curving smile found her lips. "I'm sure he does. He went to hell and back to return for me."

***

At the Easton's home, Phoebe rushed out the front door when Frederick and Lucy walked across the lawn from their automobile.

"Daddy!"

Frederick swung Phoebe around and sat her on his shoulders. "Let's go play in the gazebo for a few minutes, Princess. You can tell me all about your adventure with Nana and Papa."

Lucy knew he cleared the way for her to talk with her parents, though she would have preferred to do it right before they left rather than first off. She met her father in the foyer. After a hug and a peck on the cheek, he led her into the parlor.

"Why Lucy, I haven't seen you in red in ages! And your hair's down. You look like you did when you were around the house all day typing and Alex—"

"He's alive, Mother! And he's here in town, right now!" She couldn't help the smile that shone across her face.

Mrs. Easton's hand went to her heart. "Whatever do you mean?"

"Alexander Melling! He made it look like he died in the fire, but he was only injured. He moved to Louisiana to start fresh, to get out from his controlling family and prove to himself he could lead a decent life. After reading *Winter of My Heart*, he couldn't stay away any longer and came to me last night after the concert. We both still love each other more than anything in the world."

"What does all this mean?" her father asked. "And what of Freddy?"

Her smile faded. "Naturally, he's upset and worried, but you know how he is. He's willing to stand by my choice for a divorce and—"

"Lucille Amelia Easton Davenport!" Mrs. Easton stood, her face the color of Lucy's dress. "That fine man has been nothing but good to you and you're willing to toss him aside—the father of your children—because a man claiming to be Alexander strolls into town after all these years?"

"It *is* Alex, and I feel as if I'm finally whole. I've been broken since we parted ways but now I'm complete, or will be once things are finalized. But being in his arms is peaceful enough."

Mrs. Easton openly cried and Mr. Easton took a shot of whiskey when Frederick and Phoebe entered.

Mr. Easton stopped him and took his hand. "You'll always be a son to me, Freddy."

"Thank you, Mr. E."

"But this can't be!" Mrs. Easton cried out. "Of all the scandals, this is the worst! But to think of what would have happened if you hadn't left the church, and then tried to seek div—"

She stared down at her granddaughter.

"What wrong, Nana?" Phoebe asked.

Mrs. Easton sat back in her chair and opened her arms to the girl. "Nana's worried, but don't fret over me, Phoebe."

Mr. Easton put an arm around Frederick's shoulder and brought him out of the room. Lucy paced in front of the unlit fireplace while she waited for their return. When they came back, it was only to inform the ladies that dinner was on the table.

Frederick offered his arm to Lucy and leaned to her ear. "Your father will calm your mother. I told him you still want to buy the house after the first of the year, and he was pleased."

They ate a silent meal except for Phoebe's chatter, with Mrs. Easton giving Lucy cutting looks and handing Frederick pitying glances.

"Is your bag in the bedroom?" Lucy asked Phoebe when she was done eating.

"Yes, Momma. And Pinky's carriage."

Frederick stood and glanced at Lucy. "I'll fetch them and meet you on the porch."

"Freddy, you're too compassionate," Mrs. Easton said.

He shook his head. "You should have seen me last night. I'm afraid there's a hole in the living room wall I need to call about for repairs."

Mrs. Easton clutched her napkin to her chest. "My stars!" Then turning to Lucy, she added, "I hope you're proud of yourself, Lucille."

"They don't need pestering, dear," Mr. Easton told his wife. "They need kindness and support through this transition. We always knew Lucy was a free spirit. There's nothing we can say or do to change her mind."

Thirty-Two

Darla spent the morning reading, listening to Alice practice, and peeking out the windows toward the Davenports' house. The automobile was gone when she woke up, but then it was back before it left later in the morning. Thinking Lucy might be alone, she hurried next door at eleven, but no one answered her knock.

As the Beauchamp family left the dinner table, Alice immediately excused herself to visit Sadie—probably so she wouldn't have to see Henry arrive for Darla.

Aunt Ida stopped Darla. "Wear your yellow wool dress for your outing. And be sure you return by seven for supper."

"Yes, Aunt Ida."

She wouldn't have picked the yellow dress herself, but she was thankful her aunt chose it at the store and suggested it for her outing. The square neckline of the dress balanced her body well and it would be nice to feel the sun on her skin with the elbow length sleeves. Darla slid on a new pair of brown, low-heeled walking shoes then turned her attention to her hair. Once it was secured, she took her purse and headed for the stairs. She stopped in the parlor for Aunt Ida's approval.

"That looks nice, dear. I hope you enjoy your time."

"Thank you for the suggestion."

The doorbell rang and Darla looked at her aunt with wide-eyes.

"He's a few minutes early, but answer the door and bring him in. I'm sure Calvin heard and will meet you for a proper send off."

As she went to the door, she heard Felix snickering at the top of the stairs. She shook her fist at him, but smiled.

"Good afternoon, Darla." Henry held a fedora at his side.

"Hello, Henry. You look sharp in blue. Come in and say hello to my aunt and uncle."

"That's a nice dress you've got yourself," he said as he followed her down the hall. "I'm glad we have a sunny day to go about."

Uncle Calvin stood imposingly before the hearth but Henry wasn't shy.

"Good afternoon, Mr. and Mrs. Beauchamp. I appreciate you allowing me to bring Darla to a show this afternoon."

"No trouble at all, Henry. I checked with Mr. Davenport the other day and was pleased to hear he thinks highly of you. I'm sure you'll treat our niece with the utmost respect and have her home in time for supper."

"Yes, sir."

"All right then, I see no need to keep you two when you'd like to be on your way." He shook hands with Henry.

"We'll see you later," Darla said on their way out. As soon as they were on the sidewalk, she turned to Henry. "How much time do we have before the show?"

"Over an hour."

"Could we stop at the Davenports a few minutes? I'd like to check on them. There was quite the trouble after the orchestra last night."

"They seemed fine when I saw them before the concert. What happened?"

"A ghost from the past turned their world upside down." She ran up the Davenports' steps and knocked on the door.

Mr. Davenport opened it. "Hello, Darla. Henry. I'd forgotten you two were going out this afternoon."

"I just wanted to check on Lucy before we go. Was she able to sleep?"

"Better than me and she has no complaints today."

"Miss Darla and Mr. Henry!" Phoebe ran toward the porch.

"Sorry, my manners are off today. Would you like to come in?"

"Yes, we have a few minutes. Thank you, Mr. Davenport." Darla took Phoebe's hand and allowed the girl to lead her into the front room.

"Momma has friends coming."

Lucy sat on the sofa in a red lace tea gown—the most vibrant thing Darla had ever seen her in. Her smile was enchanting and her spirit glowed with bliss. Darla turned nauseous for the pain it must cause Mr. Davenport to see such joy on his wife's face for another man.

"Darla and Henry! You both look nice for your afternoon out. I hope you enjoy the Vaudeville show."

"Thank you, Mrs. Davenport. I've heard good things about it and I'm glad Darla is able to accompany me. You look well yourself."

"There's no need for Darla to worry over me. I feel wonderful. Everyone is coming over. They'll be here any minute if you two would like to stay and greet them."

"Everyone?" Darla asked.

"Yes, though I don't think Claudio can stay long. He has to meet Mrs. Melling for an early supper before the concert. He's lucky to see his cousin play two nights in a row."

"We don't want to intrude." Darla glanced at Henry helping Phoebe with a block tower in the corner.

"Stay, Darla," Lucy whispered. "Everything's fine now. I'm moved into the guest room and staying until I've recuperated after the baby is born. Frederick is going to talk to his lawyer Monday to get the divorce process started. I'm sure he'll talk to Dean Sachs at church tomorrow as well."

"Lucy, are you sure this is what's best? It's all so sudden."

"I've never been more sure of anything in my life. My heart's been growing toward Alex for months. It's the right thing for me, even if my mother hates me right now."

"Was it that bad?"

She nodded. "Freddy had me tell them when we picked up Phoebe."

"Mr. Davenport," Henry called when he walked by the room, "what happened to the wall?"

"I punched it last night," he said it matter-of-factly.

"You didn't tell him?" Lucy whispered.

Darla shook her head.

"Go ahead and tell him. Freddy and I have already talked it over and he's going to keep our Wednesday lunches until the baby comes, but he'll probably take lunch out the other days." Sadness crept into her eyes, but then a knock at the door echoed through the room and her smile was back.

Mr. Davenport came from the back hall and let the group in. Maggie and Douglas, followed by Claudio—sporting a black eye—and Alexander, filed into the living room.

Maggie stuck her hands on her hips. "Why are you two here instead at the show?"

"I stopped in to check on Lucy," Darla said as she stood, "but we're going now."

"Does everyone know each other?" Mr. Davenport asked.

The Campbells and Claudio nodded.

"No," Alexander said, "I was never properly introduced to Darla, though I did upset her several times. And I've not met the young man or the little angel in the corner."

"Oh," Maggie said, "we haven't met her either."

"Alexander, this is Darla Beauchamp, our mother's helper. She grew up on the island and is good friends with the Campbells. And this is Henry Adams. He's interning at my office this season to complete his accounting certificate."

Mr. Davenport walked to Phoebe's play corner and offered his hand. She clutched his thumb and walked to the center of the room with her father. "And this is our Phoebe. Can you say hello to Momma's friends, Princess?"

She curtsied. "Good afternoon. And Doff!" Phoebe pulled the tabby out from his spot behind the chair. "Doff is wizard!"

Maggie sat on the rug next to Phoebe and looked to Douglas. "Can we arrange a marriage between her and Kade? They'd be the cutest couple ever!"

Douglas laughed and stroked his beard. "Give it time, Maggie. Bring 'em around in another fifteen years and see what happens."

Alexander sat beside Lucy and took a hand into his. "She's beautiful, and that mop of blonde hair is adorable."

"Lucy's was like that until it grew down her back." Mr. Davenport smiled. "I remember Eddie throwing twigs to see if they'd stick because her hair was so poufy."

Alexander laughed. "He was always a rascal."

"Yes," Mr. Davenport said, "but I chased him away."

"Always my protector." Lucy's voice cracked at the end.

Phoebe passed Doff to Maggie after introducing the cat. She then shook hands with Douglas and Claudio, who wore huge smiles as they greeted her. Crawling into Lucy's crowded lap, she looked to Alexander with her blue-green eyes. Seeing the three of them on the sofa together gave good reason for what reality Lucy's fantasy was grounded on. Based on looks, Alexander Melling could claim Phoebe as his own without question.

"And who are you?" the girl asked.

"I'm Alex. I used to be friends with your Uncle Eddie and your parents. I've lived far away for years, but I'm moving back to Mobile soon. What's your name?"

"Phoebe Camellia Davenport. I this many." She held up three fingers.

Alexander's smile was as radiant as Lucy's. "Camellias are my favorite flowers. They bring beauty to bleak winter and remind me of your mother." He dropped his voice and leaned toward Phoebe. "One time at a party, I put a white camellia behind your mother's ear and she wore it like jewelry until her big brother threw it away."

"Right there?" She touched above her mother's ear.

"Exactly so, Phoebe. Don't you think that'd be pretty?"

"Yes!"

"Should we do it again this winter?"

"Yes!" She slipped off her perch and danced around the room.

Darla looked to Mr. Davenport. He gazed from his daughter back to the two on the sofa, fresh pain in his eyes that had her wanting to punch a second hole in the wall.

Henry came to her side. "Are you ready to go?"

She clutched his arm. "Yes, get me out of here."

He cleared his throat. "It was nice to see you all, but we need to be on our way."

"Stop in when you get back if you have time," Lucy said.

Mr. Davenport walked them to the door. "Thank you for your concern, Darla, but you can see she's quite well and happy."

"I'm most sorry for you, Mr. Davenport, and Phoebe. I tried to talk sense into that man once I found out who he was, but he was set on coming here."

"At least he has a way with Phoebe. She doesn't usually take to strangers. That will make things a little easier."

"I'll be home by supper if you need to send for me."

"You go enjoy yourselves." He looked to Henry. "Don't let her fret over us."

As soon as they were around the corner, Henry stopped in the shade of an oak and took her hands into his. "What was that all about?"

"Alexander Melling, Lucy's old fiancé thought to have died more than four years ago."

"Related to *the* Mellings?"

"Ruth Melling is his mother. He faked his death to get away and start a new life, but his love for Lucy brought him back. Being a romantic dreamer, Lucy is going to divorce Mr. Davenport so she can be with her first love."

"No wonder he punched the wall!"

"I thought he was going to kill someone last night. At least he's settled down today, even though he's pained."

"I don't blame him. He's been completely devoted to her. Some of the women that come into the office are shameless in their flirting, but he brushes them off without a hint of interest. He's a fine gentleman and I envied their marriage, but I guess that proves that not all things are what they seem."

"And poor Phoebe, what will happen to her when Lucy moves out?"

"I'm under orders not to let you fret." His hands moved to her bare forearms, then to her shoulders as he leaned in. "Forget the Davenports' drama for the afternoon and focus on our first official step in courtship."

"I'm sure I'll be able to forget once we get to Lyric Theater and the show begins."

"That's not soon enough." His fingers took her chin and he gazed down at her, his indigo eyes shining with depth. "I've wanted to do this for weeks, Darla. May I?"

She nodded. Henry's lips were warm and soft and it was over much too soon for Darla's preference, but his smile afterward made it all the better.

Thirty-Three

Frederick took Phoebe upstairs for a nap after Darla and Henry left. Once her family was out of the room, Lucy removed Alexander's gloves. He traced her jawline as she shifted toward him and he knelt on the sofa, leaning over her.

"Forgive me." Alexander's words echoed in the room like a voice of warning.

"Alex—" He cut Lucy's whisper with a tender kiss that turned to craving three seconds later. Her hands went around his waist, tugging him closer as their kiss deepened.

Then Douglas had Alexander by the collar and pulled him out of her reach. "Some things never change."

Alexander gazed at Lucy and licked his lips before turning to Claudio. "Am I forgiven, Father De Fiore?"

The priest smirked. "You have not an ounce of regret on your countenance."

"Then allow me to indulge once more." He took Lucy's hands and helped her stand. "The queen of my heart."

She fell into him and his arm went around her, one hand stroking the length of her hair, the other low on her back.

"I've missed the sight of your curving smile, the lavender scent that clings to your skin, the sweet taste of your lips, your silky hair, your warm body in my arms, your cool touch, and the silvery sound of your laughter. Lucy, you'll always be my everything and I pray I'm now worthy of your trust. Will you marry me when the time comes?"

"Yes, Alexander, you know I will." She wanted to cleave to him and feel his hands and lips all over her body, but instead snuggled against his slim chest.

"May God strike me down if I'm dreaming," Naomi said when she walked in with the tea tray. "This ain't proper with Miss Lucy already married, but y'all look like no time at all has passed."

She slid the tray onto the coffee table and Lucy and Alexander stepped apart.

"I told Lucy during our time together you understood us better than anyone." Alexander hugged Naomi, her face registering more surprise over the action than walking in on their embrace. "We talked of hiring you for our home. I'm glad she kept you with her these years."

"I do what I can for Miss Lucy and Mr. Frederick." She straightened and stepped away. "It sure is good to see the light back in her eyes. I'll return with the food in a moment so you best keep your hands off her."

A sob sounded across the room. All eyes turned to Magdalene, freely crying into a handkerchief. Claudio hurried to her side.

"I can't help it!" She clung to Claudio. "Why did life have to happen this way?"

Frederick returned and went for the Campbells. "I don't need your sympathy, though I appreciate the depth of your feelings. What I need is friendship, a listening ear, and advice from time to time." He placed a hand on Douglas's shoulder. "You two and Claudio, though mere strangers to me yesterday, are as close to this situation as anyone. You know the backstory and Alex's disposition. I'll deal with what the world flings our way with little interest, but if those closest to us find fault, we need to hear their concerns."

"You're being more level-headed than I would be with the situation," Douglas said.

Frederick turned to Lucy and Alexander with a look of resignation. "Come on, Goosy." He took her elbow and helped her to the middle spot on the sofa. "Alex, take the other end."

Lucy kissed Frederick's hand when he sat beside her. "Thank you."

"You know my pride. The sooner I accept the situation and stop fighting to hold my ground, the better off I'll be in the long-run. And, more importantly, the better things will be for the children." He laid a hand on her belly and the baby within somersaulted.

"Daddy's touch." Lucy smiled at Frederick.

Douglas laughed. "I used to keep Maggie up at night, playing with the babies like that. There's no wonder in the world that compares." He kissed Magdalene's cheek. "It was worth the scolding you'd give me for the bruising Kade gave your ribs his final month. At least Tabitha was gentler."

"Only slightly, but I always welcome your touch."

Naomi returned with the refreshments and insisted on pouring the tea so Lucy wouldn't need to lean over the low table. "And who all is staying for supper?" she asked as she handed a cup to Magdalene.

"All of them are welcome to," Frederick said. "It's a bit of an open house here this afternoon."

"I have previous arrangements," Claudio said, "but thank you for the offer."

Lucy looked to Magdalene with a smile and nod.

"Douglas and I accept."

"And I do as well. Thank you, Freddy. You're most generous." Alexander placed his hand on Lucy's knee. "I think there will be plenty to talk about."

A knock pounded on the front door and Naomi went to answer it, but Frederick stopped her. "I've got it."

When the door opened, Edmund's voice thundered down the hall. "Where's my crazy sister?"

"I believe she's locked in an asylum."

"I'm not joking, Freddy. What's this story that has Mother crying about a divorce because Lucy still loves Alex?"

"That about sums it up, but come in. We have company and just sat down with tea."

"I need something harder than tea to—" Edmund stared at Alexander. "Unbelievable! Were you too vile to merit a stay in Hell, Melling? By God, you look changed."

Edmund seemed to take in the details of Alexander's scarred hands before shaking his head and turning to Frederick. "Where's his black eye, busted nose, broken bones?"

Alexander stood and pulled aside his collar, exposing the bruising on his neck.

Frederick motioned to the hole in the wall. "I also hit through that and punched the priest. Is that enough violence to satisfy you?"

Edmund smirked and looked over the visitors. "What's this, Lucy? Are you playing at another Wonderland tea party?"

She glared at her brother. "What can you possibly accomplish by coming in here with that attitude?"

"I'm here to get answers for Mother. If her health declines, it'll be your fault!"

"She's pushing sixty and it would be called nature. I was just with her a few hours ago and she could have asked more questions or telephoned me herself."

"She's in bed with one of her sick headaches."

"That's not my fault. She's had those as long as I remember."

"But they increased when you started going with him." Edmund pointed at Alexander.

Lucy looked to the Campbells and Claudio across from her. "Meet my youngest big brother, Edmund Easton. Isn't he pleasant company?"

He laughed and bowed. "It's good to know Lucy has friends. I thought they'd all forsaken her."

"That's quite enough, Eddie." Frederick gripped his arm. "I think you need to leave."

"You're going to kick me out and let that wretch fawn all over your wife?" he roared.

"I've come to understand Lucy's always belonged to Alex. I've just been keeping her safe until he came for her."

"Then you're crazier than she is and you deserve everything you're going through!" Edmund shook free from Frederick's grip and took a swing at Alexander, who easily ducked the punch. "You poisoned her and turned her into your whore!"

Frederick tackled Edmund to the hall floor.

Lucy scrambled to her feet. "No, Freddy!"

He stood and Edmund sat upright, showcasing a split lip.

"You're not to insult Lucy, ever." Frederick glared at him. "Even when we're no longer married, she'll always be the mother of my children, and I won't stand for it. Now get out of my house!"

Edmund slammed the door when he left.

Lucy rushed to Frederick, hugging him. "You can't fight everyone that speaks ill of me—there won't be enough hours in the day."

"Family needs to understand where the limits are." He escorted her back to the sofa. "There's no excuse for him to call you names. It makes him no better than Opal when he acts that way."

"How is Opal doing?" Alexander asked as he returned to his seat beside Lucy.

"She made some improvements the first year, but when they changed her schedule to allow more freedoms and activities, she regressed. Mother and Father go up for a long weekend every month to visit, but she typically refuses to talk with them about family members, even when they want to talk about her nieces and nephews."

"She's sixteen now?"

She nodded then rested her head on Alexander's shoulder.

"Opal is Lucy's youngest sibling," Frederick told the Campbells and Claudio. "She had a nervous breakdown when she was ten. Lucy was in the hospital several days after the attack and Opal's been in an asylum ever since."

Alex fingered the back of Lucy's head to feel the old wound before clasping her hand in his. "We both have our scars."

***

By the time Phoebe woke from her nap, Claudio needed to leave.

"Why don't we ladies escort you back to the hotel?" Magdalene offered, holding a hand out to Phoebe. "It's a lovely afternoon for a walk and if we get too tired we can easily hire a driver through the concierge to bring us back."

"A walk with Momma!" Phoebe bounced on her toes. "Can we get ice cream like Daddy does?"

Frederick laughed. "You'll have to now, Goosy. There's no turning down that excitement."

"One day it's ice cream, the next day it will be a pony," Lucy said with a smile. "All right, let me go change."

"But why?" Magdalene asked. "You look lovely."

"I haven't been out of the house in red since …"

"Since I was last around?" Alexander raised his eyebrows.

She nodded. "I typically dress to blend in, not stand out."

"But thanks to Alex's autograph scheme after the concert," Frederick said, "I'm sure word has gotten out about Olive Kent, and she'd wear red."

"I told the usher not to bother you if there were other people around."

Frederick crossed his arms. "I hope you didn't tip him because Rupert and Kate Lyons were standing right behind us."

Alexander reached for her hands. "I'm sorry, Lucy. I know privacy is important to you. I'll find him when I return to the hotel and—"

"Leave him be," Lucy said. "He didn't know what a keen hunter Kate is for gossip. They were probably leaving and stopped to listen when they saw us approached. It was bound to come out sooner or later."

"I read in the paper those two got married. They're perfect for each other in the worst possible way. And as for Rupert buying out Melling and Associates, he can keep it as far as I'm concerned. The only good thing that happened in that office was spying you out the window in the fountain that summer day."

Phoebe tugged on Lucy's dress. "Momma, ice cream!"

She ruffled her hair. "Yes, Phoebe. Let me get my shoes."

Alexander took hold of Lucy's dress and lifted the trailing hem a few inches, exposing her bare toes. With a hearty laugh, he reflexively went in for a kiss, but stopped several inches from her face and gazed into her eyes with pure love. "I've missed you and all your quirks."

When the group was down the front steps, Lucy looked back at the house. "Do you think it will still be standing when we return?"

Magdalene took Phoebe's hand. "Douglas is an excellent mediator. I'm sure they'll be fine."

"He's very handsome. If I ever write a novel with a sea captain, he'll look like Douglas, right down to the red beard and arching eyebrow."

"He'd like that, and so would I. And you, Phoebe, I have a boy your age at home on Dauphin Island named Kade. He's a big brother to a baby sister, just like you're going to be a big sister to a new baby."

Magdalene shifted a few steps behind with Phoebe, and Claudio offered Lucy his arm.

"Thank you for caring for Alex and watching over him all this time," she whispered to the priest. "I'm glad he had you for a confidant."

"He is my best friend. I will miss him when he moves back."

"Will he for sure?"

"*Sí*, he told me last night he needed to see about closing down his work in Monroe so he can reestablish himself here. He will not ask you to move because he does not want to take you away from your children."

"I worry about him being here with his mother and old friends. What will they think of him for faking his death?"

"That we cannot know, but he is willing to face it all to be with you. He was haunted all this time by his actions. Every weekend he gathers the previous week's copies of The Mobile Register and pours through them for any information about you. He was pleased when you married your husband, and again with the birth announcement the next year. He did not want to think of you alone and he knew you would be well cared for."

"I have been, truly I have." She sniffed back a tear.

"I understand you forsook the church and were baptized Episcopalian before marrying Frederick. Have you had peace in that fold?"

"Not any more than possible. I've been broken all this time, a piece of my heart gone, but the people are kind. I never could go back to the cathedral with all the memories. The only time I went was for Edmund's wedding. I saw Alex there and nearly lost my mind with longing."

"You have been through many trials, Lucy. I am sure it has fortified you for what difficulties lay ahead." Claudio adjusted the cross around his neck and leaned closer. "He told me what happened with the baby. You have been through as much horror as Alex in your time apart. Be sure you lean to God, not the men in your life, for all things."

"That's good advice, one I might need reminding of."

"Would you consider coming back to the church?"

"Not the cathedral, but I could try St. Mary's. It's near my parents' house. When I move there, I could easily walk to Mass."

"That is wonderful to hear. I expect great things from you and Alex being together."

"I'll try not to disappoint you."

***

Lucy sat beside Phoebe under the electric lights in the soda parlor and gazed across the table at Magdalene, who was enjoying a scoop of pecan ice cream.

"My brother was right about one thing: I've had no friends these past years. I think Freddy hired Darla as much for me as to help with this one." Lucy kissed the top of her daughter's head. "I've enjoyed meeting you, but I'm afraid the coming weeks will be lonely after the excitement of the past two days."

"Darla, Naomi, and Frederick will be within your reach, but I've enjoyed our time together as well. I'd like to come to the city more often. Maybe we can set a regular visiting schedule. We could bring the children next time."

"I'd love that! Phoebe would, too."

The tinkling bell on the shop door rang behind Lucy.

"Why Magdalene Jones!" a familiar voice filled the space. "It's been years since I last saw you."

"It's Campbell now, but it's good to see you, Grace Anne."

"Yes, that handsome driver, you lucky lady." She stepped to the table and settled her gaze on Lucy for the first time. Grace Anne's hand went to her large gray hat trimmed in pink flowers. "I had no idea you two were acquainted."

Magdalene covered the awkwardness with a smile. "Nor did I know that you knew Lucy. The two of us were just introduced yesterday. Lucy, I met Grace Anne several times at The Point Clear Hotel while I was with Mrs. Melling."

Lucy set down her spoon. "Grace Anne and I were once close, but it's been a while."

"You had to go and ruin your reputation, though now I suppose it will serve you well. Word is out that you're none other than Olive Kent and everyone knows that creative types are allowed colorful pasts." Grace Anne's smile was as sharp as the bite of key lime pie.

"I don't expect to be treated differently than I have been." Lucy's humble words appeared to tug at her old friend.

"Well you will be. Olive Kent immortalized our city and people will be happy to claim the author as resident." She looked over Lucy. "You look well, even in your condition. I was so swollen with mine two years back I was on bedrest the final months, doctor's orders. Though I suppose that was John's way of keeping me out of the way so he could run around with his friends before settling into fatherhood. Marriage to a doctor isn't the easiest thing. You're lucky to have married Frederick. His work hours are consistent and he's as steady as anything from what I hear. Not a woman can turn his attention, but with you looking so pretty, who could blame him?"

"Is there much talk of Freddy among the ladies?"

Always one to enjoy a good story, Grace Anne slid into the open seat next to Magdalene and leaned toward Lucy. "He's the envy of the social groups! Usually at teas and card parties we talk about our husbands and people around town. It's probably because you're not there to air your complaints like the other women, but your Frederick is the golden boy of Mobile. He always looks sharp, never goes out drinking, and appears to be committed to you for eternity. Not to mention his physique from his time at the gym. Yes, he's being watched coming and going. There are several ladies who wish to become the third Mrs. Davenport."

Lucy blinked back the threat of tears. "I've never deserved his goodness."

"Nonsense. Except for your months with Alex, you were always well behaved. Well, there was that time in Bienville Square when you danced in the fountain, but it appears no one saw you after all." The smile on Lucy's face caused Grace Anne to study her a moment. "But it all turned out all right in the end."

"So it seems." Lucy put an arm around Phoebe and gave her a quick hug before letting her go back to her ice cream.

"Your daughter is precious, by the way. That's another source of jealousy among the ladies. They never cared for our blonde hair, but they think it's the cutest thing on children. My little Robert is fair-headed too, but I'm glad my hair has darkened." Grace Anne turned to Magdalene. "Do you and the driver have children?"

"Douglas. He's Captain Campbell now. But yes, we have two so far. A boy and a girl."

"Well bless your heart. John wants another, but I keep putting it off. Pregnancy was miserable for me and he hardly touched me when I was in the family way. I want to wait until after carnival season. Do you think you'll come out this year, Lucy?"

"I doubt it. The baby's due in a month and I'm not sure how quick my recovery will be."

"Nonsense. You were back to yourself within a month after her."

"Recovery is more than a waist size," Magdalene interjected.

Grace Anne shrugged. "Maybe for some. I better get back to Sadie and Marie. I left my sisters in the park to get a soda. It was lovely to see you Magdalene. And it was nice to talk with you again, Lucy. I'll be sure to let the ladies know Frederick is as wonderful as he seems. I'm sure the bounty on him will rise." She laughed and went on to the counter.

Lucy pushed her half-eaten bowl away. "There goes my appetite."

"I eat it!"

"You'll spoil your supper, Phoebe."

"Daddy says there's always room for ice cream."

The women laughed.

"Yes, and Daddy's always right." Lucy pushed her bowl to the edge of the table beside her daughter's empty dish. "Enjoy, Princess."

Thirty-Four

Darla and Henry stayed in their seats while the audience left the theater. She leaned back, staring up at the three story ceiling. "I'd almost rather sit here and enjoy the architecture than the show. It's beautiful, like so many other buildings in the city."

"But you enjoyed it, didn't you?" Henry took her hand in his and settled back to gaze at the trompe l'oeil details.

"Very much, but not half as well as I enjoy being with you."

An usher came up the aisle. "We have to ready the theater for the next show. Come back this evening if you'd like."

"Thank you, sir." Henry stood and kept hold of Darla's hand as they made their way down the row to the main aisle.

Instead of going through the door, he paused in the shadow of the alcove and placed his hands on Darla's waist. Not wanting to be caught by the workers, she leaned in for the kiss she knew he would ask for to save time. It was twice as long—twice as sweet—as their first kiss, but too soon he held the door open for her. They crossed through the lobby and out of the red brick building into the fading afternoon sun.

Darla's hand was back to being respectfully on his arm rather than in his warm grip. "I wish we were on the island right now."

"Why's that?"

"We could walk hand-in-hand down the beach with our shoes off and no one would care."

"That does sound nice. Would you settle for a soda in the park instead?"

"I'd like that, Henry. Thank you."

They stopped at a nearby drug store counter and he purchased two bottles, which they brought to a bench in Bienville Square. Across the way, Darla spied Sadie, who unfortunately saw her as well. Sadie and her sisters strolled over, curiosity plainly on their faces. Henry stood out of politeness.

"Good afternoon, Darla. Mr. Adams, it's good to see you." Sadie smiled at him. "I must say, that costume of yours at the party Monday night caused quite a stir. People couldn't tell if you were brazen or dumb. I made sure to set everyone straight that you are most extraordinarily gifted in your sense of humor."

"That's good of you, Miss Marley."

"It's the least I could do. You both know my sisters, don't you? Grace Anne Woodslow and little Marie."

"Pleased to meet you, Mrs. Woodslow and Miss Marie." Henry shook their hands. "I'm Henry Adams and this is Darla Beauchamp."

"I just ran into your employer, Darla," Mrs. Woodslow said. "She's having ice cream with her daughter and an old acquaintance of mine, Magdalene Jones. Or Campbell, rather."

"Just the three of them?" Darla questioned.

"Yes, and it's completely unfair how well she looks in her condition. And have you heard? She's Olive Kent! There will be no ignoring her or Frederick anymore. Not that the ladies ever left *him* alone." Grace Anne looked over Henry. "You're that intern at his accounting firm, aren't you?"

"I'm one, but I'm not sure if I'm the one you mean."

Darla found it wonderful he refused to play into her games. They both knew he was the only intern at the moment, but the Marley sisters didn't.

"There's a young man that Frederick insists on bringing to all Judith's appointments. She thinks he's such a dear to need a chaperone and is quite convinced he's interested in her and can't control himself in her presence."

"As client's information is private, I can neither confirm nor deny I am the said intern. But I will say Mr. Davenport is the most upright, professional man I know."

Grace Anne sniffed and looked away.

"I think it's time I got home." Sadie eyed how close Henry stood to Darla. "Are you coming back with us, Grace Anne?"

"Yes, I want to tell Mother I talked to Lucy and she didn't deny being Olive Kent."

As soon as the sisters walked away, Henry sat beside Darla. "Who's Olive Kent?"

She smiled at his earnestness. "That's Lucy's pen name. She's a famous novelist but has kept that secret hidden. That's why I was hired—to keep Phoebe occupied while Lucy writes. I wasn't told until after working there a week, but word got out after the concert last night. Once the news spreads about Alexander and the divorce, there's no telling what will happen."

Henry squeezed her arm. "It doesn't matter. It's not your concern, especially right now. I'm under orders, remember?"

"And how are you going to redirect my thoughts in the middle of the park?" she countered.

"By walking you away from here and finding a secluded spot, but only if you wouldn't find that too bold."

"Not at all." She guzzled the rest of her drink and handed him the empty bottle. "What are we waiting for?"

He ran the bottles back to the shop then offered his arm, a beaming smile on his handsome face. When they got to Joachim Street, they saw Lucy, Maggie, and Phoebe a block ahead of them.

Henry laid his hand on top of hers. "Do you wish to catch up with them?"

"No, I'm happy with our current pace, but should they see us—"

Phoebe, one hand in her mother's, turned around to look at something on the sidewalk. "Miss Darla!"

Darla laughed. "There goes that."

The three waited for the young couple to catch up with them.

Phoebe stood before Henry, arms reaching for him. "I tired. Pick me up, Mr. Henry. Please."

He squatted down and made a show of trying to lift her. "You've gotten too big, Phoebe. How much ice cream did you eat?"

"Two!"

He tickled her and Darla helped the girl onto Henry's back.

"How did you know we had ice cream?" Lucy asked.

"We ran into Sadie Marley and her sisters in the square," Darla said. "Mrs. Woodslow was eager to talk about her run in with the great Olive Kent. I had to explain who that was to Henry."

Lucy turned to him. "You won't treat me differently, will you?"

"Of course not, Mrs. Davenport."

"Do you have supper plans? You're welcome to dine with us tonight."

He looked sideways at Darla, but she refused to meet his gaze.

"We're eating at six-thirty," Lucy continued. "The Campbells and Alex will be there."

"I think I'll pass this time, but thank you, Mrs. Davenport. Darla told me we're to keep the Wednesday lunches until the baby comes. While we both look forward to that day each week, don't feel like you need to host us if things … if things get too strained."

"Freddy's the most amiable man there is. Now that the initial shock wore off, I don't foresee any issues in our future."

"So divorce isn't an issue?" Darla's tone was pointed and earned a glare from Maggie. "Sorry, that wasn't my place to speak."

Henry trotted ahead with Phoebe.

Lucy sighed. "I don't expect anyone to understand, but I have faith in what's to come. I might be naïve, I might be love-blind, but I see no other option than to live my life with Alex now that I know he's here and still loves me as much as I love him. Living without him has been difficult enough. I don't see how living with him will be any harder. Everyone loves and respects Freddy and will think me awful for leaving him, but I've not been devoted to him in my heart like he deserves. I love him too much to keep living half a life."

Her hand went to her side with a jerk.

All Darla's frustrations with Lucy collapsed. "What type of pain was it?"

"Almost like I pulled a muscle, but it's gone now."

"Should we send Henry ahead for Freddy to get the automobile?" Maggie took Lucy's elbow and looked to Darla.

"I can walk two more blocks." Lucy straightened and kept her gaze on Phoebe and Henry in front of them.

"Slow down a bit," Darla said. "Alex will still be there when we return, whether in two minutes or five."

Henry circled back with Phoebe. "Everything okay?"

"We just needed to slow Lucy's pace," Darla replied.

"Let me get Phoebe home and tell the others you're on your way."

"Giddy up!" Phoebe shouted.

Henry galloped ahead.

"He reminds me of Douglas," Maggie said, still holding Lucy's arm. "He was always willing to play with Priscilla. She's the daughter of the cook and butler at Seacliff Cottage. She was about that size when we were there. He even had a way with Lydia's baby. Seeing him with other people's children, I knew he would be a great father, and he is. Don't let Henry get away, Darla."

"Babies of my own are the last thing on my mind right now, but I do aim to keep Henry close."

"I hope my situation doesn't make things difficult for you." Lucy looked to Darla. "I know how the choices of others can affect those close to them, even without meaning to."

"Don't worry about me. Concern yourself with keeping you and this baby healthy."

When they were a block from State Street, Mr. Davenport ran around the corner. Without speaking, he scooped Lucy into his arms and started back toward the house. Darla and Maggie looked at each other, Darla with a frown and Maggie with a smile.

"He loves her, there's no doubt about it," Maggie whispered.

"God help him heal from his heartache," Darla replied.

Henry, Phoebe, Douglas, and Alexander were waiting on the front porch.

"Daddy rescued Momma! Now kiss her, Daddy. Kiss your fair maiden!" Phoebe's face shone with excitement as her father placed Lucy on her feet.

Mr. Davenport, eyes soft with feeling, looked down on his wife. "Will there come a time when it will be easier to give her a pony than to please her this way?"

Lucy gave a bittersweet smile.

He touched her cheek and placed a hand around her back as he leaned over her. He appeared to head straight for her lips, but at the last moment he angled to the side and planted the kiss on her cheek. When he straightened, Mr. Davenport looked to Alexander with a strained expression. "Let's get you on the sofa with your feet up, Goosy."

Darla let the breath out she didn't realize she was holding and took Henry's arm. "Thank you for getting him. I'll just check on her a moment and then I'd like to go home."

"I'll see to it, Darla."

Thirty-Five

After supper, Frederick took Phoebe upstairs to ready her for bed. Alexander settled close beside Lucy on the sofa, the Campbells in the chairs across from them. The feel of his hands running through her hair brought Lucy all the peace she needed.

"I'll come tomorrow afternoon," Alexander told her, "but I have to leave first thing Monday. Claudio and I need to get back to work. I'll settle things there as quickly as possible."

"But how will you survive here? Will you stay hidden?"

"No, my queen, I'll hide no more. Claudio is going to tell my mother after the concert tonight, and then we'll visit her in the morning after attending early Mass. I'll come back as soon as I leave her house."

"I don't envy you that meeting, but I'll be here with a hug for you when you return. I'd give you more if I could."

"I know you would, and I love you for it." His blue eyes studied every curve and angle of her face before leaning in for a kiss. "My Lucy, my queen, my everything. There will be nothing to stand in our way besides the world's judgment, and I've learned to shirk that."

"Not all of it. You must listen to your friends." Douglas's voice was firm.

Lucy leaned her head on Alexander's shoulder and looked to the Campbells as he put his arm around her.

"And what would you say to us right now?" Alexander's teasing tone brought a smile to Lucy's face.

"Don't be in a hurry as you tread this stormy water," Douglas said. "This situation is more volatile than the hurricane."

Alexander smirked. "Magdalene?"

"Keep your hands and tongue to yourself until the divorce is final."

Douglas arched an eyebrow and pulled her into his lap. "Not everyone is as spicy as you, Maggie."

"But Alex is." She laughed as her husband nibbled her neck.

"Yes, and watching you two doesn't help my situation."

"Sorry." Magdalene switched back to her own seat and straightened her dress. "We're leaving tomorrow. This will be the last time we'll torture you with our playfulness for a while."

"So soon?" Lucy asked.

"Captain Walker is coming for us midday. Douglas needs to be ready to work Monday morning."

"Captain Joe Walker." Alexander's voice sounded pensive. "I was jealous of him because you defended him the first day I met you."

"Poor, broody Alex." Magdalene stuck out her lower lip before smiling. "I'm glad you finally grew up."

He laughed. "So am I. Extend my good wishes to him, will you?"

"Of course, but we should go. We don't want to over-stay our welcome. Frederick is beyond generous, as a host and a man."

Lucy straightened. "The best of men."

Alexander slowly pulled his arm from around her, trailing his fingers across her back. "More than I'll ever be."

"You've always been enough for me, Alex. I tried telling you that many times."

"What can I say? I'm stubborn, and back then I was more concerned with other things than the tender feelings of my queen." He moved her curtain of hair aside and kissed below her ear.

Magdalene pointed a finger at Alexander. "That's beyond friendship."

"I *am* restraining myself."

She sighed. "I know. Believe me, I know."

The Campbells went to the foyer so Douglas could put on his suit jacket. Alexander led Lucy to the mantel and stood behind her, resting his chin on her shoulder as they looked in the mirror. He hugged around her chest, lightly squeezing her upper arms with his hands.

"Would you have kissed me under the mistletoe knowing all that you'd have to suffer?"

"It's been worth the pain to finally be in your arms again." She kissed his sleeve and smiled at his reflection. "You don't know how much I've ached for you, my angel."

"I have an idea." He nestled into her hair and inhaled. "I've craved your touch and smell all these years. The sound of your laugh, your sweet lips, that sexy smile."

Just when he pressed against her fully, the sound of little feet running down the stairs filled the space.

"God bless Phoebe for saving me tonight," Alexander muttered as he stepped away.

Lucy met her daughter in the hall. Frederick waited in the foyer to see the guests out.

"I come to say goodnight." Phoebe turned to Magdalene. "You're leaving?"

"Yes, Phoebe. We've had fun today, but tomorrow we have to get home to our little boy and girl. I told you about Kade being a big brother to Tabitha."

Phoebe twirled in her pink nightgown. "Daddy said you might come back to play one day."

"We plan to. I'll write your mother." Magdalene bent down for a hug. "Be brave."

Phoebe offered her hand to Douglas. "Drive those boats good, Mr. Douglas."

He laughed and ran his hand over his beard. "I'll do my best, Miss Davenport."

Frederick opened the door and the Campbells stepped out as Phoebe took Alexander's hand with both of hers. "Are you going on a boat tomorrow too?"

"No, I'm lucky enough to stay another day. I leave on a train Monday morning."

"Are you coming back tomorrow, Mr. Alex?"

"Yes, in the afternoon with my friend, Claudio."

"Good. I like to see Momma smile at you." She hugged his legs and then attached herself to her mother's skirt.

With tears in her eyes, Lucy squeezed Alexander's hand and he quickly kissed her on the cheek.

Frederick locked the door behind them and turned to Lucy and Phoebe. "It's been a busy day. She's just about asleep standing beside you." He took her daughter into his arms and she snuggled against his broad chest, eyes half-closed.

"Momma and Daddy put me in bed, please."

"Yes, Phoebe." Lucy touched Frederick's arm. "I'm coming."

Their daughter was asleep before they pulled her door shut. On her way to the guest room, Frederick took Lucy's arm, his brown eyes searching her countenance.

"I'm glad Phoebe likes Alex and can see his love for you." He leaned his forehead against hers. "I'm sorry for kissing you after I brought you home. I didn't know what else to do with Phoebe asking and everyone looking on."

"Frederick," she whispered his name as she wrapped her arms around his middle, "you don't have to apologize. I'm still your wife and I do love you. You'll always have a place in my heart, and you'll forever be the father of our children. As much as I've missed Alex, I wouldn't change these years with you. I wouldn't trade what we created together. You were respectful and loving and handled the situation beautifully, but I really don't think Phoebe ever needs a pony."

He laughed and hugged her to him. "Goosy, I'm going to miss you when you leave. God knows I love you." With a gentle touch, he rubbed across her belly. "May I feel the baby move tonight?"

"Yes, Freddy, anytime you want. Come in after I dress for bed. I'll leave my door open." She hugged him before turning away, not wanting to see the pain in his eyes.

After showering, Lucy pulled on a two-piece under set and propped all the pillows along the headboard, creating a wedge to sit against. She sat cross-legged and leaned back. Down the hall, the master bedroom door opened. It sounded foreign at that distance on the outside of the private space. She tucked the bottom of her chemise top under her bosom and lowered the drawers below the swell of her abdomen.

"You're glorious, Goosy. You always are, but more so when pregnant."

She patted the bed next to her and smiled. "And you're as handsome as ever. You heard about Magdalene and me running into Grace Anne, but I didn't tell you everything she said. You needn't worry about being alone. You're the biggest catch in town. There are several women already plotting to become the third Mrs.

Davenport—and I'm sure we can guess who one of them is. Once word gets out about our separation, be prepared to be mobbed."

His fingers trailed her round belly. "They can talk about me all they want, but there's not a woman in Mobile that holds a candle to you."

"Good, because I think I'd have a permanent headache if you ended up with Judith Smith."

"I could never be with someone who treated you poorly." He kissed her belly and received a kick from within. "See, the little one agrees."

The baby started maneuvering as though trying to twist his or her way out of the womb. Lucy tensed under the sensation, Frederick staring in wonder as lumps rolled under her skin in waves. She grabbed his hands and pressed them against the movements.

"Make it stop!" she gasped.

"Does it hurt?" he asked.

"No, it's just intense. I don't remember Phoebe ever feeling like this."

Frederick's hand softened on her belly. "The baby is big and strong. I wouldn't be surprised if the birth happens this month rather than next."

"What if I'm not ready? I don't feel adequate half the time."

"Goosy, you're brilliant and we make amazing babies together." Before either knew what they were doing, Frederick had her in his arms and pressed his lips to hers, his mustache tickling her nose. "You're stalwart and brave in childbirth, preferring the old-fashioned way of birthing to the drug-induced procedures doctors are selling now. As much as I marvel over our time when we join physically, your true wonder shone when you brought Phoebe into the world."

"Thank you." She kissed his cheek. "I needed to hear that. Needed to feel your love and support."

"I'm sorry if I went too far."

She shook her head and leaned back, which tugged her neckline lower and exposed the passion mark Alexander had given her.

"He didn't waste time, did he?"

"He waited five and a half years, but don't be mad at him. I held my dress aside and asked him to do it last night after he showed me his scars. I wanted him to know I'll hold nothing back from him, that his scars only make him more handsome to me."

Frederick hugged her tighter. "I need to worry about you more than him in the weeks ahead."

"I'm trying to do right, trying to be patient."

"How can I help, Goosy?"

"Will you hold me tonight, Freddy? At least until I fall asleep."

"I'll hold the baby, so you needn't feel guilty about anything you might have promised Alex."

Frederick helped Lucy up, folded the blankets back, and arranged the pillows. After she settled, he turned off the lights, opened the window a few inches, and cuddled on top of the blankets behind her, slipping his arm underneath to cradle the swell of their child with his large hand.

***

The next day, Frederick undid his tie and removed his jacket when they got home from the morning service. While Lucy fixed soup and warmed leftover rolls for their noon meal, Frederick kept Phoebe entertained by building a maze for Doff out of blocks in the living room. By the time they were done eating, there was a knock at the front door.

"Darla, come in," Lucy stepped to the side. "That's a lovely hat. Is it new?"

"No, borrowed from Alice." Darla removed the flowered hat that complimented her blue Sunday dress and set it on the entry table. "I can't stay long. Alice and I are going to Valentino's matinee, but I wanted to check on you and warn about Aunt Ida."

"Oh? What about?" Lucy settled on the sofa and motioned for Darla to sit beside her.

"I think she'll try stopping by with her books tomorrow. She wants to be the first of her friends with autographed Olive Kent titles."

"And so it begins, the train of ladies who spurned me seeking my autograph. That might last until word about Alex gets around. Then I'll be back to being 'that woman.'"

Phoebe ran in with Doff and deposited him inside the labyrinth of blocks. "Watch, Miss Darla!"

The tabby immediately jumped out and started licking itself.

"Doff, please." Phoebe tried again with the same results. "Daddy, help!"

Frederick saw the uncooperative cat and carried him to the opposite side of the maze. "When I set him down Princess, you call him."

Doff skipped a few of the turns, but he made it through. Lucy and Darla clapped for Phoebe and her trusty cat.

"And how are you feeling?" Darla asked once Phoebe settled down to fix a few of the blocks.

Lucy took Frederick's hand when he walked by. "Tell her. Tell her how the baby tried to twist a hole through me last night."

He laughed. "Her skin was stretched to the limit and what looked like a foot and—"

"And the buttocks at one point," Lucy added.

"Yes, all the parts and limbs were rolling and twisting." He perched on the arm of the sofa and placed a hand on her green blouse. A few seconds later, it was bumped off. He and Lucy laughed.

She took his displaced hand and kissed the back of it. "The baby knows Daddy."

Darla took a quick swipe at her eye and nodded. "That all sounds good. I'll see you tomorrow morning."

Frederick saw Darla out.

"She's upset with me," Lucy stated when he came back to the living room.

"Darla worries about all that could go wrong in a situation. She's concerned about you, the baby, all of us. She'll come around, but it might take time." He patted Lucy's shoulder and looked to their daughter. "Shall I put her down for a nap?"

"Will you wait until Alex and Claudio come? I'm sure she'd like to see them and they might not stay long today."

"I hope not. You've had a taxing few days."

She gazed up at him. "Thank you for helping me fall asleep last night, Freddy. I don't know how long it would have taken me otherwise. The bed doesn't seem big when there are two, but alone it's massive."

He sat beside her and put an arm around her. "Anything to help keep mother and baby happy."

The next knock on the door sent Phoebe running to answer it. Frederick helped Lucy stand and she went to the front. Phoebe already had the door open and was jumping for joy over "Mr. Alex" and "Father Claudio." She hugged each of them and brought them both by a hand inside the door.

"Take off jackets!" Phoebe pointed to the coat rack.

Alexander removed his gloves and put them into a pocket of his navy suit jacket before hanging it.

Claudio tugged at his priest's frock. "It never comes off."

"How do you bathe?" Phoebe asked.

He ruffled her hair. "You are too smart, *Principessa*. It comes off, but I have to wear it as often as possible." He hugged Lucy and kissed both cheeks. "You look well."

"Thank you, Claudio. Come in to the living room. Frederick's in there."

Then it was Alexander's turn for a quick embrace and peck on the cheek.

"Come in and tell me about your day," Lucy whispered. "Phoebe will be taking a nap soon if you'd rather wait."

"I had forgotten what Mass is like in the glories of a cathedral," Claudio said when they all gathered. "The hymns sound better, the words hold more power under the painted glass, and the sacrament seems to fill one's soul."

"It brought back many memories." Alexander took Lucy's hand into his. "Both good and bad, but there wouldn't be one without the other."

"I'm going to see Phoebe to bed." Frederick stood.

"Just a moment," Alexander said before Frederick could leave. "My mother wishes to pay a visit to Lucy. Would you prefer it while I'm here or later this week?"

"That's up to Lucy, but I must be present no matter when it takes place." Frederick scooped Phoebe into his arms, who squealed with delight as he carried her upstairs.

Lucy made her preference known. "Today please. How long can you stay?"

"We'll leave before suppertime," Claudio said.

"Let me call my mother now."

"Freddy has an appointment with Dean Sachs at four, so she needs to be here by three. The study is by the dining room. You can use the desk phone in there."

Lucy turned to Claudio when they were alone. "Was she very upset?"

"She was upset over my black eye but accepted the reality of Alexander's return quickly. *Signora* has been lonely and is more than pleased to have a part of her family back."

Lucy stood when Alexander returned, opening her arms to him.

"Mother will be here by three." He kissed Lucy's forehead and hugged her to him until the baby jabbed at the pressure. He jumped back, blue eyes wide. "Why do I feel like Freddy just punched me?"

Lucy's laugh rang out.

A look of loving concern shone on his face as he reached out to touch her belly. "Are you all right, Lucy? Does it hurt you?"

"It's uncomfortable at times, but more often amusing."

"Except last night," Frederick said as he took a seat in the armchair by Claudio. "Last night, the baby looked to be dancing in there, all moving lumps and limbs. Lucy cried out for me to stop it, so I pressed my hands to her."

Alexander looked between Lucy and her husband before speaking. "I'm glad she has you, Freddy. I know you care for her better than even her own parents could. There's no one else I'd rather have known Lucy was with."

"I wish I could say the same of you, Alex."

"I pray you'll grow to change your mind about that." His solemn expression twisted to a puckish grin before Alexander cleared his throat. "My mother will be here by three. She's invited me to move into my old room until Lucy and I settle together, but I'm not sure I can trust her not to manipulate things to suit her whims."

"What she did to Magdalene is inexcusable," Lucy said. "She needs to apologize to the Campbells."

"One thing at a time, Lucy." Alexander helped her back to the sofa. "Today, she's concerned about making amends with me, which includes welcoming you into her life if she wants me anywhere near her."

"I'll not have my children in that woman's house." Frederick crossed his arms. "I'd rather them not even be exposed to her. She's not fit company for my family."

"I don't blame you and will do all within my power to respect your wishes."

Thirty-Six

Mrs. Melling arrived at her scheduled time. Frederick saw her in and pointed her to the chair next to Claudio before settling beside Lucy on the sofa. He offered no refreshments and the group stared in silence as Mrs. Melling looked over her future daughter-in-law.

"George was right about you keeping your looks after children. Here you are, about to be the mother of two and looking every bit as lovely as you did when you were twenty."

Lucy managed a polite smile but didn't wish to comment on anything relating to Mr. Melling. As though sensing her discomfort, Alexander took her hand on one side while Frederick rested his on her other knee.

"And I was right about you and Mr. Davenport after seeing you on his arm outside the dress shop all those years ago. I must say, I'm not a fan of this situation," Mrs. Melling continued. "Divorce has never been appealing to me, no matter who it involves or why."

"Mother"—Alexander's voice held a hint of anger—"please stick to appropriate subjects."

"Perhaps," Claudio said, "if you share what moved you to come today rather than try to make small talk, it would be better."

"Dearest Claudio, you are right as usual. I am often too opinionated for those who do not see things the way I do." She gave a grim smile. "I am sorry if anything I said all those years ago gave you offense. The fact that you love Alex when he is near poverty and disfigured proves you were not after our money when you were previously engaged. I would like to let you know that when the time comes, I welcome you to our family."

"I thank you for the kind words." Lucy kept her Easton chin high.

"Of course, when your current marriage situation is settled and you are ready to be out in society after the baby comes, I'll host an engagement party and—"

"No thank you, Mrs. Melling. I have no desire to mingle with those who have shunned me since my last time with Alex."

"But with you being known as Olive Kent and Alex coming back from the grave, you two will be the talk of the town for months! It is best in situations like this to be in control of what others see and know, and the best way to handle that is by ruling the social settings."

"I'll not be part of your games." If she hadn't been weighted down with the baby, Lucy would have stood. Instead, she straightened her posture. "I don't wish to associate with those who have thought me unworthy of polite conversation. I've been at the receiving end of too many snubs to want to be welcomed back. Besides those facts, I don't appreciate how you're playing the Beauchamp girls with Valentino and I've heard what damage you did to a respectable young woman in your employment when you tried to mold her to your schemes."

"Magdalene," her whisper filled the room. Mrs. Melling cleared her throat. "I understand you met her and Douglas this weekend. That was a most unfortunate situation—one that you can be sure will not be repeated, especially with you and Alex dedicated to each other."

"The Campbells were weeks shy of marriage!" Lucy began to tremor.

Frederick took her right hand and stroked it. "I'm afraid I'm going to have to ask you to cut your visit short, Mrs. Melling. I thank you for wishing to welcome Lucy, but you can see she neither expects nor wants anything from you."

Frederick stood, releasing Lucy's hand. Claudio walked Mrs. Melling toward the hall. She paused near the sofa and reached into her purse, retrieving a lace-trimmed handkerchief.

"Eliza thought the world of you and was upset when you and Alex broke things off." Mrs. Melling unfolded the handkerchief. "This was my mother's and was to be Eliza's when she married. I would like you to have it."

She held a large gold cross inlaid with garnets on a black ribbon before Lucy. Alexander squeezed Lucy's hand twice.

Lucy accepted the heirloom. "Thank you, Mrs. Melling. I'll take good care of it."

As soon as Frederick, Claudio, and Mrs. Melling were out of the room, Alexander embraced Lucy, burrowing into her neck with a kiss.

"The pendant means more to her than the house, the Melling name, or her status. She truly accepts you, my queen. No matter what she says or tries to do to encourage you into her society, she knows our love is true and she approves that the two of us will continue my branch of the family tree."

"But I don't want it, Alex." She shifted the cross toward him. "The only thing I want that's connected to your family is you."

"Accepting it allows my mother to feel like she's contributed to our happiness. Thank you for taking it. I'll keep it with me if it wounds you to look upon."

She shook her head and looked between the man and the symbol of their faith. "I'll go put it in my room."

When she returned downstairs, Frederick, Alexander, and Claudio stood together before the hearth.

The priest stepped out of the group. "We are going to stay until your husband returns from his appointment, and then we will go." He took Lucy's hands and turned to Alexander. "Is this not like our final day in Seacliff Cottage? You, me, Magdalene, and Douglas, but this time it's Frederick and Lucy, though I hope Lucy does not punch like Magdalene."

She smiled. "I don't."

"But you've been known to playfully backhand me," Frederick said.

Alexander laughed. "I've been victim as well. The Eastons are scrappy."

Looking between the two men who held her heart, her smile faded as she realized moments like those were a blessing she wasn't worthy of. Frederick—kind, loving, supportive—didn't deserve to have his second marriage in eight years cut short. He did nothing wrong and everything right, but Lucy couldn't continue to give him partial devotion with her heart wide open for Alexander—impulsive, passionate, brave—who held the secret to her happiness even after repeatedly breaking her heart. He had loved her and set her free. Now she asked Frederick to do the same.

"Goosy, don't look so sad." Frederick came to her, arms open.

She fell into his safe hug. "I don't mean to be cruel. You were nothing but honorable to Harriet and then me, yet you're being left a second time."

"I told you not to worry. I know how to survive and I won't be alone this time around. You've given me the best gift ever with Phoebe and our new one." He cradled her cheeks and kissed her on the forehead while she continued to cling to him.

"Tell Dean Sachs I'll speak with him if he wishes. Set up an appointment for me. I can easily walk over during the day."

"You're not going anywhere alone until after the baby arrives." He kissed her forehead again and tried to pull away. "I need to get ready to leave, Goosy."

Still, she wouldn't release him.

Frederick sighed. "I can't believe I'm saying this but Alex, please take her from me—just for the hour, mind you."

Alexander laughed. "I thought you'd never ask."

"*Calmati, amico*," Claudio said, a hint of warning in his lyrical voice. "Do not ruin your chance to prove yourself changed."

"Lucy, my queen, let me comfort you." Alexander rubbed her back. "Freddy needs to go, but I'll hold you if you'd like. There'll be no complaints from me with this responsibility."

She turned to him with purpose. "You used to tell me those exact words when you wanted your way, whether me giving you a kiss or allowing you to help with something."

He offered his arm to her and brought her to the sofa. "Still true, my queen."

"I'll prepare coffee before I leave," Frederick said on his way out.

Alexander sat sideways in the corner of the sofa and brought Lucy into his lap. Pin by pin, he undid her hair, bringing each tendril to his nose before allowing it to fall between his fingers. Once her hair was loose, he gathered it into the palm of one of his hands and lifted it off her neck to kiss below each ear. Wrapping his arms around her, he tugged her back until she rested against his torso. She stretched her legs the length of the sofa and closed her eyes, her hands folded atop her belly.

"I could stay like this all day," she murmured.

"I can't begin to imagine how great it will be to stay with you without either of us having to go home. We only had a taste of that once, but I cherished it, more so because it ended up being our last day together. I'm sorry it ended the way it did."

"As am I," Frederick said as he returned. "I had to pull you off her because you'd turned vile and tried to have your way with her. Again."

"I was hungover, as I was the previous time. I've been dry since the fire. You and Lucy needn't worry about drunken violence from me anymore."

Frederick nodded and turned to Claudio. "I trust you to chaperone. Phoebe will be up before long, as well. Should I bring the coffee out before I leave?"

"We can handle it. Thank you, Freddy." After he left, Lucy sat forward and swung one leg off the sofa. "I could use some of that coffee, otherwise I think I'll fall asleep here."

"You rest, Lucy. I will get it." Claudio stood. "Alex, you need to remember Magdalene's advice from yesterday."

Alexander laughed, but his hands did roam after the priest left the room. When their kissing grew heated, he moved himself to the chair across the coffee table from Lucy.

Claudio carried in the tray. "Is the only way to control yourself by separation?"

"I've craved her touch for over half a decade. The smell and sight of her are mesmerizing, a few stolen kisses my undoing."

Lucy's smile made her cheeks ache. "You're the poet, Alex." She continued to watch him as he prepared a cup for her, his eyes bright.

Doff streaked through the room, followed by the sound of Phoebe coming down the hardwood stairs. Rather than going to her mother, she went to Alexander and laid her little hand on his sleeve.

"Momma's happy since you came. Can you stay instead of leaving on the train?"

He set down the coffee pot. "Phoebe Camellia, since we both like to see your mother happy, I think we'll make a good team. What do you think?"

"I like to help make Momma smile. I like Momma having friends. It's fun." She skipped around the table and cuddled against Lucy's side.

"You two are the prettiest girls I've ever seen."

Phoebe stood on the sofa beside Lucy and kissed her cheek. "Momma's prettiest when she smiles."

Alexander came around with the coffee cup and kissed her other cheek. "I agree, and good job, Phoebe. That's a doubly big smile, isn't it?"

She hugged her mother and plopped back onto the cushion. "Cookies?"

"Yes, Phoebe, you can have a few cookies."

"Milk?"

"Yes." Lucy shifted to stand, but Alexander put a hand on her shoulder.

"I'll get it."

"She likes it in a teacup this time of day," Lucy said.

Alexander touched the tip of the girl's nose. "And why shouldn't she? Everyone else is drinking out of one."

Phoebe giggled until he came back with her cup and an extra plate of shortbread cookies. With her practiced hand, she poured a tiny bit of milk into the saucer and set it under the table for her cat. Then she knelt beside the table to eat and drink.

Alexander settled beside Lucy. "You're blessed, Lucy. She's perfect and completely you, but with the dedicated care of Freddy."

"Are you calling me reckless?"

"In the best possible way. Reckless in love. We both were, and it was glorious while it lasted. I can't wait until we have that chance, again." The blue of his eyes shone like fire below his dark brow. Claudio cleared his throat and Alexander's smile grew. "I guess we're putting off some strong signals, my queen."

Lucy leaned against his shoulder, her lips almost touching his ear as she whispered. "It's difficult to bridle my passion for you."

He gripped her knee and shifted toward her.

"Alexander!" Claudio rattled off something in Italian.

Phoebe looked at the priest. "You talk funny."

Claudio smiled. "It is the voice of the Holy Spirit."

"I picked up a bit of Italian in my time at your parish," Alexander said, "and I can say those weren't religious words."

Alexander had to save Lucy's coffee from spilling while she laughed. He set both their cups by Phoebe's place at the table. Then the telephone rang. Alexander helped Lucy up and walked her down the hall to the wall-mounted box.

"Hello?"

"Lucy, is Claudio still there?"

"Yes, Darla. What's—"

"I need him, quick!"

"Claudio!" Lucy shouted. "It's Darla and she's frantic!"

He ran from the front room. "What is it?" he asked into the phone. His olive complexion paled as he listened. "I will be there in two minutes!"

Claudio headed for the front of the house. "We must go! Valentino disappeared with Alice after the performance."

"But what about Lucy?" Alexander asked. "Freddy didn't want her left alone."

"And he will not want you left with her, come!"

"I'm sorry, but my responsibility is to Lucy. I'll sit on the front step until he returns."

"Then I will call when I have word." Claudio ran out the front door, leaving it open behind him.

Lucy met Alexander near the foot of the stairs. "I'll stay in with Phoebe while she finishes, then we'll be out to sit with you."

Alexander looked behind him, then nudged Lucy back a few step, his hands on her hips with a tender touch. He checked toward the front of the open house again before going for a kiss. When he tried to step away, Lucy clung to him.

"Lucy, my queen, we'll have our time soon enough. Don't make this any more difficult." He kissed her once more and fingered her lips. "You're still Freddy's for the time being, even if you've given me your heart."

She followed him to the living room where he freshened his coffee and smiled at Phoebe.

"Take a cookie and sit by Momma." She offered the plate to him.

"I'm going to sit on the porch and get some air. You can come out with me when you're done with your cookies and milk."

"May I walk Pinky and Rummy in the carriage?"

Alexander looked to Lucy with a befuddled expression.

Laughing, she nodded. "Where's the carriage, Phoebe?"

"Upstairs." She shoved her cookie into her mouth.

"Could you bring it down before you go out? Freddy hasn't let me carry the doll stroller for months."

"Of course." He shoved a cookie into his mouth like Phoebe and set his cup back on the table.

Lucy shook her head at her daughter. "We'll have to set a better example. We don't want Mr. Alex or the baby picking up our bad habits."

Alexander laughed, causing a smile to grow on Lucy's face. On his way out of the room, he whispered in her ear. "That curving smile has always been capable of causing me many bad habits."

By the time Frederick walked up the street, Phoebe was happily strolling her carriage across the length of sidewalk in front of the Davenport and Beauchamp houses. Alexander sat on the front steps, a respectful distance from Lucy, who was in one of the armchairs from the living room he'd brought out for her comfort.

Frederick paused to kiss Phoebe before coming up the front walk of the small yard. "What's this?" He looked over Alexander.

Lucy took his hand. "Darla telephoned about fifteen minutes ago. Valentino disappeared with Alice after the concert and he's gone to look for them. Alex didn't want to leave me alone so we waited out here."

"Disappeared? Have her parents been notified?"

"I don't know, and I don't think it's our place to tell them if they haven't." Lucy looked to Alex. "Thank you for staying with me, but you should go help. Claudio will be upset and I remember what Magdalene told me about what he did to your father one day when he wouldn't stop pestering her."

"What was that?" Alexander asked.

"What Freddy did to you Friday night. Douglas had to pull him away."

"I'll run there now. Let me get my jacket."

Frederick helped Lucy stand and motioned her inside after Alexander. As soon as she stepped into the foyer, Frederick pulled the door almost all the way shut, staying on the porch with Phoebe.

Alexander looked up with wide eyes.

"I think he wants us to say goodbye," Lucy whispered.

Alexander dropped his gloves and fully embraced her. "I'm blessed to have you back in my life."

"It feels like you were never gone. You've been in my heart and mind all this time. I still feel like I'm dreaming." She traced the soft stubble of his beard.

"You've always been my fantasy, my living dream." He kissed her with a provocative air, but pulled back. "I'll treat you as my queen, always. I never want to see horror in your eyes when you look upon me like you did in the duplex. Your fear still haunts me, Lucy."

They shared a tender kiss and Alexander buried his head in her hair. "I'll telephone you Wednesday night. Is ten too late?"

"No, I'll try to work until then."

"But don't wait for me. You're never supposed to wait for me, remember?"

Lucy dropped her arms from his shoulders to his waist. "How can I forget? You've been my private world all these years."

"I'll try to settle things in Monroe before Christmas. When I come back, I'll rent a room somewhere. Mother's visit here proved I don't wish to be involved with her plans. She's not as bad as Father, but she's toxic nonetheless." He hugged her again. "I love you, my queen."

Lucy brought her lips to his once more. "And I love you, Alexander Randolph Melling, in spite of your name."

Thirty-Seven

Darla had paced the reception room several minutes before rushing out to check the orchestra practice room, ballroom, and lobby for Alice. When it registered that Valentino was also gone from the group of well-wishers, she wanted to do nothing more than rush up to his hotel room, but knew it would worsen the situation for her to be seen going upstairs alone. Instead, she went for the telephone in the lobby to call the Davenports' house.

As soon as Claudio ran into the hotel, he demanded a key for his cousin's room. The man at the desk didn't dare defy the agitated priest. Claudio took Darla by the elbow and hurried to the elevator.

"I don't know how they managed it," she said as they stepped into the hall and ran for the end room.

Claudio paused to cross himself and turned the key. Not wanting to see—but needing to know—Darla followed him in.

Alice stood barefoot in the middle of the room, Valentino's violin tucked under her chin and the bow mid-play. The man lounged on his bed, undressed to his trousers.

"What is the trouble?" Valentino gave a seductive smile. "I am only rewarding Alice for her good work by allowing her time with my exquisite violin."

Claudio, yelling in Italian, yanked Valentino by the arm and slapped him on each cheek before turning on Alice. "And you, *signorina!* You are old enough to know better than to go with a man unaccompanied in a hotel. You left your cousin worried so much she had to telephone the Davenports' to reach me."

"I … I'm sorry. I didn't think it wrong."

"Then why did you not bring Darla with you? Why did you have to sneak away if it was not wrong?" The priest's eyes smoldered like fire and brimstone, pronounced more with the ring of bruising around the one Mr. Davenport punched two nights ago.

Alice began to cry. "We needed time away to get to know each other better."

"*Signorina*, I do not fully blame you." Claudio's tone softened and he stepped closer to console her.

Darla chanced a look at Valentino. He winked at her and his grin returned though his cheeks blazed red where his cousin struck.

"We love each other," Alice wailed. "He trusts me enough to play his violin. If we spend more time together, he'll want me to go with him when his contract is finished here."

Claudio laughed. "He speaks of escaping together with at least one young woman in every city. That is his game. You have been his Mobile conquest, but he will take you nowhere when he leaves, of that you may be sure."

"But he spoke of Paris in the winter, Tuscany in the spri—"

"Lies! All of it lies." Claudio yanked Valentino off the bed, hands gripping his wrists as he leered at him. "Tell her the truth, Valentino! Tell her how you speak of that to all the women. Tell her of those who have written you with claims of carrying your child!"

Darla rushed to Alice's side, carefully took the priceless violin from her trembling hands, and placed it and the bow on its stand. Then she walked Alice to the chair at the desk and helped her sit.

Valentino, face ashen, spoke through gritted teeth. "You are hurting me, Claudio. You will ruin me if you damage my wrists."

"It would be justice! Maybe you would begin to understand a bit of what it feels like to the trail of women you have left behind." Claudio's arms shook with fury.

"Father De Fiore," Darla said his title in an attempt to touch his mercy, "perhaps this is not the best way to teach him. His music is a blessing to all who hear."

"Darla is right." Claudio shoved Valentino to the side as he released his hold but came against the violinist with a firm backhand that struck his face with a *thwack.* "However, you don't need your nose to play well."

Alice cried out and covered her eyes. Though he brought it upon himself, Darla cringed to see Valentino is such agony.

Claudio shoved a handkerchief at Valentino and then stomped both of his cousin's feet, causing the man to fall to his knees. "That is where you need to be. Now pray for a remission of your many, many sins." He straightened his collar and turned to Darla and Alice. "I am sorry you had to witness that."

Alice dropped her head onto the little desk and sobbed. Darla kept a hand on her arm but was too upset to speak.

"Valentino will be composing a letter this evening, letting Mr. and Mrs. Beauchamp know he will begin teaching Alice's lessons at your home rather than the hotel. Expect to see him at your house tomorrow afternoon. I do not want to hear of either of you within these walls, do you understand?"

Darla swallowed and took a breath. "Yes. Thank you, Claudio."

"Do I need to escort you two home and tell Alice's parents what type of woman their daughter is becoming?"

"No, please, Father De Fiore!" Alice threw herself at him. "I would be sent to a convent!"

Claudio shook his head. "There are worse things than devoting your life to God."

Valentino hobbled to the washroom, the blood-soaked handkerchief at his nose.

Alice looked to her cousin before she turned her frightened eyes to the priest. "Darla would be blamed. She was chaperone and if she was doing her job, we wouldn't have been able to sneak away."

"I looked away from you for half a minute to reply to Mrs. Inge rather than ignoring her. This is all on you and Valentino."

"You're just jealous that he chose me while you still think me a girl."

"Spare me the drama, Alice. I saw through his act the first hour we spent with him and warned you. If you're silly enough to come here with him, you deserve whatever punishment follows, and I'll gladly take some of the blame to see that you're taught a lesson."

"You wouldn't!" Alice screeched.

"Watch me." Darla's glare made Alice pale.

She turned back to the priest, tears returned. "Father De Fiore, have mercy on me!"

He looked to Darla. "Would you mind stepping into the hall so I may have a word with Alice? Do not shut it all the way."

Darla nodded and retreated. Valentino waited for her in the doorway to the washroom.

"She is a child. I have never heard so much crying when nothing even happened, but there is still time for me and you to—"

Using a play from Maggie's book, she slugged him in the stomach before walking out. Not caring about the state of her Sunday dress, Darla dropped to the floor, placed the borrowed hat in her lap, and leaned against the wall outside the room. With eyes closed, she thought of Henry's smiling face that morning across the aisle during Mass and how his wavy hair often curled at his forehead in a boyish way. She'd give anything to see his smile or hold his hand for a moment. The kisses they shared the day before were nice, but his smile would be more than enough to pull her through this hour's stress.

Down the hall, the elevator doors opened.

"Is everything all right?" Alexander Melling dropped to a knee beside her.

"Not really, but it could have been worse."

A gloved hand gently touched her forearm. "Do you need help standing?"

"I'm waiting until Claudio talks some sense into my cousin. Knowing that feat could take a while, I decided to get comfortable." Darla looked away from Alexander's face. "She came here with Valentino. They were alone less than a quarter of an hour and it appears nothing physical happened. That is, until Claudio got here and roughened Valentino."

"It was quick thinking on your part to call Claudio. He has much experience with situations like this. I'm ashamed to say that my family, friends, and I well prepared him for it."

His blue eyes were bright before her. It wore down the guard Darla wanted to keep between the man who tore apart her employer's marriage and any friendliness she felt toward him. "Are you ashamed of all you've done?"

"Of many things, yes. But I'm not ashamed I'm in love with a married woman because I've loved Lucy for years. She gave herself to me and vowed to marry me first. It was my fault things didn't work out back then, but our love deserves another chance." Alexander settled on the floor beside Darla and she looked away. "I know you must hate me or at least be angry for what I've done to disrupt their life. I'd be upset too if people I'm fond of were making possible mistakes."

Darla traced the scrolling detail on the carpet beside her. "It's not just for their sakes—it's for Phoebe and the new one as well."

"Phoebe is a dear."

Darla could hear the smile in his voice and committed not to turn to him.

"I'm beyond pleased that she's taken a liking to me," Alexander continued. "I haven't said anything to Lucy, but I want you to be prepared because you'll be one of the people she'll look to for help to see her through these coming weeks."

The seriousness of his tone pulled her full attention to his countenance. "What's to come?"

"I'm certain the courts will award Freddy the children. When the reason for the divorce comes to light, it will be as bad as though she's committed adultery in the eyes of the judge."

"According to her own words, she has committed it in her heart all these years. Not to mention the moments you two have shared this weekend."

"Exactly. And if asked, she won't lie, nor would I or Freddy wish her to. I fear she'll be seen as an unfit mother and it might break her."

"But she's not unfit, just emotional."

"That's not how the courts work. Even in uncontested divorces, the newspapers like one party made out to be the guilty one."

Darla slumped against the wall. "It's going to cause havoc on her."

"That's what I'm trying to prevent. I discussed it with Freddy when the girls walked Claudio to the hotel yesterday. Freddy will try to get Lucy to wait until after the baby is born before finalizing the divorce, but he's going to talk to his lawyer and get the process started as much as possible without filing. The quicker it gets through the system once it's there, the better. His lawyer might have to pull some favors, and if I can help when I get back, I'll do what I can. My father knew all the judges in the chancery court, but I'm sure my name will be in the filing information, so I should try to stay out of it as much as possible."

She studied his features—turned-down mouth and drooping shoulders under his navy suit. "You do care for her."

His deep-set eyes, though still heavy, brightened. "Yes Darla, with my whole being. And I need to get back here, not to claim her but to protect her from the storm that will come because of what we're doing. I'd wait years more for the privilege of marrying her, but I can't leave her to the mercy of the gossips. Freddy will have his hands full with the children. It will be up to me to shelter Lucy."

Valentino's door opened and a righteous-looking Claudio filled the space, a step behind him a contrite Alice.

"Alexander!" Claudio extended a hand and pulled his friend to his feet and then Darla. "Shall I walk you ladies home?"

"No thank you, Father De Fiore," Alice hastily replied and took her cousin's arm. "It's not yet dark. We can make it safely."

"And what of Valentino?" Alexander asked his friend.

"I took care of him. He is cleaning up and getting his clothes back on so we can all go to supper as planned."

Alexander raised his eyebrows and looked to Alice. "No man is worth the trouble, do you understand?"

"Yes, sir." She tugged Darla toward the elevator.

"Thank you, Alex," she called to him. "Safe travels tomorrow."

"Who was that?" Alice asked when they turned the corner.

"Alexander Melling."

"But isn't he—"

"He's been living in Louisiana all this time, very much alive."

"But he was Mrs. Davenport's first fiancé. Has he been to see her?"

"That's why he's come back."

Thirty-Eight

Mr. Davenport let Darla in the front door as he left for work Wednesday morning. She found Phoebe in the living room and they settled on the sofa with a picture book by Beatrix Potter. Just as Darla finished reading the tale of a naughty rabbit, Lucy came down the stairs in her pink column dress.

Pleased to see her taking concern with her appearance as she'd stayed in her robe the last two days, Darla smiled. "You look lovely."

"Thank you, Darla. And you look nice in violet."

"Aunt Ida will probably try to come again today. She knows we have company midday so she'll expect you to be dressed this time."

"I might as well get that out of the way, though it was nice to put it off. With the article in the paper yesterday about Alex, I'm sure more people will ask about that, as well. Did you tell your family about him?"

"Only when asked. I said I met him first with Claudio and then over here. But remember what the lawyer told Mr. Davenport. You don't have to answer something just because you're asked. You can decline or ignore."

Lucy nodded. "I'm not looking forward to my appointment with him tomorrow. Mr. Joyce has always unnerved me. All lawyers do, except Alex. I wish he still had his license here so he could handle things for me."

"But would he be able to being so close to the case?"

Lucy shrugged. "I don't know, but it's nice to imagine. I can't wait to hear his voice. Part of me thinks this is all a dream and my hopes will be crushed when the telephone doesn't ring tonight."

"It will." Darla watched Phoebe pick up Doff and set him in the doll carriage. "And if he doesn't call, I'll lose what little respect I gained for him."

Smiling, Lucy took Darla's hand. "I'm glad you've seen some of his goodness. He'll win you over if you give him the chance. I pray he does call. I need to ask his opinion on something."

"What's that?"

"Freddy wants to hold off the papers until after the baby is born. He thinks it would look bad—for both of us, but especially me—if I'm still living here after it's finalized. Something about cohabitation and morality, but I need to decide on it before my appointment tomorrow."

"I trust Mr. Davenport to guide you properly. Listen to him, Lucy. He has your best interest at heart."

The next hour, while Darla strolled the sidewalk beside Phoebe pushing the carriage, Aunt Ida came down the front steps of the Beauchamp house with an arm full of books.

"Good morning, Mrs. Beauchamp." Phoebe curtsied.

"Hello, Miss Davenport. Are you enjoying a nice walk?"

"Yes, ma'am. I keep the street safe for everyone on my patrols."

Darla didn't appreciate the narrow-eyed stare her aunt gave the child. "Well, that's nice. Is your mother home?"

"Of course."

"Would you take me to her?"

"Yes!"

Annoyed that her aunt utilized Phoebe to get in with Lucy, Darla took up the abandoned carriage and followed the others up the Davenports' front walk.

Lucy exited the study as they came in the front door. The serene smile upon her lips switched to forced politeness when she spotted Darla's aunt.

"Hello, Mrs. Beauchamp. I'm sorry I've missed you the past few days. I had a busy weekend and it tired me out more than usual." She placed a hand on her belly. "Come into the front room, please. I'll get my fountain pen."

"I must say, you look exceptional, Mrs. Davenport," Aunt Ida said when Lucy joined them. "I thought you might be troubled with the return of Alexander Melling."

"What's there to be troubled about?"

Darla set her aunt's pile of Olive Kent books beside Lucy on the sofa and joined Phoebe in her play corner, keeping a watch on the two ladies.

"Naturally, I assumed with your shared history there might have been some upset, especially when I heard he had been here. But I am glad all is well."

Lucy smiled as she opened the first book, a look of pleasure and pain in her eyes. Darla could only imagine what Lucy wanted to say at the moment. She signed the first book and set it aside to dry before closing it.

"I am hosting a tea tomorrow at two o'clock for a dozen of my friends. You are welcome to stop in, Mrs. Davenport. I am sure everyone would be pleased to see you."

Lucy signed the second book and looked to her neighbor with a cutting glance. "As long as I've lived here I've not been welcomed within your home, nor have you and your friends reached out to me in kindness.”

Flustered by Lucy’s bluntness, Aunt Ida reddened. Darla felt sorry for her before remembering all the biting remarks she’d hurled at Lucy.

“Well, I really couldn’t say, Mrs. Davenport. I am sorry if you felt unwelcomed. I assure you it was not on purpose.”

Lucy’s laughter rang out. “I’m the one who’s supposed to deal in fiction, not you.”

Darla looked between her aunt and Lucy, mouth open at Lucy’s boldness and her aunt being caught in her society lies.

“Fair enough, Mrs. Davenport. I was only trying to be polite, but you would be well received if you stop in tomorrow afternoon.”

“Thank you, but I respectfully decline.” Lucy blew on the page she’d signed on *Winter of My Heart* to dry the ink. She snapped it shut and placed it on the pile. “There you are, Mrs. Beauchamp. I’m sure you’ll be envied tomorrow. No one besides my family has owned a signed set of my books until now. I’m glad you enjoy reading the stories. Do you need Darla to help you back with them?”

“No thank you, Mrs. Davenport. I appreciate your time. And I am sorry about giving you the cold shoulder all these years. Mr. Davenport is lucky to have you.”

“I assure you it’s the other way around. I’m blessed to have had Frederick by my side.”

***

Just before noon, Lucy paced the length of the downstairs hall. Phoebe, washed and brushed from her morning of play, sat contentedly on the sofa, flipping through the rabbit book with Rummy in her lap. Darla decided the lady of the house needed her more than her daughter at the moment. She followed her toward the kitchen on her next pass.

"What are you worried about, Lucy?"

She turned to Darla, a hand on either side of her belly. Her face was completely despondent. "Everything."

Behind Darla, the front door opened. She turned in time to see Mr. Davenport's face contort into concern to match Lucy's hopelessness.

"Goosy." He rushed to her side and swept her into the study with the *click* of the door, leaving Darla staring at Henry while Phoebe jumped beside him.

"She's been anxious the last hour," Darla told Henry as he allowed Phoebe to pull him toward the dining room.

"You sit by me today, Mr. Henry." Phoebe pointed to her special chair moved to Henry's side of the table.

"Thank you for the honor, Phoebe. Let me go wash up first." He disappeared into the bathroom.

Phoebe still bounced on her toes when the study door opened. She leapt at her father and he swung her onto his back. "Come with me to wash, Princess."

They went upstairs.

"Lucy?" Darla looked in the study. "Do you need anything?"

She shook her head, a joyful smile reaching her eyes. "Freddy helped me."

Darla frowned and stepped back into the hall.

"It's not like that." Lucy followed her into the hall, but Darla stayed a step away. "Freddy holds me and whispers reassurances. He tells me he'll be by my side as long as we're married, and that he knows Alex will be there for me afterward. He'd never take advantage of me."

"I know that," Darla snapped.

"It's me you worry about—me taking advantage of him to fulfill my needs. I'm not perfect, but I never mean to be cruel. Freddy knows how I am and loves me despite my faults. If accepting his comfort makes me selfish by indulging in his care these final weeks, I'm guilty as charged."

Darla turned away and walked straight into Henry. His arms went about her, and seeming to feel the tension in her body, he hugged her to his chest and kissed her forehead. She breathed in the scent of his shirt—aftershave and clean linen—and in that moment, she understood Lucy's conundrum, as well as the sweet relief she must feel in Mr. Davenport's arms. Living in the moment, Darla clung to Henry, feeding on the energy of wholeness she experienced in his arms. He shuffled them several steps, but she kept her eyes closed and allowed herself to be moved. When a door shut, she jerked to reality. They were in the study with the door closed.

"Henry!"

"Shh, Darla, it's okay. Mrs. Davenport motioned me to bring you in." He cradled her cheeks in his hands. "You need to take a moment and focus on yourself."

"But it isn't proper for us to be here."

"You've been surrounded by men like Valentino too much lately. Yes, Mr. Davenport told me about what happened Sunday because he knew you were upset. And then everything with Mr. Melling and Mrs. Davenport on top of your Phoebe responsibilities and the worries over the pregnancy—it's too much to keep on. You're concerned about everyone but yourself. We're here with permission. Please allow me to care for you."

She looked into his indigo eyes and smiled. "I'll try, but I'm not sure I know how to relax without the sound of the surf and my feet in the sand. Walking on the beach was the only time I ever felt carefree."

He kissed her and locked his hands around her waist. "That's not often enough. What can I do for you, Darla?"

"I don't need you to do anything." She leaned away, scared to show weakness.

Henry's laugh started as a deep rumble and made its way out with a bright smile. "That's one of the things I like about you, Darla. I know you don't *need* me, but I'd like to think you *want* me." His voice dropped and he urged her closer, holding her like they were about to dance. "What would you like me to do?"

"Kiss me. Kiss me like you've never kissed another girl."

"And what if I've never kissed another girl?" He winked.

"A good-looking country boy like you, I wouldn't believe it. I bet you've stolen plenty of kisses—and been given many happily in return—during your time. Am I right?"

"I can't seem to recall any of their faces or names when I'm with you."

One of his hands slid up her back, pressing her closer as their lips met. Henry kept it sweet for longer than Darla thought possible. She held back, testing his affection. When his hand on her waist migrated to her hip, she felt her knees weaken. His mouth opened against hers and she found herself enjoying the new sensation.

After a minute, they mutually stepped back, both grinning at the other.

"Feel any better?" he asked.

"What does my smile say?"

Henry tilted his head and looked down at her. "That you'd like another go of it."

Darla laughed. "I don't want to become accustomed to moments like these right now, but I do hope there are more in the future."

"As long as I have something to say about it, there will be." He kissed her once more and offered his arm. "How about dinner?"

She held his hand instead. "I look forward to watching you dine with Phoebe at your side."

Lucy waited in the hall, all smiles for the couple when they emerged.

"I owe you an apology," Darla told her. "It appears an embrace can heal many ailments."

Thirty-Nine

After he returned from the gym

Wednesday night, Frederick settled Phoebe in bed and joined Lucy on the sofa listening to the "Sleeping Beauty" score by Tchaikovsky on the phonograph.

He pulled her feet into his lap and rubbed them to help her relax. "What exactly was all that today with Darla and Henry in the study? They didn't sneak in there, did they?"

"Of course not. After you came out of the room, Darla was upset with me. She wasn't looking where she was going and walked into Henry. Just like you always do, he reflexively put his arms around her and held her. She actually relaxed into his hug. I'd never seen her with her guard down. She's like you in that regard, always caring for others. I motioned for Henry to take her in and closed the door behind them."

"You don't need to encourage young people together, Goosy. Think of what others you know have done when alone."

"You were right the first day we met her. She's no Eliza. She's a female version of you, above the hint of scandal because her character is completely trustworthy."

"I have just as many scandalous thoughts as the next guy." His hand trailed up her leg, resting on her knee underneath her kimono as he looked upon her with a gleam in his brown eyes. "That freezing night I spent on your porch after the Mystics of Dardenne ball, Alex thought me unfeeling because I didn't go in to cover you. He thought it was because we'd promised your father not to go inside while your parents were out of town. While that did help me remain strong, the real reason was because I didn't trust myself to be alone with you."

His other hand caressed up from her feet and he stroked the length of both legs with flowing touches. "I was within seconds of marching in there to profess my devotion to you. If you would have accepted me, I would have made love to you on the settee right then and there. I both thank and curse Alex for showing up when he did. I wanted to be your lover, but God didn't agree with me."

"He knew I needed you for something more." Lucy climbed onto his lap and wrapped her arms around his neck.

His hands trailed over her silky robe in a familiar way. "Right now, the doctor's guidelines are keeping you safe. I want to make love to you one more time, knowing it will be the last so I can relish every moment and commit all your wonders to memory."

"But Alex—"

"Alex took from you what should have been mine." He grasped her hips, tugging her closer. "If it wasn't for the doctor's orders, I'd claim my privilege as husband over you right now. I'm a man, not a perfect example of humanity. That patched wall over there, Alex's bruised neck, and Claudio's black eye are testaments to that."

Lucy pressed against him. "Freddy, you know I've shirked doctor's orders before. If you need—"

His lips were hard against hers and his hands explored each curve of her body. Frederick carried Lucy to the study, setting her in front of the desk.

He gazed over her figure spilling out of her robe before speaking. "Wait here for your telephone call, and then lock your bedroom before you go to sleep." He backed out of the room, refusing to look away from her until he closed the door between them.

When the telephone rang an hour later, Lucy's raw voice scratched a "Hello" into the mouth piece as she held the receiver to her ear.

"My queen, are you all right?" Alexander's voice, though distant and slightly thin, warmed her.

"Yes, my angel."

"You weren't waiting for me, were you?"

She sniffed and fingered the letter she wrote during the last half hour. "Only at Freddy's insistence."

"I don't want to keep you long, but I'll be back in Mobile to stay next Friday."

Lucy's heart leapt in her chest with the thought of seeing him in nine days. "Do I need to find a place for you to stay?"

"No, but thank you. I'll stay in a hotel a night or two and find a room to rent somewhere."

"A story about you ran in the paper yesterday."

"Mother must have talked to someone. A reporter called me for a telephone interview at the office Monday afternoon, but I didn't mention your name. Were you listed in the article?"

"No, it was mostly a recap of the hurricane and fire, with statements from your mother about your burns and that she hoped you would settle back in Mobile."

"For your sake, it will be best to keep our information private as long as possible. Have you talked with the lawyer yet?"

"I go tomorrow. Freddy thinks we should wait to process the papers until after the baby is born. He says it would be bad for me to live here after it's filed, but I want things to be done so you and I can start planning."

"We've waited nearly six years to be married. I'd wait six more if needed."

"But I don't want to."

"A little patience, my queen. We rushed things last time, a week or two won't matter in the scheme of things. Freddy's taken great care of you, trust him to continue to do so. I'll call this weekend to check in. I love you. Stay strong and be sure to rest."

"I will Alex. I love you, too."

After she hung the receiver on the cradle, she looked over the letter on the desk. There were two tear drops staining the paper, but she refused to rewrite it. It was demanding of her emotions to write once and she didn't wish to suffer again.

My Dearest Frederick,

I want you to know that I appreciate your love and passion more than ever. Never has the world seen a more devoted husband and father. You have flawlessly cared for me through the years and I am constantly in awe of your tender attention to Phoebe and the one yet within me. God has blessed me during these years with you and will continue to do so as we strive to raise our children though separated by a few miles.

I have never given you what you deserve and I am sorry I cannot give you more, but know a part of my heart stays here with you, Freddy. Always. Whenever you decide to open your heart to another, don't be afraid. Your passion, dancing skills, and romantic ways will be more than enough to secure any eligible hand (not to mention your handsome face and athletic build—strength enough to sweep a woman off her feet and a charming smile to dazzle even the best intentioned lady). I am jubilant we are forever linked as co-creators of our amazing Phoebe and the one soon to join us. Remember I am here for you and wish to be your friend all the days of my life.

Love Forever,

Lucy

P.S. I'll always be your Goosy.

She folded the page and switched off the light. At the master bedroom, she slipped the note under the door. Frederick waited for her in the hallway when she came out of the bathroom. She opened her arms to him, pleased to see his smile.

"Thank you for sharing your thoughts with me, Goosy. You'll always have a place in my heart as well." He kissed her forehead and smoothed over her loose hair. "I hope I didn't cross a line earlier."

"No, and I'll never lock my door. I trust you, Freddy. I trusted you with my heart all this time and you've proved more than worthy."

"How's Alex?"

"He sounded fine and is returning next Friday. He'll call this weekend to check on me, but he said to go along with you on what you think best with the divorce filing. He trusts your judgment and doesn't want to rush things."

"I'll see about setting up a regular meal invitation for him once he's here. Be sure you're ready in the morning."

***

Darla arrived a few minutes early and oversaw Phoebe's breakfast so Lucy could finish readying herself. She needed to go to the office with Frederick so he could spend as much time at work without having to drive back to pick her up for the appointment. She piled her hair on her head, crowning her blouse and navy skirt.

It was her first trip out since word of her being Olive Kent spread around town, but Frederick's staff was pleasant enough. She happily settled in a corner chair behind his office door with a novel by L.M. Montgomery while he came and went, going through files and consulting with various workers while she read.

Half an hour later, there was a flurry of activity toward the front of the office. Frederick came around his desk as a shapely figure shadowed his doorway.

"Dear Mr. Davenport ..." Judith Smith's voice simpered. "I understand your need to bring the intern to chaperone our meetings, but to place me in the care of Mr. Peabody is completely unacceptable."

"Mr. Peabody is my most seasoned employee, Mrs. Smith. It's my policy to assign new clients to an accountant after I review their situation. Mr. Peabody has even more experience than I do and I felt him best qualified to handle your extensive file."

"Surely you could choose to keep me as your personal client. I know you keep the Van Antwerps and others for your own." With eyes only for Frederick, she closed the space between them, one hand fingering the pearls at her neck. "There must be some part of you that wishes to entertain my business privately."

Lucy laughed. "Oh, Mrs. Smith, that's a good line. May I use it in my next book? And how you touch your necklace to draw attention to your chest—very clever indeed."

Judith paled, then reddened. "Lucille, I had no idea you—"

"It's good to know you wouldn't plan to make a complete spectacle of yourself in front of a man's wife. That's something to be proud of." Lucy pursed her lips and raised her eyebrows mockingly.

Judith huffed and turned back to Frederick. "Please accept my apologies, Mr. Davenport. I'm sure Mr. Peabody will be more than competent in meeting my accounting needs."

Frederick shut the door behind her and gave Lucy a quick hug of thanks. "May I hire you to sit here and keep the vultures away?"

"All these years I had no idea what you were faced with, but I'm beginning to think that's a good thing. I would have been a jealous wife pacing the floors if I'd known how much you're sought after."

"I've only had eyes for you, Goosy."

A short while later, they walked two blocks to the lawyer's office. Lucy insisted Frederick come into the meeting with her, but he sat to the side and stayed silent unless asked a direct question. Mr. Joyce agreed to get the paperwork filled out as much as possible, leaving space for the information of the second child and the date of filing. He also agreed to seek information on which judge would be most sympathetic to their situation.

"But no matter who takes the case, it will be you, Mrs. Davenport, who is held responsible for the marriage ending. Your choices, your questionable behaviors in seeking a relationship with another man. Bear that in mind the next few weeks and see that you don't give the judge more reason to not allow you to have your children."

The thought of not having Phoebe and the new baby hung over Lucy like a storm cloud for days.

Besides the pressure of the baby against her ribs and lungs, her emotional state made it difficult to breathe. Not even Alexander's telephone call Saturday afternoon cheered her. By the time the following Friday rolled around, Lucy was too depressed to get out of bed for the third day in a row.

"I'm coming home on my lunch hour," Frederick told her from her bedroom doorway. "Alex will be here this afternoon and I'll not have him think I neglected you, nor will I allow him to come up here to visit. I have an inkling of what's troubling you, but unless you speak to me I can't help. If you aren't up when I get home, I'm going to come in here to dress you myself. Do you understand?"

She nodded but rolled to face her opened window.

Whether she slept, she didn't know, but the next thing she noticed was her door opening and then she was in Frederick's arms—which had increased in strength from his extra hours at the gym. He deposited her in the hall bathroom.

"At the very least, wash your face. A shower wouldn't hurt because it's been days since you've had one. If I don't hear you being active, I'll send Darla in."

She stood in shock several moments after he shut the door. Then she tied up her hair so she could shower without wetting it. When she stood in a towel afterward, there was a knock at the door.

"Would you like your clothes brought to you or you brought to your clothes?" Frederick's no-nonsense, mustached face awaited her reply when she opened the door.

"You may bring me to my clothes."

He scooped her into his arms and carried her to the guest room, setting her on the freshly made bed.

"Do I need to dress you?"

She felt a mischievous smile curl on her lips for the first time in over a week. "Only if you want to."

He threw a pair of underdrawers at her. Lucy left them hanging on her shoulder and turned serious. "I don't know what to wear. I feel completely unattractive. What looks best on me?"

"Goosy, you look good in everything. That's one of the reasons Mademoiselle Bisset likes to outfit you. I'd say just stay in the towel because you look beautiful, but you need to put something on so you don't catch a chill." He handed her a clean chemise and turned his back while she pulled on the underclothes. "Do you want shapewear?"

"There's no point at this stage and it would be too uncomfortable after days without it." She rubbed her belly through the cotton garment. "I'm worried, Freddy. Mr. Joyce said I might not be allowed the children. If I'm an unfit mother because I love two men then—"

He tucked her against his chest. "Goosy, the judge can say what he will, but I won't keep Phoebe and the baby from you, of that you can be sure. They're just as much yours as they are mine." He dropped a hand to the swell of her middle and was nudged aside with a rolling bump. "You're nurturing and caring for the little one, even if the tyke knows my touch."

"I want to nurse this one as I did Phoebe."

"And you shall, as often as possible." He looked upon her décolletage with a smile. "You think I'd deny my baby the wonders of those beauties?"

"Freddy!" She backhanded his arm with indignation.

"There's my scrappy Easton." He playfully pinned her arms to her side. "It's good to see emotion on your face. No more moping around."

Frederick released her and went to the closet, pulling out her column dress. "You look wonderful in this."

She tilted her head. "You want me to look pretty for Alex?"

"You're always beautiful, and I'm sure he thinks the same. I just want you dressed and downstairs. Is that too demanding?"

She quickly kissed his cheek. "You're reasonable and you know it. I'll be down in a few minutes."

When she stepped off the stairs, Phoebe hugged her legs.

"Momma! And Daddy is home, too. And Mr. Henry! We're all eating together!"

"Henry?" Lucy turned to Frederick in surprise.

He offered his arm and escorted her to the dining room. "I invited him back today because you missed our dinner Wednesday when you were in bed. He'll be traveling to Chatom next week for Thanksgiving."

"It's good to see you, Mrs. Davenport." Henry smiled as he pushed in Darla's dining chair.

"Will you do me a favor, Henry?" she asked.

"Of course."

"Will you call me Lucy?" She saw the surprise on his face and rushed to reassure him. "Darla does as well. And with the name change coming, I don't want you fumbling over how to address me. You'll still be friendly with me, won't you?"

"Yes, Mrs.—Lucy, though I might not see you as often."

"Thank you, Henry. It's been a blessing to get to know you."

Forty

On Saturday at half-past one, Frederick brought Lucy to her parents' house. Phoebe ran in to get a hug and kiss from her Nana and Papa, but then she was off with her father for an afternoon at Monroe Park.

"He dotes on that girl like no father I've ever seen," Mrs. Easton remarked.

"What decanters should I have at the ready for Alex?" Mr. Easton asked. "I think I remember him liking brandy."

"Nothing, Father. He hasn't partaken of alcohol since the fire. He's changed his life around, done everything he could to be sure he doesn't turn out like his father. But, yes, he did prefer brandy." She smiled, remembering the taste of it on his deep kisses.

"I don't know why I agreed to this." Mrs. Easton nervously fingered the fringe on the pillow tucked under her arm. "Once word gets out that Alexander Melling took tea here, there will be no stopping the questions. I don't even know if I can look upon the two of you together with you practically bursting with Freddy's baby."

"Mother!" Lucy's hands went to her belly as though to protect the child from the harsh words. "I have no shame for the situation. God knows I've loved Alex all these years, and also that I love Freddy. If everything happens for a reason, then God knew Alex needed time away to heal himself and Freddy and I needed to bring two precious souls into the world. If you worry too much about what other people think, you'll turn into Ruth Melling."

"Lucille Amelia, that's nothing to joke about!" She gave her husband a cutting look. "And you can wipe that smirk off your face, James."

When the doorbell rang, Mr. Easton rose to answer it. When he came into the room with Alexander, both their suit jackets were removed. Alexander's blue tie matched his piercing eyes and his white shirt set off his dark stubble. He dropped to a knee in front of Mrs. Easton, taking her hand in his gloved one.

"My sincerest apologies for all the pain I've caused you and your family, Mrs. Easton. I understand if you cannot forgive me, but please know that I wish nothing but the best for Lucy."

"Then you should have left her with Freddy." Mrs. Easton held his gaze with her blue-gray stare.

"I was ready to spend my life alone, happy that she was well provided for. But her heart called to mine through the pages of her newest book and I could no longer deny that we need each other."

Mrs. Easton's face softened and she reached a hand to his cheek. "You're still a charmer, Alexander. That boyish twinkle in your eyes and a touch of naughtiness in your grin is still there as well, though I'm sure you'd rather refute that. How can I be comfortable with you and Lucy together knowing what you did to her before and now that you've disrupted her marriage?"

"One day at a time, Mrs. Easton. Get to know me and watch my actions. I wouldn't respect you half as well as I do if you blindly accepted me back into your daughter's life."

She lightly backhanded his shoulder. "You drip charm like other men sweat in the summer."

"And now I know where Lucy inherited her spunk."

Mrs. Easton did her best to hide a smile and waved him away. Alexander leaned over Lucy to kiss her cheek before settling close beside her. Without thinking, Lucy slipped off his glove and linked their fingers together. Her mother gasped.

"I'm sorry, Mother. It's a natural reaction for me to want to—" But Mrs. Easton wasn't shocked over Lucy. She stared at Alexander's scarred skin. Lucy lifted his hand to her lips and kissed the back of it. "He's been through the refiner's fire to return to me reborn. Each mark, each scar is a testament to his change. Yes, he's still the same Alex with charm and wit, but he's even more himself because he's purged what was dragging him down."

Alexander slipped off his other glove and shifted closer to Lucy. "Your daughter has been my one true love. The memory of her smile kept me striving to be worthy to hold her once again."

Mrs. Easton rushed from the room in tears. Mr. Easton stood and nodded to the two on the settee. "She'll come around."

He quietly followed his wife down the hall.

"Oh, Lucy," Alexander said as he nuzzled into her neck, "you're blessed with them as parents."

"They'll be yours soon, though they've already said they're keeping claim on Freddy." She wrapped an arm around his waist.

He laughed. "Of course they would. They claimed him even before I came into your life. Can you believe we only had two months together? All these years apart, you've lived on in my mind, and it makes it feel like I had you for much longer than reality, my queen."

"Agreed, and being here with you brings back all the memories of our courtship, like sneaking kisses and caresses when no one was looking." Her hand trailed over his shirt as she kissed his neck.

With a little moan, he clutched her hand. "There will be time for that, Lucy, but not here, not now."

"This will be our house soon."

His hands traveled up her body until they cradled her face. "And when it is, and we're here as husband and wife, we'll explore everything together." Seeing the gleam in her eye, he smiled and responded to her unasked questions. "Yes, everything and everywhere, my queen. Like I said before, there'll be no shame when we're married."

Lucy couldn't stop herself from planting a kiss on his alluring lips. Then, in case her parents should return, she rested her head against his chest as he held her in a loose hug.

***

Though Alexander took supper with the Davenports each day, Lucy was as miserable as ever with the weight of the growing baby. She was uncomfortable at her desk, walking or doing anything that left her short of breath. Both Darla and Frederick assured a nervous Alexander that it was normal, but stress marred his face more often than his typical, easy smile.

On Thanksgiving, Lucy had to force herself to her parents' home. Her brothers and their families would be there, as well as Susan and her family—who were staying the weekend from Grand Bay. The twins, Cora and Emma, were spending Thanksgiving with their husbands' families, but were expected the next month for Christmas so they would be with their parents' for their final Christmas in the house.

The Davenports were the last to arrive. The home was noisy, crowded, and hot. Phoebe ran in happy to see her cousins, but Lucy immediately stepped back onto the porch.

"I can't do it, Freddy." She leaned against him.

"Let me fetch a pillow or two, and I'll set you up out here." He walked her to the swing outside the dining room window before dashing inside.

Edmund and Mary Margaret came out.

"What's your theatrics today, Lucy? False labor?" Edmund crossed his arms.

"You do look bad," Mary Margaret remarked.

Lucy rolled her eyes and rubbed the side of her belly through her gold and turquoise gown.

"Maybe if Alex saw you now he'd be scared off," Edmund said.

"He's seen me every day for nearly a week and will see me again in a few hours. Mother invited him to stop by after dinner to greet everyone."

"Like hell she did!" Edmund's fists turned white.

Lucy strained to keep her breathing normal as her abdomen tightened. "He'll be part of the family soon. You might as well get used to him."

"He'll be no family of mine!"

Frederick returned with pillows and stared down his former best friend before Edmund and Mary Margaret retreated indoors. He helped Lucy situate on her side, a wedge of pillows against the armrest. He then brought one of the wicker chairs over in time for Susan and her newest arrival—number six—snug in her arms.

"I heard what Mary Margaret said," Susan told Lucy. "Don't believe her. You look lovely, just tired and uncomfortable."

She sighed. "That's what Freddy tells me."

"Then it must be true." Susan passed her baby to Frederick and leaned closer to her sister. "Eddie and Mary Margaret are bitter and unhappy. He's out at least three nights a week and she's airing her grievances at socials all over town. I keep getting phone calls from friends who've witnessed her meltdowns at Bridge games. David's going to talk to him because he's shut out Max and Freddy. At some point today, I'm going to ask Mary Margaret if she wants to get Father and Mother involved."

"I do feel sorry for him." Lucy shifted on the wooden swing. "Alex tried to help him see where his path was taking him before we broke things off, but then Alex was back doing the same things before his rebirth."

Susan smiled. "His rebirth? How poetical of you to name it such. Like a phoenix, he rose from the ashes of Seacliff Cottage."

Lucy smiled. "You have a way with words, too. You should try your hand at writing."

"Try my hand? I only have two and there are six littles to care for, plus David. There aren't enough hours in the day for this old girl. But I'm happy for your success, Lucy. And I think it's a good thing people know you are Olive Kent. It shows others that wives and mothers have every right to follow their dreams as anyone else."

"Thank you, Susan. And your new one is precious. Looks like Freddy is enjoying the practice time."

He laughed and handed the baby back to his sister-in-law. "She's the cutest Shephard yet, but don't tell the others I said that."

"Are you doing well, Freddy?"

He pressed his lips together and nodded. "I'm getting on. That's all there is to do."

"If you were any more stoic, Freddy," Susan said, "we would cast you in bronze and set you as a statue in one of the public squares."

Lucy took him by the biceps. "Only if he's in his boxing shorts, shirtless. Give the ladies a chance to see what they all want to get their hands on."

Susan giggled. "I hear plenty about Freddy when I get telephone calls from the city. I'll give you a few months before sending you a list of eligible women."

"I'm not interested in any of the women here."

"There are some pleasant ladies in Grand Bay and Bayou La Batre—country sensibilities with a bit of style. Come out and visit this summer to get away from the city heat."

"I appreciate the offer, but I'm in no way ready to think about things like that, Susan."

"Just let me know. You may be losing my little sister, but I don't think the rest of the family will let you go as easily."

Lucy hugged his arm. "He's not losing me. We'll still be in regular contact and communication because of the children. Freddy will still be my closest friend, whether he wants to be or not."

"Yes, and you'll be my fair maiden." He kissed her forehead. "That is, until Susan finds me a new one."

***

After the Thanksgiving dinner, the Easton cousins congregated in the backyard. Only those under the age of two were allowed in the parlor with the adults. Maxwell's youngest drooled on his shoulder, Susan's two-month-old was content at her breast, and a disgruntled Mary Margaret bounced a toddler on her knee, eyeing Edmund while he poured himself another brandy.

Frederick held Lucy half in his lap on the settee, a pillow under her back and a supportive arm around her belly. She ate little at the table but it felt as if she had gorged.

Mrs. Easton accepted a glass of wine from her husband and gazed around the room, smiling over her children and their spouses. When her gaze stopped at Lucy, she shook her head. "I'd say you're in your final days now. Freddy, be sure you call me when things start changing. It's liable to go faster this time. You will be out of your misery soon, Lucy."

Edmund laughed from his perch near the decanters. "Her misery will just be beginning after the baby comes. She'll be throwing herself away with that cad."

Maxwell transferred his son to Lottie's arms and stood. "Don't start, Eddie."

"I'm not starting something. I'm finally going to end what began six years ago when I was stupid enough to send Lucy upstairs at the Mellings' Christmas party!"

"That's enough." Frederick's voice was calm and strong. He shifted Lucy to lean against the back of the settee so he could stand without jostling her. "If you have something to say about my wife, you can say it to me in private."

Edmund laughed and slung back the rest of his drink. "Fine. I'll just talk about you instead. You've been a dog for Lucy. She's yanked your chain for years and you're happy to sit and wag your tail until she remembers to pet you for good behavior. You're so well trained you've got all the women in town envying my ruined sister for being married to you. Sure, nobody will talk to *her*, but they love talking about *you*. Even your sister-in-law has to remind me how Freddy never goes out drinking with friends and spends his leisure time at the gym instead of the men's club or other establishments. No one, not even the striking widow Mrs. Smith, can turn his head, though I'm suspected of making eyes with everyone from the woman at the lunch counter to the secretaries in the office."

He turned to Mary Margaret and narrowed his hazel eyes. "Is that all, *dear*, or have I missed something?"

Maxwell took Edmund's arm and walked him toward the door. "That's enough, Eddie. You're a lush and everyone knows it, but you don't have to be a jackass, too."

Edmund threw off his brother's arm. "Get the children, Mary Margaret. I don't wish to speak to the creature back from the grave. Whatever Lucy is stupid enough to do with her life, Alexander Melling will never be counted as part of *my* family."

Mary Margaret held back her tears and looked apologetically at her in-laws before following her husband out of the room.

"Is he safe to drive?" Mrs. Easton asked.

"I've heard he's driven while worse off," Maxwell said. "He's been fine during business hours, but the rate he's going, things will begin to slip soon."

"Those tonics they advertise in the paper to sober people might help," Mrs. Easton suggested.

While the others spoke in a flurry of advice and opinions, Lucy groaned as the baby shifted within. She motioned for Freddy to help her up and he escorted her to the hall bathroom.

"Goosy," he said when she came out and placed his hands on her middle, "the baby must be half a foot lower than when we arrived."

"Yes, right on my bladder, but I can breathe again." She leaned against him. "I don't think I can sit any longer. Please take me home."

He walked them to the parlor door. "Mrs. E, Lucy can't get comfortable and the baby's dropped. Let Alex know what's happened and tell him he can come to our house if he'd like."

"Gracious, Lucy!" Mrs. Easton stared at her daughter's hand resting on the flat space between her belly and breasts. "The baby looks to be in position. You best get Darla over to see you when you get home. Leave Phoebe here for now. Someone will bring her home later."

Freddy lifted Lucy into his arms and carried her to the automobile.

Forty-One

The Beauchamp family gathered in the parlor after their Thanksgiving dinner, listening to Clarence and Alice play duets. Darla sat with her head against the back of the armchair, eyes closed as she thought of Henry's lips on hers. She hoped he was enjoying his time with his family, but she missed seeing him. It had been four long days since she spoke to him at the cathedral. Darla's unofficial check-ups with Lucy told her she was due within the week, and she needed to be sure of more chances to spend with Henry since their Wednesday dinners would no longer be an option. She decided to start attending the weekday morning Mass while he was out of town so it wouldn't be thought that she went specifically to see him.

In the middle of a violin solo, someone pounded on the front door. Annoyed, Uncle Calvin heaved out of his chair to answer it.

"Excuse the interruption Calvin, but we need Darla." Mr. Davenport's anxious voice carried down the hall. "The baby's dropped and Lucy's miserable. I've just brought her home from her parents' house."

Darla was up in an instant.

"Stop, Darla," Aunt Ida commanded. "I'll not have you over there in your new dress."

Darla looked at the gown she'd purchased for the orchestra performance. "Yes, ma'am." As she hurried to the stairs, she called to Mr. Davenport, "I'll be there as soon as I change!"

Darla ran next door barefoot in an old calico. She closed the front door on her way in and took the stairs two at a time. Mr. Davenport hung Lucy's clothes in her closet and she sat on the edge of the bed in her underclothes, clutching her sides.

"I bet you can breathe free and clear now," Darla remarked.

"Yes, that's the only blessing."

"Have you had any leaking?"

Lucy shook her head.

"That's liable to change when you lie down. Let's put towels down first."

As soon as Mr. Davenport had the towels out and Lucy lay in the bed with her bottoms off, wetness began to spread.

"Call the doctor, Mr. Davenport. Her water has broken."

He rushed down the stairs and Darla took Lucy's hand.

"There's no reason for me to inspect you with the doctor coming. You let me know how you're feeling and we'll take things from there." Darla adjusted the pillows behind her. "Mr. Davenport told me you're a quiet birther, which surprised me. I figured you'd be a screamer, but he insisted you never raised your voice when Phoebe came into the world."

Lucy's laugh was cut short by a contraction. "I yell in my head sometimes, and I'm afraid I nearly crushed his hands."

"That's a good thing. Many doctors won't let the fathers near for fear of them causing more anxiety. Dr. Hughes, from what I've seen, is the best sort to have. Between the two of us and Mr. Davenport we'll see you through this, Lucy."

Mr. Davenport rushed into the room. "Dr. Hughes is on his way. Do you wish me to call your mother?"

"Wait until the doctor checks me, please. But you call Naomi and let her know what's going on."

"And I'll start water boiling while I wait for the doctor. Holler if you need anything."

After the next contraction, Darla rolled up her sleeves and scrubbed her hands in the bathroom. She barely made it back in time to help Lucy breathe through the next one.

"They're coming quicker. Have you had them all day?"

Lucy nodded. "Mild ones, so I didn't tell Freddy. I didn't want to ruin everyone's Thanksgiving."

"Babies are the best thing to be thankful for, Lucy." Darla wiped her brow with a damp cloth.

Lucy adjusted the sheet across her chest and began to undo her pompadour. "I want to brush and braid my hair."

Darla brought her brush from the dresser as someone thundered up the stairs. Alexander careened to a stop, clutching the doorframe.

"Maxwell brought me over and is taking back news to your mother. Freddy said I could stay up here until the doctor arrives."

Lucy smiled and reached a hand to him. "Freddy's a dear. You're just in time to brush my hair."

Alexander moved the pillows to slip in behind her and gently set to work brushing through her golden locks.

When Lucy's face changed with the cresting of a contraction, Darla gave directions. "Keep breathing, Lucy. It will pass. Relax."

As the pain began to ebb, she tensed again and held her breath for a double contraction.

"Hug her, Alex. Wrap your arms around her shoulders and pull her back against you." She was in Lucy's face. "Exhale, Lucy. You have to breathe through it. It's almost over. The double pain is your body moving things along quicker."

When it passed, Lucy lay panting against Alexander's chest—she with a look of peace and his face advertising fear.

"Hurry and brush her hair before the next one." Darla took Lucy's hand. "And you need to do better. I can't have you fainting because you forget to breathe."

Alexander was just about to stand when the next contraction struck. Without being told, he wrapped his arms around Lucy.

"Breathe, my queen," he whispered. "You're amazing and beautiful. Breathe and allow this new baby to join our lives."

As soon as the contraction was over, Darla ushered him off the bed, quickly braided Lucy's hair, and resettled the pillows behind her. Darla turned to Alexander, but he only had eyes for Lucy.

"Alex." Lucy's voice was soft, strained.

He went for her at once and perched on the edge of her bed, hands going for her exposed middle for she'd tucked the sheet under the swell of her stomach. His discolored hands looked like a patchwork quilt upon her lily-white skin.

"Lucy," he breathed. "Thank you for sharing a glimpse of this experience with me. I wish I had been with you your first time. Maybe it would have turned out differently, for all of us."

Lucy snatched his hands and squeezed, her face contorting into a grimace.

"Deep breaths, Lucy," Darla urged as she came to the bedside. "Exhale. Good, now inhale. And relax your hands so you don't scare Alexander."

"Too late." He gazed at Lucy with such love Darla had to look away lest she soften toward him.

In the stillness after the contraction, they heard the front door open.

Darla tapped his shoulder. "You need to go, Alexander."

He and Lucy shared a deep kiss, and then he pulled the cover back over her body. "I'll not leave unless Freddy throws me out, then I'll sit on the front steps until I know you and the baby are safe."

Mr. Davenport and Dr. Hughes came in a minute after Alexander went downstairs. Lucy's husband saw to her comfort, retreating only so the doctor could examine her readiness.

"You're more than halfway there, Mrs. Davenport. And it looks like your helper has done a fine job keeping you comfortable." The doctor looked at Darla with his sharp eyes. "I've asked around about your mother and am pleased with the stories I've heard about the Dauphin Island midwife. If you're half as good as her, you'll be a fine asset to me today. Don't be afraid to speak up. If you have opinions or experiences with something I'd like to hear them."

"Thank you, Dr. Hughes."

He stepped out to speak with Mr. Davenport, leaving the door open as Darla moved closer to listen. "Is that Alexander Melling here?"

"Yes," Mr. Davenport replied, "he's an old friend of ours."

"It was quite an astonishing report in the paper about him. I heard he's checking into getting his law license back in the state, but he'll be banned from ever practicing in Louisiana since he worked under a false name. There aren't many firms that would take him on with that hanging over him, though I suppose he could return to his father's old group with Rupert Lyons."

"That will never happen, but don't worry over him. He's the type to get things done when he sets out to do something."

Lucy grabbed Darla's hands. "Help me," she whispered.

Darla climbed on the bed beside her, talking her through the next contraction, which doubled back before dying out. She held a glass of water to Lucy's lips afterward. "Do you wish to walk around now?"

She nodded. "With Freddy's help. Could you tie my robe on when I stand?"

"Yes, and I'll change out the towels."

Dr. Hughes stroked his chin as he watched Darla give instructions for Mr. Davenport to fully support Lucy when a contraction struck, then talk her through breathing until it passed.

Mr. Davenport walked backward in front of Lucy, hands gently holding hers as he watched her face for clues. When a contraction came, he supported under her arms. Lucy leaned against his chest, matching his deep breathing as he sustained her. The couple slowly made their way to the top of the stairs.

"Naomi's here," Alexander called up. "She's taking over the kitchen. Call to me if you need something and I'll fetch it from her."

"Thank you, Alex." Mr. Davenport turned Lucy and himself around for their trip back down the hall.

Before they could advance, Lucy cried out and fell against her husband.

Darla rushed from the bedroom doorway and Alexander ran up the stairs. She brought a hand between the Davenports and felt the tautness of Lucy's womb.

"It's all right, Lucy. Take your time getting back to the bedroom, no need to hurry now. Remember to breathe."

"Lucy," Alexander murmured, "God protect you."

His face was such a mess of emotions, Darla laid a hand on his shoulder. "She's doing fine, Alex. Don't worry. You can start bringing the boiled water up now and let Naomi know tea might be needed soon."

Alexander hurried to be of service and Darla followed Lucy's slow pace down the hall. When she passed the doctor outside the bedroom door, he stopped her.

"It's quite remarkable. I don't usually allow patients to move about once things are started, but it seems to have spurred the contractions along. Tell me, what position do you have the mother take to push?"

"It depends on her comfort, but often upright and squatting. There's nothing like allowing gravity to help the baby out."

Both the doctor and Darla washed up to their elbows with the hot, sterile water and a fresh bar of soap. She put on an apron Naomi sent up and watched over Mr. Davenport as he stood beside the bed, holding Lucy through another wave of contractions that lasted longer than the break between them.

The door was closed, Lucy's robe removed, and Dr. Hughes did a final check, pronouncing her ready to push when she felt the need. Darla spread clean towels on the floor and bed while Mr. Davenport supported Lucy in his arms, silent until she whimpered through an intense contraction.

"You're doing even better than you did with Phoebe, Mrs. Davenport. Truly, this is your golden birth team." Dr. Hughes motioned to the bed. "Do you wish to lie down now?"

"I want to stay in Freddy's arms."

Darla noted the bittersweet smile on Mr. Davenport's face as he closed his eyes. "I'm here, Goosy. I won't let you go."

Minutes later, Lucy gasped. "I have to push!"

Dr. Hughes motioned Darla forward as he stepped back. In a whirl of instincts and nurtured responses, Darla talked the Davenports through each step of the way as she knelt by Lucy's feet and watched for the crowning. Imagining her mother at her shoulder, she ignored the doctor's steady gaze and focused on catching the baby. As the little one came into the world, the blaring danger of the cord wrapped around the neck stopped Darla's heart. In a swift motion, she shifted the towel to one arm and hooked a finger around the cord as the baby slid the rest of the way out.

"Keep her a few minutes more, Mr. Davenport, but you two have a beautiful little girl."

Darla heard him kiss Lucy as she cleared the baby's mouth and nose, rubbing her and turning her forwards and back until a lusty cry filled the room. After inspecting the baby thoroughly, she saw to the cord and swaddled her in a fresh towel.

"The mother's looking pale," the doctor warned. "She should lie down."

"No!" Darla set the baby in her lap and pieced through the afterbirth. "Give her a drink of water, but she hasn't passed it all yet."

"It looks like plenty from here," Dr. Hughes said. "She'll fatigue if he keeps her upright any longer."

"Mr. Davenport is strong enough to keep holding her. If you lie her down now it could take hours for her body to expel the remainder. Mother always had us go through the afterbirth to make sure all the pieces were there before clearing the mother from danger."

"I trust Darla," Mr. Davenport said. "I'll hold Lucy as long as needed."

Darla wiped her hands on the apron and stood with the bundled baby. "She's beautiful, Lucy. You did great. Hang in a few minutes more."

An exhausted smile filled Lucy's face as she gazed at her new arrival. "She's all Davenport."

"But she has the Easton chin," Mr. Davenport remarked.

"Is it okay if I call Naomi in to help haul out a few things?" Darla asked.

"Yes, yes, of course." His smile was something she hadn't seen since her first weeks in their house. "And show the baby to Alex while you're out there."

Not thinking of her bloodied clothes, Darla slipped out the door the doctor opened and called for Alex. He must have been on the stairs for he was there in two seconds.

"It's another girl, but she looks like her father." The fuzz of hair was drying dark.

He grinned. "So she does. But is Lucy—"

"She's stable. I'm sure you'll be able to come in once things are cleaned up."

"Is it as messy as you?"

Darla laughed. "Very much so. Ask Naomi to bring a laundry bag and bucket, as well as ready the tea."

As soon as she returned, the doctor laid the baby on the bed for measurements and inspection while Lucy and Mr. Davenport looked on. Darla helped Lucy sip some water. A short while later, the rest of the afterbirth was out.

Darla didn't have to gloat over being correct—she saw the doctor nod his approval as she wrapped the soiled remainders in newspaper. Those went into a metal pail that Naomi brought in. Darla helped Lucy wash while Mr. Davenport saw to the baby, the doctor and Naomi collecting linens as they went along.

Later, when Lucy was propped in bed and had finished a cup of tea, the new mother watched her husband hold their newborn.

"I must admit," Dr. Hughes said, "I feel like I need to pay Darla for the experience to watch her work. This has been by far the easiest birth I've ever attended, even with the potential complications that arose. Darla made sure they were not an issue."

"Complications?" Mr. Davenport asked.

As the doctor informed him about the umbilical cord being wrapped around the baby and the possibility of infection from the afterbirth, Darla brought the infant to Lucy. She unbuttoned her gown and Darla rested the baby directly on her chest. The baby instinctively rooted for her mother and Lucy helped her latch to the breast.

Forty-Two

Lucy soaked in the peace her current position afforded—a healthy baby, a loving husband, and a fabulous midwife. If she wasn't excited about showing the baby to Phoebe, Alexander, her mother, and any other relatives that might stop by, she would have drifted to contented sleep.

"Thank you, Darla," Lucy said.

"Yes." Frederick placed a hand on the young woman's shoulder. "Thank you. You kept both my girls safe."

"Darla Beauchamp," Dr. Hughes said. "I'd like you to consider hiring on with me. I'm sure my patients could benefit from your skills. A doctor-midwife team could be very well sought after."

"Thank you, Dr. Hughes. I'll think about it."

"Now the only thing I need is the child's name, and then I can be on my way. If you need to wait, I can settle the certificate when I check in tomorrow."

"Bethany." Lucy felt the smile on her face as she said the name. "Bethany Iris Davenport."

"It's beautiful, Goosy."

The doctor took notation in his booklet with the other statistics of the birth. "Congratulations, Mr. and Mrs. Davenport. It's been a pleasure. I'll see you tomorrow. And I hope to see you as well, Miss Beauchamp, with an answer to my offer."

Frederick saw the doctor out, and a moment later Alexander was at the door. "Freddy told me to come in before the Eastons arrive."

Darla made a motion to stop him.

"No, Darla, he's welcome. He's seen me more exposed than this." Lucy watched his face flood with awe as he stepped to the bed. "Her name is Bethany Iris."

"Do you aim to plant a garden with your pretty girls?"

"Your sister was Eliza Rose. That's where I got the idea from."

"Knowing you thought of me all this time both breaks and warms my heart." His blue eyes were passionate as he brought her hand that didn't support Bethany to his lips. "You're even more beautiful right now than you were dressed for the masquerade. I'm sorry things didn't work out our first time together, but know I yearn to create a life and family with you in the future."

The bustling noise of people coming inside clattered up the stairs. Bethany slept, so Lucy passed her to Alexander to hold while she buttoned her gown. Darla cleared her throat but remained quiet. Phoebe ran in first, and Alexander was quick to show her baby sister to her.

"She doesn't have hair like me." Phoebe rubbed the baby's head. "But she's soft like Doff!"

Then the parade of Eastons came through to see to the new one. Mr. and Mrs. Easton, Susan, and Maxwell. Bethany was declared perfect and Lucy remarked over while Frederick praised Darla's good sense and skills. They stayed a quarter of an hour, then Darla shooed them out and sent word for Naomi to ready a tray for Lucy.

Alexander slipped back in once the others were downstairs. "I just wanted to say goodbye. I'll let you rest tomorrow, but I'll stop in Saturday if that's good."

"No, Alex, please come. We'll all still need to eat, though I'll be up here rather than at the table."

"That's just it. I don't want to push the limits on Freddy's rules. He's allowed me up here today, but I don't expect him to keep this door open for me after—"

"You're welcome to come, Alex." Frederick held Lucy's food tray in his hands. "You have more than proven your staying power and good intentions. Stop in the kitchen before you leave. Phoebe's eating and you may join her if you'd like. She enjoys your company. You go on too, Darla. You need a break."

"I'll camp in here tonight to help Lucy, but I'll wash up at home right quick."

"And don't worry about us," Frederick said. "Your offer from Dr. Hughes is a great step for a career. As much as we'd miss you, think of your long-term goals."

Darla smiled. "Thank you, I'll think things over tonight."

Frederick passed the tray to Alexander so he could take his daughter. He settled on the far side of the bed cross-legged, Bethany swaddled in his arms. Alexander laid the tray in Lucy's lap and kissed her on the cheek. "I guess I'll peek in after I eat supper."

Lucy drank a cup of turkey broth and ate toast while watching Frederick. "The baby's all Davenport. I think it's to make it easier for me to leave her when the judge grants you the children."

"I've already told you I'll not keep them from you, but let's not start in on that tonight."

"I thought I'd feel whole with Alexander, but now I know I'll still be broken because you and our daughters will be here and I'll be across town. Is there no way to have it all?"

"Not when your wishes are as intricate as one of your book plots." His smile didn't reach his eyes. "But I won't talk about it now.

Look at her, Goosy. Look what we made together. And you were wonderful. It was an honor to be here with you, to support you however I could."

"I couldn't have done it without you. All that time at the gym came in handy today." She playfully ran a hand over his shoulder, squeezing the thickness of it.

"I'd hold you forever if I could."

***

On the first Friday afternoon in December, Lucy nursed Bethany on the sofa, her feet resting on a pillow on the coffee table. Alexander, recently arrived for his daily visit, sat on the floor with Phoebe and her block collection.

"It needs to be this high." Phoebe stood and reached her hand as far as she could raise it. "A giant tower for baby sister!"

Alexander rubbed his stubbly chin. "I don't know if we should build one that tall inside. It would make a big crash if it fell."

Phoebe giggled and clapped her hands.

"Alex, you'll just encourage her by promising crashes and anything else remotely spectacular."

He gazed up at Lucy sheepishly. "Sorry my queen, I'm still learning."

"You'll have to take her out to build a stick fort or something now."

"Stick tower!"

Phoebe's shout caused Bethany to startle. Lucy took the opportunity to burp her, which brought giggles from big sister and a snicker from Alexander.

Lucy laughed. "You two are—"

"A great team! The best of teams to make Momma smile." Phoebe sat beside her mother and made faces at Bethany until she was satisfied that the gurgling noises meant the baby was entertained. "We made you both smile so Mr. Alex can take me outside now."

"Not yet, young lady." Naomi carried in the tea tray. "I've got your cookies and milk at the kitchen table and I'm going to hold that little bit while your mama takes her tea. Come on, now."

After the girls left with Naomi, Lucy readjusted her kimono and tucked her legs underneath her. Alexander went to pour tea, but Lucy had other ideas.

"Wait for a moment." She held her arms out to him and he dropped beside her on the sofa, embracing her. "Tell me about your day. How was the meeting?"

He leaned close, blue eyes merry and his grin as playful as ever while he shifted in for a kiss. "They'll let me know Monday for sure, but it sounds like they want me."

"Of course they want you." Lucy tugged at his tie before wrapping her arms around his shoulders.

He held her tighter in return. "Mr. Connell is willing to bring me in as a consultant until I get things settled with the state Code of Ethics, but he has to talk things over with his partner, Mr. Roberts. He doesn't mind that Louisiana has blackballed me, but they'd rather make sure the court system here will still have me. I hope if I do well enough they'll keep me even if the courts want to shut me out. I can't marry you until I have a job."

"Alex, you needn't worry about supporting me. I have more than enough for us."

"I've learned I need a profession to keep me engaged in life. I used to be content to loaf around, but part of what kept me steady these last few years was my dedication to my job and feeling like I contributed to society."

"You'll be dedicated to me and contributing to my happiness." Her fingers trailed down his back.

"Oh, Lucy …" He pressed against her, tasting of her kiss with a depth of yearning she hadn't felt with him since the night he appeared on the doorstep. "The old me would gladly accept that and pleasure you every hour, but I need balance if I'm to remain healthy. I need to do my best to maintain my worthiness to keep your hand."

She felt the stirrings within and longed to feel him completely. "I'm no saint, Alex."

"I know, but that makes me want to work harder to keep our relationship elevated from mere love affair to eternal partners." His thumb caressed her lips. "I won't allow us to make the same mistakes as last time."

"Then you better hand me a cup of tea before my hands get us into trouble."

By the time Frederick arrived, Alexander and Phoebe were in the backyard and Lucy dozed on the sofa while Bethany slept in the woven basket beside her.

"How's our girl today, Goosy?" Frederick whispered as he stroked Lucy's cheek.

"She's napping a lot, so she must be growing."

He kissed Lucy's forehead before leaning over Bethany, a proud grin on his face. "She does look bigger."

"How was your appointment with Mr. Joyce?"

Frederick sighed and pulled one of the chairs close to her side. He took her right hand in his and kissed her fingers. "We have some decisions to make this weekend."

Her stomach churned and her eyes narrowed. "What is it?"

"Mr. Joyce thinks it best to file Monday. He believes he could get a finalized date before the courts slow for Christmas. If we wait until January it could take several weeks or more with the backlog from the holidays."

"But I can't move into my parents' until after Christmas. They're hosting the twins and their families, and Susan will be at Maxwell's."

"I know, Goosy. You could stay here and we wouldn't need to worry what the courts think if I put in custody requests and they're granted with the finalization rather than letting the judge decide everything on his own. We'd only have the gossips to think of."

"Custody requests?"

"Mr. Joyce thinks if I ask for custody and you don't contest it rather than allowing the judge to decide from nothing it would help move things along and reduce the chance of you being questioned or investigated by the courts."

"But Freddy—" Her voice caught and she covered her mouth as Phoebe ran in.

"Daddy!" She flung herself into her father's lap and squeezed him. After planting a huge kiss on his cheek, Phoebe snuggled against his broad chest.

Tears welled in Lucy's eyes as nausea swept her faculties. Keeping the hand over her mouth, she pressed it to her trembling lips and squeezed her eyes shut. But even without looking, she knew Phoebe was Freddy's girl. He was the favorite parent, and no one could blame her for choosing him when Lucy had been melancholy much of her daughter's life. While Lucy hardly left the house, Frederick took her on adventures. As much as she knew Phoebe loved her, Lucy also realized she needed to commit to motherhood more this time around.

"Lucy, what is it?" Alexander dropped to his knees.

But she couldn't speak.

"Princess," Frederick said to Phoebe, "can you wash up and see if Miss Naomi needs help?"

"Yes, Daddy." She kissed him again and raced from the room, Doff streaking behind her.

Frederick repeated the news to Alexander. While he listened, he rubbed Lucy's arm through her kimono. When Frederick had explained it all, Alexander took Lucy's hands into his own and lowered them to her lap as he moved closer.

"They're looking out for you, my queen. I think it's for the best as well. And as Freddy said, he won't keep the girls from you. They'd stay with you while he works and certain nights of the week or weekends. Staying here another month would give you time to keep nursing Bethany around the clock and then you could switch to daytime nursing and Freddy can bottle feed at night, like Darla advised you the other day. Both of your bodies would adjust."

Tears rolled down her face and dripped onto her chest.

"We all knew this wouldn't be easy, but you have Freddy and I here. We're doing all we can to be sure this transition goes smoothly for you and the girls."

"I know and I don't deserve it." Her sobbing woke the baby.

Frederick paused to kiss her forehead before picking up Bethany. "Things will settle into a new normal sooner than you realize, Goosy, but we still have the month before any big changes need to be made."

He nodded to Alexander before heading toward the kitchen, swaying Bethany in his arms to calm her.

Alexander pulled Lucy to her feet and wrapped her in his arms. "Lucy, you can't have me, your daughters, and Freddy all in the same house, but we'll work together to make both homes as happy and loving as possible."

He handed her a plain handkerchief from his pocket and stood by as she dabbed her eyes and nose.

"And now I know what I'm getting you for Christmas."

"What's that?" he asked.

"High quality handkerchiefs. Monogrammed ones like you used to have."

His impish smile flashed. "And you used to sleep with."

"What do you mean *used to*?" she countered.

Alexander raised his eyebrows and dashed for the stairs. He returned a minute later, his countenance bursting with joy. "You've kept it all this time?"

"It's not every day a woman is kissed for the first time by the man she loves."

"You've told me that once before."

"And it's still true. I've been in love with you all this time and the handkerchief you gave me at the Christmas party has been under my pillow every night since then." Her arms went around his shoulders.

"Even when you shared a bed with Freddy?"

Her lips brushed below his ear. "It was tucked in my pillow case the whole time."

"I'm sorry you had to wait for me to come back. I'll make it up to you as best I can, my queen."

Epilogue

Alexander gazed at his wife across the supper table. Blonde tendrils fell over the shoulder of Lucy's red gown, but all he thought about was the moonlight on her skin in the gazebo the night before. They'd been married two weeks and there wasn't much left of the Easton's old house that hadn't been a location of their passion. What she expected from their first Saint Valentine's Day together—six years from the date their original marriage was planned—he didn't know, but he was willing to please her however necessary.

They sat on the long sides of the dining table in the center so they would only have a few feet separating them rather than a dozen. He reached a hand across and stroked her knuckles.

"You're the queen of my heart, Lucy, always and forever. It was difficult to work today with thoughts of last night causing havoc in my mind."

Her curling smile spread warmth through his chest that traveled to his loins. "I'm glad today was one of Darla's with us for the same reason. I didn't spend time writing like I should have. I used it as an excuse to hold Bethany and daydream about you."

"Lucky Bethany and blessed me for being on such an attractive mind. Is Darla doing well with Dr. Hughes?"

"Yes, she's happy to be learning and gaining more experience. Mr. Noble telephoned."

"Should I be jealous another man calls my wife on a lover's day?"

"I hope so." She tucked a strand of hair behind her ear. "He needs us to set the dates for the trip to New York. He's going to assign one of his staff members to show us around and needs to see to our reservations. What do you think about being there for Saint Patrick's Day? I'm sure we could attend Mass at one of the cathedrals."

"That sounds great. I'll check at the office tomorrow and take the maximum time they can spare me. I'm glad I don't have any court dates yet because of the trip. It will be a late honeymoon for us, as well as business for you." His foot found hers under the table and he followed the curve of her leg under her dress with his sock-clad toes.

"Are you ready for your present?" The gleam in her green eyes was infectious.

Alexander set down his fork and smiled. "Yes."

"Give me a minute, and then meet me in the study."

As Lucy moved toward the door, he studied how her body filled the gathered top of the gown and the skirt of the dress flared over her hips with a voluptuous drape. The red silk train stirred memories of masquerades and carriage rides that Alexander treasured through the years. He held back from rushing to her only because she asked for time to prepare whatever delight she had in store for him.

The study wasn't a place he spent much time as it was set for Lucy's work and she tended to only write when he was gone—a habit she needed to change once they settled into marriage. Thinking of all the wood furniture, he wondered how they could enjoy the space should things escalate when he arrived. He smiled at the thought of bringing a pillow or blanket to meet her, but decided his intentions would be too obvious and he wanted her to be in control.

He carried dishes into the kitchen and set their plates on the counter beside the sink. "It was wonderful, Naomi. I'll grab the rest for you." He returned from the dining room with the glasses and silverware. "That's all we'll need tonight."

"I know when I'm not wanted, Mr. Alex. I'll see myself out as soon as the washing is finished." She looked him over. "No shoes or jacket and Miss Lucy dining in her bare feet with that fancy dress. You two are quite the pair."

"But you love us, and we love you."

"It's true, but I miss Mr. Frederick and the girls this time of day. At least I know they're being well-cared for by my cousin and I see the sugars in the afternoons. That little one is growing like a weed."

A smile spread across his face. "I never thought I'd marvel over a baby, but Bethany is special. And Phoebe is something else."

"But what would you expect with a mother like Miss Lucy?"

"Exactly so, Naomi. I enjoy being with them before Freddy picks them up, especially the extra time on his gym days. I'll see you tomorrow."

Alexander stopped to lock the front door and turned the lights off in the parlor before knocking on the study door.

"Come in."

Across from the door sat Lucy's oak desk, her typewriter and notebooks at the ready beside the vase of red and white roses he'd sent her that morning. To the left, the rich wood grains of the built-in bookshelves were broken by a curving, sky-blue chaise in the corner. Lucy reclined on the new piece with an envelope and a smile. The door clicked shut behind him and he crawled up the lounge chair until he knelt over her.

"I loved the chaise we had in our bedroom at the duplex." He kissed her. "Remember that time you came looking for me after church? I came to you for kisses still wearing my towel."

"I relish the image of you nearly naked above me." She arched against him and he clutched an arm around her back, holding her to him as they kissed. Tapping the envelope against his thigh, she shifted. "First, you need your present. It's not me."

He nibbled her lips. "I'd be more than satisfied with you on this sofa."

"And you shall be, Alex. I bought this so you can be with me while I write or if I need inspiration." Her hand trailed to his waistband. "You're my muse, Alexander Melling."

They lost themselves, heaving touches and hungry kisses fulfilling their cravings.

Alexander sat up and straightened his half-opened shirt. "You'll need to give me the present now or you'll have to wait until we see this through," he teased while hunting for the envelope within the folds of her skirt.

Giggling, Lucy shifted away. "Alex, it's on the floor."

"What a shame." He caressed her knee and watched her eyes widen with delight.

When he turned to pick-up the envelope, Lucy stood and motioned for him to sit.

"Is it something new for my collection?"

She nodded.

"Then sit with me because I know I'll need your touch by the time I'm done reading."

She curled between his legs, head resting on his chest. "I love you, Alex. I'm glad we're finally able to share this night of love together."

"Me too, my queen." After he opened the envelope and held the paper in one hand, he wrapped his arm around her shoulders and kissed her hair before he started reading.

The One

We fell in love

And then there was winter in my heart

When you walked away

We pulled through

Only to be torn apart again.

Time can heal

But it takes more than

Days

Weeks

Years

It takes a willing heart

Sacrifice

Love

Complete devotion

You've done that for me

For us.

You've been the one for me

Since you were the first one

To kiss me

Cause me to lose sleep

Caress me

Make me cry

Tears of joy and pain

Consume me

You're the only one for me

And I pray I'm the one

For you.

Now we're back in each other's arms

Closer than ever

Tasting the passion

That brought us together in the beginning

Stronger than before

No shame for what we have

For we're man and wife at last

And I'm blessed that you're the one for me.

So come to me

My Angel

Lover

Husband

Redeemer

On this night of affection

And always

Partake of what we have

Fervently

Relentlessly

Softly

We'll meld together

As one

Always.

"You continue to take my breath away, Lucille Melling. You're the one for me. The only one the remainder of our lives." He shifted beneath her, hands roaming her silken gown as he tasted her neck. "If I had to do it all again to be here with you like this, I would, though I pray I wouldn't hurt you as I did. I don't want you to ever suffer because of me."

"You're nothing but joy and pleasure now, my angel."

He felt her body respond under his touch. "Tonight is ours, my queen. We've waited for this observance much too long."

THE END

Bonus

"Safe Embrace"

A Fortitude short/The Possession Chronicles #3.8

Claire Walker snuggled closer to her husband, eager to share his warmth in the predawn hours. Glad to have a few days of freedom with the entire family—Joe had the Sabbath off the day before and no scheduled runs from Dauphin Island until after Ash Wednesday—Claire relished the extra time in his arms.

Joe rubbed a hand across the back of her flannel nightgown. "Ain't it a shame my body won't let me sleep after sunrise when I don't have to take a boat out?"

"You and me both." Claire rested her cheek on his shoulder.

He smoothed the loose tendrils of hair off her face. "I can think of another way to spend the time."

"Save me from your unruly plans, Joseph Walker." She playfully nudged him.

Joe caught her wrist. "Don't feign shock, you redheaded cantankerous cuss. We've got four young 'uns that prove you're none too pious with your husband—not to mention all the other times in between."

Claire muffled her laugh against his chest. "It's good just lying together in the quiet."

"But it can be even nicer when we're working toward a common goal." He opened a few buttons on his long johns.

Soft footsteps padded overhead as they kissed. Joe groaned his annoyance as a solid *thunk* announced their youngest had jumped off the ladder from the loft he shared with his big brother.

Claire, once again tucked within Joe's arm, saw the outline of their nearly three-year-old son stop in the bedroom doorway.

"Whatcha need, Abraham Jeffrey?" Joe's voice was gruffer than necessary.

"Ain't ya getting up for work, Pa? Emmett told me to leave off when I woke him."

"Get yourself here." Joe opened his free arm and Abraham bound across the dark room, jumping on the bed beside his father. "You've got the soul of a captain if I ever saw it in one so young. You want a boat in my fleet one day?"

"Yes, Pa." He settled in the crook of his father's arm. "I'd be a heap better than Emmett. He sleeps too much."

"You won't be a lazy captain?" Joe teased.

"No, sir. Kade and I get up early so we're ready for captaining and fun."

Claire laughed at his earnestness but knew it was true. As soon as Abraham and his bosom friend Kade Campbell had learned to walk, they ran the island like a pair of wild boars. Had Abraham been her first child, she didn't think she'd have been willing to birth another for fear of being worn to nothing by the time she turned twenty.

"You'll be on the boats quicker than you realize, Abe, but not today," Joe said. "Tuck in for a few with me and your ma."

Abraham squeezed himself between his parents like a wriggling worm but soon dozed off.

"He's the best there is at preventing things, ain't he?" Joe whispered. "He always did love snuggling. I think you spoiled him too much with it as a baby."

Claire smoothed their son's straight red hair—the same as her own. "Can you blame me? It's the only time I had more than a minute of peace once he was mobile."

"The poor thing will be hanging on women once he's of age, seeking arms that'll make him feel as secure as yours." Joe tweaked her nose. "You've done set him up for failure, Claire Walker. There ain't another girl with arms as strong and loving as yours."

"I've been praying for Abe since the day he was born. I know God's preparing someone for him."

***

They managed another hour of rest before the lightening sky was too bright for Abraham to ignore. Joe caught him in a bear hug when he went to spring out of bed.

"Get your boots and coat, then go out to Ma's chickens and gather the eggs."

"Yes, Pa."

"And no jumping 'round once you've got 'em. We want all the eggs for a nice breakfast."

"Yessir!"

"Close our bedroom door on your way."

Abraham was gone quicker than a summer storm arriving, the door slamming behind him.

Joe laughed and knelt over his wife. "Now where were we before that hellion joined us?"

Their next kisses were overrun by the sounds of the girls tromping to the outhouse upon waking.

Joe collapsed upon Claire in defeat. "Why'd we have so many?"

"Because the Lord knew we needed three extra sets of eyes looking after Abe."

Joe rolled to his side and tugged her closer. "And I just wanted to give you a good lovin' on Valentine's Day since I ain't got flowers for ya."

Claire ran her hands over his shoulders. He was still in his prime at thirty-three, and she knew they'd be partners for decades to come. Joe wasn't the type of man she read about in romance novels, and she'd learned not to expect extravagance, but he was thoughtful and kind in all the right ways.

"Extra time with you is the best gift, Joe. But we can try for some of that other tonight."

"That's my feisty island girl." He kissed her. "You rest a bit longer while I get these mites in line for the day."

Though she would have preferred to rise, Claire decided to follow Joe's request when she saw the determined set to his jaw as he dressed. He paired an azure shirt with his brown trousers and buttoned on leather suspenders. The room was light enough to see the shine in his eyes made bluer by the shirt when he leaned over her the next time.

"Rest as long as you like." He left her with another deep kiss before the rumble of his commanding voice to the children filled the house.

Mary Louella, who had nearly three years on Abraham, came in a minute later with a fresh pitcher of water for the washbasin. "Mornin', Ma."

"Good morning, Mary." Claire smiled over the resemblance Mary and her oldest brother shared with their father, from coloring to blue eyes. "Sounds like Pa's working you all good out there."

"Clara Jane's got the biscuits in the oven and is cooking the eggs. Emmett's setting the table. Pa wants you to have a day off."

"You're all excellent helpers."

The six of them ate breakfast at the table Joe built the year they were married. When the morning cannon sounded from Fort Gaines, Abraham shot to his feet and saluted in memory of the soldiers who died protecting the island during the Civil War. They continued the meal, but from then on Abraham had a mischievous glint in his hazel eyes.

As the children cleared their dishes, Maggie Campbell came to the screened door on the back porch.

"Come in, Maggie!" Joe called. "Ain't it a bit nippy to bring Tabitha out this early?"

Maggie stepped in, a protective arm about the four-month-old she had swaddled to her chest in a tartan wrap. "She stays warm enough against me. I'm sorry to bother you so early."

"We slept in today." Claire joined her friend near the stove, noting the anxiety in her brown eyes. "What's going on?"

"Douglas got word from an early boat that Uncle Simon's headstone is ready. He's determined to collect it today since everything in Mobile will be shut down the next two days for Mardi Gras and Ash Wednesday. I don't want him going alone, but he doesn't want the children on the bay in this weather."

Though only a year younger than Claire, Maggie had a later start in life. Claire had been married over a decade, but the Campbells had only celebrated three anniversaries thus far.

"I don't blame him with your littles," Joe said as he stood from the head of the table. "How 'bout I go along and bring the oldest three with me? You're welcome to stay here while we're gone."

"Yes, please do. I'd enjoy the visit," Claire said. "We don't often get idle days."

Maggie agreed and returned home to give word to her husband. Joe and ten-year-old Emmett secured their boots and outerwear while Clara Jane packed a picnic lunch with the help of her mother.

When the Campbells arrived, Abraham immediately took Kade's hand and the boys ran out the door.

"Get your boots on!" Joe hollered after him. "Ma don't stand for you outdoors without 'em this time of year!"

As Abraham dashed back inside, Douglas Campbell—one of the captains from Joe's fleet—came in with a smile amid his red beard.

"Thanks for helping Maggie," he told Claire in a whisper. "She's been melancholy since Uncle Simon passed and worries too much about me."

"Those with tender hearts are apt to do that, Douglas."

"Aye, and Maggie's heart is the most generous of all." He turned from Claire and took his wife's hand. "You enjoy your day. We'll be home well before supper."

Douglas kissed Maggie goodbye. When he went for the door, Joe came to Claire's side.

"Now I gotta put on a good show so you don't feel neglected." Joe's merry eyes drank her in before he had her in his arms. "And I was lookin' forward to being with you all day."

"We've got tomorrow, Joe, but hurry back."

***

From the rocking chairs on the front porch, Claire and Maggie oversaw Abraham and Kade digging trenches around a stick fort in the yard. The two boys bent close as they worked their hand shovels through the damp earth. Kade had his great uncle Simon's old pipe in his mouth and Abraham swatted it.

"My troops blow up the fort!" Kade bopped his friend on the head with the pipe.

"I rally the forces!" Abraham countered with a shove.

Rocking a bundled Tabitha, Claire cuddled her friend's baby and enjoyed the fresh scent of infancy after handling the dirt and muck associated with an active boy the past few years.

"Miss Claire!" A shout came from the road.

She passed the baby to Maggie and stood as Darla Beauchamp raced into the yard. The only daughter of the island midwife was level-headed at seventeen, so it alarmed Claire to see her distraught.

Meeting her in the middle of the yard, she took the girl's hand. "What is it, Darla?"

"My family's gone to Grand Bay for the day, but Mrs. Collier sent word her grandpa's in poor shape. I'm supposed to stay at home to keep an ear out for Miss Megan next door as she's due any time, and I don't know the first thing about nursing old men."

Claire patted her hand and smiled. "It isn't so different from caring for a baby, but I'd be happy to check on him."

Darla's face relaxed and she exhaled. "Thank you, Miss Claire. I best get back home."

"I'll watch Abe so you don't need to bring him," Maggie said when Claire climbed the porch steps. "I'll bring him home with us if you don't mind."

"That would be great, Maggie."

Since marrying Joe, Claire had often assisted Virginia Beauchamp with births and newborn care. In addition, her time as a volunteer nurse during the Spanish-America War made her seem as a medical expert to their neighbors. Besides helping when she could, Claire also secured free transportation to Mobile on one of her husband's boats when the situation was beyond home remedies.

Claire collected her bag of rudimentary medical supplies and a green knit cap for Abraham. "You keep this on when you're playing outside, Abe. I'll see you at Miss Maggie's as soon as I'm done helping the Colliers. You be good and listen to her, all right?"

"Yes, Ma."

Kade tossed a rock at the pile of sticks, and both boys laughed at the destruction.

Claire kissed Abraham's face, the dirt streaks hiding his freckles, and she waved goodbye to Maggie.

She was able to provide relief to Mr. Collier by helping loosen the congestion in his chest and propping the bed at an angle better suited for his breathing difficulties. Claire watched his situation for over an hour after he settled. Satisfied there was nothing else she could do for the elderly man, Claire dropped her bag at home and walked to the Campbells.

Maggie stepped onto the porch, wiping a hand on her apron. Tabitha was swaddled her to chest once more, nursing from the comfort of the cocoon. "That didn't take too long."

"No, but there isn't much to do besides make him comfortable at this point. Did Abe give you any trouble?"

"No worse than normal." Maggie laughed then gazed about the yard. "I told them to stay put when I went inside to take the bread out of the oven. They must have run to the back."

The women walked around the little house. Claire saw the empty yard and her heart sank.

Maggie shifted Tabitha off her breast and closed her shirt. "I wasn't inside more than three minutes."

Bleats carried through the palmettos and scrub that shielded the Campbells' lot from the next. Claire turned for the narrow footpath. "Maybe they ran over to see the goats, but my parents are in the city for the day."

Crossing the yard she'd grown up in, Claire scanned the chicken coop and roaming goats on her way to the backdoor her father always left unlocked. "Abe!" she called as she walked through the house. "Abraham Jeffery Walker!"

All the rooms were empty, save a lounging cat in the front room window.

"They're not in the yard," Maggie said when they met back on the kitchen porch. "I'm sorry, Claire. I should have made them come inside with me."

"It's not your fault. Nothing can stop those two once they get an idea. You go toward town and I'll head to the shore. Let anyone you pass know the boys have gone missing."

Claire passed no one as she took the trails through the pines. At Alligator Lake she remembered a night a dozen years earlier when her younger brother went missing. Claire had found him up a tree beside the pond with a lost goat, but she shivered at remembering Kevin's fear of alligators eating him and his beloved pet. Fortunately it was too early in the season for the massive reptiles to be about since the weather hadn't sufficiently warmed.

"Abraham! Kade!" she hollered as she made her way east along the Gulf of Mexico.

One of the men who worked as a deckhand for Joe ran out from the forest. "Miss Maggie told us what happened. We've got men going in every direction, Miss Claire. We'll be sure to find your boys. I'm headed west."

"Thank you, Michael." Claire quickened her pace when he turned the other direction.

She walked close to the tree line and called out the boys' names several times a minute. Trying not to visualize her youngest in mortal danger, Claire kept her mind on her footing in the pale shifting sands.

The image of the boys building and then destroying their stick fort kept coming to her. Abraham and Kade loved to play soldiers. Many Sunday afternoons, Joe and Douglas took them to Fort Gaines at the eastern tip of the island and allowed them to run the tunnels and battlements. One time, the Colonel in charge of firing the cannon twice a day let the boys assist in the evening shot.

Claire broke into a run.

Soon the brick fort came into view. The drawbridge was down. Like a beacon of doom, Abraham's green cap lay on the weathered planks stretching across the trench. Claire snatched it to her heart and paused in the mouth of the entry.

"Abraham! Kade!"

The courtyard was empty of life. Running for the nearest tunnel entrance, Claire's booted feet struck the stone floor with an ominous sound. The dank air penetrated her wool coat as she ran the length of the hall, glancing in the open rooms as she passed them. Pausing at the juncture where the next side of the pentagon-shaped fort began, she shouted their names again.

"Ma!" A far-off cry echoed.

Claire ran to keep the terror from freezing her. The cries came louder as she reached the ammunition magazine corridor.

"Ma! Help!"

Breathless, she rushed through the arched doorway. Her eyes settled first on the sight of Kade Campbell sitting astride a field artillery cannon. His teeth clenched the pipe between his smiling lips. Beyond him, Abraham was pinned to the brick wall by the cannon's muzzle. Tears smudged his dirty face.

"Ma, please help."

"How in God's green earth did you—"

"We're blowing up the enemy!" Kade bounced on his perch, causing the cannon to shift a fraction closer to the wall on the uneven ground.

Abraham yelped.

Claire snatched Kade from the weapon and set him back a few feet. "Kade Gabriel Campbell, you better stand there until I tell you to move."

Taking hold of the carriage shaft with both hands, she heaved the wooden beam backward. The ancient wheels creaked and splintered in protest beneath the shifting weight.

Abraham took a heaving breath with the extra room. "Mama!"

"Hang on a second more, Abe." Claire readjusted her hold, ignoring the way the wood ate at the skin of her palms as she tugged against the slight incline on the floor she worked against. The next heave took all her strength. When Abraham was able to slip out from his pinned position, Claire collapsed.

Abraham ran to her. "Sorry, Ma! Don't feel bad. I sorry!"

Once her body steadied from the exertion and fright, she opened her arms and cuddled her son in her lap. "I'm not hurt, Abe. Just tuckered out from worry and having to move this iron beast."

She kissed his freckled cheek that mirrored her own, not minding the dust from his adventure.

"Love you, Ma. Thanks for saving me."

"I love you too, Abraham Jeffrey, but please follow directions next time and never run off." Claire straightened and took his hand, holding her other toward Kade. He shyly approached and she squeezed his hand as she smiled to show she wasn't mad. "Come on, Kade. You both should know you aren't big enough yet to leave home without someone."

"You here now, Miss Claire." Kade tugged on her arm. "We go see lookout posts!"

"Your mother is worried sick, Kade. We're going home."

Before they reached town, a search party found them. Claire sent the men ahead to find Maggie with word for her to meet them at her house.

***

More than an hour later, the boys were fed, washed, and tucked in for a nap on the loft bed Abraham typically shared with Emmett.

Claire stirred her coffee and looked across the kitchen table at Maggie. "So much for a relaxing day."

Maggie kissed Tabitha's brunette hair as she rested in her arms. "I hope this one's less trouble than Kade. I don't know how you juggle four."

"Lord knows the only way I'm dealing is because Abe's at the tail end. But maybe it's better you got your spitfire first while you're still young enough to handle him."

Her smooth complexion filled with smile lines as she laughed. "I might have aged a decade when they were missing."

Minutes later, Joe, Douglas, and the three oldest Walker children arrived. Clara Jane immediately wanted to hold baby Tabitha, and Joe pulled Claire into a hug.

"What's this I heard on the docks about the boys running off? I'll tan Abe's backside if needs be."

"He's had enough of a fright for one day."

Joe's blue eyes narrowed, but there was a flicker of amusement in the corner of his mouth. "You done spoiled him, ain't ya? Loved on him so good he'll expect a big production every time he's a hellion."

Claire frowned before replying. "So long as he doesn't go about stealing kisses from girls before they can freely give them, he'll turn out just fine."

"I married a cantankerous cuss." Joe's crooked grin lowered to her lips for a firm kiss. "And it's the smartest thing I ever did."

Laughing, Claire turned to the Campbells. Douglas held his wife in an amorous embrace. On the table were a bundle of hothouse roses and a jar of face cream.

"Those gifts are why Douglas was in an all-fired hurry to collect the headstone." Joe's bristly chin tickled her ear. "He wanted to buy something special for Maggie on St. Valentine's Day without her expecting it. You sorry you didn't catch a romantic fool who brings flowers and fancy concoctions?"

Claire's hands trailed Joe's solid middle and over his shoulders until she linked her hands behind his neck. "I don't need special gifts when you love me like you do every day."

"That's right fine to know before I give you this." Joe pulled out a book he'd had tucked in the back of his waistband. "Mr. Lloyd told me this was the newest sensation among the ladies in town."

Claire ran her hands over the green hardcover—*Where Birds Sing* by Olive Kent. "You know I love her books. They're half what Loretta and I write about in our letters. Thank you!"

"I can't let the Scotsman show me up on a day like today." He tucked a strand of her hair behind her ear. "I love ya something fierce, Claire."

Their kissing rivaled the Campbells' affections and cleared Emmett, Clara Jane, and Mary from the room.

"When you come up for air, I need to thank your wife for finding my boy," Douglas said.

Joe nearly crushed Claire before letting go. "She's feisty as is, but if I give her a new book, she can't keep her hands off me."

"Hush your mouth, Joseph Walker." Claire nudged him away. "You know I don't need a book for an excuse to love on you."

He grinned. "Nearly eleven years of marriage and you ain't run off yet. Either you're too lazy, or I'm doing something right."

"If I only knew back then wh—"

He cutoff her words with a pinch on her backside that made her jump.

"So help me, Joe, I'll get you for that!"

"If you ever need me to show him the higher road, let me know," Douglas told Claire.

Joe straightened his suspenders with a proud air. "Don't go on trying to beat your boss now, Campbell."

Maggie stepped forward and lightly punched Joe in the stomach. "I'd do it myself if you ever mistreat Claire."

Joe's cocky grin doubled. "It seems we've got ourselves a couple of feisty women."

"Aye," Douglas replied. "They're the best type to have."

In the doorway, Abraham's carrot top peeked around from the front room.

"And the feisty ones give birth to even more spirited souls." Joe rushed to the door and grabbed Abraham, lifting him until he was eye level. "Why'd you give your ma and Miss Maggie trouble today, Abe?"

"We had to fight the enemy!"

"And did you get 'em?"

"Yessir! We got 'em good, but I got squished."

Joe laughed but then forced himself to sound gruff. "If I ever hear 'bout you leaving without permission again, I'll put my belt on you, ya hear?"

"Yes, Pa. I'm sorry."

He hugged the boy to his chest and reached an arm out for Claire. "You're both cut from the same cloth, but this boy's got it double with my bits inside him too."

She nestled into her husband's embrace, pleased that her family was reunited with no catastrophes to mar the day of love.

The End

Author's Note

As the fourth book in the series, the list of people to thank is similar to the others. Be sure to check out those acknowledgements for more details—including special shout outs to my family, critique group, and beta readers.

This time around, I had a new editor on my side. Thank you, Cassandra Fear, for making the transition as easy as possible mid-series.

And last, but not least, virtual hugs to the members of Dalby's Darklings, my Facebook readers' group. Thanks for being as passionate about this series as I am—whichever team you're on.

About the Author

While experiencing the typical adventures of growing up, Carrie Dalby called several places in California home, but she's lived on the Alabama Gulf Coast since 1996. Serving two terms as president of Mobile Writers' Guild and five years as the Mobile area Local Liaison for the Society of Children's Book Writers and Illustrators are two of the writing-related volunteer positions she's held. When Carrie isn't reading, writing, browsing bookstores/libraries, or homeschooling her children, she can often be found knitting or attending concerts.

Carrie writes for both teens and adults. *Fortitude* is listed as a Best History Book for Kids by Grateful American Foundation. She has also published *Corroded*, a contemporary teen novel about friendship and autism, several short stories that can be found in different anthologies, as well as a multitude of Southern Gothic novels for adults.

For more information, visit Carrie Dalby's website:

carriedalby.com